MAGNOLIA MOONLIGHT

Books by Mary Ellis

⸻

Secrets of the South Mysteries
Midnight on the Mississippi
What Happened on Beale Street
Magnolia Moonlight

Civil War Heroines
The Quaker and the Rebel
The Lady and the Officer

The New Beginnings Series
Living in Harmony
Love Comes to Paradise
A Little Bit of Charm

The Wayne County Series
Abigail's New Hope
A Marriage for Meghan

The Miller Family Series
A Widow's Hope
Never Far from Home
The Way to a Man's Heart

Standalones
Sarah's Christmas Miracle
An Amish Family Reunion
A Plain Man
The Last Heiress

MAGNOLIA MOONLIGHT

MARY ELLIS

HARVEST HOUSE PUBLISHERS
EUGENE, OREGON

MAGNOLIA MOONLIGHT
Copyright © 2016 by Mary Ellis
Published by Harvest House Publishers
Eugene, Oregon 97402
www.harvesthousepublishers.com

ISBN 978-0-7369-6173-8 (pbk.)
ISBN 978-0-7369-6174-5 (eBook)

Library of Congress Cataloging-in-Publication Data

Names: Ellis, Mary, author.
Title: Magnolia moonlight / Mary Ellis.
Description: Eugene Oregon : Harvest House Publishers, [2016] | Description based on print version record and CIP data provided by publisher; resource not viewed.
Identifiers: LCCN 2016009185 (print) | LCCN 2016005606 (ebook) | ISBN 9780736961745 () | ISBN 9780736961738 (softcover)
Subjects: LCSH: Private investigators--Fiction. | Criminal investigation--Fiction. | GSAFD: Mystery fiction.
Classification: LCC PS3626.E36 (print) | LCC PS3626.E36 M34 2016 (ebook) | DDC 813/.6—dc23
LC record available at http://lccn.loc.gov/2016009185

Printed in the United States of America

16 17 18 19 20 21 22 23 24 / LB-GL / 10 9 8 7 6 5 4 3 2 1

ACKNOWLEDGMENTS

Special thanks to Captain T. McGehee of the Natchez Police Department. Never have I been treated so warmly while interviewing a very busy professional. My honorary officer's badge hangs proudly over my writing desk. Thanks also to the Cleveland FBI agents who willingly share their knowledge with local mystery writers.

Thanks to the Grand Hotel of Natchez for the wonderful hospitality. What a lovely historic gem on the banks of the Mississippi River.

Thanks to Johnny "Vegas" Sturwold, executive host at Belterra Casino and Resort, for assisting me with the game of Texas Hold'em and with poker room procedures. Thanks especially to Mike Smith, also an executive host at Belterra, for his expertise with high-stakes poker. Although the Golden Magnolia Casino is a figment of my imagination, I'd also like to thank the Hollywood Casino of Bay St. Louis, Mississippi, and its employees, who graciously and patiently answered many of my questions.

Thanks to the helpful guides inside the Bay St. Louis Historic Depot and the Alice Moseley Folk Art Museum. I'm also very grateful to Nicki Moon of the Bay Town Inn Bed & Breakfast, who shared firsthand stories of riding out Hurricane Katrina, including hanging on to a tree for dear life. Thanks also to the naturalists at Gulf Shores National Seashore in Ocean Springs and on Ship Island, smack in the middle of the Gulf of Mexico.

Thanks to my dear friends Pete and Donna Taylor, who helped with brainstorming, and my husband, who helped discover plenty of nooks and crannies in Natchez, Bay St. Louis, Biloxi, Gulfport, and Ocean Springs, Mississippi. Researching with friends and family is so much more fun.

Thanks to my agent, Mary Sue Seymour; my editor, Kim Moore; and the wonderful staff at Harvest House Publishers. Where would I be without your hard work?

⌒

AUTHOR'S NOTE

Although Natchez is home to several Baptist churches, Calvary Baptist and the events which took place there are purely fictional.

The river told its mind to me without reserve,
delivering its most cherished secrets as clearly as if it
uttered them with a voice.

MARK TWAIN

~

The river was doing what it liked to do,
just as a mule will work for you for ten years for
the privilege of kicking you once.

WILLIAM FAULKNER

ONE

$\mathcal{N}$ate Price sat down to breakfast that morning a happy man. What was there not to like about life? The sun was shining. He'd just run four miles along the levee in his best time yet. There were fresh blueberries and candied pecans in his bowl of cereal. And he had married the prettiest girl ever to graduate from their high school. Lifting the spoon to his mouth, he crunched into his whole grains and soy milk with contentment.

"Could you pour that into a to-go cup, honey? I need a ride to work today." Isabelle entered their tiny kitchen on stiletto heels in a faint mist of sweet perfume. In her silk dress with her long hair coiled into a knot, she looked like an investment banker or college professor.

Nate peered over his coffee mug. "It's cereal with milk, not a breakfast shake. What's with the snazzy getup? I thought Realty World agents were required to wear their lime green blazer at all times. And why do you need a ride when you own a perfectly good Prius?"

"There should be a limit on the number of questions before nine a.m." Leaning over for a kiss, Isabelle grabbed his bowl of cereal and dumped it into a plastic tub. "Take your spoon. You can eat while I drive." She filled her travel mug with coffee.

Nate crossed his arms and made no effort to move.

"Okay, you win." Isabelle held up her index finger. "First of all, my blazer isn't lime. That particular shade of green is called 'kelly.' Second, Mr. Randall told his agents to wear their Sunday best, no blazers today. We're attending a symposium on mortgage finance at the Grand Hotel. Me? I'm going for the free lunch." She winked a magnificent green eye.

"You usually fill up with a side salad and breadstick." Nate snapped a lid on his mug and reached for his keys. "And now for the million-dollar question—what's wrong with your car?"

"Remember that little knock in my engine? The mechanic said I would need a new transmission soon, and that was four thousand miles ago. Yesterday I could barely hear the radio over the knocking." She shrugged.

Nate halted midway through the doorway. "You should have told me sooner, Izzy. What if you had broken down coming home from an open house? Those country roads don't have streetlights."

She slipped an arm around his waist as they walked toward the car. "We're saving for our honeymoon and to buy a house. Our budget can't stretch any thinner."

"Two working people need two vehicles. With two hundred thousand miles on that car, I'd say you got your money's worth. Nothing lasts forever." Nate opened the driver's door for her.

"Well, finances are just a bit tight. You know I loved moving from Germantown to slower-paced Natchez, but fewer people mean fewer sales, and less expensive real estate means smaller commission checks." She climbed into his SUV and tugged down her skirt.

"It's nobody's fault. It's just life, my sweet bride," Nate said around a mouthful of mushy cereal.

Isabelle backed down the narrow driveway between the neighbor's picket fence and her row of azaleas. "How can I still be a bride when our second anniversary is in two weeks? I'm just another old married woman."

"Not to me you're not." Nate kissed her cheek. "New rule. You stay a bride until after the honeymoon, even if we're in our forties."

She laughed, a sound that never failed to warm his soul. "Maybe we should forget our dreams and go to New Orleans for a few days. We could stay at Nicki and Hunter's apartment while they're in Europe. They have offered the place more than once."

Nate tipped his bowl to drink the milk. "Nope. I'm not honeymooning in the French Quarter. I lived there for years, remember? Let's buy a used car with what I squirreled away for the trip and use your next commission check for a honeymoon. Saving for a new house will remain on track."

"Good idea. We'll qualify for a senior citizen discount by then." Isabelle accelerated on an open stretch of road. "Maybe we should put a bid on the place we rent. How much could the landlord want for a nine-hundred-square-foot, one-bedroom house?"

Nate slid the empty bowl under the seat. "You have illuminated the fly in your ointment—*one* bedroom. Call me crazy, but someday I hope we're surrounded by dozens of mini Nathaniel and Isabelle look-alikes. We'll need lots of bedrooms so when they cry at night my dutiful wife can hurry down the hall while I get my beauty sleep."

Isabelle shot him an evil glare. "There are so many things wrong with that mental picture that I don't even know where to start. But because we're almost at work, we'll continue this discussion at supper. Whose turn is it to cook?"

"Definitely yours. I'm hoping for a nice steak grilled to perfection over hardwood briquettes, and maybe fresh asparagus with a tangy hollandaise." He leaned back and closed his eyes.

"Nope, it's your turn. So I'll expect my usual burger, charred to a crisp, with baked beans and bag salad." Isabelle turned into Realty World's parking lot, the largest real estate brokerage firm in Natchez. "Good grief, look at the cars already! Let's hope these are all eager buyers with excellent credit scores."

Nate jumped out and jogged to the driver's side. He had only enough time to wrap his arms around his wife when Izzy's boss interrupted them.

"Good morning, Mr. Price. I'm glad you dropped Isabelle off today." Mr. Randall, looking professional in his charcoal-gray suit, approached from the back entrance. *No lime green blazer for the big shot.* "Could you step inside for a few minutes? I need another man's opinion on something. You know how these women love to gang up on me."

"Sure, I can spare a few minutes. In fact, I have all the time in the world."

Nate had finished his recent missing person investigation by locating the twenty-year-old woman in Las Vegas. The girl had agreed to call her parents but refused to come home. She was making too much money dealing blackjack to go back to selling cosmetics at the mall. And a suspected philandering spouse turned out to be someone moonlighting at a second job. The husband had planned to surprise his wife with an anniversary cruise down the Danube River. Nate felt so sorry for the guy that he had cut his usual fee in half. The agency had a corporate fraud case in New Orleans, and the suspected misuse of a power of attorney case in Vicksburg, but no new Natchez cases. He needed some more work soon, or he would be twiddling his thumbs.

"Good. I love having you around." Isabelle beamed as she reached for his hand. "Be sure to compliment Mary Jo on her new hairdo," she whispered. "Chopping off that ponytail was quite traumatic."

However, once they entered the building, Nate had no opportunity to assess Mary Jo's coiffure or do much of anything else.

"Surprise!" Shouts from at least three dozen people nearly blew the roof off the one-story building.

Dumbfounded, Nate and Isabelle gazed around a sea of familiar faces. Not only had every real estate agent beaten Isabelle to work, but Nate's new employees and his assistant were part of the crowd, along with his partner from New Orleans, her husband, and most of their friends. "Good grief," he muttered. "There's my Aunt Rose. What's going on?"

Isabelle's astonishment rivaled his. "My aunt and uncle from Clarksdale are here. I haven't seen them in two years."

In a flurry of backslapping, handshaking, and cheek-kissing, Mr. Randall herded Nate and Isabelle toward the conference table. But instead of scratch pads, pens, and printouts of recent listings, it was covered with pink paper, confetti, and bright streamers. A weighted cluster of helium balloons offered sentiments of "Best Wishes," "Congratulations," and "Bon Voyage."

"Bon voyage?" Nate asked no one in particular. "The only place I'm going is my office." He tightened his arm around Isabelle as though they were surrounded by dangerous people instead of their closest friends and relatives.

"We'll just see about that." Michael Preston, his newest employee at the agency, clamped a hand on his shoulder.

Then his partner, Nicki Galen, stepped front and center. "You're not really setting sail, but I needed a short phrase for taking a trip." She rocked on her heels, snickering. "They put me in charge of the balloons."

Nate narrowed his gaze at her. "What are you doing in Natchez? I thought you and Hunter were vacationing in France or Switzerland, someplace hoity-toity."

"Nobody says hoity-toity anymore, cousin. Anyway, we flew back early when we heard about the party. Pretty nice balloons, no?" Nicki winked mischievously.

"Check out the cakes," a voice called. The crowd shuffled them toward the table, where decorated cupcakes spelled out *Happy Anniversary*. In the center one giant cake had been emblazoned with *Have fun, Nate and Izzy*. A small white envelope protruded from the frosting.

"What is going on?" demanded Isabelle, as though beset with the same sense of peril. She leaned into his side as the crowd shouted several commands:

"Open the card!"

"Pack your bags!"

"Stop looking so scared!"

Nate plucked the sugar-coated envelope from the frosting. "Fine, but I have one question. Don't *any* of you people have work to do?"

Receiving only laughter in response, he ripped open the envelope, licked his fingers, and scanned the single sheet. Then he handed it to Isabelle, his mouth agape.

"What is it?" She read key phrases aloud. "Three weeks in a luxurious beachfront mansion in Bay St. Louis, Mississippi. Breakfast served on the porch each morning, afternoon refreshments on the lawn, true Southern hospitality. Walking distance to shops, restaurants, and the marina. Porch swing, free use of bicycles, Wi-Fi, and two bedrooms."

"*Two* bedrooms?" Michael scratched his head. "Is someone planning to join them on their honeymoon?"

"That's in case they have a lover's quarrel." A disembodied voice floated from the back of the room.

Nate recognized the voice of his Vicksburg based PI, Elizabeth Kirby. "You're here too?" He feigned annoyance. "Doesn't *anyone* put in an honest day's work anymore?"

"Not when we needed to take matters into our own hands." Mr. Randall squeezed in between Nate and Isabelle. "When it became clear you two were never going to take a honeymoon, your fellow agents and Nate's employees took up a collection. Then your cousin shook down your friends and relatives and fattened the purse." Randall drew a second envelope from his pocket and handed it to Isabelle. "We were able to upgrade you to a suite, and there's enough spending money for lunch, dinner, dolphin-watching excursions, and several bottles of suntan lotion."

Isabelle looked ready to faint. "I-I don't know what to say other than thank you from the bottom of my...our hearts." Teary-eyed, she turned to her husband.

Clearing his throat, Nate had his own lump of emotion to swallow. "We were just discussing a honeymoon this morning. Your generosity and thoughtfulness are overwhelming. As soon as we get a break in our schedules—"

"Oh, no," interrupted Michael. "That's not how this works. Read the fine print. We have prepaid three weeks during prime season on the gorgeous Mississippi coast. Clear your calendars because your honeymoon begins on Sunday."

"*This* Sunday?" Isabelle clutched her throat as though choking on a fish bone.

"Yep. You two lovebirds leave in three days." Nicki picked up a cupcake and took a bite. "I would start packing if I were you."

"But we need to look for a used car for me." Isabelle sounded more like a child than a woman in her thirties.

Marie, Realty World's assistant, took hold of Isabelle's hand. "You'll only need one vehicle while you're at the beach, and there will still be plenty of used cars here when you get back. I'll make sure your open houses or house showings are covered by other agents. I'll bet they'll even pass any commissions on to you." She scanned the room, honing in on Isabelle's fellow agents.

"Oh, no," Isabelle protested. "I could never let anyone—"

"Nonsense," said Marie. "You can return the favor sometime down the line. And when this party's over, you and I are going to Victoria's Secret and Bath and Body Works, my treat. Now let's have something to eat." Marie grabbed two cupcakes and handed one to Isabelle.

For the next thirty minutes, Nate ate sweets, drank bad coffee, and listened to advice from well-intentioned friends. He heard about every Gulf Coast landmark, restaurants worth the money, which fishing charters knew the best spots, and how to avoid sand fleas. His Aunt Rose provided tips on foot massage that made him blush. Nicki snapped a picture each time he took a bite of cupcake. And his cousin assured him she would watch the paper for great deals on used cars.

Finally, his two employees approached from the sidelines. "I hate to break this party up, but shouldn't we be getting to the office?" Michael took Nate's empty coffee cup and plate of cake crumbs. "We have a pile of cases to sort through."

Nate smiled with gratitude at the ruse. Michael was the last person one would expect with aspirations of becoming a PI, but if sheer determination and willpower were indicators of future success, someday he would be one of the best. Unfortunately, it wouldn't be any day soon.

Michael had spent his high school and college years with his nose in a book or staring at a computer screen. Nerd. Geek. Egghead. The terms for studious types might change from generation to generation, but the personality remained the same. These men didn't hunt, fish, pump iron, or race custom-built cars on dirt tracks. Instead, they made their fortunes with Internet start-up companies, investment banking, or, unfortunately, cybercrime. Michael might be an untrained PI, but in this day and age, he already possessed skills Price Investigations needed.

"Let me just say goodbye to our host," Nate murmured to the pair. He walked over to a little group of people by the window. "Thanks for organizing this party, Mr. Randall. Isabelle and I will never forget everyone's generosity as long as we live." He extended his hand to the distinguished broker.

"We all cherish Isabelle at Realty World and were happy to help."

Elizabeth stepped forward. "We're glad you included us. I don't know what we'll do while Nate and his wife are basking in the sun."

"Don't believe a word of it," he said to Randall. "These two won't even know I'm gone." Then Nate turned to address the crowd. "Thanks, everyone, for the incredible gift. Be prepared for tons of pictures when we get back." After more handshaking, Nate finally shrugged into his sport coat, waved at his wife, and headed for the door. Across the room, Isabelle was surrounded by women, all talking at the same time.

Outside in the parking lot, Nate sucked in a deep breath. "Wow, I sure didn't see that coming."

"Having lots of friends comes in handy." Michael was still staring at the back door in amazement.

"Yeah, but what goes around comes around." Elizabeth clucked her tongue. "You and Isabelle will be invited to every graduation, bar mitzvah, baptism, and retirement party for years. Not to mention forced to buy raffle tickets and Girl Scout cookies until you drop over dead."

Nate laughed. "You two sure have different perspectives on group fund-raising. Thanks for getting me out the door. Not that I'm not grateful, but that kind of party can last for hours."

"There's only so much smiling one face can handle," said Elizabeth.

Michael shook his head. "On that note, I'll take my leave. I have a class on Mississippi gun laws starting in twenty minutes."

Nate watched him putter away in his fuel-efficient car before turning to his other employee. "Beth, why aren't you in Vicksburg? Don't tell me you drove here for a going-away party. You could have sent your ten bucks through the mail."

She chuckled. "For your information, boss, I chipped in twenty-five. But your cupcake send-off isn't the sole reason I'm in Natchez." She stared at the road even though Michael was long gone. "My mother asked me to come home for Pastor Dean's funeral. She's worried there won't be enough mourners."

Nate slicked a hand through his hair. "Yeah, I heard about that. But considering the number of Baptists in town, there should be a good turnout. Isabelle and I will be there because she attended Calvary while growing up. Now we go to the nondenominational by the freeway."

Beth shrugged. "We'll see how many folks show up. Some members might boycott because the preacher offed himself."

"*What?*" Nate was shocked by her insensitivity.

"Sorry, that was crude. I meant to say some might hold it against Reverend Dean because he committed suicide. A man of God isn't supposed to take his own life."

"What are you talking about? The paper said he had a heart condition, so I assumed that was the cause of death."

Beth hiked her purse up her shoulder. "Not unless a bad ticker made him climb a stool with a rope around his neck."

Nate shuddered. "That is just awful, especially for whoever found him."

"My mom said it was his wife. Alice Dean was always nice to me. I used to babysit for their little girl." Despite her earlier detachment, Beth's eyes filled with tears.

"Well, for sure Izzy and I will be there tomorrow. Thank goodness we don't leave until Sunday."

"I sure am a downer today. When you're about to leave on the best vacation of your life, I'm talking suicide and people's fondness for being judgmental." Beth swiped at her tears. "Go to the office and clean off your desk. Tell Maxine to clear your calendar and hold your calls. Don't worry about me and Wonder Boy. We'll hold down the fort while you and Isabelle have fun in the sun."

"You do have a way with words, Ms. Kirby." Nate climbed into his SUV and lowered the window. "Will I see you at the office later?"

"I don't know. I left Vicksburg at four this morning and drove straight to the party. I haven't been home yet. Can't wait to see what else Mom has in store for me. My bedroom is probably exactly how I left it."

"You'll always be her little girl. So you're willing to stay in town while I'm gone? Michael isn't ready to be on his own."

Beth looked everywhere but at him. "If that's what you want, Nate, but I would prefer to go to the funeral, eat a chicken salad sandwich, and get out of Natchez as fast as I can."

He started the engine. "Your case in Vicksburg should be wrapping up by now. I thought you had plenty of evidence to present to the DA."

"True, but I'm following a lead for new work. I'd love to stay where I am. That town has grown on me." She started to back away.

"Any new cases had better come with a fat retainer. I know you're living as cheaply as you can, but I can't afford to set up a Vicksburg office."

"Maybe if I—"

"No, Beth, I need you in Natchez. We can talk about this when I come back, but right now I need to find a Panama hat and new flip-flops. The beach and my lovely bride are calling. Isabelle and I will see you tomorrow at the funeral." He drove away to end the argument.

Beth Kirby was a great PI, but at times she could be like a dog with a bone.

TWO

*B*eth awoke with a crick in her neck and a bad taste in her mouth. The neck pain was caused by sleeping on a worn-out mattress that should have been put to the curb years ago. And the bad taste? Too much Diet Coke, fried food, and local gossip she would have preferred not to have heard. Didn't her mother know about baking or grilling skinless chicken breasts? Couldn't she steam some broccoli or at least make baked potatoes instead of French fries? And why would she care which of her ex-friends had been dumped by their husbands?

A better question would be: *Why did I come home?* Beth stood under the shower long after the soap and hair conditioner were gone. It had been years since she attended Calvary Baptist, and the less time she sat around her mother's kitchen table, the better. Rita never failed to remind her only daughter that she had made a mess of her life. Would she never live down a past mistake? She'd moved on to a new career, while the other party continued his life without a hitch. Surely the gossips in town had found tastier tidbits by now.

Ten minutes later, dressed in navy slacks with a matching jacket, she marched into the kitchen ready to face the music.

"Slacks, Betsy? Didn't you bring a dress with you?" The furrows in her mother's forehead deepened.

"First, Mom, please call me Beth. I'm no longer ten years old.

Second, I don't have any dresses unless you count that red strapless number I wore to the prom. That's probably still in the closet."

"Don't be disrespectful. I thought you liked Reverend and Alice Dean." Rita filled two mugs with coffee.

"I did…I do. That's why I'm here wearing the most appropriate outfit I own." Beth rummaged through the cupboard. "Don't you have Special K or Total?"

"Sit. There's a ham and cheese omelet warming in the oven, along with hash browns. Who knows how long the funeral will last? It could be hours before we eat lunch." Rita carried enough food for six teenage boys to the table.

Beth noticed the stiffness in her mother's gait and deep creases around her mouth and eyes. *I'm gone for less than eighteen months, and Mom ages ten years?* "Are your hips bothering you?" she asked, taking a small portion of eggs and potatoes. "You should see a doctor."

"Why should I pay some quack sixty dollars to hear I have arthritis? I'm old. Everybody gets it if they live long enough." Rita scooped twice as large a portion onto her plate.

"A doctor might prescribe exercises to improve mobility. The co-pay would be my treat."

"Save your money. Without a husband to take care of you, you'll need it for the future." Rita patted her hand, her brows lifting in anticipation. "Will I ever meet your new boss? Is this Nate Price nice looking?"

"He's *very* nice looking in a rugged sort of way—tall, blond, and wait for it…married, for almost two years. They're finally going on a honeymoon."

"What a shame!" Rita swallowed a mouthful of coffee.

"For Nate or his bride?" Beth teased.

"For you, of course." Her mom topped off their mugs. "I'm surprised Nate found another case in Vicksburg. Doesn't that town have their own PIs? And why would you enjoy living where you don't know a soul?"

"You hit the nail on the head. Nobody knows me either." Beth ate three more forkfuls of eggs and drained her coffee. "I'll wait for you on the porch. I have surveillance tapes to review on my laptop, but I'm ready to go whenever you are." Halfway to the door, she remembered her manners. "Thanks for breakfast, Mom. It was delicious."

"You're welcome. You don't want to get too skinny. Most men like a little meat on a gal's bones."

Gal? What century does my mother inhabit?

Thirty minutes later Rita emerged from the house wearing black from head to toe.

"Let's take my car since you seldom have more than a quarter of a tank in yours," said Beth.

"I believe your father filled it up for me, but that's fine." Rita climbed in and remained lost in thought for several minutes. Then she swiveled to face her daughter. "Do you think Reverend Dean is in heaven?"

Beth kept her focus on the road. "Why wouldn't he be? He preached his faith and lived a good life."

Rita rubbed her knuckles. "Some of the ladies think suicide is an unforgivable sin, especially when committed by a pastor. He of all people should know better."

"Why would Reverend Dean have an easier row to hoe than the rest of us? Knowing Scripture doesn't guarantee anyone a bed of roses."

"What could have been so terrible? He had a pretty wife, their daughter got good grades in school, and their house was paid for."

Beth applied the brakes at the stop sign and then turned to look at her mother. "How on earth would you know all of that?"

Rita replied without hesitation. "Carol Ann works in the school office, and Pam Henderson handles mortgages at the bank they use. And the prettiness of Alice Dean is obvious."

"Have none of your cronies heard of federal privacy laws? Those women should be fired, and you shouldn't pass along private information."

Following the reprimand, both Kirby women remained silent for the rest of the drive. When they reached the church, mourners were already milling on the steps, allowing Rita to join her loose-lipped friends. Beth spotted Nate and Isabelle near the door, along with Michael, the overly enthusiastic but underachieving new PI. Nothing galled her more than when Nate referred to them as "his new hires." With her years of experience, how could Nate lump her with an unskilled wannabe?

"Good morning, Nate, Isabelle," she greeted. "Hi, Michael."

"Good morning," murmured Isabelle. "I understand Reverend Dean was your pastor, Beth. I'm sorry for your loss."

"Thank you, but it's been a number of years." Beth suppressed an uncharacteristic twinge of jealousy for Isabelle's chic dress and high heels.

With a clang of church bells, Nate herded them all inside, where they sat through two readings, three hymns, one off-key solo, and several eulogies about the pastor's zeal and humanitarian nature. The fact he chose to end his life stood like the proverbial elephant in the sanctuary. Throughout the service, Alice Dean sat with her young daughter in the front row, dabbing her eyes. Odd that no one else had joined her in the pew. Didn't she have siblings or close friends she could lean on? It would be a question for Beth's know-all, tell-all mother that evening. After the closing prayer, the assistant minister directed everyone to the cemetery and then invited mourners back to the social hall for lunch.

Outside in the bright sunshine, Beth wandered through a sea of polyester dresses and straw hats trying to find her mother. Unfortunately, Michael found her first.

"Hey, Elizabeth." He stepped from behind a white column. "Mind if I ride to Natchez City Cemetery with y'all?"

He always used her formal name. Beth considered correcting

him but decided she rather liked it. At least he didn't call her Betsy, a nickname that refused to die. "My mom is with me today," she said, shading her eyes as she peered up at him. "Can't you ride with Nate and Isabelle?"

"Nate's cousin from New Orleans and her husband will be in the backseat. That would mean squeezing five into an Escape."

Beth refrained from suggesting the cargo area because Michael was at least half a foot taller than her. "Sure, but let Mom sit up front because she gets motion sick." Beth spotted Rita's plumed hat in a cluster of busybodies and marched in that direction.

Michael remained on her heels. "Thanks. Having grown up in Brookhaven, you would think I would know my way around Natchez. But I'm still discovering what this city has to offer."

"Yep. We have ourselves a booming metropolis here. Paris, Rome, and New York must be losing sleep."

Her sarcasm only increased Michael's glibness. He chattered all the way to the historic cemetery. Even Rita couldn't get a word in edgewise. He didn't stop talking until they parked between rows of blooming crepe myrtle trees, the heavy fragrance overwhelming the senses.

Climbing out, Michael offered her mother his arm. "Would you like to hang on to me, Mrs. Kirby? There's some uneven ground ahead."

"Thank you, young man." Hooking her arm through his, Rita peppered Michael with questions about *his people* until they reached the gravesite. Then she dropped his arm and latched on to a friend, doubtlessly another gossip.

Beth sighed as Michael joined her side. "I hope my mother didn't get too personal," she said. "She feels any question is fair game."

"Not a problem. She's really very friendly."

Beth frowned without looking at her coworker.

For the next ten minutes, the stand-in pastor delivered a final homily and then invited mourners to say their goodbyes. One by one, they stepped forward to place a yellow rose atop the casket. Beth and Michael took their turn and then stood at the back of the group waiting for her mother.

"Know anything about that?" Michael asked, pointing at a stone monument in the distance. "I'll bet there's a story."

"Of course there is. This is Natchez," she said. "That's the Fallen Angel, but everybody calls it the Turning Angel. A drug company blew up a hundred years ago, killing most of its employees. The owner bought the plot and the monument to commemorate them." Beth gazed at the fast-growing kudzu barely kept at bay in the cemetery.

"Why did the name change?"

"Because like most places, Natchez has its share of nutcases who swear the angel turns whenever a car drives by. Needless to say, it has to be at night and your headlights must be aimed just right." Beth offered him an exaggerated eye roll.

"Are you usually cynical or only at funerals?" Michael squinted into the sun.

"I'm always like this, even when nobody cashes in their chips." The words had barely left her mouth when Beth heard a gasp. She pivoted around to face Alice Dean. "Oh, I'm so sorry, Mrs. Dean. I meant no disrespect. Your husband was always nice to me."

Alice's pale and pinched features softened. "I know you liked Paul, Beth, and he was fond of you. That's why I wanted to speak to you before the luncheon."

Michael shuffled his size twelve shoes in the grass. "I'll wait for you by the car, Elizabeth, and keep your mom company."

"If you work with Beth, maybe you should hear this too." Mrs. Dean shifted her weight in the long grass. "Paul didn't cash in his chips, or choose the easy way out, or any of the other euphemisms for suicide."

"Please forgive my—"

Alice waved away Beth's apology. "What I meant was Paul didn't take his own life. He would never do such a thing. He loved me and our daughter besides the fact his faith wouldn't condone such an act."

Beth glanced at Michael, who was studying the widow like a bug under a magnifying glass. "Was there a note or any kind of explanation?" she asked.

"The police found a note, but Paul never talked that way. He wouldn't have used those phrases. Either he didn't write it, or he was coerced into writing it."

Beth reached for Mrs. Dean's hand. Probably less than a decade separated the two women in age, but vastly different backgrounds and experiences provided little common ground. "I can't imagine how awful this must be for you and little Katie, but I'm sure the police will investigate your husband's death thoroughly."

She pulled her hand back. "Are you really that naive? You of all people should know judgments are made based on appearances that may have nothing to do with the truth." The woman's amber eyes filled with tears. "Please help me, Beth. I heard you became a private investigator, and I don't know where else to turn."

Now it was her turn to shuffle her shoe leather through the grass. "I am a PI, but I work for Price Investigations. Right now I'm working a case in Vicksburg—a caregiver has been misusing her power of attorney to pilfer money from an elderly woman's account."

Mrs. Dean lifted her chin. "As tragic as that sounds, I assure you the dreadful allegations levied against my husband make this case no less worthy of your time."

Michael took a step forward. "What Miss Kirby is trying to say is we're not at liberty to accept new work. Those decisions are made by Nate Price, our boss."

"Yes, that's correct, and, unfortunately, Mr. and Mrs. Price will be leaving on their honeymoon Sunday morning."

Alice consulted her watch. "I must get to the luncheon or people will talk more than they already are. Could you set up a meeting with Mr. Price? Shall we say tomorrow morning?"

Beth opened her mouth to speak, but Michael beat her to the

punch. "I'm sure Nate will be happy to meet you, Mrs. Dean. Why don't you come by his office on Jefferson Street at nine o'clock?" He held out a business card.

"I'll be there. Thank you." Alice plucked the card from Michael's fingers and walked away.

Beth held her tongue until the woman was beyond earshot. Then, "Have you lost your mind, Michael? Nate's not going to be the least bit happy. He has plenty to do before a three-week vacation."

"I think you're overreacting because you knew the deceased personally. The agency is looking for new cases, so why don't we wait to see what Nate has to say?" Michael stuck out his elbow. "Care to hang on to me on the walk back to the car?"

"You seem to have mistaken me for my mother. That's not something you should do if you're hoping for a long life." Beth marched toward the row of parked cars, annoyed with him for some reason.

Michael trailed at her heels, reminding Beth of a puppy she once owned. However, he was nowhere near as cute or lovable.

THREE

Nate didn't mind stopping at the office on a Saturday. After all, he and Isabelle had done most of their packing the day before after the funeral. Today they would stop at a discount store for new swimsuits, sandals, and inflatable rafts and then stock up on powdered tea, snacks, and fresh fruit at the grocery store to avoid high prices at the beach. They canceled the newspaper, asked the post office to hold their mail, and arranged for a neighbor to feed Isabelle's cat. Today Isabelle planned to water the plants, clean out the fridge, and place their home on Neighborhood Watch for the next three weeks. Not that they owned much that would interest thieves, but nobody wanted to return to a ransacked mess. Following his appointment with the widow, Nate would have the Escape's oil changed and tires rotated, and then they would be ready to leave early the next morning.

He was a little curious about the appointment. He'd watched the aloof Mrs. Dean at the service, the graveside burial, and the poorly attended luncheon. Judging from the number of sandwiches, apparently twice as many people had been anticipated. Alice Dean had barely said six words to any particular mourner. Grief was one thing, but the woman looked angry instead of sad, distrustful rather than despondent. So when Michael and Elizabeth told him about the meeting, Nate's interest piqued.

His two employees had very different perspectives on the case. Michael felt the new widow was hiding something and wished Price Investigations to help her finish whatever her husband started. Beth thought the woman was delusional due to grief, or the victim of a common misconception that good people deserved a happily-ever-after ending to their lives. So Nate wasn't surprised to find all three waiting in his outer office at ten minutes to nine.

"Hey, Nate," chimed Beth and Michael simultaneously.

"Good morning, Mr. Price. I'm Alice Dean." The expensively dressed woman extended a hand. "I don't believe I thanked you yesterday for coming to the funeral."

"How do you do, ma'am. My deepest sympathies on your loss." They shook hands, their fingers barely touching. "Michael, Beth, please wait out here for a few minutes. I would like to speak with Mrs. Dean privately." Michael looked crestfallen, while Beth seemed miffed, but Nate saw no need to air the widow's laundry before others if he decided not to take the case.

Once seated, Mrs. Dean launched into several reasons why her husband of fifteen years wouldn't have killed himself—not one of which refuted the stark reality that Paul Dean had been found in their garage, hanging from a rafter with a noose around his neck. A note begging her forgiveness had been left on the workbench.

After a respectful pause, Nate provided her with a logical progression of questions: Was the note in Paul's handwriting? Had there been anything troubling your husband lately? Was anyone seen near your home around the time of death? Were the rope, stool, paper, and pen items your family owned? Did the police promptly respond to the 9-1-1 call and thoroughly inspect the garage area?

Not one of her answers pointed to anything other than suicide. For several moments Nate stared at a small rip in the drapes before delivering his inevitable conclusion. "If the police found no evidence to suggest otherwise—in other words, no signs of foul play—then I'm not sure what you want us to do. You have no case, ma'am, but you do have this office's sincerest sympathy."

"I don't want your pity, Mr. Price. I need someone to believe me." Mrs. Dean tightened the grip on her purse. "The police didn't look very hard. Rumors had been swirling for days that Paul had stolen money from the church. Some of those *investigating* cops go to Calvary Baptist."

"Isabelle and I spoke to several church members during the luncheon. Everyone spoke highly of Reverend Dean."

The widow's upper lip twitched imperceptibly. "Your wife left the congregation years ago. Since moving back, you have attended the evangelical church on Main Street. No one really knows you and Isabelle, and people don't gossip with strangers."

Nate hesitated, contemplating her response. "You believe someone murdered your husband and staged his death?"

"Correct, and I wish to hire your firm to find out the truth. Paul wasn't a thief, and he didn't take his own life." Her composure started to crack as a tear slipped down her cheek. "Find out who else had access to church funds and who had a grudge against my husband." She drew a blank check from her purse and scribbled quickly. "I understand from Beth that you're leaving tomorrow. Here is an advance to get your team started in your absence. I'll pay whatever is the going rate, plus expenses."

Temporarily befuddled, Nate stared at a one followed by four zeros. *Ten thousand dollars?* "I need to consult my associates before agreeing. Michael Preston was a forensic accountant at his previous job, so he has the necessary background there. However, he's not a fully trained PI yet. It's true that Beth has investigative experience, but she's still finishing a case in Vicksburg."

Mrs. Dean's intense gaze practically bored a hole through Nate's forehead. "If money is the issue, I'll add another ten thousand to the retainer. I have my own resources from a trust fund from my father in case you're afraid our jointly held accounts might be called into question down the road."

"No, ma'am. That's not why I'm hesitant." Nate took only thirty seconds to ponder the matter. The firm needed a new case, one that paid well. None of his missing persons, or philandering spouses, or caregiver pilferers had generated enough to pay three salaries, plus their assistant. Fortunately, his New Orleans partner received free office space courtesy of her rich husband. "Very well. We'll accept the case. You can expect a full report in one week's time. At that point, I'll decide whether to return the remaining advance or continue our investigation. I will not continue to take a client's money without just cause."

Mrs. Dean rose to an impressive height, courtesy of four-inch heels. "You're a rare man if you possess the integrity you imply. I can be reached at these numbers." She laid a card on his desk. "Now, if you would ask your protégés to stop by my home in a few hours, say twelve o'clock, I won't detain you longer." Halfway to the door, she halted. "Please forgive my bad manners. Lately I haven't been able to think about anyone but myself. I wish both you and your bride a relaxing and restorative honeymoon."

"Thank you, ma'am. I'll be in touch."

When she opened the door, Nate's protégés practically fell into his office. Mrs. Dean nodded at them stiffly and then left as quickly as possible.

"Were you two eavesdropping?" Nate demanded the moment she was gone. "If I'd wanted you to hear the conversation, I would have invited you inside."

Beth strode toward the more comfortable of his two upholstered chairs. "How else can we help you decide if the case has merit?"

Michael slunk past him rather sheepishly and headed for the windows. "I thought eavesdropping was a valuable surveillance tool. I was merely honing my skills."

Nate gritted his teeth. "I'll let you know when it's time for a spy cam, Mike. And because you're a local, Beth, I didn't want to publically air Mrs. Dean's dirty laundry."

Beth's blue eyes flashed. "I understand the concept of professional confidentiality. I wouldn't talk about Alice Dean's suspicions whether or not you took the case." Her focus landed on the check in the center of his desk blotter. "And I see that you are. Ten grand is hard to pass up."

Michael's opinion was also immediately apparent. "That's great news! I can't wait to dig into the family's financial records."

"Hold your horses, cyber sleuth," said Beth. "We need signed contracts and Alice's permission to snoop into her personal affairs, or the agency could be sued for invasion of privacy."

Nate clenched down on his molars while counting to five. "You both need to settle down and remember which one of us is the boss."

"That would be you," Michael answered without hesitation.

"I apologize if I overstepped." Beth's tone contained more indignation than remorse. "I was trying to sort this out in my head and don't see much of a case here. My old preacher got caught with his hand in the cookie jar and couldn't live with the shame. End of story. Stealing is a biggie in the Christian rule book."

"'You must not steal' is the eighth commandment," added Michael helpfully.

Nate mustered his most imperious demeanor. "It's *far* from the end of the story. So while I head for fun in the sun, you two will decide if Reverend Dean took his own life. Plenty of murders have been disguised as suicides before. Look at their personal and joint accounts along with church finances. Find out what their marriage was like, and see who had something to gain by his death. Michael, I know you're already good at following a money trail, and you should be able to learn plenty from a seasoned veteran like Beth. Any questions?" Nate looked from one to the other.

"Nope," said Michael, with an expression of someone about to board the world's tallest roller coaster.

Beth, however, remained silent with her arms crossed over her chest.

"Is something wrong, Miss Kirby?"

"No, sir. I'm here to do exactly what I'm told."

"Good," Nate said, more forcefully than necessary. "As you and

Michael overheard, you will visit Mrs. Dean at her home this afternoon. Gather all the information you can. Record the conversation if she gives you permission. Otherwise, take notes."

Beth's lips drew into a thin line.

"Michael, I would like a few minutes alone with Beth. Why don't you go to the funeral home and ask for a copy of Pastor Dean's guest book? That might come in handy down the line. Then you could meet Beth at 782 Bennett Avenue at noon. If you set your GPS, you should have no trouble."

"I'm on it!" Michael pushed away from the windowsill and crossed the room in three strides. He pumped Nate's hand like a handle. "You won't be sorry you left us in charge. We'll make you proud."

After Michael left the office with more enthusiasm than ten average men, Nate locked gazes with Beth, his spunky and talented former police officer. "Care to tell me what's really on your mind?"

FOUR

*O*nce the eager beaver left, Beth's courage flagged. Why was she purposely goading her boss? She liked working for Nate…just as long as the work wasn't in Natchez. Folding her hands in her lap, she attempted a conciliatory smile. "Nothing. Everything's good with me." Neither the smile nor the response did the trick.

"Sorry, Beth. The time has come to get this off your chest." Nate rolled his chair away from his desk.

"I didn't mean to come off so argumentative. I was just wondering how I would babysit Wonder Boy when I have an open case in Vicksburg."

Nate's frown intensified. "As we discussed Thursday morning, your case in Vicksburg should be wrapping up by now. We have to be where the work is. Second, his name is Michael Preston. Mike, if you prefer. Mikey, if he permits it. Nothing else will be tolerated from you while you're in my employ. I am asking you to help train our new man in my absence. If you're half the professional you claim to be, this shouldn't be a problem."

Beth straightened in her chair. The conversation had gone from bad to worse. She'd better pull a rabbit from her hat or she would join the unemployment line on Monday. "I stand corrected regarding Mr. Preston's name and also my duties while you're gone."

"Good." Nate relaxed his grip on the chair. "Michael brings plenty of talent to the agency. His skills in forensic accounting are what we need to land good-paying clients. So unless you have a trust fund from Daddy or a magic money tree in your backyard, that's how businesses make payroll month after month."

"Understood. For the record, my dad still works the second shift at Home Depot, and all we have are oaks and magnolias."

"Let's be clear about something else too. This agency won't waste a dime of Mrs. Dean's money. If there's some type of malfeasance, we'll get to the bottom of it, but if you and Michael determine this was a suicide triggered by the pastor's guilt, we'll return the remainder of the advance."

"I wasn't questioning your ethics, Nate."

"Then Michael is your problem? Everyone has to start somewhere. The guy has been taking classes for months. What he needs is practical, hands-on training."

"Do you really think Michael is cut out for PI work?"

"He believes he is, and the will to succeed is three-fourths of the battle." Nate scraped a hand down his jaw. "I'm trying to understand you, Beth. Paul Dean was your pastor while growing up. Didn't you like him? Don't you want to make sure law enforcement didn't jump to the wrong conclusion?"

Beth picked at her cuticle. "I did like him. I used to babysit for their daughter ten years ago. They are…were a nice family. If somebody killed Reverend Dean, I want the creep thrown in jail."

"So we're back to Michael as the stumbling block. I think he's a nice guy. But even if you don't, you'll only have to work with him a few weeks. Once Isabelle and I are back, I'll find separate corners for you to play in. Surely you must have dealt with difficult men at the Natchez Police Department."

If Beth had seen that coming, she might have been better prepared. Unfortunately, she flinched as though stung by a hornet.

"So we have reached the crux of the matter. Natchez is the problem."

"I've spent my entire life here. Is it so hard to believe I want a change of scenery? You and Isabelle are unique. You worked in New Orleans, while she lived in both Nashville and Memphis. Most folks never look over their shoulder when they leave, let alone move back to where they grew up."

Nate shrugged. "Everybody's different, but we're talking about you. When I asked you about your former employment, you implied you left town on good terms. You resigned simply to spare someone on the police force embarrassment. You weren't fired, and no charges were brought by internal affairs."

"All true, but plenty of men on the force are still resentful about my promotion to detective."

"Jealousy exists everywhere people work. I'm sure even Avon ladies squabble over territories and advancements."

"Yeah, but most Avon ladies aren't accused of sleeping their way up the ranks."

"That's what was said about you?"

"By some in the department, yes. And just for the record, it wasn't true. I never had an affair with the boss or anyone else for that matter."

Nate nodded his head. "Often rather innocent work situations are misconstrued by those with corrupt minds."

"Yes, but this wasn't completely misconstrued. The chief had been my mentor, and we became friends...close friends. I would have moved heaven and earth to marry the guy. When he saw where things were headed, he stopped spending time with me. See how good *that* mentoring relationship worked?" She forced a laugh.

"You fell in love with the chief of police?"

"I'm a bit of a cliché. He liked me, and we both liked working together, but in the end I made a first-class fool of myself."

"People often behave irrationally when their hearts take over."

"Yes, but my promotion had been lined up before I started flirting with the boss."

"Workplace romances seldom turn out well."

"I wasn't worried at first. After all, we were just *friends*. Then I fell head over heels in love." Beth dropped her face into her hands. "I was raised to be a nice girl, and I behaved foolishly." Beth pressed on her stomach, which roiled from far too much coffee.

"If you say nothing happened, then I believe you. Eventually, everyone whose opinion matters will too."

"Boss, you should moonlight as a shrink when business gets slow."

Nate rose to his feet with a laugh. "Isabelle would probably disagree."

"I don't know why I'm spilling my guts to you other than my pastor is six feet under." Beth burst into tears.

Nate waited patiently for her composure to return. "I don't mind hearing your confession, Beth, but why would you ask for a job knowing we often work with local law enforcement?"

It was a logical question. Unfortunately, her answer was as lame as her rationale for bad behavior. "Because I couldn't bear the idea of never seeing him again. I didn't come to my senses until I'd been in Vicksburg for a while." She forced herself to meet his eye. "Honestly, I'm over my infatuation, but I'm not sure if Natchez PD is willing to work with me. How effectively can I train Michael if my presence hobbles the investigation?"

"We're back to where we started. For the next three weeks, throw yourself into the case. Give it your best effort. When I get back, we'll have a better grasp of the future. Maybe you'll want to keep working for me and maybe you won't. Just try not to kill Michael while I'm gone." Nate glanced at his watch. "Right now, I need to get my oil changed and tires rotated. We're hitting the highway first thing in the morning. Call me tonight after you've talked to Mrs. Dean."

Beth followed him out the door. "Thanks, for your faith in me. I haven't exactly been employee of the month in the cooperation department."

"That's for sure." He smiled to soften the words. "Give Mike a chance, will ya? He might just surprise you."

"Have a good time with Isabelle," Beth called as they separated in the parking lot. "Watch out for jellyfish, don't get sunburned, and take plenty of pictures."

With a wave Nate drove away. Beth stared into space long after he left. Was she completely over Christopher McNeil? And more to the point, could she work with her former nemeses in Homicide if Pastor Dean really had been murdered?

Ready or not, she was about to find out.

FIVE

ichael arrived at 782 Bennett Avenue by eleven thirty. Habitual about punctuality, he usually arrived early. This particular trait should prove advantageous in his new career. Today it gave him a chance to evaluate the neighborhood of his first client, the widow of the late Reverend Dean. As houses went, this one surpassed the others by a wide margin. It was hardly the traditional abode of a minister of a small church in Mississippi. Multistoried, with rambling wings and porches, the house must contain fifteen rooms, with a landscaped yard that could rival any on the cover of *Southern Living*. Michael spotted a gardener trimming the hedge alongside the cobblestone driveway. *What other Baptist preacher has a gardener and uses cobblestones in Natchez?*

Michael rang the doorbell, fully expecting a butler wearing white gloves to appear. But instead, the immaculately attired, perfectly coiffed Mrs. Dean opened the door with a slight frown. His mother spent Saturday afternoons in capris and cotton T-shirts, with Crocs on her feet and gardening gloves up to her elbows. Margo Preston didn't own suits like that or heels that high.

"Mr. Preston, correct? I was expecting you and Miss Kirby at noon." Mrs. Dean glanced at the diamond-encrusted watch on her wrist. "You're a tad early, but if you can give me five minutes, I'll be right with you."

Without waiting for a reply, she walked through the double doorway into a large living room. Sunlight streamed from floor-to-ceiling windows, giving the room an inviting feel despite the ultra-contemporary decor. "Would you like to have a seat?" Mrs. Dean pointed a long-nailed finger at the sofa before vanishing through another door.

Instead of sitting, Michael inspected the framed photographs on her gallery table. The largest was a black-and-white of Mrs. Dean, perhaps on her college graduation day. Even without makeup and designer clothes, she was an attractive woman. And the last dozen or so years hadn't diminished her beauty.

When he picked up their wedding picture, he blinked. As pretty and vivacious as Mrs. Dean was, Mr. Dean was not. Bald and spectacled, the reverend looked as exciting as graham crackers with a warm glass of milk. He was at least ten years older than his wife and needed to put on twenty pounds.

Picking up a recent school photo, he examined the couple's daughter, a child he'd only glimpsed at the funeral. Unfortunately, Katie Dean took after the paternal side of her family.

"Mr. Preston?" Mrs. Dean's voice from behind nearly made him drop the photo. "Your partner has arrived."

"Thank you, ma'am," he said, replacing the photo. Michael preferred the term "partner" over "trainer." He'd been elevated to equal status.

Judging by her scowl, Beth Kirby didn't agree. "I thought you might be early, so I came early too," she said to him. "But I didn't think you'd arrive in time for breakfast." She sat on the couch and pulled a legal pad, pen, and tape recorder from her tote.

"I didn't think it would be a problem," he murmured.

Mrs. Dean peered from one to the other. "It wasn't a problem. Would either of you like coffee?"

Before Michael could open his mouth, Beth answered for both of them. "No, thank you. We're fine. Shall we get started?"

Michael took the chair next to the widow and allowed his mentor to take the lead.

"First, I'd like permission to record our conversation. Rest assured this will be kept strictly confidential within our agency."

Mrs. Dean paled but nodded approval. "What would you like to know?"

Beth switched on the device. "I'd like you to walk us through the sequence of events on the day your husband died. Please include everything you remember. Although we will obtain photos from the Natchez police, it will be helpful if you describe each detail."

Michael reached for the tablet and pen to take notes as the widow began to talk.

"I returned home from bridge with friends around four, and I entered the house through the garage. It was later than I usually get home, but the house was empty. I called up the stairs several times for Katie, but she didn't answer. Then I found a note from her on the kitchen counter about studying with a friend."

"Did your daughter do that often?" asked Michael.

"Yes, once or twice a week. I thought nothing of it. But I was surprised Paul wasn't here—"

"Was his car in the garage?" interrupted Michael.

"Yes. It was parked in its usual spot. That's what was odd. Paul didn't usually visit the neighbors at the dinner hour."

"So what did you do?" he asked.

Mrs. Dean's forehead creased as though trying to find her place in the narrative. "I decided to telephone him."

"What happened next?" he asked, scribbling furiously.

When she flinched, Beth switched off the recorder. "Why don't we reserve our questions for the end so that Mrs. Dean doesn't keep losing her train of thought?"

"Certainly. I beg your pardon." Michael felt like an admonished child.

"I heard a cell phone ringing in the dining room and started to panic. Paul always kept his phone with him, but there it was, on the dining room table. So I looked for him in the basement and then went upstairs. From our bedroom window I saw that the shed door was open. We seldom used that spidery old space. I wanted to tear it down, but Paul insisted it had historical value." Mrs. Dean took a handkerchief from her sleeve to dab her eyes. "I ran outside as fast as I could and then found him…hanging from the rafters." She paused, her voice cracking.

"Shall I get you some water?" asked Beth. "Do you need a break?"

"No, let's just get this over with." She blew her nose and continued. "The gardening stool was on its side. Paul's feet were only inches from the ground. I remember thinking that if the rope had been longer, he would still be alive." She looked at each of them, her hands clasped in her lap. "I called his name two or three times, but he was gone."

"Did you check for a pulse, Mrs. Dean?" asked Michael.

"No. I could tell he was dead."

"Did you attempt to lift him, to take his weight off the rope?" asked Beth.

"No. I'm terrified to get close to death. I've never approached an open casket in my life or even helped bury the family pet."

Taken aback by her statement, Michael spoke without thinking. "But this was your husband, the father of your daughter."

"I know that, but your disapproval of my phobia won't help find Paul's murderer."

"We're not here to judge, Mrs. Dean. Please continue." Beth cast Michael a withering glare.

Mrs. Dean focused on a vase of flowers. "I went into the house and called 9-1-1 on Paul's phone. I forgot that mine was in my pocket. I waited on the porch, and they arrived within minutes."

Beth inched forward on the couch. "Everything that happened from the time the police showed up will be in their report. But please explain what made you think Paul hadn't taken his own life."

Mrs. Dean's gaze moved to a portrait on the wall, her eyes glassy and vacant as a porcelain doll's. "The rope," she whispered. "It had one of those nooses you see on TV. How would Paul know how to tie one of those? He'd never been a Boy Scout or gone camping in his life. And he was wearing his best suit. If Paul were going to kill himself, he would put on an old one and save his newest to be buried in." Her face contorted as her composure cracked. "I know my husband would never take his own life."

"Did you find the suicide note that Reverend Dean supposedly wrote?" Beth asked.

"No, I left the shed quickly. What if Katie came home and the killer was still nearby? When the police showed me the note later, I knew Paul hadn't written it."

"Why is that, ma'am?" Michael tried to sound respectful.

"Paul didn't use slang. He utilized only proper speech as an example for our daughter and the congregation. Many of them could use lessons in English grammar."

Beth shifted on the couch. "If we are to investigate the death as a potential homicide, we'll need written permission to delve into your personal life, including financial matters. One of the reasons the police ruled this a suicide is because money is missing from the church account. Do you know anything about that?"

"I know Paul would never steal from the building fund. A new Christian school for the community had been his dream for years. He spearheaded the initiative, spent hours studying various designs, and organized fund-raisers for years. His dream would have become a reality when the contractor broke ground next spring." A tear dropped onto her silk jacket.

"I would imagine we're talking a couple million dollars," Michael said. "That kind of money might be hard to resist, even for a man of the cloth."

Beth cleared her throat in protest. "Hold on a minute—"

Mrs. Dean didn't let her finish. "Were you raised a Christian,

Mr. Preston? If you were devout, you would never make such a comment. Paul put his congregation, especially the children, before anything else."

"I apologize for the implication, but I noticed your family lives much better than the average Baptist preacher."

"Hey, partner, Mrs. Dean is our client, not the suspect. Could you ratchet down your—"

"It's all right, Beth. He's not saying anything I haven't heard before." Mrs. Dean lifted her chin and moistened her lips. "I received substantial wealth from my father's estate. Paul insisted I keep the inheritance separate from our joint assets. I bought this house when we married, and I buy my own clothes, car, and pay for Katie's private education. Paul pays...paid for groceries, utilities, and insurance. Things like that. That's how it was in our marriage. Although my husband was content living modestly, he didn't want me to suffer because he chose a poorly paid vocation."

Even Beth's jaw dropped with that comment.

"Sounds like you didn't share his calling," said Michael.

Mrs. Dean didn't flinch, but her voice took on a hard edge. "That's not true. My faith is strong, and I was content as a pastor's wife. But is it really necessary to walk around in sackcloth and ashes to find a place in heaven?"

Beth switched off the machine. "Maybe it isn't necessary, but we're getting a little off track here, Mrs. Dean."

"Alice, please. Are you sure you won't have some coffee or tea?" She directed her inquiry solely at Beth.

"No, thanks. I would, however, like to outline how we'll proceed during our investigation."

"Do you believe my husband didn't kill himself?"

Their entire case seemed to hang in the air with her question.

Beth hesitated only a moment, her pen hovering in the air. "I have no reason not to believe. You knew him better than anyone."

Alice nodded. "Then you may proceed."

"First, we'll review the police report for omissions or misinterpretations which might have led to their conclusion. We'll also study the church's finances. Because your husband had no reason to steal, I'm betting someone else did—someone with access to the account."

"Then start with Ralph Buckley. The finance director had full access to the building fund."

"Of course. We'll speak to Mr. Buckley soon." Beth jotted notes on her pad.

"Did Reverend Dean have any enemies?" asked Michael. "Did anyone have a grudge against him?"

Mrs. Dean's lip furled slightly. "Absolutely not. Everyone loved Paul."

"What about you?" Michael tapped his pen against his briefcase. "Did anyone want your husband out of the picture for personal reasons?"

Her eyes took on a wicked glint. "Do you mean was I having a torrid affair behind Paul's back? Then my lover decided to remove our *obstacle* once and for all? The answer is no, Mr. Preston. Sorry to disappoint."

Beth jumped to her feet. "Okay, everybody just chill. Please excuse my partner, Mrs. Dean. He's new and hasn't learned proper interview techniques. Michael, why don't you wait on the porch while I finish up in here?" She pulled the agency's standard contract from her tote.

"Of course," he said. "I apologize for offending you, Mrs. Dean." Michael nodded politely at their client and walked out the door.

He hadn't meant to be rude, but something about Alice Dean had crawled under his skin. Correction, everything about the arrogant woman rubbed him the wrong way. He was familiar with the type—women who thought their wealth and beauty gave them carte blanche to say and do whatever they pleased.

But if he let his aversion to arrogance ruin his chances at Price Investigations, he was a fool. He really liked his new job. The day he'd packed up his stapler and yellow highlighters at Anderson Accountants was the best day of his life. *You should be able to learn plenty from a seasoned veteran like Beth.* Nate's advice ran through Michael's mind like a radio jingle for toothpaste. If he had a lick of his Mensa-level intelligence, he would keep his mouth shut and his ears open. Because it was unlikely he would ever get a chance like this again.

Six

"Do you have sawdust for brains?" asked Beth, the moment she stepped onto the Deans' front porch. "We gain nothing by infuriating our client, while we exponentially increase the risk of getting fired. Would you like to be the one to tell Nate? He and Isabelle should be finished packing the car by now."

"Did Mrs. Dean fire us?" Every drop of blood drained from Michael's already pasty complexion.

Beth contemplated stringing out his agony to teach him a lesson. But what if he started crying? If that got back to Nate, she would be the one in trouble. "No, not yet, but she's not inviting you back for coffee and Danish."

Michael crossed his arms over his starched shirt. "I know I was out of line, but she didn't act like a grieving widow. Every one of her answers seemed somehow off."

"*Off*—that's the best scientific conclusion you can draw? I thought you earned two master's degrees."

He shrugged. "My degrees in accounting and business management won't help me here."

"So why don't you watch and learn?" She dragged him down the stairs toward their cars.

Michael offered a three-finger salute. "Will do, Captain. I arrived at the same conclusion a few minutes ago."

Beth brushed back her bangs to scratch her forehead. "Some of Mrs. Dean's answers caught me by surprise too, but grief affects people differently. A person doesn't know how they'll react until they lose someone close. Sobbing and teeth-gnashing are often performances for the cameras or the authorities."

"Point well taken." He rubbed his chin as though deep in thought.

"Always let the person talk themselves out, especially if you think they're hiding something. Loose lips sink boats."

"Ships." Michael rolled up the sleeves of his shirt.

"What?"

"Loose lips sink ships."

"What's the difference between a ship and a boat?" Beth stared at the spot between his eyebrows, unable to decide if his eyes were brown or hazel.

"Absolutely nothing." Her partner seemed to be biting his cheek. "Did you notice the family photos on the table?"

"I didn't have to because I've known the Dean family my whole life." Beth had to plaster herself against the car as a panel truck passed too close for comfort.

"With an outsider's objectivity, I noticed that Mrs. Dean is strikingly attractive."

"You don't have to live outside Adams County to see that she's pretty. So what?"

"At the risk of speaking ill of the dead, I noticed Mr. Dean was not particularly attractive."

Beth pointedly looked at her watch. "Is this line of deductive reasoning going somewhere? Because I have a long list of errands to run before dark, especially if I'm heading back to Vicksburg tomorrow."

"I read in the training guide that intuition and first impressions should be taken seriously. My gut tells me something isn't right about their marriage. Why would a rich woman, especially a beautiful one, marry Reverend Dean? If she wants us to look for a killer, maybe it's to direct attention away from her."

Beth shook her head. "Then why hire us at all? Once the police concluded the death was a suicide, she would get away with murder."

"Maybe she took out a big life insurance policy. Doesn't a suicide render the policy null and void?"

"Well done, Sherlock. Too bad policies also don't pay if the beneficiary murders the insured." Beth tore a page of notes from her tablet. "Look, when I talk to Nate tonight, I'll tell him we'll work the case together while he's gone. But—and this part isn't negotiable—I'm the lead. You take orders from me. Can you live with that?"

"Do I still get Sundays off, thirty minutes for lunch, and two weeks of vacation after my first year of employment?"

"Keep up that humor, and my weapon might accidentally discharge into your foot."

"Will I get to carry one of those someday?" Michael pointed at her holstered Glock.

"Not if I have any say in the matter."

"Okay, Miss Kirby. I will do nothing without your express approval." He offered a small but genuine smile.

"Now we're getting somewhere. Tomorrow, I need to drive to Vicksburg and pack my stuff. On Monday, I plan to present my evidence to the DA, which should be enough to bring charges in the case I'm working. I will be ready to start training you on Tuesday. Here is what I need you to do tomorrow and on Monday." Beth plastered a list to his chest.

"I thought I had Sundays off." Michael was grinning, but she couldn't tell if he was joking or not.

"Don't worry. I'm only asking you to attend church, the Baptist in particular. Keep your lips zipped and your ears open. Sit or stand where you can hear what parishioners are saying before and after the service. If you catch someone alone, ask a few *tactful* questions. Don't drop Mrs. Dean's name or mention the fact you're a

PI. And don't divulge a word of Mrs. Dean's suspicions or anything else said inside her home."

"Give me some credit, Elizabeth. I understand the concept of client confidentiality." Michael shoved his hands into his pockets.

When traffic cleared, Beth ducked inside her car and lowered the windows. "Credit needs to be earned with me. On Monday, show up bright and early at the office of Calvary Baptist. Flash your ID and say you're working with the police regarding the death of Reverend Dean. Then ask to see the church's books. Be polite but persuasive, and the assistant will crack like an egg."

Michael bent his head toward her window. "Are we working with Natchez PD?"

"We will be because we have no other choice. Remember, without jurisdiction we can't obtain a court order to see the books. That's why you need to sweet-talk Mrs. Purdy. You can lay on the charm, can't you, Preston?"

His complexion turned rosy. "I probably have an average amount of experience in this area."

"Good. Trot out your best stuff and follow the money trail. If Mrs. Purdy leaves you alone long enough, make photocopies of everything you can."

"Tracking a pattern of pilferage can take days to find, not twenty minutes to an hour." Michael cracked his knuckles. "I know how to do my job, but without unlimited access to the church computer, I hope you haven't set your expectations too high."

"Don't worry. I haven't. Just see if the pastor or anybody else made large transfers of funds during the last year. Look for anything out of the ordinary."

"I'm on it. I'll see who else had authorization to write checks. Despite her denial, I'm curious if Mrs. Dean had her hand in the cookie jar as well." Straightening his spine, he stepped back. "Should I call you Monday evening or wait till you call me?"

"You and I will chat long before Monday night. Just don't mess up the case before I get back in town." Beth started the engine.

"I'll be industrious, tactful, and utterly charming to Mrs. Purdy. You'll be singing my praises in your next report to Nate." Michael winked and turned on the heel of his Oxford shoes.

"Hang on a minute. You never finished explaining your gut instinct about Mrs. Dean's marriage. You think she's guilty because she's pretty? Just because she is beautiful doesn't mean she couldn't fall in love with Paul. I knew him. He was one of the nicest men I've ever met. Isn't love supposed to be blind?"

Michael closed the distance to avoid being hit by oncoming traffic. "Yeah, but it almost never is. In my thirty years on earth, I've only seen gorgeous women with rich men. But hey, she's our client, and I'll give her the benefit of the doubt." With a wave he jogged toward his car, curtailing her chance to probe his sexist preconception.

However, at the moment she had more pressing matters than if Michael was a macho, good old boy. If she was moving back home, even temporarily, she needed to make peace with her mother or find somewhere else to live. Unfortunately, she'd given up her apartment in town when Nate assigned her to the Vicksburg case. So she planned to hit the ATM, stop at the drugstore, and fill her tank with gas. And a visit to the farmer's market made sense. Because her mother wasn't a health-conscious cook, if she didn't intervene, Pops would suffer a coronary before he turned fifty.

Two hours later, with her backseat loaded with fresh produce, Beth punched in her mother's number. Rita picked up on the first ring.

"Have you started cooking yet?" Beth asked.

"Goodness, no. Your father and I ate a big lunch before he left for work. He works late on Saturdays."

"Why don't I pick up something on my way home? Then we can put away my groceries and relax tonight."

"Could you swing by Popeye's for a two-piece white meat meal? I'd like red beans and rice and mashed potatoes with gravy for my sides. Don't forget honey for the biscuits." Her mother didn't sound like someone who had eaten a big lunch. "Don't worry. They have grilled things on the menu that you'll like."

"Sounds good," said Beth, foregoing an opportunity to spar. No doubt there would be others that evening.

On the drive to the restaurant, she passed many of her old haunts. A few triggered painful memories, but most brought back a wave of nostalgia. She had spent the past year buried in her work and out of touch with her old life. Unfortunately, her decision to enter the restaurant instead of using the drive-through proved to be a mistake.

"I'll have the two-piece white meat meal with mashed potatoes and red beans, a three-piece meal of blackened tenders, and an order of Cajun rice," she said to the clerk. "And a large unsweetened tea."

The teenager had barely entered her order when a singsong drawl called her name. "Beth Kirby, is that you, or are my eyes deceivin' me?"

Beth turned to face her three closest friends during high school. "Hey, Kim, Cheryl, Nina. How y'all doin'? It's been a while."

"Just a plain ol' 'hello'? You can do better than that, girl." Kim wrapped her arms around her and squeezed.

Beth smelled her raspberry shampoo and *Light Blue* perfume, the same Dolce Gabbana fragrance she'd worn in high school. Her feelings of nostalgia notched up a level. Cheryl and Nina crowded in, creating a four-way hug.

"You still livin' in Vicksburg?"

"Natchez ain't been the same without your sense of humor."

"Looks like the old band is getting back together!"

Comments and questions were flying, but Beth's tongue suddenly tangled in her throat.

"Give the woman some breathin' space," demanded Kim. Taking charge, she extracted Beth from the other two. "Pay the girl and grab your chow. We already have a table by the windows."

Beth dutifully paid and picked up the bags. "Sorry. I can't stay.

I have to get this home to Ma. She'll throw a fit if her chicken gets cold."

"Your sweetheart of a mother?" Kim dragged her by the arm. "Sit and give us a five-minute update with a promise of more to come later."

Beth slipped into the red leatherette booth. "I'm not sure if you heard, but I'm a PI now, working for Nate Price. Remember him? He was a few years ahead of us in school."

All three women shook their heads.

"Well, I just finished a case in Vicksburg. A nurse had been ripping off an old lady. When her family got suspicious, they hired me to—"

"Are you dating this Nate Price?" asked Cheryl.

"No, he's just my boss. Anyway, I found enough evidence to get the nurse arrested. Too bad she had already spent most—"

"I hope you're back in Natchez for good." Kim reached for her hand. "Nobody thinks badly of you, Beth. Nobody who counts, anyway. There was no call to run off and hide upstate."

"I was working, not hiding."

"Okay, but since Big Chief Christopher is getting along fine, why should you be separated from your family and friends?" Kim squeezed her fingers.

For some odd reason, Beth was shocked by Kim's question. Although she'd been fond of her gal pals, she hadn't lost much sleep over being friendless in Vicksburg. "That's nice of you to say, but I have to go where the boss sends me."

"Well, you're back now and that's what counts."

"How do you know Christopher is getting along fine?" asked Beth, unable to stop herself.

To her credit, Kim didn't exchange glances with the other two. "Because I see him from time to time, washing the car or cutting grass, when I walk Miss Daisy. Don't you remember? J.T. and I bought a house in Oak Knolls, around the corner from him."

Beth gulped her tea and stood up. "Okay, I'm out of here. If

I don't take this fried bird to the lovely Rita, she'll send out a search party. Give me a week to settle in, and then we'll do lunch, a movie, anything as long as we don't discuss Chris McNeil."

"You got it, girlfriend. Welcome home." Cheryl jumped up for a final hug across the table.

Beth blew kisses to them and fled as fast as possible. Despite their repeated references to the past, she felt warm and cuddly inside. It never occurred to her she would be missed by her friends. Apparently, she'd been too busy feeling sorry for herself.

She drove the long route home so she could update her boss in private. Nate patiently listened as she described in detail the meeting with Mrs. Dean, omitting her partner's stupid questions and inappropriate comments.

"So you believe we have a case?" Nate asked. "The pastor's death might not be a suicide?"

"Too soon to say, but I agree with Mrs. Dean about the suit of clothes. That doesn't sound like something he would do. Tomorrow I'll drive up to Vicksburg and clean out my rented room. On Monday I'll present everything to the DA. It should be more than enough to bring charges against Nurse Ratchet. Then I'll start working with Wonder…er, Michael on Tuesday. Are you and Isabelle ready to go?"

"We're packing the cooler and snack bag now."

"They'll have food where you're going." Beth chuckled.

"Are you kidding? It's a four-and-a-half-hour drive to the coast. A person can starve in that amount of time." They shared a laugh. "I appreciate your help in training Michael. You mark my words. That man will be a great asset to our team."

"No problem, but just so we're clear—I'm here for only as long as this case lasts. I don't see myself moving permanently back to Natchez."

"Understood. We'll cross that bridge when we come to it. Stay in touch."

Nate hung up as Beth pulled into the driveway of her parents' three-bedroom bungalow. She saw her mother peeking between the curtains, watching as though she were sixteen years old. As much as she enjoyed reconnecting with her friends, twenty-seven was *way* too old to return to the nest.

SEVEN

Bay St. Louis, Mississippi

*I*f the expression on his wife's face was any indication, their friends and family had made a great choice for their honeymoon destination. The town was charming, with a historic, old-world feel, despite the fact almost everything had to be rebuilt after Katrina. And they both fell in love with Aunt Polly's Bed and Breakfast at first sight.

"Look at these rocking chairs!" squealed Isabelle. She jumped out of the car and ran toward the porch.

By the time Nate parked and carried up their bags, she was rocking as though making up for lost time. "Take it easy. Don't wear out in the first ten minutes."

"According to the brochure, breakfast can be served in the dining room or here on the porch," she said. "We can watch the sunrise over the bay, or maybe the sunset, depending on the direction we face. Isn't it beautiful?"

Nate climbed the steps and dropped their bags. "It's lovely, but don't get too comfortable. Let's see if our room is as pretty as that brochure." The moment Isabelle stood, he swept her into his arms and unlocked the door to their suite.

Isabelle giggled as he carried her across the threshold into a

Victorian sitting room with fourteen-foot ceilings. "Wow, I would say that's a definite yes. Put me down this instant so I can explore."

Nate complied, equally impressed with the furnishings. "Look at the antiques and family heirlooms. I hope I don't break anything."

"Stick with me. I'm seeing what's behind door number two." Isabelle entered a huge bedroom where a massive bouquet of gardenias, a bottle of champagne, and two flutes sat on the table. "Look at those flowers."

Nate plucked a card from the ribbon and read aloud. "Congratulations! Relax and have fun. Don't even think about us working stiffs back home. Your friends in Natchez."

Isabelle stuck her nose in the flowers and breathed deeply. "What do you say? Should we try a glass since they went to so much trouble?"

"Maybe just half a glass. I don't want you getting tipsy." Nate popped the cork and poured the bubbly. But before they had a second sip, she disappeared into the third room.

"Look at the size of the bathroom shower," she called. "Everything looks from a different era, but with every modern convenience."

"Did you notice the TV hidden inside the antique armoire?" Nate opened the paneled doors like a game show host. "I can keep up with ESPN."

Isabelle perched a hand on her hip. "With the Gulf of Mexico at our back door, you want to watch sports? Just smell that salty sea air. I can't wait to go fishing."

"I didn't know you fished," said Nate, shutting the armoire doors. "Are we talking swordfish or bluegills with a bamboo pole?"

"Either will be fine. I can't believe we have a real four-poster bed." She threw herself down on the bedspread, her arms stretched over her head. "I feel like Scarlett O'Hara."

Nate plopped down beside her. "That makes me Rhett Butler." But before he could enfold her in his arms, Isabelle bolted from the room.

"Let's walk the beach," she called from the porch. "No, let's rent bikes and get a feel for the area. No, let's walk to town and go shopping. I don't own enough vacation clothes."

When Nate found her on the porch, leaning over the rail, he wrapped his arms around her waist. "Tomorrow we'll pick out bikes. I vote for walking along the beach to town. By the time we get there, we'll be hungry for supper. We do need to keep up our energy." He wiggled his eyebrows.

"Let's not get sidetracked, Romeo. You bring in our bags while I take a quick shower and put on a sundress. I want our first night in paradise to be perfect. After all, this might be the best vacation we ever have."

"And the most romantic?" He tightened the embrace.

"And the most romantic." Isabelle kissed his cheek and squirmed away.

An hour later, they strolled hand in hand down the beachfront. In the marina, sailboats bobbed like toys in a row, while offshore, larger yachts sparkled like jewels. "How would you like to own one of those someday?" Nate asked, pointing at a speedboat.

Isabelle watched it cut through the waves. "I'd prefer something quieter and more relaxing, where I can throw out a fishing line and catch us dinner."

"Speaking of which, what's your pleasure tonight?" Nate pulled the guidebook from his back pocket. "There are restaurants ranging from gourmet Italian, to casual burgers and fries, to tacos with fresh guacamole."

Isabelle leaned in to study the pictures. "All the fishing talk gave me a hankering for seafood. Find me one of those."

"Your wish is my command, sweet bride." After a short perusal of the map, Nate pointed her shoulders in the correct direction.

"Could we cool the bride and groom stuff? If we mention the word 'honeymoon,' the next question from someone's mouth will be, 'Oh, did you get married over the weekend?' Then, if we say a weekend two years ago, people will think we're nuts."

"Are we the only people in America living on a budget? Okay, mum's the word unless someone notices the dewy look in your eye." He kissed the top of her head, her silky hair tickling his nose.

Once they reached the seaside café, they were shown to the best table in the house. Or maybe there were no bad tables. Nate was so happy, he didn't know which. The service was impeccable, the food delicious, and the conversation livelier than he and Isabelle had shared in months. But as Nate finished his last bite of his entrée, he realized his wife had grown quiet.

"What's wrong, Izzy? Don't you like your dinner? We have enough spending money for you to order something different. Just this once, of course." Nate winked at her and received a disappointing reaction in return.

"Could you excuse me a moment?" Isabelle rose from the table so abruptly her napkin and handbag fell to the floor.

"Shall I have them box this up for you?" he asked, reaching down to retrieve her tiny purse.

She shook her head and disappeared down the hallway.

With his companion gone, Nate's legendary appetite vanished as well. Maybe they ate too many snacks on the drive down. Honey peanuts, strawberry Twizzlers, and Cherry Coke might have been inappropriate appetizers for gourmet seafood. Or perhaps the long car ride or too much sun on their walk upset her stomach. For whatever reason, Isabelle had looked green around the gills when she bolted from the table. When Isabelle's absence stretched into twenty minutes, he began to worry. *Should I call 9-1-1 so paramedics can check the ladies' room or start breaking down stall doors myself?* Nate pulled out his phone.

But before he chose his course of action, Isabelle staggered back to their table and slumped into her chair. "Are you all right?" he asked.

"Not really. I might have food poisoning. Suddenly I felt very sick, and then my expensive dinner went down the drain, so to speak."

"Can't be food poisoning. We both ate the same thing, and I feel fine. In fact, that was the best snow crab I've ever had." Nate scanned the room for their waiter.

"An allergic reaction then. I feel like I'm floating on high seas during a hurricane. Sorry to cut our first romantic evening short, but could we go back to the B and B?" Isabelle sounded downright desperate.

"Right this moment." Nate wrapped an arm around her waist and lifted her from the chair. Together they shuffled toward the hostess station, where he slapped his credit card on the podium. "Miss, could you help us? I don't see our waiter and we need to leave. My wife doesn't feel well."

The hostess took one look at Isabelle, grabbed the card, and hurried through the swinging doors. Isabelle laid her head against Nate's shirt. Her eyes were shut, her skin flushed, and she was breathing through her mouth. A minute later the hostess returned with a man in an expensive suit.

"I'm Mr. Ochs, the general manager. Your meal is on the house. I hope you'll return another night when your wife feels better." He handed back Nate's credit card.

"Thank you, Mr. Ochs. I'm sure we will." But before Nate could put away his MasterCard, Isabelle broke from his embrace and ran out the front doors.

He caught up with her on the sidewalk, halfway down the block. She was leaning against a palm tree, clutching her belly. "Good grief, Izzy. Don't run away from me like that. You scared me witless." He put a steadying arm around her.

"I didn't want to be sick in that restaurant's nice lobby. I must be allergic to crab. Who knew?"

"How could you *not* know you're allergic to crab?"

"I guess I never had it before. Lobster, shrimp, oysters, crawfish—yes, but not crab. Could we not talk about food until tomorrow? Plenty of people out walking haven't had dinner yet. I'd hate to spoil it for them."

"Let's get you back to a rocking chair on the porch." Nate tugged her hand in the direction of the B and B.

"Hold on. I need to tell you something." Isabelle peered up at him with moist, glassy eyes. "Right after I was sick in the bushes, I thought I saw Craig drive by. Of all people to see down here, right?"

"Craig from Nashville?" Nate's incredulity stemmed not from her ex-husband being in Bay St. Louis, but from the fact she was telling him now. She still looked greener than a well-fertilized lawn.

"One and the same. Only his hair was long, and he'd grown a scruffy beard and mustache." Holding her stomach with one hand, Isabelle started to walk. "It almost looked like he was in disguise."

"Then the guy in the car probably wasn't Craig. After all, you were...indisposed."

"But the car was an old blue Toyota. That's what Craig bought when we were married. He kept the Toyota, and I got my Prius in our divorce."

"There are plenty of Toyotas on the road. At any rate, we're on our honeymoon, so let's not worry about Craig or anything else. At least not until you feel better." Nate lifted her chin and kissed her nose.

Isabelle offered a weak smile. "I've ruined our first night in paradise, haven't I?"

"Don't be silly. Nothing is ruined, dear heart. And we have twenty more nights to rekindle the romance." Nate wiggled his eyebrows again, but Isabelle was far too distracted to notice.

EIGHT

*I*sabelle awoke several hours later, groggy and confused but feeling infinitely better. She wasn't sure if it was the can of ginger ale, the soda crackers, or the fact that every trace of crab had left her system, but her stomach felt almost normal again. She gazed around their well-appointed room. The air-conditioning had been turned up and a lightweight quilt pulled to her neck. Moonlight streaming through slits in the wooden blinds danced across the bed, a bed she occupied alone.

Once fully in charge of her faculties, Isabelle headed to the bathroom to wash her face and brush her teeth. Poor Nate! He'd had such high hopes, but her stomach had other plans for the evening. Thankfully, she'd married a thoughtful and considerate man.

Isabelle found her husband asleep in the sitting room recliner, the volume on the TV turned low. ESPN's continuous loop of updates rolled across the screen. After studying his face in repose, Isabelle didn't have the heart to wake him. Although he'd rest better in bed, he might have trouble falling back to sleep. She consulted her watch and made an impetuous decision. Taking her phone to the porch, she settled in a rocker and punched in a number. Craig told her several times that his new wife was a night owl. Cassie liked to read into the wee hours and then take afternoon naps when she got home from work.

"Hello, Cassie?" she whispered when the other end picked up. "It's Isabelle Price from Natchez. I hope I didn't wake you."

"Izzy? Are you and Nate finally on your honeymoon? Of course you didn't wake me. It's barely midnight." Cassie released a cheerful laugh, not sounding at all sleepy. "It'll be hours before I sleep, to quote Robert Frost."

"Thank goodness. I wanted to catch you before things got hectic here. First, thanks again for the thousand dollars you and Craig sent last month. We plan to put that toward a new car for me. At long last, the Prius gave up the ghost."

"You're welcome. Craig regretted sticking you with half the credit card debt in the divorce. Most of it had been cash advances to feed his habit. It's only fair that Craig pays you back."

Isabelle noticed two things about Cassie's reply: Number one, she didn't drop her voice when referring to her husband's addiction. Even though Craig's problems were out in the open, a wife usually spared a husband's feelings by not referencing them. And two, she had used past tense to describe Craig's mind-set. "Well, those checks have been a big help to us. We might have cut our honeymoon short if not for Craig. My car broke down right before we left Natchez." After a moment's hesitation, Isabelle's prodding yielded the intended results.

"I'm glad you were able to get away, but that check might be the last one for a while."

Patiently Isabelle rocked, watching lights twinkle across the bay. "We can get by without the money," she said at last, "but I sense there's something you're not telling me. If you want me to respect your privacy, fine, but if you'd like to talk, I'm here to listen."

"It's a short story, actually. Craig left me. That's why I'm not sure if there'll be any more checks. Apparently, he fell in love with a law clerk where he works." Cassie emitted a bitter laugh. "She's probably more fun than me, but it's hard to stay cheerful while digging out of a financial hole."

Isabelle's heart broke for her ex's second wife. What a nightmare to fall in love with a man with so much baggage and then be left on the sidelines. Yet despite Cassie's frank confession, something niggled in the back of Isabelle's mind. Craig might have an addictive personality, and he might have problems with money management, but he didn't have a cruel bone in his body. And to suddenly tell your new wife she was being replaced was cruel.

"I truly hate to ask, but do you think Craig might have moved to Bay St. Louis with this other woman?"

"Where on earth is Bay St. Louis?" Cassie sounded bewildered.

"It's a nice little town on the Mississippi Gulf Coast, close to Gulfport and Biloxi, but not as well-known."

"Oh, no. Craig would never move to an area that has casinos. He joined Gamblers Anonymous after we got engaged and still regularly attends meetings. Why do you ask?"

Isabelle stopped rocking. "Because I thought I saw him drive by earlier tonight. Did he happen to grow a beard and mustache?"

"You must be mistaken, Izzy. You know Craig hated facial hair. He was even fanatical about five o'clock shadow, remember? He would shave if we were going out. I'm sure he and whoever-she-is still live in Nashville."

Cassie's voice contained so much sadness Isabelle couldn't press the matter any further. "Thanks for clearing that up, and I'm sorry for your loss. Craig didn't deserve you."

"Ditto, wife-number-one. Have fun on your honeymoon, Izzy. Don't give that lowlife we both had the misfortune to marry another thought."

After they hung up, it was a long time before Isabelle could fall asleep. Despite Cassie's and Nate's assurances, she knew whom she had seen on South Beach Drive. Craig Mitchell was in Bay St. Louis. She would know that slimeball anywhere.

NINE

Natchez
Monday

Michael rose at the crack of dawn to begin his new exercise regimen. Although he'd been on the high school track team, his respectable hundred-meter dash hadn't paved the way for a lifetime of physical fitness. Truth be told, he was about the flabbiest skinny guy in western Mississippi, maybe in the entire state. He pulled his brand-new pair of Brooks running shoes from the box. Paying a hundred fifty bucks for a pair of sneakers should prompt him to take this phase of his reinvention seriously. Every cop, private detective, and bounty hunter in the business needed to be in as good shape as the criminals. According to television, felons spent their days pumping iron and playing basketball in the prison yard in preparation for illegal activities upon their release. He hoped he wouldn't encounter any serious bad guys until the regimen improved his strength and endurance.

Slipping on a sweatshirt, Michael jogged down the riverfront trail at an easy pace. All of Natchez lay within easy reach of his second-floor apartment above a law firm. Moving from his parents' house in the suburbs, surrounded by families, had been a good idea. Frugalness kept him living at home longer than most men his age. Even after paying his parents rent, he was able to amass a sizeable down payment. But because he no longer needed a house, moving to Natchez put him close to work and far from his mother's disappointment. Judging by her sorrowful face, you would think she'd been the one jilted.

After a head-clearing run and a hot shower, Michael drove to the office of Calvary Baptist. After yesterday's disappointing service, he was bound and determined to make progress in the investigation. Parishioners before and after church were friendly enough… to each other. But they hadn't exactly poured out their hearts to a stranger. His explanation that he recently relocated here earned him a weekly bulletin, along with info on VBS and the women's club. When he explained that he possessed neither wife nor child, interest in him waned. Or maybe he imagined it. Either way, nobody volunteered anything helpful about the Deans, and his eavesdropping yielded solely how to remove gum from a child's hair. *Elizabeth will not be impressed,* he thought. And Michael wanted nothing standing in his way at Price Investigations.

"Good morning. You must be Mrs. Purdy. I'm Michael Preston." He flashed a smile as he walked through the door.

"What can I do for you, Mr. Preston? I heard you were interested in joining our church." The middle-aged woman dropped what she'd been doing and pulled a brochure from the drawer. "I understand you're from Brookhaven."

Instead of gleaning tidbits from the congregation, he had provided conversation fodder. "Yes, ma'am, but I already have the brochure. I'm here on behalf of Mrs. Dean. She hired our firm to tie up some loose ends regarding her husband's death."

Mrs. Purdy returned the brochure to the drawer. "Are you with the marble engraving company? I thought the funeral home would handle the headstone."

"No, I'm here to look at the church's financial records. I understand there's some confusion, and I'd like to straighten it out."

She blinked several times. "Financial records?"

"Yes, ma'am. Most likely, you have an accounting program that manages receivables and payables, and separates the contributions into various funds."

"Well, sure, we have a separate account to pay salaries, utilities, and maintenance. Then there's a mission fund and the building fund for the new school. But I don't have the password to those files. I just handle prayer requests, email, the daily devotion, and the weekly newsletter." She pushed up from her desk. "Care for a cup of tea, Mr. Preston? I was about to make one for myself."

"I would love one, ma'am." Michael followed her to a tiny kitchen. "I want to do anything I can to help. I feel so sorry for Mrs. Dean."

"My, yes. Paul was such a good man." She sighed as she filled the teakettle with water.

"I don't know how she'll manage without the pastor's salary." He leaned one shoulder against the doorjamb. "It's expensive to raise a daughter these days."

"Money is one problem she won't have." Her voice lost its tender concern.

"Oh, does Mrs. Dean work outside the home?" Michael took two mugs from their hooks and set them within easy reach.

"Of course not. Women like her don't *work*," Mrs. Purdy sneered. "She had a million-dollar policy on her husband. I know, because I witnessed his signature on the application. Paul told me not to talk about this, but with him gone, why should I protect her reputation? What does a God-fearing woman need with that big a policy? You need enough for a decent burial and to put the kid through college. More than that would be greedy. The premiums must have been through the roof." She took the mugs and filled them from a hot-water dispenser by the sink.

"It does sound a tad extravagant. Do you remember which insurance company issued the policy?" Michael tried not to sound as though he were on the verge of an investigative breakthrough.

She tapped her lips with an index finger. "Hmm…I'm not sure. It's been a while."

"Unfortunately, most policies won't pay in cases of suicide."

"Oh, my. What a *shame*," she said, dunking her tea bag vigorously. The glint in her eye underscored her words' true meaning.

"Who did have the passwords to the accounts, ma'am?" he asked to get back on track.

"Only the reverend and Ralph Buckley, our finance director. But Ralph left town right after the funeral. I suppose he needed time to mourn."

"May I see the checkbook register for the church account?"

"Sure, but it isn't here. Paul took it home to get bills caught up. He worked in the evening after supper."

"Was that normal? I mean, didn't you say Ralph Buckley was in charge of finances?"

"Yes, but Ralph's been under the weather due to his angina."

Michael sipped his tea to hide his disappointment. *No access to the church hard drive or the checking account. Zero for two.* "Thank you. I'll stop back after Mr. Buckley returns. For now, please accept my condolences on the loss of your friend."

Her face brightened. "Thank you, young man. Paul was my friend. And Lord knows that man needed all he could get. See you on Sunday," she added when he was halfway down the hall.

Michael received a less cordial reception at stop number two.

Alice Dean opened the front door barely enough to hold a conversation. "Mr. Preston? I understood Miss Kirby wouldn't be back until tomorrow."

"Correct, but she asked me to start reviewing financial records in her absence. According to Mrs. Purdy, the church checkbook is here." He smiled. "May I come in, please?" For one dreadful moment, he thought she would refuse.

"Very well, as long as you don't need my help. I'm quite busy today, as you can imagine."

Actually, he had no idea what recent widows faced but thought it prudent not to ask. "Could you point me in the direction of Reverend Dean's study?"

Mrs. Dean turned on one heel and marched down the hallway, stopping at the last door. "The church account is the red leather-bound book on the right. All checks have an old-fashioned duplicate copy. Payables are entered into the computer on a daily basis. Take as long as you need and then let yourself out. I'll be upstairs emptying out closets."

The moment she disappeared, Michael relaxed. He sat down at the pastor's cluttered desk and immersed himself in papers, files, and ledgers. Finally, a world he was comfortable in.

Although his eyesight was excellent, Michael slipped on a pair of readers. Magnifying whatever he focused on allowed him to concentrate on details. But after an hour of poring over the last six months of checks drawn on Calvary Baptist's account, he'd found nothing out of the ordinary: utilities, payroll for Mrs. Purdy, insurance, plumbing repair bills, a new air-conditioning condenser— the endless costs of maintaining a public building. Then he noticed one troubling discrepancy. Although the person authorized to sign on the account was Paul A. Dean, the signatures weren't remotely the same. At least half the checks had been written by someone else—someone who made little attempt to emulate the pastor's hand.

And Michael had a good idea who forged the pastor's name. With a shiver of excitement, he pulled out the agency's signed contract from his briefcase. He might not be a handwriting expert, but considering Mrs. Dean's fondness for mixing block letters with cursive, none would be necessary. *Who beyond the sixth grade still uses a snowman for the numeral eight?* Some of the checks to pay church expenses had been signed by Alice Dean. Correction, forged by Alice Dean. With the barest twinge of shame, Michael rummaged through the pastor's desk until he found the Deans' personal checkbook register. Although both names were on the account, hadn't she stated that her husband paid the household bills? Not according to the signature on most of the checks.

Alice Dean held the financial reins of the family, and maybe for the Calvary Baptist Church of Natchez too. She might already be rich, but if she played her cards right, she was about to add another million dollars to her coffers. All she had to do was find someone to take the rap for her husband's death.

And she thought he and Elizabeth were here to help.

TEN

Bay St. Louis

When Nate awoke Monday morning, his bride was still sleeping soundly, so he left her that way. Her first night on the Mississippi Gulf Coast had been rough. No one liked to be sick to their stomach, especially away from home. He placed another bottle of water and pack of crackers on her nightstand, dressed in shorts and sneakers, and tiptoed out the door. Outside the sun reflected brightly off the calm water, while a breeze offered relief from the high humidity. In the bay, boats trawled for shrimp, hoping to fill their nets before seagulls ate up their profits for breakfast.

After debating his choices, he decided it was already too hot for his usual morning run. With bikes available at no charge at the B and B, he could ride around the peninsula for an hour and be back about the time Izzy should wake up.

Nate headed north on North Beach Boulevard, past the yacht club and around Coward's and Cedar Points. The faster he pedaled, the freer he felt, as though his entire world consisted of land, water, wind, and the bike. He definitely would invest in a twelve-speed when he returned home, and maybe one for Isabelle too. He turned down Engman Avenue to shorten his trip by cutting inland and ran smack into the Golden Magnolia Casino.

What an extravaganza of a resort, with a high-rise hotel, an RV park, a marina, and golf course, besides the main attraction, which separated tourists from their money. Nate had nothing against gambling per se. He just never had the desire to lighten their already anorexic bank account. But maybe he and Izzy would stop in since he heard casinos had the best buffets in the business.

Circling the parking lot, Nate decided to head down Golden Magnolia Boulevard, confident it would lead him back to Route 90 and Old Town. But as he rode past the grand entrance, he spotted a familiar face exiting the casino. At least the man looked like Izzy's former husband. Or had her suggestion simply put ideas in his head? With a scruffy beard, long hair, and a ball cap pulled low, Nate couldn't be sure.

He rolled to a stop under a tree and watched as the man climbed into a beat-up Toyota and backed from the parking space. He'd only seen two or three photos of Isabelle and Craig taken at long-ago barbecues. Isabelle said she'd burned their wedding album in the fireplace after he filed for divorce. She was lucky her rashness hadn't burned down the house. When Nate saw the photos, he thought her ex looked like the quintessential lawyer—clean-cut, buttoned down, and almost nondescript, at least from a mildly jealous perspective.

Today Nate was the lucky one. When the early gambler drove away, he passed right by where Nate backpedaled in the shade. Even though a closer look wouldn't do Nate much good since he'd never met Craig in person, recognition clearly registered on the man's face. Izzy's ex stared, blinked, and then punched the gas pedal.

So much for Isabelle being mistaken.

But what difference did it make? Craig was water over the dam. If Nate remembered correctly, Craig had remarried and was living happily ever after in Nashville. It was unfortunate if he had succumbed to his gambling addiction, but was that their problem? He and Isabelle had worked so hard lately, maybe too hard. Long before Nate reached downtown Bay St. Louis, he'd made up his mind to say nothing about his discovery. This was a chance to put their marriage first. And maybe—just maybe—let nature take its course.

When Nate skidded to a stop in front of Aunt Polly's B and B, his bride was sipping a cup of tea on the porch.

"Sneaking off for a bike ride without me?" she asked, her dimples deepening with her smile.

He leaned the bike against a tree and jogged up the steps. "I thought I'd let you sleep, but if you're willing, there's a three-speed with your name on it. Good morning, my queen." He leaned in for a kiss.

"Hello, my prince. Breakfast will be out in a few minutes. It was last call, and I am famished." Isabelle pointed at a table set with crystal and china.

"You should be. Hunger is a good sign." Nate held out his elbow to escort her to her chair. "What would you like to do today? How about a dolphin-watching excursion or maybe deep-sea fishing?"

Isabelle shook her head. "Nothing in a boat on water."

"How about a drive along the beach road to Alabama? We'll see the entire Mississippi Gulf Coast. Or we could ride bikes and learn our way around."

Her smile turned apologetic. "Could we avoid riding on either two or four wheels until I'm sure my stomach is back to normal?"

"Then why don't we walk to town? That should keep your feet planted on solid ground." Nate sat down just as Mrs. Russo delivered their breakfast—pecan French toast, crisp bacon, and fresh fruit with cream.

Smiling, Isabelle picked up her knife and fork. "Thanks. I promise not to be a stick-in-the-mud for the entire trip." She munched a piece of bacon.

"We have all the time in the world," he said.

Actually, Nate couldn't wait to start vacationing. Now that they were here, he wanted to leave no stone unturned. He consumed his breakfast as though he hadn't eaten in days.

Isabelle dawdled, as usual. When she finally went inside to do her makeup, Nate took a two-minute shower and then tapped his toe on the porch for another fifteen.

But the leisurely stroll to Old Town was worth the wait. Inside the historic train depot they found one room filled with Mardi Gras costumes and another dedicated to Mississippi blues musicians.

Isabelle stopped in front of a portrait of several legendary greats. "Do you think my brother might have become famous one day?" she asked softly. "Danny had just started composing music before he died."

Nate wrapped an arm around her waist. "No doubt in my mind. Everyone said he was the most talented sax player they had ever heard."

"They could have put his picture here, next to the twentieth-century bluesmen." Her fingers hovered over an empty area in the painting. For several moments Nate and Isabelle were alone in the museum, surrounded by ghosts from a bygone era. Then a shrill voice pierced the melancholy mood.

"Where were you folks during the hurricane of 2005?"

They pivoted to find a sweet-faced volunteer named Joni, according to her name tag.

"I was finishing college at Mississippi State in Starkville," said Nate, thankful for the interruption.

"I was at Vanderbilt University in Nashville," offered Isabelle.

"Me, I was living here." Joni pointed at the tile floor. "This area east of New Orleans was ground zero during Katrina. Would you folks like to see our album of before-and-after pictures? Wait until you see the progress we've made in ten years."

"We would love to." Isabelle took a final look around and hurried from the room of guitars, trumpets, and ghosts of what-could-have-been.

Nate wasn't nearly as excited to see a bunch of old photos, but halfway through the album he changed his mind. To say Bay St.

Louis had made strides was an understatement. After being wiped off the map, residents returned to rebuild the Bay Bridge, the roads, and almost every building to equal or exceed the original charm. Joni shared harrowing tales of those who rode out the storm, clinging to tree limbs for hours or hiding in attics until the water receded. Nate and Isabelle were rendered speechless.

"Well, that's enough about the past," she said, closing the album. "Be sure to tell your friends about us, and don't miss the art gallery upstairs. It's the work of a local gal who knew that life shouldn't be taken too seriously."

When Joni moved off to a new batch of visitors, Nate whispered in Isabelle's ear. "If it's the same to you, let's skip the room of wannabe Renoirs."

"We'll do nothing of the sort." Isabelle slapped his wrist for good measure. "That tour guide made me feel part of her family in five minutes. I don't want to hurt her feelings." She pulled him toward the elevator.

"All right. We'll check out the artwork. I'm curious about anyone who can keep an upbeat attitude during a hurricane."

Upstairs, the work of Alice Moseley surprised him as much as the photo album. Considering the woman had never picked up a paintbrush until her fifties, her extraordinary life gave hope to retirees wishing to reinvent themselves. When Isabelle wandered off in search of a restroom, Nate bought her a whimsical print of cotton fields, sharecropper shacks, and a balky mule. Alice Moseley sure had a humorous way of seeing the past.

Nate found Isabelle by the railroad tracks behind the museum. "I got you a souvenir to remember our trip." He produced the bag from behind his back.

Isabelle smiled as she pulled out the print. "This one was my favorite too. Thanks, honey." She buzzed his cheek with a kiss.

"Where to now?" Nate unfolded his map of Old Town.

She took little time to peruse. "Let's go shopping here and

here and here." She tapped on a vintage clothing shop, a fair trade importer, and a jewelry store whose name he couldn't pronounce. "And, of course, the bookstore."

"Did you win the lottery when I wasn't looking?" he murmured as she pulled him down the street.

"Relax. I'll only ogle and drool. And I'll let you pick where we have dinner tonight. Anything but seafood."

After what seemed like six hours of browsing shops, Nate was ready to eat the stale breath mints in his pocket. When Isabelle finally wore out, he selected the first place they came to, North Beach Restaurant. Fortunately, Monday was a slow day, and they were seated on the patio with a view of the bay. "See anything on the menu you like?" Nate realized too late that most of the choices were seafood. "If not, we can go somewhere else."

"And give up this view?" Isabelle shook her head. "I'm having the eggplant parmesan."

"Good choice. I'm going with the rib eye. Now, show me the books you bought." Nate leaned back in his chair.

By the time Isabelle showed him her five books, the waitress appeared to deliver their drinks and take their orders.

With a glass of lemonade in hand, Nate settled back to appreciate the ambiance and admire his lovely wife. But instead, guilt crawled up his spine like a millipede. He didn't like keeping secrets, especially not one that struck a personal chord with her.

"I have a confession to make," he blurted out. "I saw Craig this morning while you were still sleeping."

The breadstick halted halfway to her mouth. "When you were riding your bike? Where was he?"

"I rode to the north end and ended up in the parking lot of the Golden Magnolia Casino. Craig had just walked out and was getting into his car."

Isabelle dropped the breadstick onto her plate. "So I wasn't seeing things last night. He has fallen off the wagon." Her complexion lost much of its color.

"I wasn't sure it was him because he didn't look like the guy in the photos I've seen. But when we made eye contact, he reacted. I thought he might have a stroke." Nate crossed his arms over his chest. "I can't believe he went gambling that early in the morning. We hadn't eaten breakfast yet."

"You don't understand gamblers. Craig probably played all night. He would grab something to eat and then hit the sack, not to surface again until late afternoon." Her shoulders slumped. "What a shame. I had high hopes for his second marriage."

Nate leaned back as the waitress delivered their first course. "It is a shame, but check out these salads. Just how you like it, with fresh mozzarella, radishes, and chickpeas." He chewed a leaf of romaine. "Tastes like it was picked yesterday. Dig in, Izzy."

His enthusiasm had little effect. Isabelle speared a cherry tomato, but left it on her plate. "I have a confession to make too," she said after a pause. "I woke up last night around midnight feeling a whole lot better. You were asleep in the chair, so I called Cassie Mitchell."

Nate almost choked on his food. "Your bridegroom falls asleep and you call your ex's second wife?"

She smirked. "Sounds ridiculous, but I wanted to thank her for their generous check."

"You already wrote a thank-you note. Besides, the money was a payback, not a magnanimous gift." Nate stuffed his mouth to keep from saying something he shouldn't.

"I know that, but still, some exes wouldn't make the effort. Anyway, Cassie said that Craig left her for another woman. Someone in his office. She was heartbroken."

"Tigers will never change their stripes. Eat, Isabelle. This salad is delicious."

"You're right." Picking up her fork, she ate a single chickpea.

But after two years of marriage, Nate wasn't fooled. By the time he finished his salad, and hers had wilted from being poked at, he leaned back in his chair. "Okay, Izzy, out with it. What's on your mind?"

Her green eyes peered up at him through thick lashes. "I can't help thinking we should do something to help. Poor Cassie is alone in Nashville, totally unaware Craig is here in Bay St. Louis."

"This is not our business." Unfortunately, that came out a tad stronger than necessary. "I mean, we're here on our honeymoon, at long last."

"I'm not suggesting we play marriage counselors, but shouldn't we see if Craig needs our help?"

"Intervention is what you're suggesting. And from everything I've read, you can't help someone who doesn't want to change."

"That's what I was told too." She pushed away her salad as the waitress delivered her eggplant parmesan. "My, doesn't this look yummy?" But her merry tone fooled no one. From her expression, she might have been gazing at pizza sat on by an elephant.

Nate felt his temper starting to boil. He took a few deep breaths before reaching for her hand. "Please trust my judgment. You can say a prayer for Craig, but this trip is about *our* relationship. I want us to forget about jobs and ex-husbands and concentrate on us. Aren't women supposed to be into romance?"

Izzy squeezed his fingers. "You're absolutely right. I can't speak for the rest of my gender, but I'm into it for the next three weeks."

Nate picked up his knife and fork and attacked his steak. He had no desire to gauge her inner feelings or discuss her ex-husband any further. Sometimes a man had to put his foot down. And beyond a shadow of a doubt, this was one of those times.

ELEVEN

Natchez

"Are you awake, child?"

Beth opened one eye to see her mother's lined face. "I am now."

"There's a young man waiting for you on the porch. I told him you got home from Vicksburg very late last night, but he said he would keep himself busy until you were ready." Rita ruffled the back of her head. "He said he's your partner. Is that true?"

"Just for a while." Beth bolted upright and kicked off the covers. "Why doesn't he meet me at the office?" She peeked through the curtains. Sure enough, Michael's tiny Fiat was parked on the street.

"That's what I suggested, but he said Maxine is taking a few days off. The office is locked up tighter than a drum. Should I invite him in for pancakes and bacon?"

"If you do, we'll never be rid of him. I'm jumping in the shower. Then I'll take breakfast to go. Thanks, Ma." Beth kissed her cheek on her way into the bathroom.

"What should I do in the meantime?" Rita whispered as though Michael might be within earshot.

"Nothing, trust me. Like a cockroach at a garden party, just pretend you don't see him."

When Beth emerged twenty minutes later, Michael was in the

porch swing, his laptop propped on one knee. "How did you find me?" she asked.

"Maxine gave me your address. She made sure I had everything before she left on vacation. Did you need anything from the office?" He slipped his laptop into his bag.

"If I do, I have a key." Dropping into a chair, she opened a waxed paper packet and handed him one just like it. "Breakfast from my mom. Don't get used to it."

"What is this?" Michael unwrapped his curiously.

"A bacon, egg, and pancake sandwich, perfect for on-the-go lifestyles."

"Is this an ethnic concoction?" He sniffed and took a small bite.

"I have no idea. Eat or don't eat, but tell me what you found out."

While Beth enjoyed her breakfast, Michael explained in great detail what she already knew. "We already talked about insurance," she said. "Why would Mrs. Dean want it to look like a suicide if she had a large policy? And the fact she signed her husband's name to pay bills means nothing."

"That's forgery and potential fraud, which isn't nothing."

"Do you have any idea how many wives sign their husband's name in this country? We'd have to build a lot more prisons. Don't call the FBI unless you saw a forged signature on a bank transfer to a Cayman Island account." Beth tipped up her travel mug for a mouthful of coffee.

"Roger that, but wire transfers wouldn't be in a checkbook register. I need access to the church's hard drive." Michael pulled out a piece of bacon and ate it separately.

"All in good time. At least you ingratiated yourself to Mrs. Purdy. That woman doesn't usually cotton to outsiders." Beth finished her sandwich and scrambled to her feet.

"So where to today, partner?" Carefully rewrapping his pancakes, Michael tucked them in his briefcase.

"That's what we need to discuss. When I ask the chief for copies of the police report and Pastor Dean's autopsy, I'd like to be alone."

Michael shook his head like a stubborn mule. "No way. Nate told you to train me while he's gone."

"Try to be mature about this, Mikey. I will train you, but just not today." Beth walked down the steps toward her car.

Michael shuffled his feet behind her. "Might I know the reason for my exclusion and what I should do in the meantime?"

Turning to face him, Beth peered into his soft brown eyes. "Do you know that I used to work for the Natchez PD? There were some hard feelings when I left. This will be my first conversation with the boss since my resignation."

"Ah. I understand. Sorry if I pushed too far."

"No problem. You can't be expected to read my mind." Beth opened her trunk to lock up her firearm.

His face brightened with a smile. "Why don't we spit on our palms, shake hands, and call it even?"

She slammed the trunk and stepped back. "You're kidding, right?"

"Yes, Elizabeth, I'm kidding. I'll look into Calvary Baptist Church in case any financial dealings made the papers. Then I'll check the backgrounds of Alice and Paul Dean and this Ralph Buckley. When you're done at the station, how about if I buy us lunch...or dinner?"

"After that gourmet meal? You better hope Mom doesn't find out you stuck it in your briefcase."

"If I can sweet-talk Mrs. Purdy, I can handle your mother. Tell her thank you, by the way."

"I bet you can. We'll talk later." With a wave, Beth drove off and laughed halfway to her destination. Who would have guessed Michael was the type to handle Rita Kirby? He just earned one point on the tally board. But as the one-story brick building loomed into view, Beth forgot about tally boards and eccentric mothers. She thought solely about Christopher McNeil, a man who had wormed his way into her heart and ruined her life.

She should have made an appointment instead of marching

in and demanding to see such an important man. Unfortunately, preplanning had never been her strong suit. Inside the outer lobby, she picked up the wall phone and waited for the dispatcher. "Good morning," she greeted. "I'm Elizabeth Kirby. May I see Chief McNeil for a few minutes?"

"Who?" came the standard reply as the woman searched for her pen.

"Elizabeth Kirby." She omitted saying she was a former employee so she wouldn't be frisked or scanned for explosives.

"Do you have an appointment, Miss Kirby?" The dispatcher asked politely, despite already knowing the answer.

"No. I just arrived in town, but this shouldn't take long." Beth drew a breath and held it.

"Let me check if Chief McNeil is in the building." It was the standard reply so that undesirables could be avoided.

While Beth waited, the heavy steel door swung open and the shift sergeant appeared in the doorway. The man wasn't one of her loyal fans. "You carrying a firearm, Miss Kirby?"

"I certainly am not."

"Wait here," he barked, and the door swung shut.

During the several-minute interim, Beth pictured Chris as balding, fifty pounds heavier, and twenty years older. When the sergeant reappeared, she was led down the hallowed hallway into an office that once held great significance for her. When she stepped across the threshold, her heart seized in her chest.

"Buzz if you need backup, Chief," said the sergeant, closing the door behind her.

Chris hadn't grown paunchy, or bald, or dissipated during the last twelve months. If anything, the additional gray at his temples made him look more distinguished. How unfair was that?

He rose to his feet and extended his hand. "Beth, what an unexpected pleasure! Have you moved back to Natchez?"

Beth shook hands clumsily. "No, I'm just here temporarily for a case." Like a bashful schoolgirl, she shifted her weight between her hips.

"Please make yourself comfortable." He pointed at a chair and sat down.

"I hope I'm not interrupting." Beth perched on the edge of her seat as though prepared for quick flight.

"Not at all. How have you been?" He offered the same snake-charmer smile that made her hear wedding bells.

Remembering how easily she'd fallen for him, Beth stiffened her spine. "I'm fine, but this isn't a social call. I've been hired by Mrs. Paul Dean to investigate the pastor's death."

He looked flummoxed. "I'm not sure what there is to investigate. All indications pointed to suicide, as tragic as that is for the Dean family."

"Did your officers scratch beneath the surface or just go by their gut instincts?"

Chris's pleasant demeanor slipped a notch. "My detectives did their job, Beth. I personally reviewed the evidence connected to his death. Paul was my pastor as well as my friend."

Beth felt her face grow warm. "Sorry. That was about the rudest thing I could possibly say." She focused on the wall clock, trying to regain her composure.

"You're forgiven. I'm sure approaching me on behalf of Mrs. Dean wasn't easy for you. Tell me what you need."

Somehow his attitude struck her as condescension. "A copy of the police report, along with the coroner's autopsy report. Mrs. Dean believes her husband was a victim of foul play. Certain details of the reverend's death don't fit his character." *Foul play. Did I really use that term with my old boss?*

He folded his hands over his flat belly. "Such as?"

"Such as the perfectly tied hangman's noose around his neck. How would a minister know how to tie one of those?"

He nodded in agreement. "That also struck Detective Lejeune

as odd. Apparently, instructions on constructing one are online, and the detective found the website in Paul's browser history."

Beth felt her shirt sticking to her back. "You've got to be kidding."

"I assure you, I'm not. What else troubles Mrs. Dean?"

"Her husband was wearing his best suit of clothes. Wouldn't he have saved that to be buried in?"

He leaned back in his chair. "Frankly, if I'd reached so low a point that I wanted to end my life, I wouldn't care what outfit I wore."

She swallowed hard to erase the mental image. "Mrs. Dean also thought the wording on the suicide note didn't reflect her husband's speech patterns."

Chris focused his gaze on her as he drew a manila folder from his drawer. His piercing gray eyes were the ones she'd seen in her dreams for months. "I still have Paul's file handy. That's how hard it is for me to let this go." He shuffled through until he found a piece of notebook paper. "Shall I read this aloud or would you like to see it?"

"Could I see it, please?" Beth's stomach clenched with apprehension as she read the short note. "I'm so sorry, Allie. This sure is a coward's way out. I hope you and Katie will forgive me. But I can no longer forgive myself. If God's merciful, I'll see you again someday." Mutely, she laid the note on his desk.

"The wording sounds normal to me. What did Mrs. Dean object to—sure instead of surely, or maybe the contraction of God with the word is?"

Beth shrugged. "I don't know, but I had to follow up with you."

"I'll have copies made of the autopsy, the police report, and the note, but regrettably Detective Lejeune found strong motivation for Paul's suicide." Chris slicked a hand through his wavy hair. "Close to five hundred thousand dollars appears to be missing from one of the church's accounts. According to Ralph Buckley, Paul had taken control of the building fund. Because the money wouldn't be needed for another year, it was to have been prudently invested.

If the reverend suffered serious stock market losses, he might have been unable to face the congregation."

"That's a whole lot of assumption, Chris."

His crow's feet deepened with his smile. "It certainly is, but right now I have nothing else to offer you."

His choice of words took her back twelve months when she'd wanted everything he couldn't offer. Beth scrambled to her feet. "I appreciate your making time for me. I'll wait for those copies in the outer office."

"It was good seeing you, Beth. If anything changes on my end, I'll let you know. And I'd appreciate the same courtesy from Price Investigations." He tapped the papers into a pile. "How do you like being a PI? I heard Nate Price is a stand-up kind of guy."

Once again his casual nonchalance annoyed her. *Does he expect me to discuss my new boss like we're old friends? Or that we can just pick up where we left off?* "Things at work are hunky-dory, Chris. Life sure has a way of marching on."

And though she was shaking on the inside, she left his office without a backward glance.

TWELVE

*M*ichael could have kicked himself the moment Beth drove away. Why had he badgered her about her appointment? Nate had mentioned that she'd worked for the police department. She wouldn't have left a regular paycheck with great benefits to work for a new PI firm unless there had been trouble. If this was a personal hot button, he wouldn't make any friends being nosy. And with Nate out of town, he needed someone to teach him the ropes.

Back in his apartment, Michael settled into what he did best—ferreting out information on the Internet. Almost everyone had something to hide…a risqué photo taken during college, a bankruptcy due to a spendthrift spouse, a reckless driving conviction. But try as he might, he found nothing sketchy about either the reverend or Mrs. Dean. Not from their college days or spring break vacations or anywhere they lived prior to their current residence.

Paul Dean graduated from seminary in the top five percent of his class and had been halfway to his doctorate in divinity when he accepted his first position as pastor. During summers he volunteered at soup kitchens, literacy programs for new immigrants, and built new homes with Habitat for Humanity. He had paid back his student loans and regularly donated more than ten percent to his church.

Alice Dean wasn't a stellar student in high school, but she had been the homecoming queen. In college her academics weren't much better, but she had joined a sorority and earned a bachelor's degree within the normal time frame. Her parents had plenty of money, with a second home in Orange Beach, Alabama, along with a condo in Vail. No surprise there. The Deans' move to unpretentious Natchez must have been disappointing for a bona fide debutante who had skied during Christmas vacations in her youth. Yet on the plus side, the former Alice Parker had zero scrapes with the law, owed not a dime for her four years at Auburn, and participated in several mission trips to Haiti with her church. Most likely that's where she'd met and fallen in love with Paul Dean.

Michael couldn't find any information about her trust fund, but her credit rating was top-notch. Nothing in their backgrounds suggested the Deans were anything but the perfect American couple. Likewise, Calvary Baptist Church wasn't running a crooked bingo parlor in the basement or selling counterfeit CDs of Christian pop music. Michael padded into the kitchen for a Coke before beginning his background check on Ralph Buckley, whose absence following the funeral placed him high on the suspicion meter. But before he could pop the top, his cell phone rang. Caller "Unknown" killed his hopes of it being his partner.

"Hello, Mr. Preston?" asked a cheery voice. "Natalie Purdy from Calvary Baptist. How are you, dear?"

"I'm well, thank you. How about you on this fine day?" Michael trotted out his seldom-used small talk skills.

"I'm fine. Just a bit wilted from this heat. I remembered that you wanted to look into our church financial records on behalf of Alice."

Michael nearly choked on his mouthful of soda. "Yes, I do. Did Mr. Buckley return from his trip?"

"No, and I'm peeved he still hasn't called here. So I checked a few places in his desk, and sure enough, I found his password to the Excel files. Typical man…he left the password in plain sight in a little notebook in his bottom drawer. If you're not busy, you could swing by and check those accounts."

"That's very nice of you," he said, smiling at the notion that a closed bottom drawer could be considered "plain sight." "I will be there in ten minutes."

Michael stopped at a bakery for a key lime pie and arrived in fifteen. He almost purchased pecan but remembered his mother's complaints about fat grams in nuts. *Anything made with limes must be low cal.* "I brought you a little something for break time," he said, stepping into the church office.

"Oh, my word. Key lime—my favorite." Mrs. Purdy read the label on the string-tied box. "I knew you were a nice man the moment we met. Too bad my daughters are both married, or I would fix you up. Let me put this in the refrigerator." Carrying his gift into the small kitchen, she called over her shoulder. "I stuck the password on the monitor with a Post-it. Why don't you get started? If you don't mind being here alone, I need to make a quick trip to the post office."

Mind? It was a forensic accountant's dream to be alone with data with a flash drive in his pocket. "Not at all. Take whatever time you need." But before she could leave with her armload of letters, Michael's conscience kicked in. "Do you think Mr. Buckley would mind if I backed up the information onto a memory stick? I promise it will be kept confidential." "Backed up" sounded much better than "pirated" or "stole."

Mrs. Purdy took little time to decide. "You go right ahead, young man. If money is missing from one of the accounts, Ralph had no business picking now to take his vacation. Someone needs to track down those funds so poor Paul doesn't look like a crook. Our pastor wouldn't steal a pen from the bank, let alone money from the school fund." She bustled out the door.

At the computer, Michael cracked his knuckles like a concert pianist before a tricky concerto. Yet his scan of the operations account yielded nothing. All maintenance expenses seemed normal, and regardless which Dean actually wrote the check, the reverend had entered the debit into the correct column. At first glance, the mission fund also appeared legitimate, although he wouldn't know for sure until he verified that those missionaries actually worked in the field. Michael copied the data onto his flash drive and turned his attention to the third account for the new school. It proved to be the mother lode of investment activity.

Since the account's inception four years ago, money had been accumulating at an amazing rate. Unless this was the largest Episcopal or Catholic parish in New York City, Michael couldn't imagine donations this generous in a town like Natchez. As he reviewed the month-by-month balance sheet, he realized growth had come not from the collection plate, but from risky investments in junk bonds, short-term commodity futures, and nondiversified sector mutual funds. Such investments were for the rich or those who were savvy in the stock and bond markets.

Considering his education and a life devoted to spiritual pursuits, Paul Dean was neither. And nothing in his wife's background would have provided the know-how. Michael finished copying the rest of the files just as Mrs. Purdy returned from her errands.

"How are you doing?" she asked. "Ready for a cup of tea and a slice of that pie with me?"

Slipping the stick into his pocket, he closed the open files on the church's computer. "I would love to, ma'am, but another appointment demands my attention." He offered a sincere smile. "Perhaps another time?"

"I'll hold you to that, young man. See you in church on Sunday."

～

The appointment demanding Michael's attention was with his laptop in the comfort of his own apartment. He couldn't check

Buckley's background without leaving a search trail on the church's system. He found out that the current finance director of Calvary Baptist had held the position for four years. Before that, Buckley had worked at an insurance agency specializing in high-commission policies for those who were practically uninsurable. Those firms preyed on people desperate for insurance due to serious preexisting conditions. Prior to that, Buckley worked as an investment broker that hawked penny stocks to those seeking quick returns, and as a telemarketer for a get-rich-quick set of DVDs, a company later dissolved by a watchdog agency. Although Buckley had never been charged with any crime, his background certainly prepared him to spin the church's basket of straw into a pile of gold. Did success also make him greedy?

Michael printed copies for the case file and leaned back with a satisfied sigh. He had done well yesterday and today on his own—a fact even Beth couldn't refute. But he wasn't about to repeat past mistakes. Working twelve- and thirteen-hour days might have provided advancement and generous raises at his prior job, but it had allowed little time for extracurricular activities.

And that had made him physically weak, emotionally immature, and socially inept. At least, according to his former fiancée. And how could he not believe the woman he loved?

Changing into sweatpants and a T-shirt, Michael headed for the hotel along the riverfront. Because many business travelers had little time or energy to work out, the upscale property allowed locals to use their well-equipped fitness room. In exchange for a small monthly fee, he hoped to turn his flabby muscles into arms of steel by next spring. Michael was a patient man, and he planned to eventually leave every trace of his boring self behind.

THIRTEEN

As soon as Beth had copies of the Dean reports in hand, she ran, not walked, from the Natchez Police Department. She couldn't wait to get away from Chris. She'd forgotten how great looking he was, the way words rolled off his tongue, and how electricity spiked up her spine whenever he spoke her name. Actually, she hadn't forgotten. She'd simply forced those memories to a dark corner of her mind to be revisited late at night when sleep wouldn't come. How had he managed to undo all the progress she made during the last year in less than fifteen minutes?

Shaking off the feelings their encounter had generated, Beth forced herself to concentrate on the case. She shuddered as she read Detective Lejeune's notation that Reverend Dean studied noose-making on a website. Someone had once told her you can learn to do anything on the Internet—construct a bomb, grow vegetables without dirt, build a house. So Pastor Dean could have figured out how to hang himself as though Natchez were the Wild, Wild West. *I suppose if you were planning to end your life, you wouldn't bother to clear out your search cache or worry about ruining your best suit of clothes.*

Chris was right. Most men didn't concern themselves with such things. When her parents were about to take their twenty-fifth anniversary cruise, Mom had organized her outfits in the guest room to make sure each piece was clean, pressed, and mended, but Beth's father packed only the shorts he washed the car in and a few logo T-shirts. Fortunately, her mother had taken over the task or they would have dined poolside on the ship's formal night. So it was entirely possible Reverend Dean forgot to change into old duds before heading to the outbuilding.

As Beth parked next to her mother's minivan in the driveway, she reread the suicide note a second time: *I'm so sorry, Allie. This sure is a coward's way out. I hope you and Katie will forgive me. But I can no longer forgive myself. If God's merciful, I'll see you again someday.* To her that sounded exactly like Reverend Dean. He'd always talked about God as though they were on a first name basis. And one night when she was babysitting, she'd heard him call his wife by the nickname "Allie." Maybe it was just once, but she'd heard it nonetheless. Beth slipped into the kitchen, poured a glass of sweet tea, and sat down to study the police reports. However, she'd barely skimmed the coroner's conclusions when her mother interrupted her solitude.

"Why are you home from work so early?" she asked, shuffling to the refrigerator.

Beth kept her focus on the crime scene photos. "I don't work at the bank, Ma. Secret agents and private detectives keep odd hours. Their time is their own."

"Secret agents, bah. Next will you tell me your new partner is James Bond?" Rita pulled out a package of frozen pork chops.

The question made her laugh. "Michael isn't exactly Roger Moore or Sean Connery. He's not even Daniel Craig." Beth regretted her unkind comparison the moment the words left her mouth. She owed her partner loyalty, at least for the next three weeks.

Rita sat down with a familiar look on her face. She wanted to chat.

Beth did not. Glancing at her watch, she shoved the police reports back into the folder. "I have just enough time to work out," she said, strolling toward the door. "I'll be home for supper."

"You plan to exercise in that outfit?" Her mother didn't miss a trick.

"My gym bag is in the car." Beth sprinted for her car before Rita could tack half a dozen errands onto her trip to the Grand Hotel.

Twenty minutes later, in her favorite shorts and shirt, Beth had just stepped onto the stair-climber when she heard her name.

"Elizabeth!" Michael called from across the room. "Funny running into you here." Jumping off the treadmill, he headed in her direction.

"Are you following me, Preston, like some sleazy stalker?" Her tone conveyed little camaraderie. Exercise for Beth was akin to meditation for Hindu mystics. It cleared the mind, connected a person to their inner self, and prepared the body for the next challenge.

"Of course not," he said, his cheerfulness gone. "But how many places to work out do you think there are around here? I only found this fitness room and one in the Hampton Suites. I can't believe this town has no gyms."

"Natchez is in between gyms at the moment. The last two closed."

"Yet you found it odd that I'm here."

"I didn't take you for a treadmill kind of guy."

He shrugged, looking everywhere but at her. "I didn't used to be, but it's not too late to give up my sedentary lifestyle."

"Because now you're a PI instead of an accountant?"

"Yeah, that's part of it, but mainly I'm ready for a change."

"Well, good luck with that." Beth switched her machine back on.

Michael walked to the end of the row and climbed on a bike. After adjusting the dial, he pedaled at a rate that guaranteed he wouldn't get out of bed tomorrow. At least, not without a massive amount of pain relievers.

Beth wondered if her bad temper was due to seeing the man she had once thought of as the love of her life. But no matter what the reason, she needed to get along with her partner. Turning off the bike, she approached Michael with a contrite expression. "I'm sorry. Things didn't go well at my appointment. I'm one of those females who turn cranky when they don't get their way."

Michael paused to study her. "I have a sister like that—sweet as can be for hours. Then she suddenly explodes without provocation. So I accept your apology."

"What's your sister's name?"

"Elizabeth. Isn't that an odd coincidence?"

Beth's chin snapped up. "You've got to be kidding!"

Cool as dew on a lawn in January, Michael smiled. "Yes, I am. My sister's name is Caitlyn, but I decided to mess with you." He resumed his frenetic exercising.

"Okay, I had that coming. But if you're serious about getting in shape, you need to slow down. Like most beginners, you're starting out too aggressively. Either you'll hurt yourself or you'll lose interest before you see much improvement."

Michael flushed a deep shade of red. "Aren't you just an unlimited font of criticism? I think I'll check if the Hampton Suites accepts local residents." He crossed his arms over his chest.

Beth glanced around. They were attracting attention from the other patrons. "Honest, this is me trying to be helpful, not critical. If you want to build stamina, you have to slow down. It's just a suggestion."

"I'll take it easy on the machines. Anything else, Miss Kirby, while you have my attention?"

"No, that'll do it."

Beth slunk back to the end of the row. For the next hour, she concentrated on her workout without gauging his progress or to check if he'd passed out on the floor. But, oddly enough, they both finished their showers and headed to their cars at the same time.

Michael pretended not to see her, but she closed the distance in a few strides. "Look, Preston, I'm here to apologize and give you the number for the best personal trainer in town. When I first joined the force, I used this guy for two years. He's reasonably priced and very nice. Nonjudgmental. He'll take you from your current condition to wherever you want to go without injury." Beth held out a business card.

"Nicer than you, Elizabeth?" he asked, arching an eyebrow.

"By leaps and bounds."

"Then maybe I'll give him a call." Michael plucked the card from her fingers, stuck it into his pocket, and walked away.

"Wait!" she demanded. "I still owe you for my rudeness. How about if I buy dinner tonight? We can discuss what we found out on the case."

He turned back slowly. "What kind of dinner?"

"Anything you like, or I can invite you to eat with the Kirbys. Mom's fixing her specialty—stewed possum with turnip greens."

His smile was slow in coming. "The Carriage House out at Stanton Hall looks interesting. Can you afford that on your salary?"

"Yes, even if I have to sell my plasma to make it happen. Anything you want to order is on me."

"All right, but we'll take separate cars. My male ego can't handle any more insults in case my driving doesn't measure up." Michael opened the door to his Fiat and climbed in. "Lead the way."

"You won't be sorry." Beth skipped back to her car, happy for two reasons: One, she would finally try a place she'd wanted to for years, and two, Michael probably had the healthiest ego she'd seen in a long time, which made a world of difference with partners.

FOURTEEN

Bay St. Louis

*I*sabelle opened one eye to a handsome face.

"Good morning, sunshine." Nate kissed the tip of her nose.

"I'll take your word for it." She snuggled deeper under the silky sheets.

"How are you feeling?" He drew circles on her back.

"Great. Just a little tired."

"You can go back to sleep. I'm going for an early run before breakfast. The humidity is at its lowest point for the day."

"Take all the time you need," she said from beneath the sheet. "I'm dreaming of hot oil massages under a beach cabana."

However, the moment Isabelle heard the door close, she jumped out of bed and into the shower. She didn't have much time, but she hoped she wouldn't need much.

With a map of Bay St. Louis in hand, she backed the Escape from its assigned spot and drove north on Beach Boulevard. Ten minutes later she was parked outside Golden Magnolia Casino in a spot where she could watch the main entrance. *Who's the sneaky little PI today?* She basked in her ingenuity.

Fifteen minutes later, with her blouse plastered to her back,

Isabelle decided to abandon her ridiculous idea. Just as she started the engine, her ex-husband walked out the door. Craig squinted in the bright sunlight and slipped on mirrored sunglasses, disguising his already bizarre appearance. But after four years of marriage, Isabelle couldn't be fooled. She jumped from the car, crossed the valet lanes at a full run, and hurtled herself at him.

"Craig Mitchell? Is that really you?"

"Izzy?" he sputtered.

"Yes, but you may call me Isabelle," she sniffed, stopping inches from his face.

"Sorry, *Isabelle*. What are you doing here?"

"I'm honeymooning in Bay St. Louis with Nate." She glared at him.

"That much I figured, but why are you at a casino? You don't drink, smoke, gamble, chew gum in public, spit watermelon seeds, or anything else that could be considered vulgar." Craig pulled off his glasses to pinch the bridge of his nose.

Isabelle noted the deep creases under his bloodshot eyes. She considered his question and opted for the truth. "Nate said he spotted you while bike-riding yesterday. I wanted to see for myself."

"Are you satisfied? It's really me. Now you may carry on with your life." He tried to walk around her.

"Wait a minute," she said, blocking his path. "Why are you getting mad? I thought we parted friends. Why not come back and have breakfast with us? The inn where we're staying serves delicious food."

"We *are* friends, and I'm not mad. But you need time alone with Nate and I'm busy today."

Again he tried to circumnavigate her, but she grabbed his arm. "Craig, you look terrible. When was the last time you slept or ate a decent meal? Or called your wife?"

He reared back as though she'd slapped him. "Don't you recall the part where we got divorced? You no longer get to sit in judgment of my appearance or bad habits." His face flushed a warm shade of red. "And the frequency of my phone calls home is none of your business."

Isabelle loosened her grip. "You're right. It's not. I just wanted to make sure you're okay."

Craig removed his cap and scratched his scalp, his expression changing to one of resignation. "It's nice of you to be concerned, but things are under control."

"Didn't you join Gamblers Anonymous?"

"Yes, but turns out I wasn't the compulsive addict everyone thought I was. I'm down here to blow off steam before starting a new job. Cassie couldn't take off work right now, so I came alone. The Gulf Coast is too hot this time of year for her anyway. When I'm back in Nashville, I'll start GA meetings again just to make sure my life doesn't spiral out of control."

Isabelle was no expert on gambling addictions, but she'd become an expert at when Craig was lying. "I spoke with Cassie on the phone. She said you left her."

"Oh, Isabelle. What have you done?" He moaned as though in physical pain.

"I called Cassie to thank her for the money...and...and that's when she told me you'd fallen in love with another woman." Isabelle tasted something sour in the back of her throat.

Craig seemed to be silently counting to five. "Think back. Did you tell her I'm in Bay St. Louis?"

"I said Nate thought he saw you, and she knows where we're honeymooning. Cassie said Nate must be mistaken because you're living in Nashville with a woman you met at work. None of that is true, is it?"

He sighed wearily. "Things just didn't work out with Cassie. We fell out of love, and I needed to get away. I thought it would spare her feelings if there was another woman. She would be angry instead of hurt." Craig met her gaze briefly.

"Speaking from experience, the truth is usually best," she said, bitterness edging her tone.

"Maybe for you, but Cassie's different. She's thin skinned. Please stay out of this. Whatever you do, don't confirm where I am. She'll come down and insist we see a counselor or some nonsense like that."

"It's not nonsense. A professional can—"

"No, I'm telling you nicely to butt out. Trust me when I say it's for the best." Despite his harsh words, Craig looked on the verge of tears.

"Very well. It's your life." She stepped back, repulsed.

"Forget you saw me, Isabelle. Cassie's better off without me. Enjoy your vacation with Nate. I wish you two nothing but the best." This time when Craig stepped around her, he moved with the force of a steamroller.

She stood sweating under the marquis of the Golden Magnolia Casino, knowing that her ex had told her nothing but a pack of lies. And she wanted to know why.

FIFTEEN

*N*ate had already showered, dressed, and was drinking coffee on the porch when Izzy pulled into the driveway. She bounded up the walk, carrying plastic sacks from a grocery store.

"Greetings, husband. I feared we wouldn't have enough snacks, so I bought chips, salsa, and two six-packs of Peach Snapple."

Nate met her at the steps to relieve her of her burdens. "Wow, plus boiled peanuts and two kinds of Twizzlers. Your stomachache must be past history." He set the bags inside the door of their suite.

"It is. I feel on top of the world— Oh, good morning, Mrs. Russo. Let me get that for you." Isabelle held open the door for their innkeeper.

"Did I hear someone mention they're hungry?" Mrs. Russo set down her silver tray in front of Nate. "We have spinach and cheddar omelets, hash browns, and turkey sausage. What kind of juice would y'all like?"

"Tomato for me, and coffee, please." Izzy settled into the opposite chair.

"Couldn't fall back asleep after I left?" Nate shook his napkin across his lap.

"I was just tossing and turning, so I decided to make myself useful." She cut her omelet into pieces.

"Good thing we have a small refrigerator in our room."

"What do you mean?" She swallowed her first bite.

"For the twelve Peach Snapples you couldn't live without." Nate studied her over his coffee mug.

"I already forgot what I bought," she said, chuckling. "I see you've been studying the brochures. Where to today, Skipper?"

"It's going to be a hot one, so I narrowed it down to the water park in Gulfport or snorkeling from a catamaran. They take you out over a coral reef where we're guaranteed to see fish."

"Oh, I don't know, Nate. I'd hate to get sunburned and look like a lobster all week."

"We brought plenty of sunblock, and you have a swim T-shirt. Which reminds me, how about seafood tonight as long as we avoid any crab dishes? I thought I'd get a lock on supper before we finish breakfast." Having beaten Izzy to the punch with her favorite joke, Nate laughed uproariously. She loved to plan their next meal while eating the current one.

But Isabelle missed his clever humor. She was eating mindlessly while staring at a dish of butter.

Nate cleared his throat. "Or we could sign up for the submarine that dives off the continental shelf. It's a battery-powered submersible that two people operate themselves. We can bounce along the ocean floor in search of giant squid."

Isabelle picked up her glass of tomato juice. "Whichever excursion you prefer," she murmured. "I'll let you decide. All three sound great."

Nate set down his fork. "Out with it, Izzy. What's bothering you? You haven't heard a word I've said."

Instead of denying the allegation, her eyes filled with tears. "I'm sorry, Nate. I've been trying to figure out how to explain where I went this morning."

"I thought you went to buy food we don't need," he said softly.

"That was just a ruse by a deceitful woman." Isabelle's chin quivered. "I was staking out Golden Magnolia Casino, watching for Craig."

Nate blinked like an owl under a spotlight. "Why would you sneak off to see your ex-husband?"

"Because I was worried about him." With a shaky hand she brought her coffee cup to her lips.

"Did you find him?"

She nodded. "Yes, and he told me lie after lie. He said Cassie encouraged him to come here, and that his gambling was under control. I know it isn't. He's fallen off the wagon or whatever they call a relapsed gambler. He's lost weight, his hair hasn't been cut in weeks, his face is scruffy, and the bags under his eyes could hold enough clothes for a month."

Nate struggled to keep his voice level. "That's how he looked to me too."

"Craig said he's fallen out of love with Cassie, but there's no other woman. I think he's flat broke and ashamed to go home." Isabelle wrung her hands in her lap.

"He has a right to mess up his life, Izzy."

"That's what he said. He told me to butt out. I feel sorry for him."

"You can't force a person into treatment. Craig must be willing to change."

"What about those staged interventions, where family and friends insert themselves between the addict and their compulsion? Are we not our brother's keeper?"

"Not this week we're not. Enough, Isabelle. Craig is becoming *your* obsession."

That stopped her like a brick wall. "Is that what you think?"

"It's starting to sound like it. For the rest of our honeymoon, I want you to relax and have fun." Nate threw his napkin down and pushed away his plate. "At home, you worry whether your clients can obtain financing. You worry about your coworkers' money troubles. You worry about the ozone layer, global warming, and the country's national debt." Nate's voice lifted with intensity. "Maybe carrying the weight of the world has affected your health."

"What do you mean?" Isabelle sipped her water, the ice cubes long gone.

"I mean we've been married two years, and it's still just the two of us." Nate spotted Mrs. Russo dragging the hose to the front of the house. *Must she water the begonias and pansies now?*

"I didn't think you were ready for a family. We're still renting, we need to replace my car, and I still owe three grand on a credit card from my divorce."

"If people waited until their financial ducks were in a row, the birthrate would drop to zero. I'm ready to be a dad. I can provide for us while you take some time off. And we can buy a house this fall as long as you're not thinking mini mansion." Nate wrapped his hand around hers. "What do you say?"

Isabelle's smile said it all. "I say forget the submarine ride under the ocean. Let's go make a baby."

Mrs. Russo inched precariously close to the porch, eavesdropping shamelessly.

"Simmer down, Mrs. Price," Nate cautioned. "I didn't collect these brochures for nothing. Pick something out for today."

"Had you going there, didn't I?" She winked. "Let's put on our swimsuits and head to Gulfport. I can't wait to get water up my nose on the giant slide."

Nate carried their plates to the tray by the door. He couldn't wait to spend a day alone with his wife. And it had nothing to do with rafts floating down a lazy river.

Sixteen

Natchez

Michael slept like a baby last night, at least after he took two ibuprofen tablets and a dose of an over-the-counter sleep aid. Beth was right. If you exercised as though getting in shape took only five rigorous sessions, you ended up in the hospital. Even though he'd slowed down after her warning, every one of his muscles felt on fire. Today he would rest his wounded body. And when he went back to the gym, he would take her advice.

Although conversation with his partner had turned ugly in the fitness room, dinner turned out better than expected. There was no more discussion about her personal trainer, doubtlessly a testosterone-driven caveman, and Beth didn't criticize his appearance, choice of beverages, or the way he chewed his food. She talked about her meeting with the Natchez chief of police, and he described his enlightening peek at the church's Excel spreadsheets. With Ralph Buckley juggling a half-million dollars like tennis balls, Mrs. Alice Dean no longer looked like a suspect.

Michael swallowed several anti-inflammatories with coffee and headed for the shower. He hoped that by the time the pleasant effects of hot water on sore muscles wore off, the pills would have kicked in. Then he planned to call Beth. He had some ideas on tracking down Buckley, but wasn't sure how far PIs could stretch the letter of the law regarding privacy issues.

However, Calvary Baptist's helpful assistant took that decision out of his hands. "Hello, Mr. Preston? Natalie Purdy calling to say that was the best key lime pie she ever tasted. It was so rich, especially with extra whipped cream on top. Thanks again."

Michael chuckled over her use of third person—a habit she shared with his mother. "You're welcome, ma'am. Glad you enjoyed it."

"I hope you don't mind me calling so early, but guess who was here when I got to work?" she whispered into the phone.

"I have no idea," he said, pain muddling his imagination.

"Ralph Buckley, that's who. Weren't you anxious to question him?"

Michael missed the cup and poured hot coffee on his hand. "I am. Are you saying he just showed up unannounced?"

"Yep. I asked what he was doing. He said the last time he checked, he still worked here. That was a little snippy, don't you think?" Indignation sharpened her words. "If you still want to talk to him, I'll make sure he doesn't leave, even if I have to bar the door with my body."

"My partner and I will be there in twenty minutes. Please don't put yourself in danger. Just try to act natural." Michael hung up the phone and immediately called Beth.

"How fast can you get to the Baptist church?"

"Why?" she asked, with an audible yawn. "Good morning to you too, by the way."

"Good morning. Ralph Buckley is back in town, but who knows for how long. I think we should talk to him."

"I think so too. I'll meet you there in twenty minutes." Beth hung up before he could ask his list of questions.

Fifteen minutes later, Michael pulled into the parking lot in wrinkled Dockers and loafers over bare feet because he couldn't find clean socks. His partner was already there with her thick auburn hair still damp from a shower. It was the first time he'd seen her without makeup.

"Wow, Kirby, you've got freckles, millions of them. Who would've thought?"

"Pay no attention to my appearance." Beth bounded up the church steps. "If I didn't leave while Rita's back was turned, you'd be getting another breakfast sandwich. Today's creation was Eggo waffles stuffed with peanut butter."

Michael opened the door for her. "Is this your mother's normal behavior—force-feeding your work associates?"

"Not usually, but I told Mom you *loved* her bacon and pancake sandwich." Beth smirked like a child.

"You're quite the fibber. I'll keep that in mind." Michael pointed down the hallway. "Come meet my new friend in town."

"I already know Mrs. Purdy. You're the stranger in Natchez, Preston, not me."

"We'll see about that." He led the way into the main office.

"Michael, right on time. Good to see you, but what are you doing with Beth?" The assistant's smile faded.

"Miss Kirby is my partner at Price Investigations. And a man couldn't ask for a better mentor than Elizabeth."

"Yes, I suppose she would have plenty to teach someone young and impressionable." Mrs. Purdy flipped through a stack of mail.

"Could we talk to Mr. Buckley, please?" Beth asked politely.

Without making eye contact, the assistant angled her head to the left. "Last office down the hall, unless that crook saw you and crawled out the window."

"Thank you, ma'am," said Michael. He followed Beth but waited to speak until they were out of earshot of the assistant. "She sure doesn't like you much. You used to be a member here. Any story you care to share?"

Beth made a face. "None that's important to our case." She stopped in front of the closed door. "You were great with Madame

Defarge, but I'll take the lead with Buckley. We don't want to tip our hand."

Michael saluted, something he picked up from his father, but Beth's gesture was the real surprise.

She applied a thick coat of lip gloss, fluffed out her hair, and then swept open the door. "Mr. Buckley? Might we interrupt you for a few minutes?" She crossed the threshold smiling like a beauty queen.

A small, dark-haired man turned from his computer. "Certainly, and whom do I have the pleasure of addressing?"

"Beth Kirby." Stretching out her hand, she shook energetically. "This is Mike Preston, who's a trainee in my office. We've been hired by Mrs. Dean to sort out the pastor's affairs after his unexpected death."

Trainee—what happened to partner? Michael swallowed back his disappointment. "How do you do, sir?"

"Fine. How can I help you help Alice today? I felt so bad leaving right after the funeral."

"What was the reason for your sudden departure?" He leaned a shoulder against the doorjamb.

Buckley finally pulled his focus from Beth. "I was best man in a wedding. The bachelor party was my responsibility." He didn't look pleased with having to explain himself.

"We understand perfectly," said Beth. "When you make promises, you must hold up your end." She shot Michael a glare. "We're sorting through Reverend Dean's finances, and they appear tangled up with Calvary Baptist's. Apparently, money was moved from the school account to an unknown location. Folks in the congregation are pointing fingers at the pastor. If you could help us track down those funds, it would take the pressure off Mrs. Dean. She can't settle his estate with church funds temporarily…misplaced." Beth flashed another smile, the caliber of which Michael had never witnessed.

Buckley nodded. "I've heard the rumors. Very sad for a respected man of God to fall from grace so quickly. But I'm afraid I have no idea where Paul invested the money."

"We checked your background, Mr. Buckley." Michael couldn't tolerate his lies another moment. "You're the one experienced in buying and selling stocks, junk bonds, commodities—everything but pork bellies in Chicago. And you're the one with a broker's license, not Pastor Dean."

Beth pressed down on his instep. "Please excuse Mr. Preston's exuberance. He hasn't learned that things aren't always how they appear."

Buckley rocked back in his chair. "It's all right, Miss Kirby. He's only looking out for Mrs. Dean. And yes, I'm the one who had been in charge of investments for the last two years. Thanks to me, the fund for a new school grew from less than a hundred thousand dollars into close to five hundred thousand."

Michael pulled his foot from beneath Beth's smaller one. "Which now seems to be missing."

"The operative word being 'had' in my statement. Paul took a look at the books and didn't like my investment strategy. Churning, he called it."

"Your choices were anything but conservative, even to my unsavvy eye," said Beth, rather sweetly.

"True enough, but look at the results. I took a pipe dream from a small church and turned it into a real possibility. Why does everyone think making a killing in the market is somehow unholy? Criminals do it all the time. Why can't good people?"

"The money, along with the pipe dream of a new school, seems to be gone." Michael narrowed his eyes.

"As I was saying, Paul didn't like my aggressive strategy, so he took control of the building fund a few months ago. Check the books again, Mr. Preston. You'll see no money transfers by me during that period. I have no idea what he did. I washed my hands of it."

Michael felt Beth's eyes boring a hole in the side of his head.

"We will look into this further, sir. On behalf of Mrs. Dean, thank you for speaking with us."

"Yes, thank you *very* much," said Beth, offering her hand.

The sleazy guy enfolded it inside his. "You're very welcome. Say, didn't you used to be a member here? I haven't seen you in church in quite a while."

"I've been living in Vicksburg, but maybe I'll pencil it into my Sunday schedule." Beth slowly withdrew her hand. "Thanks again."

Michael couldn't wait to get out of there. He waved goodbye to Mrs. Purdy and practically stomped out the door. When they reached their cars, he turned on his heel. "What was with the sugar-sweet routine? You all but batted your eyelashes at Buckley."

"You catch more bugs with honey than with vinegar." Beth braced both hands on her hips. "If we alienate the guy, he'll clam up and not tell us anything."

"It's *flies*, not bugs," Michael said after a moment.

"Flies, bugs…you should worry less about analogies and more about learning interrogation techniques." Beth jabbed a finger into his chest. "I told you to keep quiet and let me take the lead."

"I couldn't stand his bald-faced lies. He was trying to pin this on Reverend Dean."

"Maybe they're not lies. Were there any financial transactions in the last couple months by Buckley?"

Michael felt blood rush to his face. "I might have stopped checking details too soon."

"Great. And Nate thinks forensic accounting is your strong suit."

"It is." Michael lifted his palms. "I just got overexcited with my discovery. It won't happen again, Elizabeth."

"Okay. I'll say nothing to Nate as long as you say nothing about me flirting with Buckley." She clicked open her car door. "I hate it when I use my feminine wiles like that. Maybe I should rethink my own interrogation techniques."

"Feminine wiles? I must have missed that part."

"Oh, shut up." Playfully, Beth punched him in the arm.

"Ouch. My arms are sore." Michael exaggerated his grimace.

"Sorry, but I did try to warn you." Beth climbed in behind the wheel. "Go home and study those police reports I gave you and the financial records you pirated from Mrs. Purdy. Let's see if Buckley is telling the truth. Tomorrow you might have to pay Mrs. Dean another visit and look deeper into their finances."

"Will do, but where are you going?"

"To the firing range to log in some hours. Give me a call after supper."

"Aren't we both still on the time clock? I know that the cat's away, but I could use a few pointers on handling firearms."

"I don't think so." She put the car in reverse. "You weren't very receptive to my advice."

Michael leaned level with her car window. "You blindsided me at the fitness center. This time I'm asking for your expert guidance."

"Sign up for classes at the firing range. Professional instructors are better prepared to handle newbies without insulting them."

As she started backing up, Michael trotted alongside her car. "I've taken classes on cleaning and maintenance, safe handling and transport, and the laws governing open carry in Mississippi. What I need is someone to let me shoot."

Beth rammed on the brakes. "You have never fired a gun? Not even a BB gun as a child?"

"Never. My mom wouldn't allow them in the house. Seems like we each have crosses to bear with our parents."

She burst out laughing. "That's for sure. Okay, Wild Bill, but an indoor range is no place to shoot for the first time. Have you bought a gun yet?"

"No. I've studied them online, but I can't decide what would be a good fit from pictures." He flexed the fingers on his right hand.

"No problem. You can work on your computer tomorrow. Today, let's go out to my aunt and uncle's farm for your first lesson. That way no one will witness you shooting yourself in the foot."

"What I love best about you, Beth, is your total confidence in me. I'll follow you to the farm."

Michael sprinted to his car and then practically crawled up her bumper several times along the way. He didn't want to chance losing her either in Natchez traffic or on twisty country roads. And he didn't want to do anything else to annoy her. He was starting to like Elizabeth Kirby. As long as he could laugh at himself, they might survive the all-thumbs stage of his transformation.

SEVENTEEN

*B*eth checked her rearview mirror several times, but her partner had no trouble keeping up. At least his driving was top-notch. He didn't ram on the brakes before a hairpin turn like most city slickers. He coasted into the curve and then accelerated midway to maintain optimum control. Thirty minutes later, they reached the pothole-riddled driveway of her Uncle Pete and Aunt Dorrie. Surrounded by two hundred acres of low-lying delta farmland, suitable for rice and little else, the rural Kirbys enjoyed complete privacy. The sound of gunfire on a Wednesday afternoon would draw no attention whatsoever. Beth parked in the shade under a sycamore, leaving just enough room for his Fiat.

"I'll leave my guns in the trunk while we go say hi to my kinfolk."

"Guns?" Michael asked. "You carry an arsenal of weaponry?"

"Not normally, but I'd planned to shoot a variety at the range today. By the way, keep your hands where my uncle can see them and don't make any sudden moves," Beth teased as they climbed the wooden steps.

"Hey, y'all. It's me," she called through the screen door.

"Are these your father's relatives or your mother's?" he asked.

"Pete is my dad's brother. Why?"

But the sudden appearance of the pair curtailed any response.

"Good golly, girl, you know better than to knock." Aunt Dorrie wrapped her muscular arms around Beth and squeezed. "It's been way too long, child."

Beth spotted her uncle over her aunt's shoulder. He was leaning against the refrigerator with a big grin on his face. "What's up, Uncle Pete. You get your crop in?"

"All in. I'm just waitin' for the sun to work her magic. Your ma said you came back to Natchez. Thanks for paying the country folks a call."

When Dorrie finally released her, she turned her attention to Michael. "You Betsy's new boyfriend?" Dorrie let her gaze travel from his shiny loafers up to his sandy-colored hair.

Shamelessly, Beth did the same as though seeing him for the first time. Actually, Michael Preston wasn't a bad looking guy.

"Unfortunately, ma'am, I am not," he said. "We work together. She's training me this week. Nice to meet both of you." He shook hands with her uncle.

"Too bad." Dorrie stopped ogling and shuffled to the stove.

Beth thought she'd better nip this in the bud. "Training—that's why we're here. Is it okay if we shoot some targets in the west pasture? Mike wants a few pointers."

"Of course," said Pete. "Nobody leased those acres this year. Don't forget the bucket of soda cans in the barn." Turning to Michael, Pete said, "If anybody can give marksman lessons, it's my niece. Her cousins called her Deadeye for years. Too bad she had no stomach for hunting. Betsy could've kept us in venison and rabbit stew forever."

"We better get started." Grabbing Michael by the sleeve, Beth headed for the door. "Thanks for the trip down memory lane."

"Don't you dare leave without eating supper," Dorrie hollered through the screen. "That boy needs something sticking to his ribs."

"Sorry about the wisecrack about your being skinny," Beth said once they were out of earshot. "Why do relatives think they can say anything that pops in their heads?"

"Don't worry about it. I certainly won't take offense with a crack shot who has guns for every occasion."

"Dorrie and Pete are good people. They are just not loaded with sensitivity." Opening her trunk, Beth picked a gun from her assortment and handed it to Michael. "This is what you're going to shoot today—a forty caliber Mini Glock. Medium weight, not a lot of recoil, but it has plenty of stopping power." She selected a second weapon. "I'm going to use this—a nine millimeter Glock. I can't understand why this isn't standard issue for the force." Beth slammed the trunk on the rest of her arsenal.

Michael examined the gun gingerly. "She's a beauty."

"It's not loaded, but keep the barrel pointed at the ground. Never joke around with a firearm. Plenty of fools have shot themselves or their friends with supposedly unloaded weapons."

"Will do. That part was thoroughly covered in class." Michael double-checked that the safety was on.

"Watch your step along the way. Remember, this is a farm."

When they reached the barn, temporarily devoid of livestock, Beth pointed at the overflowing bucket of cans. "You carry the targets and I'll bring the ammo."

Michael shifted the mini Glock to his other hand and grabbed the bucket's handle. "Thanks for not telling your uncle I never shot before."

"Pete wouldn't have believed me. Then he would have insisted on seeing for himself. I love my uncle, but we don't need him launching into one of his two-hour stories about the good old days."

Michael suddenly halted on the path. "It's really beautiful out here. Does all this land belong to Pete and Dorrie?"

Beth shaded her eyes to appreciate the familiar view. "For as far as you can see. It might be beautiful, but it's hard to make a living farming. Agribusiness has too much control. See that fence?" She pointed at a sturdy split-rail fifty yards away. "It's there to keep cattle back from the steep drop-off to the creek. Pete replaced the top rail with a flat board for target practice. We'll be shooting downhill with a high embankment on the other side. Stray shots won't go anywhere. You can set up a row of cans while I load our guns."

Michael remained rooted in place. "How do the cows get a drink of water?"

"Downstream. It's only steep right here."

As though pleased with the answer, Michael walked downhill to line up two dozen cans. When he returned, Beth reviewed basic safety instructions and then aimed her weapon at the fence rail. She fired nine shots at the row of cans. "Your turn. Try to duplicate my manner and interval between shots."

Michael lifted his weapon, took aim, and pulled the trigger nine times. He didn't flinch or blink or do a single thing wrong.

"Perfect, that was great," she said.

"You might need glasses, Elizabeth. Neither of us hit a thing." The corners of his mouth turned up.

"We weren't meant to. I filled the clips with blanks for the first round to get you accustomed to the recoil and sound of discharge. And, in case any small critters were in those weeds, they're long gone by now."

"Very smart of you, Deadeye. Your uncle said you weren't fond of killing animals."

"Bambi and Thumper are safe, but the same can't be said about those who call me Deadeye. And since we're on the subject, forget about calling me Betsy. That honor is reserved for relatives over the age of fifty." Beth loaded live ammo into her clip, met his gaze for a brief moment, and then turned and fired. The first nine aluminum cans fell from their perch. "Now it's your turn, Mr. Preston."

Michael stepped up, aimed, and fired. However, his result duplicated his clip full of blanks. "How can that be? You made it look so easy."

"Nothing in life is easy. We're going to move up to twenty feet and use that upturned log to brace your arm. You must keep your arm steady when you fire, or you won't hit the barn, let alone a moving target. When you can hit nine out of nine, we'll move back to thirty feet. Eventually you'll be able to keep your arm steady without bracing it."

His forehead furrowed. "All that in one afternoon?"

"Nope. Take all the time you need. We can even come back here if you want to take a chance with my relatives."

Michael watched as she reloaded his gun. "What kind of chance? I think they're very nice."

"They are. They'll graciously welcome you back, invite you to supper on the back porch, and maybe even send a sweet potato pie home with you. Then one day Uncle Pete meets us in the yard with a shotgun. You notice tables and chairs have been set up, like they're ready for a shindig. On the porch will be the preacher and my girlfriends in matching dresses. You will be forced to make a choice, Mikey."

He hooted with laughter. "People don't do things like that. Anyway, he's your uncle, not your dad."

Beth shrugged. "All I know is Dorrie and Pete have four daughters—all younger than me, but every one of them is married. Uncle Pete always complains that my dad is too lenient." She handed him the loaded gun. "So I suggest you either improve your aim or your hundred-yard dash. Because Uncle Pete never misses."

EIGHTEEN

Bay St. Louis
Wednesday

*I*sabelle tried to remember the last time she'd relaxed and enjoyed herself so thoroughly and came up empty. Certainly not in high school when insecurities about her hair-clothes-makeup and who-was-saying-what behind her back interfered with any sense of security. And definitely not in college when she became obsessed with meeting and marrying the "right" man. Who didn't want a future filled with sunshine, blue skies, and shopping malls? She married Craig two weeks after graduation and then worked two jobs to put him through law school. Whatever free time they had was spent arguing about his gambling. Perhaps if she had pulled her head from the sand sooner, his debts might not have mushroomed out of control.

After their divorce, Isabelle moved to Memphis and filled every waking hour with work to pay off her share of their debt. Meeting Nate Price had been a gift from heaven, although it hadn't seemed so at the time. Thanks to Nate's persistence and patience, her emotional wounds healed. With a husband who loved and respected her, Isabelle didn't mind evening open houses or manning the agency every other Saturday. She and Nate were building a life together with each deposit into their savings account.

Yesterday, splashing through the waves at the water park and walking the beach at night, Isabelle had never felt so happy. Nate had become more than her husband and partner in life—he'd become her best friend. Nothing else in life could compare to that.

Today they chose Ship Island for their adventure, an uninhabited island owned by the National Park Service. They caught a ferry in Gulfport for the hour-long trip to miles of pristine beaches, along with a historic fort to tour. She and Nate played in the surf, ate a picnic lunch surrounded by hermit crabs, and spotted bottlenose dolphins on the ride back. Seagulls followed in their wake, watching for fish in the churned-up water. Neither of them wanted the day to end.

"Where should we have dinner?" she asked as the boat docked.

Nate withdrew his trusty tour guide from their daypack. "How about Captain Frank's? Menu looks good, prices look great, and they have every kind of seafood imaginable."

"Perfect." Isabelle attempted to apply makeup over her sunburn using the car's rearview mirror.

Once they were seated at their table with a view of the Gulf, Nate ordered peel-and-eat shrimp as their appetizer and iced coffees. "I'm going to miss looking at water every day." He interlocked his fingers behind his head. "Should we get a plastic pool for the backyard?"

Isabelle laughed at the mental image. "Maybe we'll just save the money for a weekend trip every year."

Soon a heaping platter of boiled shrimp was placed between them, along with their drinks. They dug into the feast as stars appeared in the evening sky, one by one. Midway through entrées of red snapper, Isabelle felt her cell vibrate in her pocket. "Let me answer this on my way to the ladies' room."

In the time it took to dig the phone from her pocket, she decided upon two possible callers—Nicki from New Orleans with an update on life with Hunter as parents-to-be, or Marie from her office, checking to see how the honeymoon was going.

Unfortunately Caller ID produced a third and unforeseen choice—Cassie Mitchell. For a brief moment Isabelle considered ignoring the call and letting voice mail kick in. But how charitable would that be? After all, she was the one who had called Craig's ex-wife and set plates spinning on sticks.

"Hello, Cassie?" Isabelle rallied a pleasant tone of voice.

"I'm so relieved you picked up." Cassie sounded breathless, as though she'd just finished a marathon. "I didn't know who else to call. You were my only option."

"What's going on?" Spotting a door to the patio, Isabelle altered her path to the ladies' room.

After a brief hesitation, Cassie released a verbal flood. "I haven't been able to stop thinking about Craig. Something smelled fishy from the start, but my pride didn't let me acknowledge it. After our conversation, I started poking around where he worked and found an intern willing to talk to me."

Isabelle's stomach tightened into a knot. "What did you find out?"

"Craig took a leave of absence from the company. According to his file, it was for an unspecified medical reason. All this time I believed he was still a law clerk until he was reinstated to the bar. Why would he leave, Izzy? They are one of Nashville's biggest law firms. The senior partners really liked Craig, despite his past problems. His boss had been willing to give him another chance."

Isabelle had only straws to grasp. "Maybe he took a job elsewhere for more money. Maybe you should—"

Cassie wasn't interested in maybes. "The intern said Craig left town. She had a number to reach him in an emergency, but under no circumstances was she allowed to give that number out. Just relay the information back to him. All very cloak-and-dagger, don't you think?"

"Yes, I do. That's why you should forget about him, at least for the time being."

Cassie continued as though Isabelle hadn't spoken. "That's

not all. I asked the intern point-blank if Craig was involved with another woman at the office. She said no. Her exact words were: 'When would Craig have time for an affair? He was the first one here in the morning, the last to leave, and worked all the overtime he could get.'"

"They could have been very secretive, Cassie. People go to great lengths to be devious."

"That's basically what I said, but the intern insisted nothing in that office stayed a secret. The women were gossip magnets and spread every bit they heard. She said Craig was a stand-up guy at work. He *never* flirted or even laughed at sexist jokes. The intern thought the medical issue had something to do with me, but federal law prohibited the partners from asking specifics." Like a leaky balloon, Cassie finally ran out of air.

Racking her brain for the right thing to say, Isabelle listened to the second wife sniffle.

"There is no other woman, Izzy," Cassie continued. "I believe my competition is the queen of clubs or maybe a royal flush."

Isabelle closed her eyes and sucked in a deep breath. How could she keep silent now? It would be the same as lying to a woman who had never caused her a bit of grief. "You're correct. Craig fell off the wagon. He's definitely in Bay St. Louis. I saw him coming out of a casino. He'd been playing cards all night."

While Cassie processed the information, Isabelle listened to birds twittering in overhead branches, children giggling at a nearby table, and customers calling to their waitress for extra napkins.

"You weren't planning on telling me this?" Cassie asked in a stiff voice.

"I wanted to, but Craig specifically told me not to call you. He doesn't want you to know about his backward slide."

"He's sick, Isabelle. If Craig had cancer or dementia, people would be horrified if I abandoned him. How is this disease different? We're not divorced. He's still my husband, and I married him for better or for worse."

Isabelle was temporarily flummoxed. "That's true, but what if there is another woman? I didn't see anyone with him, but he could be keeping her under wraps. I don't want you to get hurt."

"I'm already hurting, so I might as well know the truth. I will ask for time off from work. Then I'm finding out exactly where Bay St. Louis is and driving down to help him get straight. I don't know when, but as soon as I can. Don't say anything to Craig. This is between him and me. You and Nate enjoy your honeymoon and forget about us. You deserve a nice vacation. Take care, Izzy." Cassie ended the call.

Isabelle pondered Cassie's words on her way to the ladies' room. Hadn't Craig given her the exact same advice? But on her walk back to the table, the only question on her mind was, *How will I explain all this to Nate?*

Nineteen

*N*ate had a bad feeling the moment Isabelle returned from the restroom. If eating in restaurants was upsetting her stomach, they needed to stock up on fresh fruit and vegetables and maybe cold cuts from a local deli. They both hailed from middle-class families and were unaccustomed to heavy sauces and exotic spices.

"Are you all right, Isabelle?"

"Yes, I'm fine." She offered a weak smile and picked up her fork. But from that point on, she consumed less than a sparrow on a diet.

Nate finished his meal, declined dessert, and asked for the check. During the drive back to the B and B, he asked again, "Are you feeling okay? Should I pull to the side of the road?"

"Don't be silly. I'm fine." Isabelle patted his knee and then fixed her focus on the road until they reached Bay St. Louis. Once inside their suite, she locked herself in the bathroom for at least twenty minutes.

Nate couldn't sit on the porch watching boats forever if his bride was queasy. He knocked timidly on the door. "Can I bring you some peppermint tea or a can of ginger ale? There are Pepto Bismol tablets in the glove box."

"No, thanks. I think I'll just hit the sack." The door opened, and she emerged wearing a long nightgown. She headed straight to bed and crawled under the covers.

Nate returned to his rocking chair on the porch until he couldn't keep his eyes open any longer, and then he, too, headed to bed. When he awoke at midnight alone, he started to panic. He found Isabelle in the third place he looked. Wrapped in a terrycloth robe, she sat on a bench close to the water. "Was I snoring, dear wife?" he asked. "Is that why you abandoned me?"

She turned her tear-streaked face in his direction. "No. You were as quiet as a mouse for a change."

Nate plopped down next to her. "Why don't you tell me what's bothering you. And if you say 'nothing,' I'm going to pull your hair."

"Oh, it's something, all right. I just don't know how to tell you."

"Why not start with the honest-to-goodness truth?"

Isabelle released an exhausted sigh. "My stomach is fine, but that was Cassie Mitchell calling at the restaurant."

"What did she want?"

"She'd been asking questions at the last place Craig worked. One of the interns said he was away on a medical leave of absence, but he hadn't taken up with another woman. Cassie knows Craig fell off the wagon and that he's here in Bay St. Louis." Isabelle met his gaze for a moment. "She called me, Nate. Not the other way around. I respected your wishes about butting out."

"I believe you." He took hold of her hand. "You have no control over her."

A tear ran down Isabelle's cheek. "Tomorrow she's requesting time off from work. She plans to confront Craig and encourage him into rehab. She considers this her wifely duty and feels sorry for him because addiction is a disease."

Nate tipped back his head and considered the stars. Amazing that the bright lights of Biloxi fifteen miles away didn't interfere with the billion-piece light show overhead. Nate sensed they stood at an important crossroad in their marriage, so he chose his words carefully. "And you feel sorry for Cassie."

Isabelle nodded. "I can't turn my back on either of them. Craig seemed miserable the other day, as though he'd lost control of his life."

"And you want us to somehow intervene before Cassie gets to town? Or at least find out if Craig has fallen in with loan sharks again?" asked Nate, without letting himself think about the questions.

"Could we?" Isabelle jumped up, revitalized. "Maybe Craig doesn't owe too much money yet. Maybe we could get him into treatment before he leverages their entire future."

Nate stifled a wry laugh. "How do you suggest we manage this? Go undercover at the Golden Magnolia Casino?"

"Well, yes. You're a PI. You've had training in these things."

"Neither of us knows anything about gambling. We'd stick out like vegans at a barbecue rib cook-off."

"We'll pretend we're bumpkin tourists trying to learn the games." Isabelle pulled him to his feet.

"No pretending necessary. Where are you going in such a hurry?"

"To bed. If we're going undercover, we both need a good night's sleep."

And that was the sanest idea they would have for quite some time.

～

Nate waited until breakfast to point out that mornings—or even afternoons—weren't the best time for casino surveillance. Because Craig preferred all-night marathons, Isabelle agreed to spend the day at the beach followed by a long afternoon nap. That evening Nate and Isabelle showed up at the Golden Magnolia with a camera slung around his neck and Isabelle in a huge straw hat. Looking like quintessential tourists, they strolled through the elegant lobby as though they had all the time in the world. Nate stopped at the first row of slot machines they came to.

"Should I get a roll of quarters from the cashier window?" Isabelle asked, hooking her arm through his elbow.

"Machines no longer take coins. This one doesn't even have a handle. You insert paper money here…like a fifty or a hundred-dollar bill." Nate pointed at a slot on the Triple Wild Cherry machine.

Isabelle squeezed his arm. "Don't you dare! We'll wager a ten-spot. That should be enough to get the idea."

Nate inserted a crisp Hamilton, pushed the button, and watched the electronic wheels spin. Taking turns at the button, Nate and Isabelle watched their forty quarters dip precariously low, soar to a high-water mark of sixty-two, and then steadily diminish to zero. But plenty of flashing lights and sound effects livened up the ten-minute session.

"Well, that was fun. Now let's go find the poker tables." Isabelle dragged him down the center aisle. "Craig's favorite game was Texas Hold'em."

"Those look like poker tables in the middle of the casino." Nate read the brass placards as they passed each table. "Caribbean Stud, Pai Gow Poker, Let It Ride, and Texas Hold'em on the end."

"We can watch from here," whispered Isabelle, pulling him behind a marble pillar.

They moved from one clandestine vantage point to the next, studying the faces of the gamblers, but Craig was nowhere to be found.

"This might be his night off," Nate observed. "What do you say we hit the buffet? I could use a bite to eat."

Isabelle wasn't easily deterred. As a well-dressed casino employee walked by, she stepped into his path. "Excuse me, sir. We're Isabelle and Nate Price from Natchez. Are these your most expensive poker tables?" She produced a megawatt smile. "I see the minimum bet is only ten dollars. Where can we win bigger jackpots?"

Elliott Lacey, casino host, according to his name tag, was momentarily speechless. "How do you do, Mr. and Mrs. Price. Welcome to the Golden Magnolia." He shook hands with Nate. "We have a poker room if you wish to play against other players. Opening bids vary, as well as the size of the pots."

"Would you mind terribly escorting us there?" asked Isabelle, her drawl thickening. "I would like to observe so that I might properly advise my daddy back home. I promise not to stay long or disrupt anyone's concentration." She made an *X* motion across her heart.

Daddy? Nate had never met his father-in-law because he had passed on years ago.

Mr. Lacey smiled and extended his elbow to Isabelle. "I'm on my break, ma'am, so it would be my pleasure."

Nate wouldn't have believed her flirtatious behavior if he hadn't witnessed it himself. He fell in behind them, eager to see what she would do next.

Inside the high-stakes room, the lighting and furnishings were expensive, the waitresses better attired, and the mood subdued. Two tables were active with eight players at each. No bells and whistles, no rock music in the background, and nobody jumping up shouting, "Jackpot!" It didn't take them long to realize Craig wasn't one of these players either.

"Thank you, Mr. Lacey. I've seen enough."

"You're welcome, Mrs. Price." He bobbed his head politely and wandered into the crowd.

Isabelle sagged into Nate's side. "What are we going to do?" she wailed.

"Wait here a moment." Nate hurried after the helpful casino host. "Excuse me, sir. We're trying to track down an ex-husband who plays poker here. Are these the *only* poker games taking place inside this casino?"

Mr. Lacey studied him and then glanced back at Isabelle. "There are private games in the high-stakes rooms any given night of the week, but those are by invitation only. A player doesn't just walk in, and *no one* observes the games. If your wife knew her ex-husband's casino host, he or she might be of more assistance."

"Thanks. We appreciate your help." Nate shook the man's hand, but he refused to share that with his wife until they were seated inside the buffet restaurant.

Isabelle mulled over the new information as she ate a modest portion of baked chicken, potato salad, and peach cobbler. "That has to be where he is—in one of those all-night games in a hotel room. Oh, my. Craig could get into plenty of trouble if he doesn't know when to hold 'em, when to fold 'em, and when to walk away."

"Are you going to break into a Kenny Rogers song?" Nate dug into his self-made ice-cream sundae.

"Would you please take this seriously?" Isabelle sounded like a feral cat.

"I *am* taking this seriously, but we've hit a brick wall. We're not rated players, and we don't have a fat wad of cash. So we're not getting inside those games, no matter *how* much you bat your eyelashes. Let's go back to our room."

She blushed with embarrassment. "I don't want to play poker. I only want to find out what Craig's up to. Let's buy a foo-foo cocktail and stake out the elevators. Maybe we'll get lucky."

"Fine, but only for the duration of one drink." Nate pushed away his remaining dessert, his stomach at maximum capacity.

After purchasing virgin mai tais, they settled onto a banquette in the lobby. Amazingly, Craig strolled into the Golden Magnolia Casino a few minutes later wearing dark glasses and a baseball cap. Nate hid behind a copy of *USA Today*, while Isabelle peeked from behind a brochure for parasailing. Craig walked to the elevator and pressed the button.

The moment the elevator door closed, Isabelle jumped up to follow him. Nate watched the numbers light up on the overhead display. Craig's elevator stopped at the seventeenth floor. When the adjacent door opened, Isabelle practically bowled over the people exiting. "Excuse us," Nate mumbled as he squeezed past. "Bit of a family emergency."

"We need to hurry to see which suite he enters," she said, pressing the numeral seventeen. Yet no matter how many times she punched the button, Isabelle couldn't select the seventeenth floor.

"Izzy, stop. You need a key card to access floors fifteen and above." Nate pointed to a small sign.

"Oh, dear, what are we going to do?" His wife sounded close to tears.

Another passenger, a young cocktail waitress, took pity on them. "You don't want to play up there, honey. The minimum buy-in is thirty *K* for tonight's game."

"Buy-in?" Isabelle asked, wide-eyed.

"The amount needed to get in the game. Thirty thousand, minimum," the waitress repeated.

"Ohhh." Isabelle dragged out the single syllable. "We were playing Triple Wild Cherry slots, and I thought it might be fun to play Texas Hold'em like on TV. We're on our honeymoon."

"Save your money. Only one person walks away from the table a winner. Everybody else had better be rich so they don't need the cash. I have something you'll enjoy more." The girl dug two coupons from her pocket. "Free buffets on the house. Good anytime."

"Thank you," they said simultaneously.

On the way back down, the cocktail waitress stepped out on the ninth floor. "Enjoy your honeymoon, folks. Thanks for coming to the Golden Magnolia."

Nate and Isabelle rode the elevator to the basement and then up again.

"Thirty thousand dollars," Isabelle muttered as they reached the lobby. "Where on earth would Craig get a buy-in like that?"

Where indeed?

Before leaving the casino, Nate bought two more fake mai tais to take back to their B and B. Sitting by the water, sipping something coconuty, he felt content. But something told him the new sleuth of Bay St. Louis was just getting started.

TWENTY

Natchez

*M*ichael drove to the office of Price Investigations on Friday with confidence he would succeed at his newfound career. At long last he had something to offer besides stupid questions and demands for special training as though this was summer camp for thirty-year-olds. He and Beth had spent yesterday apart, studying evidence, following leads, and sorting out the suspects. Today he would present his case.

When Michael walked into the office, Beth was sitting at Nate's desk studying the doodles on his desk blotter. "Trying that out for size?" he asked, settling in a guest chair. "Nate is too young to retire."

Beth rocked back and forth with a big grin. "I expect rapid advancement up the ranks, mainly because I'm so cute."

"There goes political correctness out the window." Michael broke eye contact, her overconfidence effectively undermining his. "Is Maxine still on vacation?"

"She is. I'm hoping she's someplace fun and not home washing windows." Beth poured a handful of M&M's from a bag in a drawer.

"Aren't those Nate's? And did you know you left the front door wide open?"

"Yes, on both counts. Crime is nonexistent in Natchez before

noon. Bad people always sleep late. Anyway, I'm ready for whoever walks in." Beth lifted her foot to the desktop and pulled up her
pant leg. "Twenty-two caliber with seven in the clip." She turned
her ankle to show off the holster.

"How many guns do you own?" he asked, dumbfounded.

"Six or seven, plus a bazooka and a cannon." Her blue eyes
sparkled.

"You're joking about the artillery, right?"

"I am. What did you find out yesterday?" She lowered her foot
to the floor.

Michael took the file from his leather briefcase. Clearing his
throat, he concentrated on his notes. "First off, I called Mrs. Dean
and asked if I could revisit the pastor's study. She wouldn't allow it
because she was leaving town. She's taking Katie to her sister's for
a few days. I asked if I could borrow their computer, and she said
absolutely not. When I mentioned Buckley had returned, she grew
incensed." He paused, waiting for Beth's reaction.

She stopped rocking. "Do tell all, Mr. Preston."

"Mrs. Dean asked if he was still spreading nasty rumors about
her husband. Apparently, Buckley thought Reverend Dean was
either losing his mind or had early onset Alzheimer's. She insisted
the allegations were 'a crock' and 'who doesn't occasionally forget
where they left their keys or wallet?' I had to agree with her."

"Me too, for what it's worth. Just yesterday I put a roll of waxed
paper in the fridge. Distraction makes us look silly. Sounds like Ralphie's trying to regain control of the money."

"That's what I thought. Mrs. Dean knew about Buckley's aggressive investments and suspected he was also skimming profits."
Michael reached for the bag of M&M's. "Not that I've found evidence of that. I'm just repeating Mrs. Dean's conjectures."

"Duly noted, Sherlock."

Michael felt himself blush, a habit he couldn't seem to break.
He refocused on his notes. "Mrs. Dean also provided verbal

confirmation that her husband controlled the account for the past several months."

"Works for me. What else?" Beth grabbed the bag for another handful and returned the bag to its drawer.

"I spent the rest of yesterday studying the detective's report and the autopsy results for the alleged suicide. Thanks, by the way, for giving me copies. They helped to clarify the case. And thanks for target practice and supper at your aunt's house. The meal was delicious."

Beth burst out laughing. "It was chicken and rice with corn on the cob. Not exactly nouvelle cuisine from the Food Network."

"It was gourmet by my standards. I live alone and never learned how to cook."

"Also duly noted, and you're welcome. My aunt really liked you." Beth wiggled her eyebrows. "Don't say you weren't warned, Preston."

"Getting back to the police report…" Michael refused to reveal how easily she embarrassed him. "According to Detective Lejeune, no fingerprints were on the rope. Isn't that odd? Why would some-body planning to kill himself bother to wear gloves? No gloves were found at the scene, but if somebody *helped* Reverend Dean, he or she would certainly have taken them with them." Michael looked up from his notes.

Beth remained devoid of expression. "Go on," she prodded. "I'm listening."

"I checked with Mrs. Purdy. On the day Reverend Dean died, he left the church before two o'clock. He told her he was needed at home, but neither his wife nor his daughter was home until much later that day. The pastor had given his wife the impression he would be visiting shut-ins. But there were no appointments on either his office calendar or his day planner at home. I checked into this—Paul Dean was meticulous about writing appointments down, both at church and at home. He even wrote 'take out trash' on the calendar."

Beth cocked her head. "Okay. What conclusion can you draw?"

"Somebody was coming to the house, someone the pastor didn't want anyone else to know about." Michael spoke the words as quickly as possible, as though confessing to a personal crime.

"That's valid because the timetable doesn't line up with what he told his wife and assistant. Keep talking. You're on a pretty good roll."

Her flippancy hit a nerve. "Facts are facts, Elizabeth. Reverend Dean told two different stories."

"I agree." Beth pulled a bottle of water from her bag and chugged down half of it. "What else?"

Michael collected his thoughts. "According to the coroner's report, two separate bruises were found on the victim's neck. They were close together yet distinctive. As though there were two separate incidents of hanging. The first attempt damaged the windpipe and would have made it difficult to talk or breathe, but it wouldn't have incapacitated the victim. Reverend Dean would have had to shorten the rope and climb back on the stool for another try. This time he succeeded in breaking his neck and dying within moments."

Beth flinched from the mental picture painted with his description. "How awful," she murmured.

"Truly, if that's how it went down. But I don't think a scrawny man like Reverend Dean had the physical or emotional wherewithal to try again. I believe someone else shortened the noose and forced the pastor back onto that stool. Furthermore, Buckley possesses the upper body strength along with sufficient motive to carry this out. Reverend Dean probably figured out that the guy was trying to regain control by spreading rumors. If Reverend Dean decided to confront him, Buckley might have panicked and taken matters into his own hands."

"Could you make this sound less like a game of Clue?"

Michael felt his blood pressure begin to rise. "Sorry if my delivery doesn't live up to expectations, but I think I'm on to something."

Beth straightened in her chair. "Actually, your conclusions

surpassed my wildest expectations, and your delivery was fine. I just have the bad habit of making jokes out of things that upset me. I'm sorry."

She'd spoken the final two words softly, but Michael heard them clearly. "Then this will be good for us both," he said after a few moments. "I might need to lighten up."

"And I'll be the first Kirby to develop a sensitive side." Beth pulled open the drawer. "M&M's as a peace offering?"

"Not unless they actually belong to you, and I sure hope you plan to replace Nate's candy."

"Fair enough." She shut the drawer. "What should we do with your conjectures?"

"Let's ask the detective if this type of rope retains fingerprints. If someone in the Natchez PD agrees with my assessment, maybe we can raise reasonable doubt in the mind of the coroner. We need another medical opinion about the second hanging attempt. Of course, Mrs. Dean would have to agree to exhume the body, but she might be willing based on the evidence. I believe if the pastor failed during his first attempt, Mrs. Dean would have found him injured but alive when she got home."

"Or their daughter." Beth covered her face with her hands. "What an awful thought. Paul Dean never would have subjected his family to that." She jumped to her feet. "You done good, partner. I'll go talk to Detective Lejeune. He was the lead detective during the investigation."

"Let's both talk to him. I can learn a lot from watching you interact with Natchez's men and women in blue."

"No, I must do this alone."

"I'll keep quiet and listen this time, Elizabeth. You have my word."

"I believe you, but Detective Lejeune was my old partner on the job before his promotion. In fact, his promotion came mainly because I left. We have plenty of past history and most of it isn't warm and fuzzy."

"So this has nothing to do with me?"

"Not a thing, honest. We'll meet later after I talk with Lejeune." Beth strode toward the door and then stopped in her tracks. "I owe you more explanation than that."

"You owe me M&M's purchased with your own money. Nothing more." Despite his denial, Michael secretly hoped she would spill her guts.

"Jack Lejeune was a headache the entire time we partnered together. He's very competitive and can't tolerate the idea of a woman besting him at anything. When we both took the detective's exam, I scored higher in every category. Yet when I made detective instead of him, he whined that my promotion came because of my...relationship with the chief."

"Some men have more ego than intelligence. Surely other officers on the force recognized the truth."

"People must have been nice wherever you worked last." Beth forced a sad smile. "Anyway, thanks for understanding. No matter what happens today, this is the last time I go without you. Lock up on your way out," she called over her shoulder.

Michael sat alone in Nate's office, mulling over the case and his partner's comments. When his thoughts drifted back to the last place he worked, he jumped to his feet. He suddenly had the urge to pound the pavement and burn up energy.

One person in particular at his last job was anything but *nice*.

TWENTY-ONE

*B*eth wasn't sure why she'd made such a promise to Michael, but now that she had she felt better. She was tired of the innuendos and backstabbing for something that had never happened. Why should she be persecuted for something that existed only in people's imaginations? Whether or not Jack Lejeune resented her until the day he died, she had a responsibility to Mrs. Dean and to Michael. With renewed determination, she drove to the station and marched up the front walk.

But before she could pick up the phone in the lobby, Sergeant Mendez walked through the door. "I take it you're here to see the chief?"

"You take it wrong. I'd like to see Detective Lejeune, please." Beth straightened to her full five feet six inches.

"You got an appointment?" Mendez spoke as though suffering with indigestion.

"I don't, but is Jack here? This won't take long." She hiked her purse higher on her shoulder.

"Won't take no time at all because he ain't here."

"In that case, I'd like to make an appointment."

"If I remember right, Detective Lejeune has an opening a week from Tuesday. Does that work for you, Miss Kirby?" Mendez's grin turned malevolent.

"It does not, but I'll call and leave a message for him. Thanks anyway." Feeling her face grow hot, Beth turned and hurried from the building. Before leaving, she checked the lot and saw that Lejeune's vehicle was gone.

Because it was too early to go home, Beth bought the largest latte and stickiest cinnamon bun available and parked across the street from the station. Two hours later her patience was rewarded. Jack drove into the lot and parked cockeyed in a spot. As he strolled toward the back entrance, Beth intersected his path.

"Hey, Jack. Can a have a word with you?"

"I'm kinda busy, Kirby." He pulled his sunglasses down with one finger. "Didn't the sergeant make you an appointment for next Tuesday?"

"This can't wait a week," she said, unsurprised that news of her visit had already reached him. "My partner and I noticed some irregularities in your report of the Dean suicide."

His smug grin vanished. "Oh, you did? You're no longer on the force, Kirby, so nobody cares what you think. The chief had no business giving you the case file."

"Price Investigations represents Mrs. Dean. She believes her husband was murdered and so do I." Beth divided her weight between her feet as though ready for a fistfight.

"Based on what?" Jack spat the question. "You got me curious."

"According to the police report, the rope was a braided natural manila that had been looped over the beam. I checked. That stuff picks up fingerprints, yet none were found. Also, Reverend Dean was meeting somebody at the house that afternoon, someone neither his assistant nor wife knew about."

"That's it? The lack of fingerprints and a mysterious visitor? Maybe the preacher had a girlfriend on the side. Maybe she'd broken up with him, and that's what sent him over the edge."

Beth's hands balled into fists. "Look, sleazeball, Reverend Dean didn't have a lover. What about the two parallel bruises on his neck? That would indicate two separate hanging attempts. You're telling me an out-of-shape man, gasping for air, shortened the rope and tried again?"

"No, Beth. *I'm* not telling you anything." Jack jabbed his finger into her collarbone, an action that surpassed audacious. "That's the conclusion of the coroner who examined the body. If he says death by suicide, and I've got no evidence to the contrary, then that's what we got."

She knocked away his hand. "We need a second opinion on cause of death. Maybe the ME in Jackson can take a look."

"Reverend Dean is already in the ground. It costs a bundle to exhume a body. The county ain't going for that without probable cause, and we don't have that."

"Says you?" Beth was losing patience.

He glared down at her. "That's right. Says me. I'm the lead detective on this case and you're not. Oh, wait. You're not even on the force anymore. Or did you happen to forget that?"

"I know exactly who I work for. I want you to run our concerns by Chief McNeil. Let him make the call as to whether or not we have probable cause." Beth shifted her weight to the other hip, ignoring the attention they were drawing.

"You just won't give it a rest, will you? Back off and leave the chief alone."

Beth shook her finger in front of his nose. "This has nothing to do with Chris or me or even you. Other than the fact that you're the laziest cop I know," she added, her patience running out. "This has to do with Alice Dean's suspicion that her husband was murdered. Will you talk to Chris or shall I?"

Jack offered an unexpected smile, which improved his bland features tremendously. Someone might even find the guy handsome if he didn't have the personality of a toad. "Sure. I'll talk to him before my shift ends. But if I were you, Kirby, I wouldn't get my hopes up." Ambling away, he entered the station without a backward glance.

Beth drove home, gritting her teeth as the double latte burned a hole through her stomach. That evening, all she wanted to do was eat and then curl up in front of some mindless sitcom on TV, but her mother's sullenness at dinner was a harbinger of a coming storm.

"Good meat loaf, Mom," said Beth, adding more catsup to the crust. "And these mashed potatoes are great."

"Then why don't you eat more?" Rita aimed her fork at Beth's plate. "You haven't tried any of my succotash. Have you got man problems on the mind?"

Beth choked on a burnt piece. "Man problems? I haven't had a date in years." She glanced at her father, but he was watching the ball game on the kitchen counter.

Rita took another spoonful of mixed vegetables and added some to Beth's plate. "I heard from a friend that you went to see Chief McNeil. You can't possibly think something good can come from that."

"I hope the dispatcher didn't put any 9-1-1 calls on hold while your friend called you five minutes after I walked out the door. Doesn't anyone mind their own business anymore?"

"Barbara worries about you, the same as me. She's known you since you were born."

"Yes, and she's always been nice. So you may tell Barbara that my visit was strictly connected to the case I'm on." Beth added more gravy to her potatoes. "I'm a PI working in Natchez. I can't avoid law enforcement if I want justice for my clients."

"Then you should talk to Chief McNeil with his door open. Don't give people a reason to gossip about you, not if you want your reputation to recover." Rita dabbed her lips with a napkin. "And you wonder why you haven't had a date in years."

"I don't wonder, Mom. Boys don't like girls who are smarter than them, or shoot better, or run faster, or jump higher. Never have and never will." Beth stuck her knife and fork into the meat loaf and pushed away her plate.

Stan switched his attention from the Atlanta Braves to his

daughter. "Pay no attention to those inferior specimens." He patted Beth's arm. "When a man worthy of your affections comes along, you'll recognize him on the spot."

"Thanks, Pops." Beth buzzed his cheek with a kiss on her way to the sink.

The ring of the wall phone curtailed Rita's initial comment. "Who would be rude enough to call during the dinner hour? Kirby residence," she barked, and then in a gentler tone she said, "One moment, please." Pressing the receiver to her chest, Rita said to Beth, "It's Chief McNeil for you."

Beth grabbed the phone, asked him to call back on her cell, and ran to her room. Sitting in a yoga pose between the wall and her bed, Beth stared at her phone as though she were in high school. When it rang, panic shot through her veins like electricity.

"Hello, Chris."

"Hey, Beth. Sorry I interrupted your supper." As usual, the sound of his easy drawl raised goose bumps on her arms.

"Your timing couldn't have been better. Did Jack explain my request on behalf of our client?"

With his usual proficiency, Chris repeated her words to Jack practically verbatim.

"Wow, I didn't think he was even listening to me," she said.

"He listened, but he doesn't agree with either your assessment or Mrs. Dean's suspicions."

"Actually, it was my partner at the agency who found the discrepancies." Beth refused to take undeserved credit. "What do you think?"

There was a pause, as though he took a sip of something. "I didn't like the double injuries to his throat either, but that, along with a lack of fingerprints, won't be enough for a judge to order an exhumation. However, if Mrs. Dean requests another opinion and is willing to pay for it, that would take care of it. It's unfortunate that it comes down to dollars and cents, but I must be realistic with you."

"I appreciate that. I will talk to Mrs. Dean tomorrow and let you know."

"Very good. In the meantime I'll instruct Jack that if Mrs. Dean demands an exhumation, he will talk to the coroner along with you and Mr. Preston. You must work with Jack on this, Beth, because I want the letter of the law followed when the state medical examiner gets involved. Will you be able to put past differences aside and defer to him during your investigation?"

"Absolutely. I can behave as a professional on behalf of our client."

"Fine. Then you'll have no problems with Natchez PD. If foul play was involved in the death of Pastor Dean, we'll help you find it. Jot down the number to Jack's cell."

Beth grabbed a pen and wrote the number on her palm. "Thanks, Chris, I appreciate your intervention."

"No thanks necessary. It's my honor to serve Natchez to the best of my ability. Good night, Beth." He hung up without waiting for her reply.

It was just as well, because she couldn't think of a single clever thing to say.

TWENTY-TWO

Bay St. Louis
Friday

Isabelle kissed her husband's forehead and cheek without a response. Then she planted a kiss firmly on his lips and received only a sleepy grunt in return. Growing impatient, she shook his shoulder. "Na-ate," she sang. "Time to get up."

He turned over, pulling the sheet over his head. "No, Ma. I don't want to go to school today."

Isabelle took hold of his nose and twisted. "I am not your mother, and you're getting up this minute."

Nate bolted upright so fast Isabelle fell off the bed. "You little troublemaker. I'll teach you a lesson you won't soon forget." He tickled her ribs through her cotton top.

She slapped his hands away. "I knew you were faking. Now go jump in the shower so we can be in position by zero seven hundred."

Frowning, Nate crawled from the bed. "Mrs. Russo won't even have breakfast on the table, and I'm starving."

"I asked her to pack breakfast to go. We can eat while on surveillance." Isabelle ignored Nate's grumbling as she fluffed up their pillows.

Twenty minutes later, parked outside the Golden Magnolia, she pulled ham and egg croissants, two containers of fruit salad, and a thermos of coffee from a wicker hamper. "Mmm," she said, open-ing one sandwich. "This smells delicious."

Nate unwrapped his and took a bite. "What, no orange juice?"

Isabelle lifted out an orange plastic bottle. "Mrs. Russo thinks of everything. I wish I could live at her B and B forever."

Nate took a long swallow and smiled. "Me too, sweet thing. That's why I don't like wasting our time with Craig."

"Looks like we won't waste much today." Isabelle pointed at the entrance where Craig strolled from the casino, unaware of the approaching storm. She dropped her sandwich into the bag and jumped from the car.

Nate did the same, although with far less spring in his step.

"Good morning, Craig. Looks like another perfect day in para-dise," she said cheerily.

He sighed mightily. "Izzy, Nate. What are you doing here? I thought I made myself perfectly clear—"

"Relax," she said. "We just want to buy you breakfast and see if you want to spend the day with us. Why don't we take one of those fishing charters and catch a huge herring for supper?" Isabelle spread her hands to indicate a three-foot fish.

"No, no, and no. Just for the record, a herring is a tiny fish, barely enough for a pelican's supper." Craig slipped on his sunglasses and marched across the parking lot.

Isabelle quickly dogged his steps. "Please, Craig? I remember you once loved fishing but rarely had time for it. This is your big chance before your new job starts."

"No thanks, Isabelle."

As Craig dug for his keys, she cast her husband a pleading look.

"Come on, buddy," said Nate, rallying to her cause. "Why not get away from the tables for a while? Let's grab something to eat and talk sports. Izzy knows football like she knows fish." Nate slapped Craig on the back.

"As appealing as that sounds, I've got to hit the sack. I've been up all night. Maybe before you two head back to Natchez." Craig climbed into his car and lowered the window.

"Everybody's got to eat. If you have breakfast with us, Izzy will stop dragging me out of bed before the sun's up. You know how persistent she can be."

"All right. One breakfast, but I pick the place. Follow me to the best food in Bay St. Louis." Craig started the engine.

On the way to their car, Isabelle bumped Nate with her hip. "Later you'll have to elaborate more on my personality. I'm utterly fascinated."

"Just trying to convince him to join us. It worked, didn't it?" With a wry smile Nate fell in behind Craig's Toyota for the short drive.

Isabelle couldn't argue with success, but their battle with Craig was just getting started. In the small diner with the biggest menu she ever saw, Craig gave his order the moment the waitress appeared.

"I'll have three eggs, scrambled, bacon extra crispy, two flapjacks, wheat toast, and coffee," he said.

Isabelle thought about her uneaten croissant in the car. Despite her aversion to wasting food, she ordered blueberry pancakes to be sociable. Nate selected shrimp and grits with a side of ham. While they waited for their food, the two men chatted about Saints and Titans football, and ran through the draft prospects for Ole Miss, Mississippi State, and LSU for good measure.

Isabelle tried to be patient, but when she started to nod off from boredom, she broached the topic on her mind. "The Gulf Coast has recovered nicely since Katrina. Why don't you come sightseeing with us? We don't mind company, and if you stay out of the casino, you'll have money to take back to Nashville."

"I'll pass, Izzy." Craig leaned back as the waitress placed a mounded platter in front of him. Then he picked up his fork and attacked the food as though he hadn't eaten in days. Isabelle and Nate began to eat as well but with far less gusto. After several minutes, Craig took a slurp of coffee. "I've seen all the attractions I came here for. I've played a few tournaments. Now I'm getting invited to serious games. If I drop out of sight, I might lose my chance to win big."

Isabelle arched her back against the vinyl seat. "Well, perhaps after Cassie arrives, you can tear yourself away long enough to walk the beach."

Craig choked on the piece of bacon he was chewing. "*What*? You called Cassie after I told you not to?" He threw his fork down with a clatter. "Why are you still tormenting me after all these years?"

"I didn't call her. She called me."

"If you would have minded your own business in the first place—"

"Wait a minute, Craig," Nate interrupted.

"No, you wait. You have no idea what trouble your wife has caused. If there's any way to stop Cassie, you must do so. It's not safe for her here." Craig looked so anxious, so desperate, that Isabelle felt a jolt of fear run up her spine.

"If it's not safe for Cassie," said Nate, dropping his voice to a whisper, "it's not safe for you, either. Let us help you for old times' sake, before you're in over your head."

"Man, you are totally clueless. I'm already in over my head. It's too late for *intervention*." Craig imbued the word with derision. "I know you mean well, Nate, but please talk sense into Izzy. Keep her away from me. I don't want her, or you, or my wife to get hurt. Trust me when I say there's no other way." Craig jumped up from the booth and ran out the door.

Isabelle and Nate stared at each other. Then Isabelle started crying, unsure why she cared so much about her ex. "Well, that's it. No matter what happens, we tried our best."

Nate shook his head. "No, my love, I don't think we've seen the last of him. Not by a long shot."

TWENTY-THREE

Natchez

Michael awoke to a ruckus below his window on the street. Either the trash haulers were trying to wake the dead, or someone irate was attempting to gain entry to his building. Stretching lazily, he padded to the coffeemaker in time to see a rock bounce off his kitchen window. A rock large enough to rattle the glass but small enough not to break the pane.

Michael pushed up the window and stuck out his head, becoming an easy target for the hooligan in the alley. "Who's down there?" he shouted.

"Your partner." Beth's voice drifted skyward. "Why aren't you answering your buzzer? I've been standing here for ten minutes." She moved from under the overhang to the Dumpster.

With her red hair curly from the rain, she would have looked adorable if not for her frown. "No need to break my window just because the buzzer's broken. They're coming tomorrow to fix it."

"How do you know when you have company, Preston?" she called, arching her neck and shielding her eyes from the rain.

"Never had any so far. You're my first guest. Why didn't you call me last night with an update?"

Beth lifted both hands in supplication. "Could I please come upstairs so we can discuss this out of the rain?" Her voice intensified with each word.

"Sure. Why didn't you just say so?" He shut the window, released the door lock, and pulled on a sweatshirt. His daily exercises hadn't yet produced bodybuilder results, but he could feel his endurance and stamina improving. When he opened the door to the hallway, Beth was at the top of the steps, shaking like a poodle.

"Come in, Miss Kirby. Did you not notice today was Saturday?" He handed her a towel for her hair.

"Until Nate comes home I'm the boss, and I mandate Saturday a workday. You're not a nine-to-fiver anymore." Beth headed straight to the coffeemaker. "I didn't call you last night because I played rummy with my dad until midnight. I seldom get to spend much time with him. However," she drawled, filling a mug to the rim, "I've already been on the phone with Mrs. Dean. She returned from her sister's last night and said we could come over this morning, as in now. So go put on something classy." She flourished a hand at his workout clothes. "I'll tell you about my conversation with Detective Lejeune along the way."

Michael grabbed his coffee and bolted to the bathroom for a shower. Odd how working weekends hadn't been half as appealing at his old job. Not even while engaged to the office assistant.

"Is it okay if I have some of this apple Danish?" Beth shouted from the kitchen.

"Eat all you want. There's juice in the fridge too."

Ten minutes later, he yanked on clean clothes and towel dried his hair. "Are you sure Mrs. Dean knows I'm coming too?" he called.

"Yep. I smoothed things out between you two. Just don't say or do anything to annoy her."

Michael appeared in the doorway. "That implies I can recognize annoying statements in advance. How's this? Decent enough?"

"Wow, the speed at which men get ready astounds me. Yes, chinos and a polo shirt are perfect." Beth popped the last bite of pastry in her mouth. "Thanks for breakfast, Mike. I escaped Hotel California before mealtime."

"You're welcome." Picking up his briefcase, Michael opened the door for her. "Ready to go?"

"I'll drive since we're in a hurry. You look nice, by the way." Beth ran down the steps at breakneck speed.

"Thank you, Miss Kirby. I'm hoping for a good report to the boss. Tell me about your visit with Detective Lejeune and Chief McNeil."

Beth drove so fast Michael barely had time to process the conversation before they arrived at the Deans'.

"Here's our plan," she said, braking to a stop in the driveway. "Alice said you may check her husband's computer in his office. She's furious about what Buckley had been doing behind the pastor's back. While you're digging up dirt on Ralphie, I will talk Alice into an exhumation of her husband's body and convince her to pay for it."

"Can't I help with my newfound tact and finesse?" He winked as he slicked the damp hair back from his face.

"Let's postpone your demonstration of those skills for another day. I need you to comb through Paul's emails to board members. Look for anything having to do with the finance manager." She jumped out of the car.

"Will do. I'm the man for the job." Michael trailed her up the walk.

"Ready?" Beth waited a split second and then knocked.

Whether he was ready or not, the widow swept open the door. Although perfectly groomed in a tailored suit, Alice looked as though she hadn't slept well in days.

"Good morning," she murmured. "Please come in. Mr. Preston, you know the way to Paul's study. Beth, you and I can talk in the family room. I have a carafe of coffee waiting for us." She turned and led the way through the house.

Michael had to slink off, coffeeless, down the hallway. But his endeavors in the pastor's study were not in vain. He soon found emails between Reverend Dean and several board members about Buckley's devious scheming. The copy machine whirred as he printed off page after page of potential evidence, including one major break in the case. Like a schoolboy hoping to impress his teacher, Michael couldn't wait to show Beth.

For the next hour he combed through the pastor's private correspondence, gaining insight to a man he knew only in death. The picture which formed was of someone dedicated to his faith, tireless in serving his church, and fully committed to his wife and daughter. Michael saw no signs of dementia. Just the normal mental commotion from juggling too many balls in the air.

"Are you about done, Mr. Preston?" A voice over his shoulder broke his concentration.

Michael turned to see Alice in the doorway with Beth hovering behind her.

"I am, ma'am. And I believe we have enough for the police to get an arrest warrant for Mr. Buckley."

"You found proof that snake was poisoning the board against Paul with lies about Alzheimer's?" she asked.

"Yes. A string of emails between Buckley and several board members. One of them didn't buy into the allegations and forwarded the entire thread to Reverend Dean. Buckley was definitely trying to regain control of the building fund."

"I knew something was bothering Paul, but he refused to discuss it with me. I'm in your debt, Mr. Preston," she said, meeting his eye. Then she reached for Beth's hand. "Thank you for your kind words, Beth. Please keep me informed of any new developments." Alice turned on one high heel, cutting short the warm-and-fuzzy moment. "If you're finished in here, I'll see you to the door."

Michael shoved the printouts into his briefcase and followed Beth down the hall. On their way to the car, she returned his earlier wink.

"I take it you have good news too?" he asked.

Beth waited until they were inside the car to hoot with joy. "Alice not only agreed to the exhumation, but is willing to pay for it as well. She fears Buckley might flee the country with the congregation's money if he's not caught soon. Her only stipulation is that her daughter not be told."

"Well done." Michael slapped her on the back. "Buckley bolting for the border is a distinct possibility. His passport is up-to-date, and he speaks both French and Spanish."

Beth started the car and pulled into traffic. "You learned a lot about Mr. Wheeler-Dealer in a short amount of time."

"I don't watch much TV. What comes next?"

"With the exhumation going forward, I'll call my friends on the Vicksburg police force. One of them might be willing to contact the state medical examiner to speed things along." Beth stopped at the end of the block and swiveled to face him. "You find anything else on the computer other than proof Buckley was stabbing Paul in the back?"

"I believe I hit the mother lode," Michael murmured, trying to prolong the drama. He nodded at a young mother pushing a stroller in the crosswalk.

Beth arched one eyebrow. "Spill your guts, Preston. Or as soon as these witnesses are gone I'm beating it out of you."

He made a dismissive cluck. "You do realize I've been back to the workout room several times."

"You do realize I hit every can along the fence rail dead center."

"True. Okay, I found a recent email from Pastor Dean to one of the elders. Attached was an Excel file showing Buckley had transferred sixty thousand dollars to his personal account."

"No kidding?" Beth pushed her sunglasses to the top of her head.

"No kidding. Sixty thousand from the building fund into the joint account of Tamara and Ralph Buckley. Tammy is his lovely wife of twenty-six years, by the way."

"We've got him on grand theft!"

"Even better. When Reverend Dean read Ralph's slanderous emails, he looked deeper into the guy's financial shenanigans. Up until that point, he thought Buckley simply invested too aggressively. That's when he found the bank transfer and demanded, in an email, that Ralph replace the funds immediately. Buckley went to talk to him the next day, unaware that Reverend Dean had already sent proof of the theft to another board member."

A slow smile bloomed on Beth's face. "We've got motive for murder."

"We've got motive, all right. And while we wait for autopsy results, the police can keep him in jail on the theft charge. Old Ralphie isn't taking off with sweet little Tammy."

Beth turned onto the road along the river. "Well done, Preston. I'm recommending you for a raise when Nate gets back. You've all but tied a bow on this case."

Michael hoped his blush blended into his tan. "In the meantime, why don't you buy me lunch? And I'm not talkin' the drive-through lane."

"Fine, but let's eat fast. I can't wait to talk to Jack. Correction, for both of us to talk to him. He will soon be eating crow instead of a double cheeseburger and fries like us."

TWENTY-FOUR

*B*eth would have given anything not to speak to Jack in front of her partner. She knew it would not go well. The detective would try to demean her, embarrass her, and undermine whatever evidence they had found. But considering Michael's progress in the last few days, there was no way she could exclude him.

She waited until they were at the restaurant and had ordered lunch before punching in the cell number supplied by Chris.

Jack picked up on the first ring. "That you, Nancy Drew? Or are you Sherlock Holmes along with your sidekick, John Watson?"

"It's Beth Kirby with Michael Preston, and you're on speaker, so don't say anything unprofessional. The chief promised full cooperation."

"Of course he did. And you'll receive every bit of cooperation I'm capable of." Jack's cackle set Beth's nerves on edge. "What did Mrs. Dean say?"

"She agreed to an exhumation. In fact, she insisted if it will shed light on her husband's killer."

"Clinical depression, temporary insanity due to a guilty conscience, fear of exposure over some misdeed—any one of those could be the killer, but he acted alone. And when Paul Dean didn't succeed the first time, he simply tried again." Jack spoke with the ambivalence of a cynical veteran.

Beth paused as a young woman delivered their tray of burgers and Cajun fries. "I don't think so, Jack. And because Mrs. Dean's willing to foot the bill, we'll get that second opinion."

"I'll begin the paperwork for the Mississippi crime lab and alert Doc Pallota. The local coroner needs to be present when we open the grave. I suppose you and Preston want to be there for the festivities."

"Of course we do. While you do that, I'll contact friends on the force in Vicksburg. Maybe their medical examiner might want to drive down."

"Why am I *not* surprised you have friends on the force in Vicksburg?"

"Why wouldn't I have friends in the police department? I was investigating a case involving a caregiver stealing from an old lady. Plenty of cops are willing to work with PIs."

"Including this one," Jack said. "When the chief tells me to play nice, I do what I'm told. But let me ask you something, Beth. Any of those cop pals wear skirts? You know, women?"

Beth doused her half of the fries with catsup as her temper flared. "What does the fact Vicksburg has mainly men on the force have to do with anything?"

"Nothing. Just asking a simple question." Jack chuckled like an old friend, something he never was. "Involving Vicksburg is a waste of time. If there's been a possible crime, that body has to go to Jackson. Period. Anyway, your second opinion is going to match the first. I spoke with Natalie Purdy at the church. She told me Pastor Dean had been forgetting to write down plenty of appointments lately. Not just this *one time* as you implied to Chief McNeil."

Beth lifted her gaze to Michael, who shrugged and shook his head. "Wait for the full autopsy, Jack, with your *usual* open mind." Beth's tone dripped with sarcasm.

"Fine. If that's it, I'll call you with the date and time of the exhumation."

"There's something else. Michael found emails to Buckley on

Reverend Dean's computer insisting that Buckley pay back the money he stole. We found proof that he transferred church money into his own account. Paul was ready to blow the whistle. That's why Buckley went to see him that day. Ralph Buckley is the church finance—"

"I know who Buckley is," snapped Jack. "How much money are we talking? If it's just a couple hundred—"

"Sixty thousand dollars." Beth interrupted, taking her turn at rude behavior. "That's reason enough to murder someone, especially if they would regain control of the remaining assets."

"Let me look at your so-called evidence. I'll decide whether or not we have a beef with the finance officer."

Beth grinned at Michael over her sweet tea. "You won't be disappointed, but time is of the essence. We believe Buckley to be a flight risk. Where should we meet you?"

"I'm staring at you two gumshoes right now. Look to your right."

Simultaneously, Beth and Michael swiveled toward the window. Jack Lejeune was parked at the curb, munching a burger he must have bought at the drive-through window. "Are you following me?" Beth screeched into the phone.

"In your dreams, Kirby. How many places to eat lunch do you think this town has? Here I was, enjoying my midday break, and who do I spot thirty feet away? We're destined to be joined at the hip."

"Doomed, not destined. Come inside and meet Michael."

Tossing his trash into a barrel, Jack sauntered in with his usual arrogance. Michael watched him as though memorizing the details.

"Be prepared for anything," Beth warned under her breath.

But the detective was a model of manners. "How do you do, Mike. Jack Lejeune. I'm looking forward to working with you." The two men shook hands, and Jack made small talk for a few minutes.

Finally, Beth cut him off. "Give it a rest, Jack. Mike's from Brookhaven, not Natchez."

"In that case, did you discover the gym inside the Grand Hotel?"

Jack gestured for Beth to scoot over and then sat down in the booth. "I'll tell management you're helping law enforcement, and they'll waive your monthly fees."

"I work out there four times a week, so I appreciate that." Michael grinned with joy not commensurate with saving thirty bucks.

"That's awfully nice of you, Jack," Beth cooed. "In the meantime, take a look at these." She cleared a spot and laid three computer printouts across the table.

The detective picked up the papers one at a time, studying each one carefully. "Good work, Preston," he said upon completion. "Did you obtain permission to collect evidence from both the church and the Deans' home computer?"

"I did," said Michael, his lunch forgotten.

"Then we've got enough to arrest Buckley for grand theft. Unfortunately, Miss Kirby, this does not implicate the guy for murder. Sorry to burst your bubble."

"I know that, Einstein." She tapped the papers into a pile and handed him the file. "But it's enough to arrest him. If the judge denies bail because of Buckley's risk of flight, you can keep him locked up until the crime lab completes the second autopsy."

Jack picked up her tea and sniffed. "What have you been drinking? No way will a judge deny bail to an upstanding, churchgoing member of the community. You're fishing without a pole or bait in the Great Salt Lake." He smiled smugly at Michael. "In case you haven't heard the news, that lake's got no fish."

Beth collected her dignity and rose to her feet. "Let's go arrest Buckley. Then we'll worry about making a more serious charge stick." She tossed the rest of her meal away, her appetite vanishing in Jack's company.

He gave her a head-to-toe perusal. "You would still be a cop today—a good cop—if you could only separate fact from fiction. I'll call the chief to get the wheels turning on the arrest warrant. Stay close to the phone. I'll call you when the warrant's ready. Then we'll meet at Buckley's house. He's probably home on a Saturday afternoon." The detective left the restaurant with as much swagger as he entered.

On their way back to the office, Michael said little, but his mind seemed to be whirring a mile a minute. Beth couldn't bad-mouth Jack without revealing their past history, something she wasn't prepared to do. So she allowed her partner to be impressed with a petty, lazy, narrow-minded blabbermouth. For the rest of the afternoon they caught up on paperwork and filled Nate in on their recent progress with the case.

When they reconnoitered three hours later in front of Buckley's house, Jack continued on his best behavior. "I appreciate your work on this, Mike, but I'll take the lead at this point."

"You've got it, Detective."

"Keep your weapon holstered, Kirby," Jack said to her when they reached the front steps.

The door opened before Beth could reply. "You guys want my mom or my dad?" asked a sullen-faced teenager.

"Your father, please, young lady." The detective smiled at the girl.

"I'll show you where he's at and then I'm outta here. You'd better not have blocked my car in." She issued a rather dire warning to fully armed adults.

"We parked on the street, so lead the way," said Beth. She watched every doorway as they moved through the house.

"Dad, you got company!" the girl hollered.

Good thing nobody just stepped out of the shower, Beth thought as Buckley's daughter threw open a door.

The finance director froze, holding a wrinkled shirt over an open suitcase.

"You Ralph Buckley? I'm Detective Jack Lejeune of Natchez PD. These are PI consultants to the force, Kirby and Preston."

"I'm acquainted with Beth and Mr. Preston." Buckley dropped the shirt.

"Going somewhere, Mr. Buckley?" Jack moved to the other side of the room.

"No, I just came home and haven't had a chance to unpack yet. What's this about?" Buckley blinked through his thick-lensed glasses.

"This is about us having a warrant for your arrest. You've been charged with grand theft. You have the right to remain silent…"

As the detective recited the Miranda rights, Buckley fixed his gaze on Beth, his expression sad rather than surprised. "Funny how I'm being arrested for a small pittance, while Paul got away with the church's entire future."

"Paul didn't get away with anything," said Beth. "He's dead, or have you forgotten?"

"A fact which gives me no pleasure whatsoever," he said, not resisting as Jack snapped on handcuffs. Buckley walked from the house with his head down and without stopping to lock his door.

For the sake of his wife and daughter, Beth turned the knob on her way out. *How odd that the finance director would refer to sixty grand as a small pittance.*

TWENTY-FIVE

Bay St. Louis
Monday

For the next three days the honeymooners walked the beach, rode their bikes, swam in the ocean, and read novels by the pool—all the fun things vacationers were supposed to do. Every evening they dined on fresh seafood, with sweet potato fries, coleslaw, and, of course, dessert. Tonight they had split a piece of key lime pie with vanilla ice cream, and washed it all down with sweet tea.

"Ugh," Nate moaned on the drive back to their B and B. He held his gut with one hand as though in pain. "Tomorrow I'm going for a run at dawn. I feel as if I've gained ten pounds since we arrived."

"Ditto about putting on weight, but I sure don't want to run in this heat. I'll cut back to five hundred calories a day for the next three months to make up for it."

Nate handed her a restaurant mint. "Five hundreds calories a day. Is that even possible?"

Isabelle pulled her glasses down with one finger. "Only if I staple my lips shut."

Back at Mrs. Russo's lovely home on the bay, they parked under the protective arms of a live oak tree. Overhead, thousands of stars and the bright moon lit the flagstone path to the porch. A cool breeze off the water brought relief on the humid night. With his arm around Isabelle's shoulder, Nate felt like the luckiest man on earth. "What's your pleasure, Mrs. Price? Shall we walk the beach or maybe swim to Cuba?"

"Let's sit in the rockers for a spell and then head to our suite. Maybe we'll turn in early…and maybe we won't." Turning her face up to his, Isabelle winked impishly.

"Sounds like a perfect ending to another day in paradise."

They had barely settled against the cushions when Mrs. Russo appeared in the doorway. "Sorry to interrupt, folks, but someone is waiting for you in the parlor."

"At *this* hour?" asked Nate, his romantic notions curtailed.

"Yes. Apparently, the matter couldn't wait. The woman said her name was Mrs. Mitchell."

Isabelle jumped to her feet. Nate followed at a more leisurely pace.

"Izzy, Nate, forgive me for disturbing you, but I couldn't sleep until I spoke with you." Sitting in an upholstered chair, Cassie Mitchell looked miserable.

Nate immediately regretted his selfishness. "Are you staying here tonight?" he asked.

"No. I found a less-expensive place along Highway 90, less than fifteen minutes away."

Isabelle pulled up a chair and reached for Cassie's hand. "What have you found out about Craig?"

Cassie burst into tears, making decipherable conversation impossible. Finally, she choked out a skeletal update of her husband's life. "An assistant in Craig's office has always liked me. I wouldn't say we were friends, but when I went there she wanted to help. Colleen insisted Craig wasn't involved with someone at work." Cassie blew her nose in a tissue. "She told me that two men came to see him a couple months ago. They wouldn't give their names but said they were personal friends. Craig wasn't thrilled to see them. Then two weeks before he left, those men came back. Colleen didn't know what was discussed, but they were in Craig's office a long time. Three days later, Craig showed her an airline ticket and asked if it was possible to cash it in. She examined the fare and said yes. The next day Craig called the office and said he needed a leave of absence because his brother was sick." Cassie broke into more sobs. "Craig doesn't even have a b-brother."

While Isabelle comforted Cassie, Nate surreptitiously glanced at his watch. "Who do you suppose those men were?" he asked.

"They *weren't* old friends. By her description, one was a bookie named Mickey Pierce and the other probably a hired thug. Craig once showed me a picture of Pierce—the man had a crooked nose and looked as if he was sweating. That's exactly how Colleen described him."

"Talk about a cliché," said Nate.

Cassie nodded. "I suppose so, but this is worse than anything I feared. I can handle being left for another woman. I can even handle Craig falling off the wagon and gambling. But this man must be forcing Craig to do something against his will."

"Hold up, Cassie," said Nate. "Nobody can make somebody gamble. It isn't like holding up a bank. What if he gambled and lost? Even if Craig owed this guy money, there's no way he could make the cards fall a certain way."

"How could you be so sure? Pierce probably recruited my husband to cheat the casinos down here."

Nate rolled his eyes. "Some small-time bookie from Nashville isn't going to rip off the Golden Magnolia of Bay St. Louis. These big casinos employ professionals to spot card sharks within minutes of them sitting down."

Cassie struggled to her feet. "I don't know what's going on, but those men bought his plane ticket here. Craig hates to fly, so he cashed it in and drove down instead. All that nonsense about another woman was smoke and mirrors to keep me away. Craig could be in real danger."

When Nate heard the pain in her voice, his chest tightened. "If

Pierce and your husband are up to no good, we can hope they'll be banned from the tables before they do something illegal. As much as I respect your loyalty to Craig, there isn't anything you can do. Why don't I follow you back to your hotel to make sure—"

"No, thank you. I can find my way around a small town like this. I just wanted you and Izzy to know I'm here. If you see Craig before I do, I would appreciate a phone call."

"Of course." Isabelle patted her shoulder. "Please call us if you'd like to meet for lunch or dinner sometime."

Cassie forced a smile. "Nothing would make me happier than the Mitchells taking you two to dinner. Thanks for listening to me, especially since this is your honeymoon. Good night." She left the parlor without another word.

Nate and Isabelle walked to their suite in a somber mood. Nate fell asleep wondering if it was something in the salty air that put a damper on romance.

TWENTY-SIX

Natchez

After a restful Sunday, Beth and Michael worked fever-ishly on Monday to get Reverend Dean's exhumation set for Wednesday. The state medical examiner agreed to conduct a criminal autopsy at the request of Natchez PD. Fortunately, Mississippi was experiencing a temporary dearth of suspicious crimes, freeing up the facility and the ME's time. Beth, however, had little chance to celebrate the good news.

Detective Lejeune had been correct in his assumption. The judge refused to deny bail for a financial crime involving a life-long community member, although he did express contempt for people who stole from religious organizations. Bail was set at two hundred fifty thousand, and the Buckleys were forced to surrender their passports. Ralph's Spanish and French would be of little use in Natchez.

Their last duty of the day before leaving the offices of Price Investigations was to call Nate. With Michael practically sitting in her lap, Beth brought the boss up to speed on their case. Nate was overjoyed, but Beth tried to divert all praise toward her partner.

"Sounds like Nate is pleased." Michael danced around the office.

"I wouldn't get too excited if I were you. Let's get out of here." Beth hurried out the door, almost forgetting to lock it behind her.

"Why not?" Michael kept pace at her side. "Reverend Dean's body will be on its way to Jackson in two days, and Ralph Buckley has been charged with a felony. Since that thief probably had to mortgage his house for the ten-percent bond, I don't think he's going anywhere."

"Because Mrs. Dean hired us to prove her husband was murdered and to find his killer, not catch some financial flimflammer with his hand in the cookie jar. Remember, we're PIs, not the police."

Michael rubbed the dark shadow along his jaw. "Good point, but Rome wasn't built in a day. Say, what are your plans for tonight?"

"Let's see...a quick workout, dinner with Mom and Pops, then maybe *Castle* reruns in the living room. Mom's cooking pinto beans and cornbread with tea so sweet I'll need a dental appointment next week. You want in on this fun?"

"As enticing as that sounds, I thought I'd take you to dinner. Consider it a token of my appreciation. The trainer you recommended has been working with me three nights a week."

"You actually called him?" Beth asked, regretting the question immediately.

"Haven't you noticed a difference? I follow his instructions to the letter—five one-hour workouts a week, a daily four-mile run, and fifty chin-ups using a bar I installed. I hope the landlord doesn't evict me over holes in the door frame."

"That's fantastic, Mike." Beth dug for her keys as they stood between their cars. "I doubt I could do thirty."

"Here, feel my muscle." Michael pushed up his sleeve and stuck out his arm.

Beth dutifully squeezed his bicep. "Wow. Charles Atlas as I live and breathe."

"Who's he? Anyway, I'm grateful for the introduction, so let me spring for dinner. I heard Breaud's has good food."

"Let me think...a bowl of pinto beans or charbroiled oysters under the stars?" Beth pretended to ponder her options. "Okay, I'm in as long as you ask for a courtyard table and understand this ain't no date. I never go out with coworkers."

"Or anybody else, for that matter," he murmured, ducking into his car.

"What did you say?" she demanded.

"You heard me, Elizabeth. If I'm wrong, you can set me straight at dinner."

She glanced at her watch. "Let's see…exercise and then a shower. How about if I meet you in an hour and a half?"

"Perfect. I'll go for a run. In a few more weeks I'll be ready for the office smackdown. See you in ninety at Breaud's."

Beth watched him drive away, charmed by his sense of humor. Most male egos wouldn't tolerate self-improvement jokes, especially not from a woman. She respected Michael's desire to gain strength and endurance, but she liked his outlook even more.

After a grueling workout and quick shower in her parents' cramped bathroom, Beth slipped on a mint-green sundress from a wedding long ago and high-heeled sandals. She wound her hair in a knot at the nape of her neck and headed for the door. Unfortunately, her escape wasn't quick or easy.

"Where you goin' in that getup?" asked her mother.

Her father glanced up from his bowl of beans and ham. "Wow. You look nice, Betsy."

"Thanks, Pops. I'm having dinner with a coworker." Beth grabbed a bottle of water from the fridge.

"With that nice Michael Preston?" Her mother made no attempt to be subtle. "Thank goodness you wore something other than jeans."

"We'll be discussing the case, Ma. That's it." Beth let the screen door slam behind her.

"Of course. Hence the high heels and fancy hairdo!" Rita called after her.

Beth laughed all the way to the restaurant. *Mom using the word 'hence'? What is the world coming to?*

After finding a spot on the street, Beth walked toward the entrance as Michael climbed from his tiny Fiat. Dressed in well-tailored slacks and a white shirt open at the neck, he looked…European. At least in the estimation of someone who had never left the country. Far too sophisticated for Natchez, Mississippi.

"Who were you expecting, Preston?" she asked, the moment he reached her side. "I told you this was no date."

Michael glanced down at his clothes. "Is this too fancy for a weeknight?" He folded back his cuffs. "I just wanted to get my money's worth out of some expensive duds. Nobody's quite as practical as an ex-accountant. Besides, I wouldn't dream of asking you out." He opened the door for her. "I see you're not in sweatpants and flip-flops."

"Fair enough. The dress is too cha-cha for church, and I seldom attend garden parties anymore." Beth smoothed out a wrinkle as they approached the hostess stand.

"Preston," he said to the girl. "I requested an outdoor table."

Beth bit her tongue until they were seated close to the fountain. "Okay, what did you mean by 'I wouldn't dream of asking you out'? What's wrong with me?"

Michael shrugged. "Not a thing. I'm simply honoring your earlier request. The curious part is why you don't date anyone. You're not bad looking, and this is a small town. You must have attracted somebody's attention by now."

She gaped at him, both shocked and amused. "You do realize that 'not bad looking' isn't a compliment."

"I suspect you're immune to flattery. But if you'd rather not talk about this, we could discuss sports, religion, politics, or the worst ten TV shows ever made."

"Nope. I need to come clean about my past and answer your questions. Then you'll understand the bad blood between Detective Lejeune and me." Beth took a long sip of water. "I got…involved with Chief McNeil while I was on the Natchez police force, while Jack was my partner."

"Did you two have an affair?"

"No, it never went that far. At first we were friends. He was my mentor, but I became infatuated with him. I orchestrated ways to spend time together. Other cops started to talk, but I didn't care. I was such a fool. I built this fantasy in my mind that we would run away together. I still feel so ashamed." Beth stared at her place mat where a wine stain hadn't fully come out in the wash.

"Most people are fools at some point in their life." He sounded very matter-of-fact.

"If I truly loved him, I wouldn't have made trouble for him on the force. Long before rumors started to swirl, I took the detective's exam and scored high. I was already up for the next promotion, based on merit and nothing else." Beth emphasized the final two words.

"I believe you, Elizabeth. Your interview and organization skills are top-notch. Certainly your marksmanship would be hard to beat."

She crossed her arms, wishing she'd brought a cardigan. "Jack was more popular on the force than me. If he said I had slept my way into the promotion, many were still willing to believe him." Beth felt herself blush with shame. "And do to this day."

"Once a professional reputation is compromised, it's hard to restore."

"You aren't kidding. By the time Chris set me straight, the damage was already done. He didn't want me to resign. He insisted the rumor mill would eventually find another victim, but I couldn't face looking at *him* each day." Beth lifted her chin and met Michael's eye. "Too bad my schoolgirl crush didn't happen at sixteen when consequences are far less serious."

"I'm surprised your partner didn't have your back."

Beth scoffed. "Jack blamed me for getting passed over. Not once did it cross his mind it might have been his laziness and incompetence."

"That's usually how it goes." Michael picked up his menu.

"Being forced to work with the newly appointed Detective Lejeune is my just reward. See what happens when people get involved at work? Lives are ruined."

Michael looked as though he might comment, but then changed his mind. "You're absolutely right. Shall we order? I'm getting hungry." He waved at a passing waiter.

"Fine with me. I get the same thing each time I'm here." Beth pressed the menu to her chest. "And since I've monopolized the entire conversation, why don't you tell me about the special occasion which warranted those clothes?"

Michael's face registered surprise for a fleeting moment. "I bought them for my engagement party. Considering I've never been married, and I'm no longer engaged, there'll be another true confession session in our future. But if you don't mind, we'll save that one for another night."

"Works for me." Beth dug through her purse as a distraction until the waiter appeared to take their order. *Stood up at the altar?* That had to score a ten on the pain scale, while her romantic delusion with the boss didn't rate higher than a seven.

TWENTY-SEVEN

Bay St. Louis
Tuesday

Isabelle awoke at five a.m. and couldn't fall back to sleep. After thirty minutes of tossing and turning, she crawled from the tangled sheets, grabbed her bathrobe, and tiptoed out to the porch. No need to disturb Nate just because she wouldn't get any more rest. Seated in her favorite rocker under a moonless sky, Isabelle listened to the foghorns of freighters out at sea and the mournful whistle of a train. As humidity wrapped around her like a blanket, she realized she'd done nothing *but* disturb Nate since the day they met.

First, she hadn't been very nice to him in high school. Then, when he came to Memphis to find her brother's killer, Nate ended up saving her from a psychopathic stalker. After they married, Nate opened an agency in Natchez and then carried the lion's share of their financial burden. And what had she done since arriving at their three-week romantic getaway? She'd been obsessed with "saving" her ex-husband, a man who expressly told her to leave him alone.

As the progression of events marched through her head, Isabelle dropped her chin to her chest. *Poor Nate. What did a hardworking, God-fearing man like him do to deserve a wife like me?* All he wanted was to spend some quality time with her away from work and household responsibilities. Their family and friends had taken up a collection for a relaxing vacation. Instead, she had looked for another mess for him to straighten out. As much as she hoped Cassie and Craig would get through these dark days, she had a responsibility to the man who had pledged to love, honor, and cherish her forever.

And the rest of their life started today.

Isabelle sprang from the rocker, letting it thump against the wood. She took one of each tourist brochure from the rack and tiptoed back to their suite. By the time he woke up, she would be ready with a plan.

Two hours later she was showered and dressed. She set a cup of coffee on his nightstand, gave his arm a shake, and then bolted from the room. A note propped up on the mug read: *Dress casual. I have big plans for us, honey. Meet me on the porch for breakfast. I'll be wearing a pink sundress at a table with purple amaranths.*

Isabelle was sipping her second cup of coffee when Nate strolled outside, mug in hand. He perused the porch, where two other couples and a family of five were dining on croissants, omelets, grits, and fried ham.

"It's a good thing you told me the color of your outfit, Izzy, because I would have had trouble spotting you in this crowd. And I have no idea what an amaranth is." Nate dropped into the opposite chair.

"This is an amaranth." Isabelle lifted the vase. "But today isn't about horticulture. I have a fun-filled agenda for us. And you'll be pleased with breakfast too—no fussy chick food today!" Isabelle lowered her voice to a whisper as Mrs. Russo appeared with two heaping plates. The woman must have built-in radar, considering she always knew when all members were present.

Nate leaned back and inspected the food. "Breakfast looks great. Tell me what's on your mind." His tone revealed little enthusiasm for what was to come.

"How would you like to drive up to Kiln to the Lazy Magnolia Brewing Company? They give family-friendly tours with samples of their craft brews at the end. Doesn't that sound like fun?"

Nate ate a forkful of eggs. "Absolutely, if one of us liked the taste of beer. Because we don't, it's not worth the drive."

"You have a point." Isabelle slipped the brewery brochure to the middle of the stack. "How about Biloxi Schooners? They have a sixty-five-foot, double-mast replica for a two-and-a-half-hour cruise or a half-day charter." She read the caption beneath the picture.

"Do you even know what a schooner is?" Nate cut his ham slice into pieces. "It's an old-fashioned sailboat. What if a big storm develops while we're out in the Gulf? You'll be hanging your head over the side for the entire trip."

Isabelle tucked that brochure on the bottom and selected her next candidate. "What about the Hurricane Katrina Memorial on the Biloxi Town Green?"

Nate leaned over to inspect the brochure. "I would like to see the Katrina Memorial and pay my respects. Lots of people along the coast lost their lives while we watched hurricane coverage on CNN, safe in our living room. That one's a yes. Got anything else?"

"We could rent bikes in Ocean Springs and do the fifteen-mile tour through the historic section, maybe grabbing lunch along the way."

He wiped his mouth and stared at her. "I can't believe you want to rent bikes in this heat. We'll get halfway out and need to call a taxi with a bike rack."

Isabelle felt her hopes for a fun day slipping away. "I've always wanted to see an alligator."

"What do you mean? One of those roadside attractions where they're kept in pens? Or maybe somebody wrestles one in the mud?" Nate smirked and dug into his grits.

"No, I want to see one in the wild." She tossed her last brochure across the table. "Let's go to Gulf Islands National Seashore. They have nature trails along Davis Bayou and boat rides with a park ranger. We're bound to see plenty of wildlife." Isabelle took a bite of croissant, waiting for objections to roll in.

"Is this far away?"

"Fifteen minutes past the Biloxi Town Green."

"Then get a move on, Izzy. We have places to go, and I'm ready right now. Well, at least as soon as we're finished here."

Isabelle ate all she could, her appetite still not back to normal, and filled their cooler with bottles of water. Changing from her sundress into a T-shirt and shorts, she decided that no matter what happened today, she would smile and have a good time.

After the Katrina Memorial they drove into the lush, serene world of a national park, well removed from the hubbub of the coast. The helpful guide at the visitor center pointed out the best spots to view herons, osprey, terrapin, and fiddler crabs.

"Where can we see a gator?" asked Isabelle, opening her map on the counter.

The ranger considered for a moment and then drew a big red X on the map. "Big Bob hangs out here most mornings expecting tourists to throw him marshmallows. Not that I want you to do that." She shook her finger at them. "It's against the law to feed our wildlife, but poor Bob still waits patiently, snacking on frogs and crabs in the meantime."

"Thanks so much," said Isabelle to the ranger. She grabbed the map and they jumped in the car.

"Slow down, Izzy," Nate warned at the next curve. "We're not allowed to run over tourists either."

"I can't wait to see a gator," she said, dutifully slowing her speed. "I sure hope Bob doesn't pick today to lower his expectations."

Although they had no trouble finding the indicated spot, after a full hour of watching from the platform at the swampy pond below, Bob failed to make an appearance. As their skin turned pink and their clothes dampened with sweat, Nate finally spoke the voice of reason.

"Sorry, Izzy. Looks like it's not to be. Let's head to where we catch the tour boat."

"Where's a marshmallow-packing band of hooligans when you need them?" she muttered, pulling out her map. "Why don't we leave the car where it is and take this trail inland? It should be a shortcut to the fishing pier." She tapped her finger on a dotted line.

Nate leaned over her shoulder. "I don't know about that. What if the trail turns swampy or we get lost? We left our water in the car. According to the brochure, cottonmouths live in this park."

"Nate Price, I cannot believe this. You were a big, brave PI in New Orleans and Memphis—unafraid of anything, according to your cousin. Now you're scared to leave the pavement? If we're going to see gators in the wild, we must be adventurous."

He narrowed his gaze. "Lead the way, missy. I'm right behind you."

Isabelle stuffed the map into a pocket and started down the path. Their second hour of gator patrol produced sightings of crabs, turtles, fish, and a fat raccoon. Even though they saw no alligators, Isabelle did find a nest of fire ants. While she was watching for movement among the reeds and cattails sixty feet away, dozens of red bloodsuckers crawled up her legs. Before she could react, several burrowed into her socks and under the legs of her shorts. With little alternative, Isabelle dropped her shorts in the middle of nowhere, while Nate swatted and batted to his heart's delight.

It wasn't a very dignified moment.

They left the backwoods as quickly as possible, found a spray bottle of Benadryl in the car's glove box, and caught the park's last tour for the day. When Isabelle climbed into the flat-bottom boat, she tried her best to smile...and not to scratch.

The ranger's narrative about life in the swamps and bayous took her mind off her ant bites. Nate loved hearing about life on the

Gulf Coast, and Isabelle loved seeing him so happy. One of their fellow passengers, a former schoolteacher, asked many questions the ranger happily answered.

"What about alligators?" Nate asked during a break in the conversation.

The ranger nodded. "We had several nests in the area this past spring, each one producing a dozen or more offspring. The female will guard her clutch for the first year against predators, usually other adult alligators."

"Any chance of seeing a mama gator with her babies?" asked Isabelle.

The question caused the schoolteacher to pivot around on her seat. "Mothers are highly protective of their young. This boat won't go anywhere near one of those nests for *our* safety, along with theirs." The woman frowned at Isabelle as though she just proposed mass suicide. "I'm glad there are places in the world they can live unmolested. Every square foot of land shouldn't be landscaped."

"I agree, ma'am," murmured Isabelle, "but I'd still like to see one."

"Try the gator ranch in Moss Point." The schoolteacher returned to her face-forward position.

Nate rolled his eyes and slipped an arm around her. "You thinking about a gator pond in our backyard someday? That rules out miniature poodles for pets."

"I'd be satisfied with goldfish and a few bird feeders." Isabelle released a weary sigh. "I wanted today to be perfect, but my big plans turned into one disaster after another."

"I enjoyed every minute of it, especially fire ant extermination." Nate tickled her neck. "And the day's not over."

"Let's just get back to Aunt Polly's before this boat sinks with all hands lost." Isabelle curled into his shoulder to watch the scenery on the return trip.

"Look there, Izzy." Nate extended a finger to indicate a long, watery aisle between tall rows of cordgrass. The former schoolteacher and everyone else were distracted by a flock of pelicans.

Isabelle glanced up to see a scaly reptile gliding through the water with a miniature replica of itself on its back. It lasted only a moment, not enough time to alert the group, but Isabelle knew for certain—a mama gator was taking her baby for a ride through the bayou.

"Still think today was a disaster?" Nate whispered in her ear.

"Not anymore," she croaked, overcome with emotion.

She decided then and there to forget about Craig and the mess he'd created. If Cassie called, she would encourage her to hire a local investigator or call the police. Nate deserved a wife who paid attention to him, not one who worried endlessly about a man bent on self-destruction.

On the drive home they stopped at the Biloxi lighthouse, a shining beacon against the night sky, and then ate fish tacos and fried green tomatoes at Shaggy's on the beach.

"Anything else on your agenda?" asked Nate. "Maybe a nighttime dive for sunken treasure in the bay?"

"Nope. Let's head back to our suite at Aunt Polly's before we run out of steam." Isabelle winked at him.

"I'll go pay the check while you start the car." He tossed her the keys. "This day keeps getting better and better."

TWENTY-EIGHT

Natchez

*M*ichael couldn't believe he'd pushed Beth to talk about her personal life. What was the matter with him? He was worse than the ladies who worked at the bank with his mother. They could sniff a marital problem at fifty yards and then badger the person for details. Maybe misery did love company. Those unlucky in love took comfort from those equally challenged. He'd left himself wide open with his comment about the clothes. He hoped his partner would forget all about last night.

As for him? It would be a long time before he forgot how nice she looked in that green dress.

Michael downed a cup of coffee, punished his body with push-ups and sit-ups, and then ran five miles at an easy pace. After a shower and more coffee, he considered his workday. With Beth on her way to Vicksburg to talk to old contacts, he was a boat without a rudder.

When his phone buzzed, he answered on the second ring. "Michael Preston."

"Hi, Mike. Jack Lejeune, Natchez PD. How's it going?" Beth's nemesis greeted him as though they were old friends.

"Good, thanks. What can I do for you, Detective?"

"Nothing. It's what I can do for you. Lo and behold, Ralph

Buckley, with legal counsel present, gave us a videotaped confession last night."

"You've got to be kidding." Michael tossed the rest of his coffee in the sink.

"Caught us by surprise too. Maybe Buckley got the idea that if he's up-front, the DA might charge him with a lesser crime, maybe even a misdemeanor. And he could be right."

"He confessed to murder and wants a misdemeanor?" Michael barked into the phone.

"Simmer down. No, not murder. I told you and your partner Buckley was no killer. He ain't the type. He wouldn't want to get his hands dirty or rip his shirt."

"What exactly did he confess to?" Michael dropped into a kitchen chair.

"Come down to the precinct. I'll let you watch the video. Because Buckley asked to make a statement, nothing on that tape is confidential. It'll be good for your training. And who knows? Maybe you'll want to apply to the police academy. You're the right age and all that."

Michael considered his response carefully. Having Lejeune on their side would be advantageous. "I appreciate your offer, Detective, but my partner is in Vicksburg today. Can we come by the station tomorrow morning? Will that work?"

There was a raspy laugh before Lejeune answered. "It will not. This is a one-time offer which will soon expire. Come this morning or kiss your chance goodbye."

"I'll be there within the hour."

"Good. You'll find me at my desk. Oh, and Mike? You've probably heard that Beth and I are no longer besties. Since the chief ordered me to cooperate with Mrs. Dean's ridiculous investigation, I thought you and I would make a better team. Catch my drift?"

"Loud and clear. See you soon."

Michael hung up, feeling sweat soak his shirt despite a cold shower less than ten minutes ago. He didn't like Lejeune. Maybe it was because the guy didn't defend Beth with the backstabbing good old boys. And Lejeune still was sneaking around her back. Or maybe his irritation stemmed from Lejeune's eagerness to dismiss the case. Lazy, just like his partner described. Either way, he had a job to do. Sixty minutes later Michael was buzzed through the reinforced door and shown to the detective's cubicle.

Lejeune smiled and shook his hand heartily. "Follow me, Mike. I've got the camera set to replay." With his boot heels clicking on the tiles, Lejeune led the way to the conference room.

Michael took a chair on the opposite side of the table and opened his binder to a fresh sheet.

"Taking notes for your new boss? Betsy won't be happy when she gets back to town. She was ready to tie the noose around Buckley's neck. Too bad Mississippi uses lethal injection for their mode of execution."

"I'm still new on the job. I want notes to review for my sake."

"A fine idea." Lejeune started the camera and leaned back in his chair.

For close to two hours, Michael watched Buckley admit to stealing sixty thousand dollars from the church he attended. According to his testimony, his wife had run up a huge credit card bill with a vicious interest rate. After their son moved back home with his wife and new baby, Tammy demanded a two-story addition be added to their house. After all, Ralph Junior had bravely served his country overseas and now needed a decent place to live. Ralph Senior decided sixty thousand would be sufficient for both requests.

"Why didn't you take a second mortgage like every other American?" asked Lejeune during the interview.

Buckley had a ready answer: "The bank wasn't issuing new loans until after the first of the year. The manager told me to reapply after January first but assured me that with my credit score it would be approved."

"Why didn't you request a short-term loan from Pastor Dean and the board? You were a longtime member of the church."

"You seem to know very little about the rules governing nonprofits, Detective. The board was in no position to grant such a request. Otherwise, half the congregation would be lining up for loans."

Michael had to agree with Buckley's assessment. He glanced at Lejeune. The guy's mood was almost gleeful.

"So you helped yourself from Calvary Baptist's account to keep the little wife happy."

Buckley shook his finger at the camera. "I planned to pay back every dime as soon as I got my loan. No one would have been the wiser, but Paul decided to check the books with a magnifying glass. He called me on the phone all furious, threatening to call the church attorney. That hypocrite!"

"Why would you call Reverend Dean that?"

"Because he was doing the same thing but on a much larger scale. Paul demanded I come to his house to discuss this. When I agreed, I had no idea he'd already told Robert Scott, one of the church board members."

"Was this the day Reverend Dean died?"

Buckley glanced at his attorney, who nodded his head. "It was, but in the meantime I got a call from Bob Scott. Reverend Dean had forwarded an email about the sixty thousand dollars. So the night before my meeting, I did my own audit of the church accounts, including the building fund."

"Didn't Reverend Dean take control of that account because he didn't like your investment strategies? Weren't they pretty fast and furious for a small Southern church?"

Lejeune pressed "Pause" and slapped the table with his palm. "I got that info from you, Preston. Good background prelims."

"Thanks," said Michael, unable to take his eyes off the monitor. Lejeune pressed "Play."

"Yeah, and my fast and furious investing turned two hundred *K* into half a million in less than four years. If I'd been left alone, I might have tripled the amount by the time we broke ground for the new school."

"Or you could have lost it all in a market crash."

"We'll never know now, will we?" Buckley set his mouth in a tight line and glared at the camera.

"Let's talk about your meeting with Reverend Dean on the day he died."

"I'll tell you one thing, I didn't go there alone. Bob Scott picked me up at my house and drove me. Paul looked surprised that I brought him along. The three of us hashed out more than one problem that afternoon."

"Did this conversation take place in the barn out back?"

Buckley blinked into the camera. "No, it took place at his dining room table with my Excel sheets spread across the table."

"What was the outcome of this meeting?"

"I agreed to pay back every cent within seven days. If I did, they would keep the matter quiet. I'd already cut up Tammy's credit cards and told my son he could move into the basement."

"What about this other evidence you found, regarding money missing from the building fund—the account Pastor Dean had sole control of. Tell us about that."

"Bob Scott demanded an explanation from Reverend Dean, but Paul just sloughed it off. He said the money was currently in transit and would be posted soon. In transit—what did that even mean? But Bob was willing to give him the benefit of the doubt. After all, the guy is a landscaper. What does he know about financial transactions?" On camera, Buckley had grown agitated, his face mottled with sweat. "Both men knew I was leaving town for a bachelor party. I was given seven days to pay back the loan, but Pastor Dean was to produce a corrected balance sheet in the same amount of time."

"Was Reverend Dean alive when you left, Mr. Buckley?"

"What are you talking about?" Spittle flew from his mouth. "Of course he was alive when *both of us* left the Deans' home. Bob Scott dropped me off in my driveway. Even my nosy neighbor saw me get out of his car. Most likely Mrs. Taylor was still spying when Tammy drove me to the airport an hour later. Check the airlines. I was on a flight from Baton Rouge to Las Vegas."

"Oh, we will, Mr. Buckley. And thanks for coming in today."

Lejeune switched off the camera and grinned at Michael. "Then the lawyer produced proof Buckley had indeed paid the operating account what he owed and yada yada."

"So Buckley walks away from this free and clear?" Exasperated, Michael ran a hand through his hair.

"Nope. What the finance director did was illegal, but my guess is the DA will reduce charges to a misdemeanor. Buckley will be barred from similar jobs in the future, but I doubt he'll spend another night in jail." Lejeune stretched his arms over his head. "But the real upshot of this is that Buckley is off the hook for murder. That is, if there was any murder in the first place."

A cat with his whiskers in a bowl of cream couldn't look smugger than Detective Lejeune.

TWENTY-NINE

After leaving Detective Lejeune in the conference room, Michael drove to Calvary Baptist Church. He spent the next several hours poring over the church's financials again without even plying Mrs. Purdy with another pie. He explained he had urgent business and headed straight to Reverend Dean's office.

Urgent, indeed. With Buckley's confession of an illegal loan of sixty *K*, half a million bucks was still unaccounted for. And poor Pastor Dean didn't have his pockets full of cash when he took his last breath on earth. The longer the money floated in the ether, the less likely it would be returned to the congregation. Buckley's alibi would most likely check out. Lejeune wouldn't have called if he had any doubt about that. Which brought up another reason for urgency. Michael wanted something to show Beth when she got back to town, other than a morning spent consorting with the enemy.

Although Price Investigations and the Natchez PD were on the same side, Lejeune calling him to view the confession videotape might not sit well with Beth. *The new partner getting chummy with the old partner?* That smelled like betrayal, whether they were on the same team or not. So Michael was glad to have something good to report when she called on her way back from Vicksburg.

"Hi, Mike," Beth said in a chipper voice. "Did you miss me today?"

"More than I thought humanly possible. How did it go up north?"

"Despite bureaucratic wheels turning at the speed of glaciers, if the ME receives Reverend Dean's body by Wednesday night, she'll start the autopsy on Thursday, Friday for sure. Certainly before snow flies in the Bahamas. I've got friends with their ears to the ground. What did you do today—work on a tan to go with your new body?"

"It's hard to improve on perfection, so I spent the day looking for the missing half-million dollars."

"Good idea. I'm sure Alice wants the funds for the new school tracked down. As soon as that autopsy is finished, we should be able to lock up Buckley and throw away the key."

"Let's just follow the evidence and not jump the gun. Isn't that what you taught me from day one?"

There was a hesitation before Beth asked, "What's going on? Did something weird turn up today?"

"Where are you, Elizabeth?"

"Just outside of town on Route 61."

"Good. Why don't you come straight to my place? I'll have a deluxe pizza, plenty of Coke, and a six-pack of orange soda so you can take your pick of what you would like to drink when you get here. I prefer to discuss this in person."

"My protégé has gone mysterious on me."

"All will be revealed when my assistant drops the black cloth. Come alone and make sure you're not followed."

"You better not be referring to *me* as your assistant." Beth laughed as she hung up.

However, Michael was no longer smiling. With his interim boss on her way, he needed to choose his words carefully. Twenty minutes later, Beth parked on the street and pressed his buzzer. Michael watched her from his window but counted to five before buzzing her in. He heard her clattering footsteps long before she appeared.

"You sure do make enough noise in those clogs," he said once she reached his doorway.

"I'm a noisy kind of girl." Beth strode inside and flung her purse in the direction of his sofa. "What did you find out, Preston?"

"First, let's take our gourmet cuisine and something to drink out to my verandah." He hooked a thumb toward the sliding glass door.

Without a word Beth walked into the kitchen, put two slices of pizza on a plate, and popped the top on a Coke. "Lead the way."

Michael duplicated her actions and headed to his tiny balcony overlooking the alley. Fortunately, the Dumpsters had been recently emptied.

Beth sat in a webbed chair. "We're on your verandah with our cuisine, so spill your guts." She tucked a napkin into her shirt.

"Ladies first. Why don't you want to tell me about your eventful day?" Michael had to sit sideways to fit his legs behind the railing.

Beth swallowed a mouthful of pepperoni, mushrooms, and hot peppers. "I told you my news on the phone. Either you explain why Buckley dropped off your radar or I'm cracking one of your ribs."

He clucked his tongue. "Wait until Nate hears about your politically incorrect behavior. Things won't go well at your next review." When steam began pouring from Beth's ears, Michael delivered his semirehearsed speech about the videotaped interview that Lejeune had been unable to postpone.

"That skunk preferred me being out of town. But it probably was better that way—less chance of gunplay in the conference room." Beth spoke more to herself than to him. "So Buckley's off the hook for swiping the mega-amount. I doubt he would kill his friend over sixty thousand dollars. Plus a solid alibi will remove that possibility altogether."

"Lejeune would have called by now if it hadn't checked out. You're not sore at me for seeing him alone?" Michael relaxed his neck and shoulders.

"Of course not. Like I said—Jack and I don't play well together." Beth took another bite. "You implied on the phone you discovered something interesting about the missing school fund. Talk, Preston, while I eat. This pizza is delicious. I might eat the whole thing."

"When I learned Reverend Dean controlled the building fund for the last six months, I got a hunch this could be the key to his murder. I went through the church accounts again but saw nothing I hadn't seen before. Reverend Dean wasn't keeping those files up-to-date like Ralph Buckley had done during his wheeling-and-dealing days."

"Go on." Beth sipped her Coke without taking her gaze off him.

"Then I found something in Reverend Dean's saved emails under the tab 'Social.' The other files were videos of the church bake sale, the membership open house, and last year's harvest party."

"The threat of cracked ribs is still on table." She wiped her hands on a napkin, wadded it into a ball, and bounced it off his chest.

"I discovered a string of emails between the pastor and a non-profit called Spare the Children. When Reverend Dean took control of the four-hundred-seventy thousand, he apparently invested it with an international charity. The website states their organization aims to save kids from starvation and abject poverty, and to prevent teenagers from falling victim to human traffickers. All noble causes to be sure. They offered investors one- and two-year bonds at an interest rate of twelve percent. Being from the financial sector, I can say normal bonds don't pay that much. Only junk offerings with a high risk factor do that."

"Thank you, Warren Buffett. Now *get on* with it."

"When I googled this charity, I found several complaints from small churches in the South. Every one of those churches was clamoring to get back their initial investment."

"Hold that thought. I'm going inside for an Orange Crush. Care to join me?"

"Yes, bring out two. They're in the fridge." Try as he might,

Michael couldn't wipe the smile off his face before she returned. "Shall I continue, Miss Kirby?"

"By all means." Beth handed him a beverage and sat back down.

"Reverend Dean wrote many emails to this organization before his death. At first he praised the good work they did and how Calvary Baptist was proud to help such a worthy cause."

"So Paul believed he was helping a good cause while earning twelve percent on the investment." Beth's expression registered recognition of what was coming.

"Exactly. He had loaned the money for a twelve-month period before they broke ground for the new school. Reverend Dean didn't steal the money or hide it away. He invested it in what he thought was a win-win situation."

"And he was too naive to smell a scam," Beth concluded. "He wasn't a thief. He just didn't know any better."

Michael didn't need to affirm her deduction as Beth's eyes filled with tears. When she dropped her face into her hands and sobbed, he thought he might cry too.

"Do you need a break or should I continue?"

"Continue." Beth wiped her eyes with a napkin. "Please ignore my emotional breakdown."

"Reverend Dean suspected something wasn't right when they stopped sending monthly statements as promised. None of his emails had listed a person's name, only the charity as an entity. Then a week before he died, he demanded to speak with the person in charge and left a phone number. He threatened to contact Mississippi's attorney general and every watchdog agency for nonprofits in the country. In their final email, Spare the Children indicated someone would be getting in touch with him shortly. That's the abbreviated version of the story," Michael concluded. "I'm so sorry, Elizabeth."

With tears streaming down her face, she met his eyes. "Why are you sorry? You didn't steal the money, and you didn't kill my pastor. You did well today, Michael—better than me. Tomorrow the waterworks will be gone, and then you and I will track down the real killer. Right now, I'm getting more pizza. This is the best I've had in a long time."

Michael watched her until she disappeared into the kitchen. She was beyond a great mentor or the friend he never had. She was a unique human being, one he could easily fall in love with. And that scared the wits out of him.

THIRTY

*B*eth regretted crying like a baby in front of Michael last night. Nothing looked less professional than bawling in front of your coworker. She was supposed to be training him as a professional PI, but picturing Reverend Dean duped by an agency he would have naturally trusted broke her heart. Had one of those charlatans killed him over the scam? They would just have to wait for the second autopsy. If any evidence led to someone at Spare the Children International, she would take special pleasure seeing them brought to justice.

She arrived at the office of Price Investigations juggling three extra-large lattes: two plain and one mocha with whipped cream.

"Beth, you're the best!" said Maxine, lifting the mocha from the carrier. "Nate *never* brings in morning treats."

"That's because he and Isabelle are saving for a house. Me? I'll probably live with Mom and Pops my entire life."

"Nonsense. Someday a handsome man will knock you off your feet."

Beth wrinkled her nose. "Not unless he's driving a bulldozer. Where's Michael? He usually beats me here. We have that exhumation in less than an hour."

Maxine wiped away a foam mustache. "He'll be a few minutes late due to 'an extraordinarily cool surprise.' His words, not mine."

Beth blew on her latte, but before it was cool enough to drink she heard a cacophony on the street. Some idiot was laying on his horn at nine o'clock in the morning. "What on earth?" She jumped to her feet.

"Your ride is here, sweetie," crowed Maxine, peeking from between the blinds.

The assistant's joke wasn't far from the truth. When Beth reached the street, a shiny red convertible idled in front of the building with Michael Preston behind the wheel. "Whose car is that?" she demanded, shading her eyes from the sun glare.

Mike reached out the window and patted the door. "Mine, Miss Kirby. All mine."

"No, it isn't! You drive a little green Fiat—forty-five miles to the gallon, room for two people with a dog in the back."

"Not anymore. I traded in that peanut for a man's car. Jump in and we'll go for a ride."

Beth narrowed her gaze as she processed the information. "Did you forget today's the day we disinter Paul's body?" She pointed at her subdued black slacks and white blouse.

Michael immediately sobered. "Of course not, but the delivery date for the car had already been set. Please, Elizabeth, just a quick ride across the bridge and back. I promise we'll be at the cemetery before anyone else."

"Okay. A short ride, but no more horn blowing." The moment Beth climbed in the passenger seat and clicked her seat belt, Michael peeled away from the curb. "Are you sure you didn't steal this?" she asked, glancing in the rearview mirror.

"Of course not. I have the bill of sale if you want to see it. This 2016 Dodge Charger SRT 392 is all mine." Michael turned onto the road that followed the river.

"You paid cash instead of making payments like everyone else in America? Did you win the lottery, or maybe your rich uncle died?"

Michael kept his gaze fixed on the road. "Neither. Let's just say I spent every year since college fiendishly saving money. I have more savings than the average sixty-year-old. One thing about an accountant, they know how to pinch every last penny." His tone contained scorn instead of pride.

"That's a good thing. Most folks can't even save five bucks a week."

"It's only good if you have something or someone to save for. Since I don't, my frugal days are behind me. You want a cup of coffee to take to the cemetery? I'll even spring for a donut with sprinkles on top."

"No, thanks. I already bought three lattes for the office. Yours and mine are getting cold while you burn more gas than that Fiat used in a week."

Michael accelerated on the ramp to the bridge. When he encountered surprisingly little traffic, he opened up the Charger for the entire expanse before turning into the riverside park on the Louisiana side. "Do you think I'm wrong to change my ways?"

Beth reflected before she answered. "I guess not, since you're not hurting anyone. But what brought this on?"

He shrugged. "I woke up one day and didn't want to be the skinny nerd who gets sand kicked in his face."

"Which beach did that—"

"Metaphorically speaking, Elizabeth. I like myself better since I started getting in shape. This car is my reward."

"I usually get a DQ sundae after a punishing workout. Have you considered the high cost of insurance or your likelihood of speeding tickets?"

"Wouldn't a banana split defeat the purpose? I thought you'd be happy for me."

"I am, but who goes out and pays cash for something this expensive?"

Michael shrugged and pulled a computer printout from the sun visor. "My personal trainer gave me this recently. I plan to take part in this competition eight weeks from now."

Beth gazed at the fuzzy pictures, trying to make sense of them. "Looks like some kind of marathon, but I can't tell if it's running or biking or swimming in the ocean."

"You hit the nail on the head. It's sort of an Iron Man contest off the coast of Louisiana."

"Have you lost your mind, Mike?" Beth swiveled in the bucket seat. "People train for *years* before participating in this kind of competition. I think you're making great progress, but you could die trying something like this."

"Stop worrying. Tony set this up over a three-day weekend for his clients, not for anyone else. It's a personal best kind of race. But your concern touches me deeply." Michael held his hand over his heart. "If I didn't know better, I'd think you're starting to like me."

"If you want to put yourself in a hospital, that's your business. But Nate will be gone for another week and, frankly, we're getting along fine, much to my surprise. So I would appreciate not having to train your replacement."

"The competition is still weeks away, and I promise to wear a crash helmet, knee and elbow pads, and a life vest in the water. Satisfied?"

"Relieved, actually. And now you have a get-out-of-jail-free card for the future."

"What do you mean?" He cast her a sideways glance.

"One free chance to stick your nose into my business. Now if you have nothing else to show me, let's head to City Cemetery. I want to be there when Alice arrives so she doesn't face this alone."

Michael put the car in gear and headed up the ramp. "We're less than ten minutes away. Regarding that Monopoly card? I plan to play it when you least expect it."

They rode to the cemetery in total silence. Beth wasn't sure why she wasn't happier for Michael. Maybe it was due to the somber occasion or maybe she was jealous. She'd never ridden in a nicer set of wheels in her life. But once she was at the gravesite, surrounded by men with shovels, a backhoe, and the coroner, all thoughts of fast cars were forgotten. Beth held Alice's hand throughout the exhumation until the hearse drove away with her husband's body.

On their way back to the office, Beth's sense of guilt kicked in. When Michael pulled into the lot, she blurted her confession. "I didn't handle your good news very well. Seriously, I'm happy for you about the car. Life is short. Since you can afford it, why shouldn't you drive something cool?"

"Thanks, Elizabeth."

"And I'm proud of your self-improvement. Most people only talk about changing, but you're doing it. Truth be told, I'd like to get rid of a few bad habits too."

"I can't imagine what those might be." Michael leaned across her to open the door.

"Maybe I'll start today. Aren't you coming inside?"

"I promised Maxine donuts, and this guy delivers. We need something to eat with our cold coffee. I'll be back in a few minutes."

Beth closed the car door and watched him drive away. Is this what it meant to have a real friend? Michael had every reason to be mad at her but he wasn't. *Become a nicer person* moved to the top of her to-do list. Or was something else simmering beneath the surface? She had to admit there was something appealing about a man without pretense, someone comfortable in his own skin. If she wasn't careful, she could become attached to her new partner. And if she'd learned anything from the past, falling for someone at work was a bad idea.

THIRTY-ONE

*B*eth had approximately half an hour to pull herself together—the time it took to get to Donut Scene and back. Considering what Michael found out about Paul's investment in Spare the Children, she needed to bring Natchez PD up to date. And in light of her recent decision to change, she needed to face Chris alone. She wanted all the cards on the table, hers and his, so there would be no further dancing around the elephant in the room. They both lived and worked in Natchez. Most likely, she wasn't moving anytime soon.

"Oh my gosh! What do you have in that pink box?" Maxine's exclamation caught Beth's attention exactly thirty minutes later. She emerged from her cubicle as Michael opened a bakery box.

"Cream-filled éclairs with caramel frosting and chocolate sprinkles," he said. "Ten for you, one for me, and one for Beth."

"You are a man after my own heart." Maxine reached for a stack of napkins from atop the filing cabinet. "If I wasn't already married, I'd be chasing you all over town."

"Story of my life, Miss Maxine." Michael handed the donut box to Beth.

"Thanks, Mike. Put one on my desk while I reheat our lattes." Beth walked into the kitchen amazed by how women in their fifties could say whatever they wanted to men. If she lived that long, she would enjoy that particular perk. When she returned, Mike and Maxine were talking LSU football like old pals. Beth pulled up a chair and bit into her treat.

"Did Nate call this morning?" she asked during a break in their conversation.

Maxine offered a one-word negative reply.

"Did you call Jack about Paul's involvement with that charity?" Beth directed this question to her partner.

"Not yet, but I will after I finish another éclair. These are too good to be true." Michael flipped open the box.

"I'm only letting you have a second one because you're so cute." Maxine imbued her final three words with special emphasis.

Beth swallowed a mouthful of donut. "When Nate gets back, we need a seminar on sexist comments in the workplace. It's been brought to my attention the womenfolk here don't know the federal guidelines."

"Lighten up, missy. What Nate doesn't know..." Maxine finished her mocha with a satisfied slurp.

"I changed my mind about a second donut," said Michael, brushing sugar from his shirt. The rest are yours to share with your lucky husband. I'll go make that call," he said to Beth.

She scrambled to her feet. "Wait. I decided to go to the station for an in-person conference."

Michael stared in confusion. "Are you mad because I was late to work?"

Beth felt like Mean Mom, who never let the kids have any fun. "Absolutely not, but while you were picking up breakfast—thanks, by the way—I realized it was time for a showdown with Chris. I'll give him an update and clear the air of past issues."

For several moments no one spoke. Beth had never referenced her crush on the chief in front of Maxine or anyone else. But the time had come to lose a few insecurities. "After today, all conversations will be with Jack, the detective in charge of the investigation. But I'd like one final solo meeting." Beth finished her coffee, wishing she'd requested chocolate syrup too. The drink had turned bitter on her tongue.

"Of course," Michael said softly. "Should I continue to research that charity?"

"No. Please book us on the earliest flight to Denver tomorrow. Let's go meet the director of Spare the Children in person."

Maxine dropped the rest of her éclair into the box. "I'll take care of those tickets, Beth, so Michael can complete the case report before your trip. When you talk to that slimy Chris McNeil, remember you have the full faith of Price Investigations behind you." Maxine laid a tentative hand on Beth's shoulder.

"Hear, hear," added Mike.

"Thanks, you guys." Beth walked out with a feeling of camaraderie, something long absent in her life. But her new paradigm received its first test at the Natchez police station. When Beth asked to see Chief McNeil, she was buzzed through the front door by Sergeant Mendez.

He blocked her path like a guard dog. "Don't you mean Detective Lejeune? He's the one you're supposed to talk to."

"Please see if Chief McNeil can spare five minutes." Beth heard notes of panic in her voice.

"I'll see if he's available." Mendez glowered as he punched in the chief's extension and then turned his back to her. "He has a few minutes before a meeting with the mayor, so I suggest you make it snappy, Miss Kirby."

"Thank you. I will."

At her knock on the partially open door, she heard, "Beth, come in." Always the gentleman, Chris rose to his feet. "Does your visit involve the exhumation? I'll see if Jack is available to join us." He lifted the receiver of his phone.

"Hold up there, Chris. There's nothing to discuss. The body is barely on its way to Jackson. When I do have information, I'll contact Jack directly. I'm here to clear the air between us."

"In that case, have a seat." He pointed at the closest chair.

"I woke up this morning feeling as though I'd been laboring under a false assumption for years, to use my mother's expression."

His friendly demeanor faded. "Speak your mind."

"I realized everything that happened was my fault—my resignation, my leaving town with my tail between my legs, the bad blood between me and other cops."

"I never wanted you to resign. I knew the 'bad blood' as you call it would die down. Unfounded gossip is an unfortunate work hazard."

Beth ignored his reply and continued. "I chose to resign and I'm not sorry I did, but I need one straight answer from you. Then I will never bring this up again. Were you ever in love with me?"

He paid her the respect of not answering quickly. "I loved you as a person, as clichéd as that sounds. I stupidly thought we could be good friends without offending other employees. But no, I didn't feel that way toward you."

Beth gazed out the window, absorbing his words. She felt neither sadness nor disappointment, only mild embarrassment. It was as though her subconscious knew the truth while her mind insisted on going through the familiar motions. "Yeah, a smarter girl would have realized that. I'm sure you tried to make it clear, but I refused to believe."

"No, Beth, this isn't all on you. I knew where we were headed, but I was flattered by your attention. I should have curtailed our relationship much sooner than I did." He rolled back from his desk. "I'm sorry you paid a higher price for our foolishness."

She waved away the notion. "Don't be. I love my job. It's better than being a cop. The money's not great, but I have real friends now, something I didn't have on the force."

"I wish you all good things in life."

"Okay, before we start singing 'Happy Trails,' let me update you on our case while I'm here. Then you can get to your meeting with the mayor."

"What meeting with the mayor?"

"I must have misunderstood Sergeant Mendez. No matter."

Beth explained Michael's discovery of the paper trail leading to Spare the Children. "Paul had control of the building fund, just as Ralph Buckley said, but he didn't steal the money or stash it away for his and Alice's retirement. He invested it for a twelve-month term with a Colorado charity. Because Calvary Baptist wouldn't need the money until then, Paul thought he could help a worthy cause while earning decent interest."

"Sounds too good to be true."

"Apparently it was. My partner and I are flying to Denver tomorrow to meet the director of Save the Children. Michael is a forensic accountant. He's gathering evidence to prove this is nothing but a shell game out to dupe unsuspecting churches."

Chris scratched his chin. "He's probably right, but this is out of our jurisdiction. I'll put you in contact with the FBI in Jackson. Their Financial Crimes Division will take whatever evidence you've gathered and contact the SEC if necessary."

"Hold off until I get back. I'll question the director solely as Alice's agent in the settlement of her husband's estate. I promise not to compromise any federal investigation should one arise in the future."

Chris stood and extended his hand. "I trust your judgment. I'll inform Jack of today's discussion and tell him you'll be in touch with the second autopsy report."

Beth shook hands and left with her chin up. She even thanked Sergeant Mendez on her way out. For the next hour she drove around putting every bit of the past into perspective. Briefly she wondered if Chris would tell Jack about their *entire* conversation. With a sense of freedom, Beth discovered she didn't care.

As often was the case when she drove into the country, Beth ended up at her aunt and uncle's farm. Funny how an afternoon of shooting aluminum cans off a fence rail burned away the last of her pain. When she kissed her aunt goodbye and drove home, Beth discovered a new outlook on her life…along with Michael sitting on her porch.

"Chicken, Miss Kirby? I have beans and slaw too."

"What are you doing here?" she asked, unable to stop grinning.

He shook the tub. "Waiting for you with dinner. I thought you might be hungry after a trip to Dorrie and Pete's."

"How did you know I went—"

"Please, when you didn't come back to the office, I figured that's where you went. Maxine also packed up two éclairs. She said they would taste good with a glass of milk before bed."

"I wouldn't make a very good spy. Too predictable." Beth plopped next to him on the glider. "My mother didn't drag you in to eat?"

"She tried to bribe me with baked chili-mac, whatever that is, but I said we had important business to discuss over dinner."

"Do we have something important to discuss?"

"Nope, but Maxine thought you might need a friend tonight. She had a garden club meeting, so here I am." Michael opened a cooler by his feet. "Coke, Pepsi, or water?"

"Pepsi." Beth started the glider moving. "Funny. I was just talking about my new friends. I'll take a chicken leg. Did you get fried or grilled?"

"Grilled. I'm in training for the mini Iron Man, remember?"

"Just checking your dedication, Preston."

Michael handed her a plate with a leg and scoops of both side dishes. "We even have dinnertime entertainment." He pointed at a yellow moon rising over the treetops.

"Looks like it's almost full." Beth settled back to eat and watch the moon as though it were a rare occurrence. It was an odd feeling to have on her parents' front porch. But there was no place she would rather be.

THIRTY-TWO

Bay St. Louis
Wednesday

Good morning. You're up awfully early."

Isabelle's cheery greeting, along with a peck on his cheek, jarred Nate awake. "Good grief, wife. Don't sneak up on a man like that." He grinned sheepishly at the sight of her fresh, well-rested face.

"Good grief is right. How late did you stay up? You've got bags under your eyes that could hold a king's ransom."

"I'm hoping today's plans include time in a chaise catching a tan or a cool breeze in the shade."

Isabelle spun his chair around and looked at him squarely. "Nate, are you saying you didn't sleep at all?"

"Relax. After a quick shower I'll be good as new." He turned back to his computer and tapped the screen.

"What has so captured your attention that you stayed up all night?" Isabelle leaned over his shoulder.

"Researching a complex topic from a position of total ignorance isn't for those who need beauty rest." Nate pinched the bridge of his nose.

Isabelle read aloud from the web page: "Any guy who thinks a pair of eights is a great hand and then folds after running up the pot is a total jerk." She stopped abruptly and stared, unable to repeat the next expression if her life depended on it. "Where can I find this Joey K person? I plan to wash his mouth out with soap."

"You'll have to bring several bars and buckets of water." Nate scrolled down the message board to reveal a plethora of bad grammar and an appalling selection of descriptive phrases.

"Goodness, Nathaniel Price. Turn this computer off this instant and go to bed." She crossed her arms and glared at him.

Nate focused a bleary eye on her. "With no breakfast and no TV for a week, Ma?"

Isabelle chuckled and perched on the edge of the settee. "Seriously, what are you researching that involves people who talk like that?"

Nate pushed away from the desk, stretching out the kinks in his spine. "The time has come for full disclosure, for better or for worse. I'm researching the game of poker, specifically high-stake poker tournaments at casinos."

"Have you lost your mind? Gambling ruined my first marriage and is about to ruin Craig's second. Do you think this is a healthy pastime for our honeymoon?" Isabelle lowered her voice to a harsh whisper.

"Simmer down, woman. I didn't even buy raffle tickets to help the SPCA's spay-and-neuter program. When I couldn't sleep last night, I decided to investigate the world of poker. I'm curious as to what a well-educated man like Craig finds so irresistible, and frankly, I'm a little ashamed I showed little compassion toward a man I should pity. If you two hadn't divorced, I could have never married the woman of my dreams."

Isabelle covered her face in her hands. For one horrible moment, Nate thought she was crying before he realized she was laughing hysterically. "Care to let me in on the joke?"

"If ever two people were at cross-purposes during the most romantic three weeks of their life, it's us." She wiped her eyes with the hem of her T-shirt. "Night before last, I reached the conclusion that I've been selfish this entire trip. Instead of making my *current* husband my top priority, I was focused on fixing Craig's life. I'd decided that if Cassie called again, I was going to tell her to contact the local police or hire a private detective. Craig deserves nothing more than a mention in my prayers."

"You haven't neglected me." Nate pulled her onto his lap. "And there's no reason we can't help the Mitchells and still enjoy some fun in the sun."

"Cassie is here in Bay St. Louis now. If anyone can bring Craig back to the straight and narrow, it's her."

Nate tapped the computer screen. "Ignore the vulgar language and read a few of these poker room chats. I've trolled message boards, Facebook groups, and blogs dedicated to serious poker players. Craig might have fallen into something he can't climb out of."

Isabelle scrolled down, skimming the contents with a grimace. "Ugh, can't you give me a summary? I'd rather not read their nasty rants this early."

Nate shifted his wife's one hundred twenty pounds to the other chair. "Part of the reason for the foul language is that these gamblers are furious. Most serious players are at least casually acquainted with each other. Poker players in Shreveport and Tunica are complaining they were cheated. Nobody knows how it happened, but in both cities high-stakes games were won by card sharks no one recognized."

"Could just be sour grapes from losers. I thought you said casinos have high-tech security systems, making it impossible to cheat at cards."

"Difficult, yes, but not impossible. After my crash course on how to play poker at three o'clock this morning, I learned that rules are different in high-stakes games than on the casino floor. Gamblers play against each other, not against the house, and you must be invited to those games by one of the hosts. No casino wants to harbor cheaters, so security keeps a watchful eye, but a player's privacy must also be taken into consideration."

"Remember when we saw a clip from the World Series of Poker? That one young man in dark glasses and a hoodie looked like a bank robber. But I fail to see what the rants from sore losers have to do with Craig."

"To help Craig we need to understand the fundamentals of the game. A few whales that got burned in April in Shreveport were later burned in Tunica in May."

"I take it whales are the big-money gamblers. We lost ten bucks at the slot machine. What species of fish does that make us—pickerel?" Her grin lit up her whole face.

"More like guppies. Problem is, not one of the players remembers the same winner at both places."

Isabelle shook her silky mane of hair. "There's your answer—sour grapes. You go to bed while I head to the porch to see what specialty Mrs. Russo cooked up today. You can eat your share of breakfast for lunch."

"Maybe it's not sour grapes. I think it's some kind of an organized poker ring, but I don't understand the game well enough to see how Craig ties in."

"Craig is an addicted, compulsive gambler with only himself to blame. He would probably waste his last dollar on a long shot."

"Nevertheless, I have an appointment at the Golden Magnolia Casino in a few hours. I want to know if Craig is winning or losing fairly. I'm buying the head of security lunch in exchange for information as a professional courtesy."

"What *professional courtesy*? Your agency's ongoing case involves the murder of a Baptist preacher."

Nate rubbed his tired eyes. "I said I'd been hired by an ex-wife to investigate a compulsive gambler and possible card cheat. I'm doing this for you, Izzy. You're just not paying me. Care to come with me? Lunch will be fabulous."

"You can stretch the truth thinner than cellophane." Isabelle placed both hands on her hips. "I'll pass on lunch and go shopping instead. I need to pick up something for the other agents, my broker, and your assistant. Plus, I still haven't found a gift for your cousin yet. Nicki and Hunter's baby shower is in a few weeks. Set your alarm for noon and get some sleep. I'll see you this afternoon." Isabelle waved and closed the door behind her.

Nate was left alone with a dull headache. If ever he needed her to come with him, it was today. Whether whale, pickerel, or guppy, he was a fish out of water. Having a beautiful woman along when he talked to casino security might have been an ace up his sleeve.

THIRTY-THREE

*I*t didn't take Isabelle long to feel guilty. Was guilt genetically hardwired into female DNA? Or was it something every American mother felt it her duty to instill in daughters? Personally, she would have preferred the ability to make a soufflé or speak multiple languages or solve a Level 3 Sudoku puzzle. She should have accompanied Nate to his appointment. Neither of them knew much about poker, but she was the one who had dragged him into this mess.

Isabelle began shopping for gifts like a crazy contestant in a reality show. She ran up and down boutique aisles grabbing gifts while ticking off the recipient's name on her mental tally board: embroidered tablecloth for Maxine, Bay St. Louis golf shirt for her boss, hand-painted scarves for the other real estate agents—each unique in pattern and color. Her biggest challenge was finding an appropriate gift for Nate's cousin. Nicki and Hunter were expecting their first child in a few months. The baby shower could be the season's biggest event in New Orleans' Garden District. Isabelle found a hand-crocheted sweater with matching hat and booties at an adorable but overpriced children's boutique. Pale yellow would be perfect for the new baby whether boy or girl. Grabbing a half-dozen "Life is better on the Gulf Coast" T-shirts for miscellaneous souvenirs, Isabelle practically ran back to the B and B.

When Nate padded onto the porch foggy-brained at noon, she was curled up in a chair reading a novel. "Hi, handsome. Is that offer of lunch still open? I worked up quite an appetite spending your money."

"Done so soon? I didn't think I'd see you till suppertime, unless the bank canceled our credit card." Nate combed his hair with his fingers.

"I decided to go with you. If I hadn't stuck my nose into my ex's business, you would only have your tan to work on this trip."

Nate offered the smile that won her heart the first time she saw it. Or maybe it'd been the second…or the twenty-third, but nonetheless it had won her heart. "Skin cancer should be taken seriously. Your nosiness might have saved me from painful treatments down the road. I'll jump in the shower and then we'll be off." Nate ducked back into their suite.

Thirty minutes later he reappeared, looking splendid in chinos, a linen sport coat, and a silk shirt open at the neck. "What an improvement," she said, remembering his baggy shorts and ripped MSU shirt at yesterday's breakfast. "How come you don't get this spiffy when we go out to dinner?"

"Casino executives are always dapper. Haven't you ever watched a James Bond movie? The better I dress, the more respect I'll receive."

On the drive to the Golden Magnolia, Isabelle had no idea what to expect. But when the head of security met them at the front entrance, she had to agree her husband was right. Although not as handsome as the actors who played James Bond, his charcoal-gray suit was impeccable and his silver hair expertly cut. Art Lewis greeted them warmly.

"Do you have a preference where we have lunch?" he asked.

"Yes, I'd like to eat at the Champion Grill here in the hotel," said Nate. "The reviews are great."

Isabelle wasn't sure when Nate had done his homework, but Mr. Lewis was pleased with his choice. "My favorite! Why don't I lead the way and share some stories about the changes we made after

Hurricane Katrina? Although the casino was totally destroyed, this beautiful old gal is now better than ever."

Over entrées of chicken Caesar salad and iced tea, Nate first explained his line of work and then described what was going on with Craig Mitchell.

"I'm certain he's involved against his will with pressure from a gang of card cheats," Isabelle interjected. "Craig loves Cassie—that's his second wife—and he wouldn't just up and move to Bay St. Louis to resume his old lifestyle."

Mr. Lewis, who had been listening politely, dabbed his mouth. "I'm sure you know the man better than anyone, Mrs. Price, but gambling becomes an addiction for one to two percent of the population, no different than drugs or alcohol. Relapses, unfortunately, are commonplace until he or she kicks the habit for good."

"I'm surprised to hear a casino executive admit this. You derive your income from folks losing their hard-earned money at the tables and one-armed bandits." Isabelle felt Nate's leg bump her under the table. "No offense, Mr. Lewis."

"None taken, Mrs. Price," he said, smiling. "Although it's been years since I heard them called that. The Golden Magnolia offers a complete entertainment experience—golf, spa facilities, a marina and RV park, delicious dining, exciting shows, and yes, gaming for those who wish to wager discretionary dollars. We have no desire to bankrupt people or break up families. For those who think they might have a problem, information about Gamblers Anonymous is available throughout our facility, along with our voluntary self-exclusion program."

"Good to know. That's what Craig needs to do." Nate reached for another crusty roll.

"Besides, it would be very hard to force someone to play Texas Hold'em, especially if you wanted them to *win*." Mr. Lewis punctuated the sentence with a wink, aimed straight at her.

Unconvinced, Isabelle pressed the issue. "Craig is a good poker player. He's also very lucky. Maybe someone is forcing him to keep increasing his bets each time he's dealt a good hand until the pot is huge." She used her fingers to indicate a large pile of chips. "Then Craig throws down his winning hand and sweeps in everyone's money." Isabelle raked the imaginary pot of gold toward her lap.

Mr. Lewis looked at Nate, both men momentarily speechless.

"We only watched poker a short while one evening," explained Nate. "Isabelle doesn't exactly understand the game." Wisely he omitted the detail about their ten-dollar loss at Triple Wild Cherry.

"Truly great hands are few and far between, ma'am." Mr. Lewis's focus returned to her, and his tone turned solicitous. "Poker is all about reading your opponents without revealing your own hand. Bluffing, if you please. I've seen people win a hundred thousand dollars on a pair of jacks because the other players folded, including some who would have won had they stayed in. Usually, you don't find out what the folded hands contained, but once in a while a player loses his cool."

"Do you play poker?" asked Isabelle.

"Occasionally, but not in Mississippi. If I get the urge to play, I fly to Las Vegas."

Nate stopped eating his salad and set down his fork. "So you're saying Craig is most likely playing of his own volition."

"I can't imagine it any other way." Mr. Lewis pushed away his half-eaten lunch.

"Thugs might be blackmailing him," blurted out Isabelle. "And forcing him to count cards."

"You're thinking of blackjack, Mrs. Price. You can't count cards in Texas Hold'em." He discreetly glanced at his watch.

"Are you saying it's impossible to cheat at poker?" she asked.

"I've been around long enough to know anything is possible." A dimple appeared in Mr. Lewis's cheek. "Although I hope your ex-husband reconciles with his wife, my job is to protect the financial interests of this casino. Would you like me to plug his photo into our system? Facial recognition will alert security when he walks through the door. If he is cheating, he won't be cheating for long."

"No, please don't do that." Impulsively, Isabelle grabbed the man's arm. "If Craig finds out I tipped you off, he'll kill me."

Apparently giving up on her, Mr. Lewis swiveled around to Nate. "I'm unsure what you want me to do, Mr. Price."

"My wife uses the term 'kill' euphemistically. Craig wouldn't hurt a fly." He paused a moment and then said, "Is it possible for me to observe Craig play just to make sure he's operating on his own? I would consider it a professional courtesy. My agency will be at your disposal if you ever need help from a PI." Nate handed him a business card.

Mr. Lewis tucked the card in his pocket. "If we suspect a crooked game might be underway, we might employ a PI who is an expert poker player. Although we have no control over games in guest suites, we don't want cheating anywhere inside the Golden Magnolia. But you don't understand the game of Texas Hold'em well enough for us to stake you to a night's play. And, of course, Mr. Mitchell would recognize you."

"Do you have any suggestions?" asked Nate.

"Why don't I give you the name and number of a retired PI here in town? Johnny Herman is also an avid poker player, although he prefers tournaments to high-stakes games. He might be willing to play a few hands with Golden Magnolia's money to get a feel for Craig. Johnny can usually spot a cheat before too much damage is done. But if Mrs. Price's ex-husband is doing anything illegal, he'll be prosecuted to the full extent of the law, the same as any thief." Mr. Lewis jotted down a phone number on his business card. "Why not give Johnny a call?"

Isabelle had remained quiet long enough. "Craig won't do anything stupid if he sees me there."

"What are you talking about?" Nate squawked. "You know even less about poker than I do."

Mr. Lewis looked equally perplexed. "These are private games, Mrs. Price, by invitation only or arranged by the hosts. Spectators aren't allowed."

"I've seen poker on TV. Don't you have women serving beverages and handling a buffet? Why not hire me for a few days? I waitressed at Applebee's every summer during college and never spilled a single drink."

He nodded. "You're right. The casino host will usually request two hospitality girls to make sure players remain in the game for hours, but I'm not sure working a private poker game is the same as working at Applebee's."

"Forget it, Isabelle. Let's go talk to that retired PI." Nate signaled for the check and reached for her hand. "We appreciate you making time for us, Mr. Lewis."

Isabelle pulled her hand from Nate's grasp. "Where would I get one of the uniforms?" she asked Mr. Lewis.

Nate stared at the ceiling as he thought. "But what if the Sunday school superintendent saw you serving drinks?"

Isabelle crossed her arms defiantly. "I doubt that Mr. Nash frequents the high roller room at the Golden Magnolia."

"You could break your neck in those stilettos." Nate remained equally stubborn.

"I'm sure I can survive long enough to find out what Craig has up his sleeve. Hey, I cracked a poker joke," she added, pleased with herself.

Art Lewis's dimple deepened as he took another card from his wallet. "Why don't you two talk this over? Then, if you still wish to give it a try, ask for Mrs. Doucet in Human Resources. Show her my card and ask for a temporary position as cocktail hostess as a special favor to me. Mrs. Doucet will measure you for a uniform and teach you enough to work a couple sessions." Lewis turned to Nate. "If Johnny Herman agrees to play at the same table as Mr. Mitchell, have him call me. You and I can watch the action on security cameras. You'll be doing me a favor if we nip this in the bud, besides preventing a lengthy jail sentence for Mr. Mitchell. Thieves and cheats always get caught. It's just a matter of time."

As the waitress arrived with the bill, she stopped at Mr. Lewis's chair. "May I have that, ma'am?" said Nate. "This lunch is my treat."

The executive scribbled his name on the check. "That's very kind of you, but the Golden Magnolia wouldn't dream of letting you pay. Please consider staying with us the next time you visit the Gulf Coast. And let me know if I can be of further assistance. It was a rare pleasure meeting you both." Mr. Lewis rose to his impressive height and bowed to Isabelle. "And I'll remember your offer, Mr. Price, should I ever need help in Natchez."

The honeymooners exchanged a look after he had strolled away. "That guy knew that we weren't staying here," whispered Isabelle, "and also where your agency is located."

"Art Lewis probably knew as much about *us* as about his own mother before we walked through the door, including what size uniform you would wear." Nate spoke under his breath as they left the restaurant. But Isabelle caught his meaning loud and clear.

THIRTY-FOUR

Natchez
Thursday

Last night Michael had the most enjoyable evening since his fiancée had dumped him. Maybe even better than any with Rachel. That woman never knew how to relax. Rachel dressed far fancier than what the occasion called for, as if she wanted to be ready for a last-minute better offer. No wonder a lifetime with an accountant from Brookhaven eventually lost its appeal. Beth, on the other hand, seemed surprised he didn't pick his teeth or watch streaming sports scores during a meal. *Something to be said about a woman with low expectations.* He liked Beth and liked how relaxed he felt in her company. While they had shared his bucket of chicken, he updated her with what he learned about the director of Spare the Children.

This morning, they decided to take her car to the airport. How would it look to the insurance company if his new Charger was stolen during the first week? While they drove to Baton Rouge through the beautiful Mississippi countryside, she talked about her visit to Uncle Pete's farm.

"Did you hit any cans this time?" he asked.

"Forty-eight out of fifty. I lay blame for missing the other two on a horsefly and a cousin who sneaked up on me."

"I hope your cousin is still among the living."

"My cousin, yes, but that fly won't be bothering any more horses."

"Next time I'm tagging along so I can show off my new nine millimeter Beretta ninety-two. My instructor at the range recommended the make and model."

Beth whistled through her teeth. "Look at you, Jesse James. A Beretta is a fine weapon. We'll plan for an evening of killing Coke cans soon. Of course, you'll be allowed only one more visit after that. If I bring the same man a fourth time, Uncle Pete will be waiting with a shotgun and the preacher. Just giving you fair warnin'."

"Good to know." Michael took a sip of coffee as she accelerated on the open road.

After a period of companionable silence, Beth brought up an unexpected topic—her conversation with Chief McNeil. "Basically, I imagined half of what happened and painted the other half a particularly *rosy* hue. Though it was painful, I'm grateful Chris disabused me of my fantasies. Otherwise, I'd be one of those sad old ladies forever stuck in the past. Now I'll be a sad old lady pining over expired coupons and the neighbor's dog tearing up my flowers."

They both laughed, but Beth's grip on the steering wheel betrayed her emotions.

"Don't be too hard on yourself," he said. "What happened to you happens to the best of us."

"Even you?"

Michael wouldn't have chosen now for his personal true confession, but he realized too late that he'd set himself up. "Even me."

"We have almost an hour if you care to elaborate."

"My story will take about five minutes. I fell in love with the office assistant fresh out of college. Rachel was bright, ambitious, and beautiful. Not sure what she liked about me—maybe my salary, maybe my potential for *fast-track advancement*." He heard the scorn in his voice. "Whatever, I fell hard for her. I started saving every penny I could for a down payment on a house, our kids' college education, and a nice retirement down the road. Talk about living in a dream world. After we'd dated eight months, I bought a two-carat diamond and asked her to marry me. Right about the time I booked our honeymoon cruise, she called off the wedding. Not exactly at the altar, but close enough."

Beth glanced in his direction. "Wow. Rachel sounds like a real charmer. However, I must disagree with your assessment. She might be beautiful and ambitious, but bright? Not by a long shot if she let you get away."

"Thanks, Beth. You and I are better off without those two losers."

She laughed. "You've got a cool car. And I found someone to shoot Coke cans with. It don't get better than that in Natchez."

Their good mood lasted throughout the flight to Denver, up until they reached the offices of Spare the Children International. Michael took one glance at the slick furnishings, the expensive prints on the wall, and the view of the Denver skyline from the twenty-third floor, and he smelled a scam. Doubtlessly everything they saw had been rented or leased. He'd seen 'fly-by-night opera-tions before where the operators packed up and disappeared within a twenty-four-hour period. Vanished, right down to shredding the documents into the trash. His partner, however, gazed around the executive suite as though in awe.

"Miss Kirby, Mr. Preston? I'm Elliott Rayburn, director of Spare the Children."

"What a lovely view you have, Mr. Rayburn," said Beth. "I could get used to Denver if I didn't need to breathe so often."

"Ah, my assistant mentioned you're from the Mississippi Delta. Yes, quite a difference from sea level, but trust me when I say you grow accustomed to the thin air after a while."

"And you can always rent an oxygen tank in the meantime, right? Mike Preston, sir." Michael extended his hand. "Kind of you to see us on short notice."

Rayburn shook halfheartedly. "Not at all. Please have a seat."

The silver-haired man gestured toward the two leather chairs in front of his teakwood desk. His work surface contained no business accoutrements other than a sliver-thin laptop and one folder of papers. "My assistant said you're here on behalf of Mrs. Alice Dean, widow of the late Reverend Paul Dean. I was very sorry to hear of Reverend Dean's passing. Such a tragedy when a pastor succumbs to depression. What hope do the rest of us have in dealing with life's sorrows? Mrs. Dean has my sympathy."

"Thank you," said Beth. "His passing affected the congregation deeply."

Rayburn straightened his tie. "May I ask in what capacity you represent Mrs. Dean? Are you the attorneys who will settle the estate?"

Beth shook her head. "No, nothing like that. We're brand-new private investigators, but we're here as friends of Mrs. Dean more than anything else. Reverend Dean had been my pastor."

"Then you have my sympathy as well, Miss Kirby. Ask me whatever you like." Rayburn folded his hands, his nails trimmed and buffed.

"We understand Calvary Baptist had invested our building fund with your charity. Was that like one of those bond funds?"

Michael glanced at Beth. Her expression rivaled that of a ten-year-old auditing an applied calculus class.

"In a manner of speaking, the investment was similar to how a bond fund works. Reverend Dean was promised a decent rate of return for funds that the church didn't need for a while. If I recall, construction of a new school was eighteen months away at the time of his initial investment. Twelve months is the minimum term required for the work we do." Rayburn's smile revealed straight teeth, bleached to perfection.

"Why is that, Mr. Rayburn?" Michael was unable to remain silent any longer.

"Elliott, please. Our charity operates on a global level. The demand for money is often urgent and substantial. At the same time, fund-raising efforts take place at sporadic intervals. Our war chest can swell or shrink tremendously on a daily basis."

"What do you mean by war chest?" Beth leaned forward in her chair.

"Make no mistake about it, Miss Kirby. Drug lords, human traffickers, and political despots who commit genocide have declared war on decent human beings. If we are to spread the word of God's love, we must first provide safe haven for those who suffer. Whether it be from starvation, forced prostitution, or landmines left behind after a forgotten war."

"Spare the Children fights against all that?" asked Beth.

"Our aim is to protect God's most vulnerable creatures, His children. Let me show you what we're all about." With the press of a button beneath his desk, a panel opened in the wall and a video began to roll.

Michael sat mesmerized by an audio/video extravaganza that would bring a tear to the most jaded eye. As proof positive, Beth was soon dabbing her baby blues. He wasn't quite as overwhelmed because he didn't believe a word of what he saw and heard. If this charity accomplished what they claimed, why hadn't he heard about it on *Sixty Minutes* or the nightly news?

When the montage concluded, Rayburn waited to receive the usual kudos. "As you can see, for our global work to continue, benefactors must commit to a specific time frame. All of this was explained to Pastor Dean before the initial investment and during subsequent conversations. I hope our inability to pay early dividends didn't exacerbate his depression."

Beth was quick to answer. "Oh, surely not. Mrs. Dean just wants to tie up loose ends. According to emails from Spare the Children, her husband was supposed to receive regular statements."

Rayburn's mouth dropped open. "That is absolutely correct. Calvary Baptist should have received quarterly statements, including the account balance at that point, along with an update on recent success stories."

Michael cleared his throat. "I found nothing like that in Reverend Dean's papers. Could you furnish Mrs. Dean and Calvary's board members with copies of those statements?"

Rayburn's smile faded. "Unfortunately, I use several different accounting firms for record keeping. With contributors spread across the globe, people prefer to get statements from someone closer to home. If I remember correctly, a Mississippi firm handled that state along with Louisiana, Tennessee, and Alabama. I will get you their name."

"You don't keep copies here at headquarters?" Michael asked.

"Yes, I'm sure we do, but it's my job to see those funds get where they're needed to save young lives." Rayburn stood and glanced at his watch. "I will have to text or email you that company's name. Right now, I'm late for a teleconference with Asia." He rounded the desk to take Beth's hand. "My assistant will provide copies of those statements if we have them. Please pass my condolences on to Mrs. Dean."

"I sure will." Beth pumped his hand. "Thanks for making time for us, Elliot, and keep up the good work. The world needs more men like you and fewer pimps and drug dealers."

With a final smile, Rayburn vanished through the door behind his desk. Moments later, his gracious assistant appeared to hustle them out of world headquarters.

In the elevator for the ride down to the first floor, Michael cocked his head to the side. "I take it you weren't as mesmerized as you seemed."

"By that snake oil salesman?" Beth hiked her purse up her shoulder. "I wouldn't invest a dime with someone who claims he saves kids yet wears a suit that expensive. I bet it cost a thousand bucks. Lesson number seventy-eight, partner: Never let the bad guy know you're on to him. You find out more if they think you've been buffaloed."

"Good point, but that suit was closer to three grand. And as heartbreaking as those videos were, it looked like a cut-and-paste job to me with a movie soundtrack."

The elevator door opened onto the plush lobby. "What if the whole thing's for real?" asked Beth, grabbing hold of his sleeve.

"That assistant promised she'd track down those statements, and I believed her. With any luck, your church can get its original invest-ment back. What's the plan? Are we heading back to the airport?"

Beth shook her head. "Didn't you check our return tickets? Eight o'clock tomorrow morning was the best Maxine could do. We're booked into the Hampton Suites by the airport. We have a free night in the big city, along with two hundred bucks expense money."

"Did Maxine book two rooms or one?" Michael asked as he tried to hail a taxi.

"Two, of course. Don't be stupid. And the two hundred is for both of us, so google something appropriate for dinner." Beth perched on the curb, waving at every taxi that passed.

"How about Japanese at one of those hibachi tables—the kind where you sit on cushions?"

"Sounds good. Since it's my first time west, I'm ready for any-thing. I'll even try those tidbits of raw fish."

"You've never eaten sushi?"

"Didn't you hear the part about never leaving Mississippi?"

Michael smiled. "You are in for a treat, Miss Kirby, because I'm ready for just about anything too."

THIRTY-FIVE

Friday

*B*eth walked into a kitchen she barely recognized. Every flat surface was covered with green beans, Mason jars, or some sort of cooking utensil. Her mom's usually tidy kitchen had been turned upside down.

"What happened in here?" Beth pivoted in place to assess the disaster. "Did you have a fight to the death with vegetables and the green beans won?"

Startled, Rita pressed a palm to her chest. "Gosh, you scared me, Betsy. It's canning day. I plan to put up twenty quarts or die tryin'. What on earth are you doing here?"

"This is where I live unless you carried my stuff to the curb in the last twenty-four hours." Beth pulled the pitcher of iced tea from the fridge.

"Why are you home at one o'clock in the afternoon?" Rita resumed snapping the ends off beans, the floor already littered with stems that had missed the trash bag.

"Mike and I had a very early, very long trip back from Denver, thanks to a layover in Dallas. Don't they have direct flights anymore? Then we were stuck behind every slow-moving vehicle on Route 61 from Baton Rouge." Beth pressed an icy glass to her forehead. "I told Mike I'd complete my report and update Nate from home. Besides, we had a late night. Dinner at a hibachi restaurant takes forever. They cook your food one piece at a time. If you give me some beans, I'll make myself useful."

Rita dumped a pile in front of Beth and added more to her own heaping mound. "Did you catch Reverend Dean's killer in Denver? I hope you slapped the cuffs on him."

"I don't even own cuffs because I'm no longer a cop. But now we know where the church's money went. And who knows? The director of that charity might turn out to be a murderer as well as a thief. Mike didn't believe a word the guy said. Elliott Rayburn was far too slick to be a humanitarian."

Her mother arched one eyebrow. "Why were you out late at a fancy restaurant? I thought this was a business trip for your murder investigation."

Beth looked up from her pile of beans. "It *was* a business trip. We went to the charity where Reverend Dean invested the money for the new school. All restaurants in a big city are fancy. Denver isn't like Natchez. Not my fault the meal took hours. As soon as Save the Children sends Mike the quarterly statements, we'll have a better idea of their scam."

"Mike, Mike, Mike. Do you realize you mentioned his name four times since you walked in the door?" Rita dumped her colander of beans into a pot of boiling water.

Beth stopped zealously snapping ends. "What's the matter with you? He's my partner. If I'm talking about an event he was part of, of course I would mention his name. I thought you liked *Michael.*"

"I do like him. That's why I don't like where this is headed." Rita emptied the basket in the center of the table, burying them in a mountain of beans.

"Are you having some sort of menopausal episode? Where *what* is headed?" Beth's voice rose with agitation.

"You two play nice in there," Stan Kirby called from the other room. "Or I'll send you both to your rooms." Roused from his nap, her father padded into the kitchen. "Hey, daughter, we don't usually get to see you in the afternoon." He planted a kiss on Beth's head and headed outside.

"Hey, Pops, I hurried home to help Mom on bean day," Beth called after him. Then she locked gazes with Rita. "No good deed goes unpunished."

Rita softened her tone. "Where your relationship with your partner is headed. I've seen this before. I've seen this with *you* before."

Beth wiped her hands on a towel. "Mike and I are friends. This is nothing like what happened with Chris."

Rita snapped a dozen ends before replying. "I know you believe that, and it might even be true. But I've lived long enough to know men and women can't be friends."

"That is the most ridiculous thing I ever heard."

Surprisingly, her mother laughed. "I would have said that too at your age."

"There's nothing wrong with having an amicable relationship with people at work. Partners have to get along to make an effective team. But I couldn't become romantically involved with Michael in a million years. We're from opposite ends of the spectrum."

Rita shrugged. "Perhaps I'm wrong and times have changed. If you can honestly say Michael Preston isn't seeing something more to this, I will butt my nose out."

"He's not, Mom. Mike just came off a bad relationship. He's all about self-improvement, not falling in love on the rebound."

"Good to hear. Now be a dear and pick the last two rows of beans. That afternoon sun will give me a migraine."

"You have more beans in the garden? This is already enough for every family in Natchez."

Rita patted her arm. "Seeds were on sale last spring. Then we got perfect weather for a bumper crop. I'll fill jars with what I just blanched."

"Sure, I don't mind." Beth swept her stems into the trash and grabbed a hat by the door. The afternoon sun could give anyone a headache, but she didn't mind a couple of hours in the garden.

It would give her time to think. Although she had protested her mother's allegations, deep inside she knew Rita was right.

It was something about Michael's behavior at dinner: He listened to her every word as though she spouted pearls of wisdom instead of offhand comments from someone who had never eaten Japanese food. He insisted on paying for the taxi, tipping the van driver, and buying her snack during the flight, even though she had their expense money. Any one of those niceties could be written off as simple kindness, but if she added them together, along with a few surreptitious glances in her direction, she reached a frightening conclusion—her mother was right. Michael might be developing a crush on her. And she'd found out the hard way that work relationships don't end well.

Beth knew she needed to reconcile herself to snapping beans in her mother's kitchen for many years to come. Her father would totter in on his walker, ordering them to behave or suffer the consequences. The mental picture made her laugh, but Beth knew there was nothing funny about the situation. She really liked Michael. He was twice the man Chris was. He just wasn't the right man for her.

THIRTY-SIX

Saturday

Michael punched in Beth's number the moment he started his powerful engine. Just as voice mail was about to pick up, a sleepy voice answered. "Hello?"

"Elizabeth? It's Mike. Want to meet me for breakfast? I've got a rather interesting development to share." He switched the phone to Bluetooth and pulled onto the street.

"What time is it? Why are you bothering me so early?"

He glanced at his watch. "It's eight fifteen, Miss Sunshine. How about getting a head start on the day over blueberry pancakes and turkey bacon?"

"Better stop throwing your money around, Preston. Premium gas for your fancy car can eat through a paycheck in no time." Beth's tone had morphed from sleepy to irritable.

"Who are you, and what have you done with the nice person I had sushi with in Denver?"

"That person stayed up past midnight canning green beans with her mother. I hope you like veggies because you and Maxine are each getting six jars."

"I love healthy food. Green beans have few calories as long as they're not dripping in butter. But what about breakfast? I promise not to order anything green."

"Thanks, but I'm going to pass. See you at the office later."

She hung up before Michael could ask if she wanted takeout. So instead of wasting time at a restaurant, Michael picked up a dozen multigrain bagels with low-fat cream cheese and drove straight to Price Investigations. He and Maxine were on their second bagel when Beth strolled through the door forty minutes later.

"Sorry I'm late. I overslept." Beth opened her tote bag and lined up six jars on Maxine's desk. "Six for each of you, courtesy of Rita. And, Maxine, why are you here on a Saturday?" She handed Michael the bag before reaching for a bagel.

"I wanted to catch up on paperwork. Yummy, home-canned are the best," enthused Maxine. "Tell your mama thank you."

"I will, Maxine. Could someone pass me the cream cheese?"

Michael picked up the cheese spread and a stack of napkins. "Thanks for the beans, but could you bring that bagel to my cubicle? I'm eager to show you the last three statements for Calvary Baptist's investment."

Beth scrambled to her feet to follow him down the hall. "They actually sent copies? I thought we'd need a court order before Rayburn complied, especially if it's a scam."

"See for yourself." Michael tapped a few keys and three statements appeared side by side on his monitor. He moved away as Beth pulled up a chair.

"Spare the Children sent these?" She leaned in to study the screen, her bagel forgotten.

"Rayburn's assistant first emailed that their in-house bookkeeper had left on vacation, but she gave me the accounting firm who prepares the Mississippi statements. 'Left on vacation' sounds fishy, doesn't it?"

"Like a boatload of catfish left in the sun."

"Then she emailed back with these statements attached. Rayburn left strict orders she should be helpful, so she found them herself."

"Could you explain what I'm looking at?" Beth rolled back from his desk.

"It would be my pleasure." Michael handed her the cream cheese. "Reverend Dean invested almost half a million dollars, just like he said he did. These quarterlies were furnished by a company called D.K. Financials out of Jackson. I don't know if they have a brick-and-mortar office or just an Internet operation, but their address is a post office box. These statements were attached to a generic email from the company. No particular employee seems to be in charge, which I find unusual. From what I learned, D.K. Financials handles investments for Mississippi, Tennessee, Alabama, and Louisiana, just like Rayburn said." Michael tapped figures on the screen. "Take a look at the weekly fluctuations in the account."

Beth leaned forward again, holding her bagel aloft. "Honestly, Mike, I can't make heads or tails of this."

"That's because the statements are gibberish. These quarterlies reflect fluctuations in the value of the *charity*, not the individual deposit from Calvary Baptist of Natchez. That doesn't make sense for an investment, even if they don't pay interim interest or dividends until the end of term."

"I'll have to take your word for it. Balancing my checkbook is a monthly nightmare."

"Most investment quarterlies are straightforward. The summary page shows the amount you either gained or lost due to market volatility since the last statement. With one quick glance, you'll either crack open the bubbly or toss and turn for many sleepless nights." Michael hooked his thumb toward the computer. "Those statements are purposefully cryptic, and that usually means one thing." Using his index fingers, Michael drew a shape in the air.

"Is that an isosceles triangle?" asked Beth. "I got an *A* in geometry."

"I believe it is. In this case it represents a pyramid marketing scheme. Dubious swindlers convince people to invest their savings with the promise of better returns than they can get elsewhere. Investors are told their money is safe, that they can't lose if they stay the course for a certain amount of time. Victims are often lured by the promise of doing humanitarian work. Being fairly unsophisticated, Reverend Dean would have watched that video and taken the bait—hook, line, and sinker."

"Hey, watch who you bad-mouth, buster. Elliott Rayburn even had me going for a while. Besides, you don't know for a fact this is a scam." Balling up her sticky wrapper, Beth tossed it at the trash can and missed.

"Sorry. I meant no implied disrespect to your pastor." Michael leaned down to retrieve the wrapper. "To be honest, the director of Spare the Children was very convincing. That's what makes charlatans as dangerous as thugs sticking up convenience stores. They can wipe out retirement accounts, wreak havoc on credit unions, and ruin a church's dream for a new school."

"You think Rayburn doesn't use the money for his charity?"

"I suspect there is no charity, Elizabeth. It probably exists only on paper. The scammers register as a nonprofit to obtain tax-exempt status and then go to work fund-raising. They amass a fortune by making big promises. If an investor smells a rat, or needs to cash out due to unforeseen circumstances, they're paid back with money from new investors. The scammers might even add a small profit to keep people happy so nobody blows the whistle too soon."

Beth's forehead furrowed. "Sounds awfully complicated. The cons must know they'll eventually get caught."

"White collar thieves see this as a faster road to riches than working for the next forty years. It's very complex, but an exit strategy is part of their plan. They set a date to stop raising funds, grab their fake passports, and head to the airport."

"You mean leave the country forever?"

"Elizabeth, you don't think like a criminal. We're talking millions of dollars. Do you have any idea how well you could live on that in Costa Rica or Brazil or some country without extradition to the United States?"

"Everybody involved can't be willing to leave the country, not in an operation this large." Beth jumped up and started pacing between cubicles. "That's ridiculous."

"You're right. Only the top two or three will take the money and run. Other people involved are either oblivious to the scheme—duped like Reverend Dean—or paid handsomely to do their job. If they blow the whistle, they can be charged with aiding and abetting fraud. Most will keep their mouth shut, at least until they get caught. By the time the pyramid crumbles, money will have moved around the world, potentially beyond the reach of U.S. law enforcement."

Beth stopped pacing and walked back to the computer. "Do you think you found proof of a scam?"

"I'm looking at just the tip of an iceberg, but this is now an FBI matter. Their Financial Crimes Division needs to take a look at Spare the Children International, which could already be on their radar. Nate hired me as a PI to investigate a murder. And as crooked as I believe Rayburn is, I see no evidence that he's a killer. Not yet, anyway. He might very well have killed Paul Dean to avoid paying back so large a sum. Most churches wouldn't have had a fraction of what Buckley amassed with his day-trading in the stock market." Michael hit the button to print copies of the statements.

Beth picked up one of them. "You and I need to keep looking before this case is taken away from us."

"We can't impede a federal investigation, but there is something we can track down." Michael leaned back with a sly grin.

"What is that?" Beth placed one hand on her hip. "I'm too crabby today to play guessing games."

"Reverend Dean demanded to talk to someone in charge because he wasn't getting regular statements. D.K. Financials sent them out, but not to the pastor. They sent them to the financial director. I'd bet Ralphie took some kind of commission for leading the lamb to slaughter. And if the investment went south, Reverend Dean would take the blame instead of him."

"You think the money is all gone?"

"Maybe not yet, but if it *is* a scam, those thieves won't stick around forever. Buckley might have an alibi for when Reverend

Dean died, but he's in this deeper than a short-term loan to pay off Tammy's credit cards or add to his home."

For the first time that morning, Beth smiled. "Okay, you follow the money trail so we'll have a better case to hand over to law enforcement. I'll question Mrs. Purdy and Alice for what they know about Spare the Children or D.K. Financials. They might have filed away something that came in the mail. People still use snail mail for business correspondence. Then I'll track down other churches in the four-state area that might also have invested with this charity." She headed toward the doorway.

"I'll be happy to get you those names."

Beth halted midstride. "I know how to use a computer and the Internet. I was doing Google searches long before you came to work for Price Investigations." Her words hung in the air like ice crystals.

"I didn't mean to imply otherwise. Just trying to be helpful." Michael sat down at his desk before she saw how rattled he was by her comment.

For several seconds he stared at his computer until he was certain she was gone. Then he racked his brain for what he'd done wrong since leaving Denver, but he came up empty. Everyone was entitled to an occasional bad day, especially someone who'd stay up half the night helping their mother in a hot kitchen. But if something else was happening behind the scenes, he needed to know. He really liked Elizabeth. He knew the dangers of falling for someone on the rebound, but that rule couldn't possibly count in this case.

His partner was as unlike his former fiancée as two women could possibly be.

THIRTY-SEVEN

*B*eth worked the kinks out of her neck and checked her watch. More than three hours had passed, and yet she was still on the outskirts of nowhere. Alice had remembered her husband talking about Spare the Children and its mission to stop human trafficking, while providing food, clothes, and medical care to the thousands of orphans around the globe. But if the charity had fallen from grace, her husband hadn't shared that information with her. Furthermore, Alice had never heard of D.K. Financials. Nor had she come across any correspondence from them while going through Paul's papers.

Natalie also had little to contribute. She promised to check every drawer in the pastor's desk, but any mail that appeared to be financial in nature would have been given to Ralph Buckley. Because he kept his files at home, only a search warrant could access them. And no judge on earth would give one of those to a PI. Beth's attempt to locate other churches affiliated with D.K. Financials was also an abysmal failure. It was time to admit defeat. It was also time to make amends with her partner.

Beth found Michael where she'd left him—bent over his computer in the back cubicle. "Hey, partner. I'm here to beg forgiveness for my chronic and compulsive rudeness."

Michael glanced over his shoulder. "Sounds like a new-age disease that requires years of expensive therapy."

"Either that or a strawberry banana split with extra whipped cream."

His smile was slow in coming but worth the wait. "I'm betting you hit a wall with your Google search, so you've come to offer an olive branch."

"You know me well."

Michael pulled off his glasses and rubbed the bridge of his nose. "Actually, I don't know you at all. You put up roadblocks at every corner."

"In that case I'll grant you three questions. Ask me anything and I will give you honest answers."

He leaned back in his chair. "Do you really prefer strawberry ice cream with bananas to hot fudge with toasted almonds?"

"Most definitely. That was your first question." Beth wiggled two fingers.

"What do you really think of my Charger SRT 392?"

She stared at the ceiling. "At first I thought it was extravagant and not worth the high cost of fuel, insurance, and possible speeding tickets. Then I changed my mind. Life is short, so why not drive something you like? Me, I'm saving twenty bucks a month for a Dooney and Bourke purse—a real one, not a knockoff." Beth lifted a third finger. "One to go, buster, so make it count."

"What did I do to annoy you? We got along fine in Denver. Now there's a wall around you a mile high."

"Why, because I didn't want pancakes first thing this morning? Am I not allowed to be in a bad mood? Why would this have anything to do with you?"

Michael crossed his arms. "You just asked three questions before giving me my final straight answer."

"Some questions are tougher than others," she said after a tense few moments. "Why are you pushing this?"

"Because I spent the last two years with my head in the sand. Everyone around me saw the breakup coming. Everyone but me."

Beth waved her hands through the air like an irate basketball referee. "You and I are work partners. This is nothing like you and what's-her-name."

"Rachel. Her name is Rachel. And I know that. But even my friends never clued me in that I was a fool."

"You can't be sure. Maybe your friends didn't want to make trouble based on speculation."

Michael shrugged. "Regardless, I want people in my life who'll let me know when I have broccoli in my teeth, or my jokes aren't funny, or that I'm not giving them enough space. Otherwise, I might as well get a dog from the pound."

"First the car, now a dog? You're putting roots down in Natchez."

"Maybe, we'll see. Or maybe I'll move to Hollywood and become a rock star. Talk, Kirby. Is my know-it-all personality getting on your nerves?"

"Nope. A true know-it-all wouldn't ask that. It's something stupid my mother said." Beth averted her gaze, hoping the answer was written on the ceiling. "I had fun in Denver too and came home with the idea we could be good friends. We have the same sense of humor."

"So what did Rita say to change that? I thought she liked me."

"She does like you, but she thinks it's impossible for men and women to be just friends." Beth let a few moments spin out. "One of them will develop feelings the other doesn't share."

"Sounds like she bases her conclusion on your relationship with Chief McNeil."

Beth didn't like where this was headed, but she couldn't turn back now. "Maybe, and judging by my past history, she could be right. I read too much into the chief's attention."

"He probably didn't try very hard to discourage you."

"Whatever," she said, rolling her eyes. "How do we know I won't develop a mad crush on you?"

Michael threw his head back and laughed. "That would have already happened by now. I know you don't fall asleep thinking about me."

"I dream solely about all-you-can-eat dessert buffets."

"As for me, I enjoy your company and have nothing but respect for you."

"Sounds like how I'd describe my Aunt Colette."

"I describe you like a partner and hopefully a lifetime friend, even if I end up in Hollywood."

"That's the best offer I've had in a long time." Beth felt herself relax.

"We create our own future. You and I don't have to fall into any pigeonhole your mom or anyone else creates. Let's just be honest with each other. Then we won't go too far off track."

"I gave a few pointers in the gym and on the firing range, and you teach me a new paradigm about relationships. Who knew you had this inside you?"

"Sometimes I surprise even myself." Michael turned his attention back to his computer.

Beth pushed papers aside to perch on his desk. "One more thing…could you help me find the names of other churches that might have been defrauded? None of my search engines turned up even an irate blogger."

Michael reached for a piece of paper in the printer tray. "One step ahead of you. These are clients who contributed to Elliott Rayburn's charity from Mississippi and the adjacent states."

Beth grabbed the sheet to peruse. "How on earth did you get this? Did you hack into their database? Is that legal?"

"Probably not, but we won't be submitting these names in any court of law. If those on the right side of the law don't use the same tactics as criminals, we don't stand a chance against cybercrime. This is a new world. The days of Pretty Boy Floyd sticking up a bank in Oklahoma are over. All it takes now is a geek with a poorly developed ethical code and high-speed Internet."

"Ah, you paid attention in PI school. The Fourth and Fifth Amendments protect citizens from the government, but not from one another. Private police, if not deputized, are just citizens and can legally do things public police cannot." Beth pushed up to stand. "Thanks. I'll start checking these right now. In return I'll buy you a sundae after work."

"Any kind I want?"

"Yep, and price is no object."

"Let's go now and have ice cream for a late lunch. You can check into those churches later." Michael rose to his feet.

"What about your Iron Man competition? Aren't you on a protein and plain vegetable diet?"

"I'm so far ahead of the competition I can afford one high-fat meal." He flexed a bicep. "Wrap your hand around that if there's any doubt."

"I'll take your word for it." But as she stepped past him, she punched him squarely in the solar plexus. "Wow, hard as a rock. You have been taking the workouts seriously. Good thing I'm still a better shot." Beth grabbed her purse on her way down the hall.

Gentlemanly as ever, Michael opened the door for her. "Soon none of the females will be able to kick sand in my face."

Beth doubted any could now and knew for a fact this one didn't want to. A friend like Michael Preston was worth a barrelful of boyfriends any day.

THIRTY-EIGHT

*M*ichael ordered a three-scoop chocolate sundae topped with sugared pecans and whipped cream. His trainer would have a heart attack just looking at the extravaganza. Beth ordered a banana split with two scoops of strawberry ice cream and extra whipped cream. She passed on the nuts. Seated at a metal table fashioned to look like something from the 1950s, they devoured lunch with zeal never shown romaine lettuce and grated carrots.

After five minutes, Beth pushed her bowl across the table. "Wanna try mine?"

Michael paused, his spoon midway to his mouth, and swapped bowls. "Sure, as long as you eat some of this." Rachel had hated it whenever someone wanted to sample her food. She refused to give up as much as a French fry even though more than half her meals went uneaten.

"It's good, but it's still no match for strawberry," Beth concluded after a three-bite sample. "Tell me what's on your mind. I think you had another reason to leave the office."

"I want to talk to Buckley this afternoon. According to Mrs. Purdy, he's supposedly collecting files from his home to return to the church. Apparently, the board wasn't happy about his short-term loan. Let's make sure he doesn't destroy evidence before I can turn over what I found to the police."

"I just went to see Natalie and yet you know this?" Beth switched the two desserts.

"Mrs. Purdy called me as soon as you left. She doesn't trust you, but there's no accounting for taste, Elizabeth."

"Okay, how do we prevent Ralph from destroying evidence?"

"I have a few tricks up my sleeve. Sit back and trust me."

"I suggest we finish up and get a move on. You're all full of surprises today."

Forty minutes later they pulled into the Buckley driveway. "That Pontiac is registered to Ralph, so I believe we're in luck," said Michael, turning off the powerful engine.

"Real luck will be in not dealing with his obnoxious daughter," Beth muttered as they approached the front door.

Their knock was answered by none other than the crooked financial director. "What on earth could you two want?" he snapped. "Haven't you made enough trouble for me? I've been fired from the church staff and must appear in court for nothing more than a big misunderstanding."

"None of that was our intention," said Beth, in a tone which couldn't get any sweeter. "Could we come in and talk about this for a few minutes?"

"No, you cannot come in." His emphasis left little doubt. "Why would I let you in to nose into my business?"

Michael decided it was his turn at bat. "Because we're probably the only ones who can help you right now, Mr. Buckley. Once the FBI's Financial Crimes Division becomes involved, the case will be out of our hands."

Buckley paled to the color of skim milk. "What are you talking about? I've done nothing that could be considered a federal crime. My attorney assured me everything can be straightened out with restitution and probation *if* this mess even advances that far. I'm cooperating with the board of elders' request to turn over my files."

"Would those financial files include statements you received from the accountants hired by Elliott Rayburn?"

Buckley seemed to shrink before their eyes. "What are you talking about?"

"Don't waste our time with lies. We have copies of the last three quarterly statements you received from D.K. Financials of Jackson. Although they're nothing but smoke and mirrors to buy Spare the Children time to scam more congregations, they prove one thing. You were in on it with them. Despite Reverend Dean's request to be kept in the loop, D.K. Financials sent their statements to you."

Buckley tried to slam the door, but Michael was too quick. Shoving his boot heel next to the jamb, he grabbed hold of the door. "What's your hurry, Ralph?"

"You're not cops. I don't have to talk to two PIs hired by that snooty Alice Dean. Just because she comes from money, she thinks she can—"

Michael didn't like Buckley's harsh words against a widow who only wanted justice for her dead husband. He threw his shoulder against the door and shoved it open.

Buckley staggered backward, while Michael and Beth practically fell into his living room. "You've got no search warrant and no right to push your way in. I'm calling the cops." With a shaking hand, Buckley pulled a phone from his pocket.

"By all means, Ralph, call Detective Lejeune. It'll save him the trip back to the station once he's done at the DA's office." Michael inched forward until he loomed over the smaller man.

Beth pulled on his shirtsleeve. "Maybe we should wait on the porch until Detective Lejeune arrives with that arrest warrant."

"Why should we stand in the hot sun when I distinctly heard Mr. Buckley invite us in?" Feeling more confident by the minute, Michael thumped an index finger against Buckley's chest. "We'll stay right here while Mr. Buckley gathers the financial records for Calvary Baptist. And while you're at it, why not print a copy of the payment you received for handing Reverend Dean on a platter to Elliott Rayburn?"

"How could you have found out about that?" sputtered Buckley as he staggered back into a hall tree. "If Paul had butted out his nose, the church would have gotten their investment back with interest. He knew the time frame involved. If he would've left well enough alone, he'd still be alive."

Michael looked at him with contempt. "How much did they pay you?"

"Not enough to end up dead like Paul. You'd better watch your step, Preston. You too, Beth. You don't know how dangerous these people are."

With his protective instincts kicking in, Michael stepped in front of his partner. "Are you threatening us?"

"It's not me you need to worry about!" Buckley screamed without concern as to who overheard. "I didn't kill Paul, but you're right—somebody did." He pivoted on his heel and strode down the hall. "Sit, stand, search my cupboards for all I care. I'm not sticking around until somebody makes sure I suffer a fatal *accident*."

Michael started after him, but a tight grip on his arm slowed him down.

"Where are you going?" Beth hissed in his ear.

"To his office. Buckley invited us in and said we could snoop all we want. Let's see what else he has in his filing cabinet."

"Come outside right now. Don't make me pull a gun on you." Beth didn't sound like the sweet woman who shared her strawberry sundae with him.

Once they reached the front porch, Beth grabbed his shirt with both hands. "What were you talking about? Jack isn't getting a search warrant. He doesn't know about the connection between Buckley and Rayburn. Sounds like the DA offered Buckley a plea deal and he plans to take it. Do you have proof Buckley took some kind of kickback?"

"Easy, partner." Michael pried her fingers off his newest wardrobe addition. "No, I was bluffing. I had my suspicions and the ploy worked."

"To what end?" Beth stomped her foot. "Once again you tipped our hand. All Buckley needs to do is deny taking payola. Then the burden will be on you to find proof of conspiracy—the proof he's probably shredding right now. We should have updated Jack before you broke down Ralph's door." Grabbing his hand, Beth dragged him down the walkway like a five-year-old.

"He's scared, Elizabeth, but I doubt Buckley is so desperate he'll destroy evidence—"

"He's scared all right, and you should be worried as to why."

"Rayburn didn't look like a cold-blooded murderer. He wouldn't want to wrinkle his suit."

"Considering the church invested half a million dollars, Rayburn could afford to pay someone to do the dirty work. Hitmen out in the sticks work for a couple thousand."

"How do you know that?" Michael pulled free from her grasp.

"Don't ask." When they reached his Charger, Beth held out her palm. "Give me your keys," she demanded.

"You want to drive my car? This ain't no four-cylinder Chevy, little missy. This is a man's car." Michael held out his fists like a sleight-of-hand game in a carnival. "Choose correctly and I'll let you drive."

Beth's face looked like it might ignite. "Give me those keys this instant!"

"Fine. I was merely concerned for your safety." He opened the hand containing the keys.

Beth snatched the ring, unlocked the driver's door, and then hesitated. "On second thought, I'll walk back to the office. Checking the other names on D.K. Financial's list can wait till later." She tossed him the keys. "You get to drive the man's car after all."

"You can't be serious. Walking will take at least half an hour."

"Exactly. I'll need that much time to figure out what to say to Nate. We need to explain this without sounding like you messed up. In the meantime, call Jack with a full update of what you found out. You probably have his number on speed dial." Her face scrunched into a scowl.

"I already see the error of my ways. Ride back with me, Beth, and we'll call Lejeune along the way." Michael opened the passenger door.

Beth shook her head like a stubborn mule. "No, for two reasons. One, you'll do better talking to Jack alone. That man doesn't like me. And two, by the time I call the boss and he asks, 'Did you inform Natchez PD of what you discovered about D.K. Financials and Ralph Buckley's involvement,' I don't want to be lying when I say yes. Knowing Nate, he will ask."

Michael climbed into his low-slung car and lowered the window. "As usual, you're right. I guess I still have more to learn."

Beth's expression softened. "The thin line that a private detective must walk with law enforcement takes time to master. Don't beat yourself up for getting excited. I'll see you in thirty minutes." Beth marched off at a pace a notch slower than a jog.

Michael appreciated her foresight. If it was the last thing he did, he would prove himself worthy of her faith in him. *Might as well get this uncomfortable phone call over with.* He punched in number seven on speed dial and switched to hands-free communication. By the time his Charger passed Beth power walking down the street, Detective Lejeune answered the call.

His gruff, "What's up, Dick Tracy?" didn't bode well for the rest of Michael's afternoon.

THIRTY-NINE

*M*ichael paced the floor of Price Investigations until Maxine issued a loud sigh.

"I cannot work with you wearing a groove in the floor tile. I'm going on break. You want anything to drink?"

"No thanks, Miss Maxine. Not unless they sell hemlock juice." Alone in the office, Michael tried to figure out why he'd approached Buckley without inviting the police to the party. Unfortunately, he still had no logical explanation when Lejeune squealed to a stop in the back lot.

When that man says, "I'll be right there," he's not using a figure of speech.

Michael swept open the door the exact moment Lejeune reached the top step. "I hope no one set up radar between the police department and Price Investigations." He offered a friendly smile.

"Cut the jokes, Preston, and spill what you found out about Buckley." Lejeune stomped inside and glanced around. "Where's your mentor, Miss Ne'er-Do-Well?"

"Miss Kirby will be here soon. I found the evidence, so I can fill you in." Michael wanted to make sure Beth took no blame for his overzealousness.

Lejeune leaned his bulk against a filing cabinet. "That's what I'm here for."

"Our assistant will be back shortly, so why don't we talk in my office?" Michael picked up the folder from Maxine's desk that he'd put there five minutes ago.

"Lead the way."

Halfway down the hall Michael decided against his claustrophobic cubicle. "Actually, we might be more comfortable in here. Please have a seat." He waved him into Nate's office.

Lejeune did as instructed without taking his eyes off Michael. "Are you going to give me that file or not?"

"Yes, but I want to provide some background first." Michael sat in Nate's upholstered chair. "Since our last update, I visited the Denver charity where Reverend Dean invested the church building fund." He omitted Beth's name to keep any hostility aimed at him. "The pastor hadn't spent the money like we'd originally assumed. He was trying to do a good deed until they broke ground for the new school. I've been unable to determine whether this charity is a legitimate nonprofit."

Lejeune crossed and uncrossed his legs but didn't interrupt.

"As I examined the days leading up to Reverend Dean's death, I discovered his requests for investment progress had been ignored. Recently, I found out the charity issued statements, but whether or not they're accurate remains to be seen."

Lejeune exhaled a breath. "Yeah, I got the picture, Sherlock. Move along."

Michael ignored the insult. "The quarterly statements were sent to Ralph Buckley from an accounting firm in Jackson, D.K. Financials, which handled Mississippi and three other states. I believe Buckley received a commission for lining up Reverend Dean and Calvary Baptist Church. When I confronted Buckley today, he didn't deny the allegation. In fact, he became highly agitated. Here are the bogus statements and copies of emails between Buckley and D.K. Financials, and between Spare the Children International and Reverend Dean. Buckley's bank account should show a deposit from Elliott Rayburn or some officer at the Denver charity."

Michael handed Lejeune the folder. "I've done a preliminary background check on D.K. Financials. All that seems to exist are a post office box, a fancy website less than a year old, an email address, and an answering machine. Inside the file is proof Buckley was part of a scam to defraud the church. He made sure Reverend Dean was left holding the proverbial bag."

"Oh, is *that* what you believe?" Lejeune sputtered out the question. "A charity scam that involves churches in four different states?"

"This could stretch across the globe, Detective. According to their executive director, Spare the Children raises money all over the world."

"Across the globe?" Lejeune slammed the folder down on Nate's desk, his eyes bulging. "Yet you thought it savvy to march up to Buckley's front door and gloat, '*Nah-nah-nah*, I caught you now, you bad, bad boy.'"

Michael expected a reprimand for his hastiness, but he hadn't expected humiliation. He bit the inside of his mouth to control his temper.

"Because you're new at this, Preston, I'll spell it out for you. After you found proof, as you described it, your *sole* responsibility was to notify law enforcement. That would be me. You're not a sworn officer of the law, and thus you acted without authority. What's more, this case is no longer the jurisdiction of the Natchez PD. I'll have to turn your so-called evidence over to the FBI office in Jackson. All this was spelled out to your partner by Chief McNeil before you two went gallivanting off to Denver." Lejeune waited for his reaction before continuing. "Yeah, I know Beth Kirby went with you. Did you two have fun in the mile-high city?"

"I don't appreciate your insinuations, Detective," Michael said, tightening his grip on the arm of his chair.

"No? Well, I don't appreciate you tipping off Buckley. By the time I present this *evidence* to the feds, that crooked conman could be long gone. We could have saved the American taxpayers plenty if Buckley believed he got away with a slap on the hand. Now he's probably on his way to Nebraska with a new identity." Lejeune rose to his feet and tucked the file under his arm. "Great work, Preston."

Michael walked him to the door, grateful Maxine hadn't witnessed his scolding. Unfortunately, Beth reached the end of her half-hour walk at an inopportune moment. She ran up the steps and paused, breathless and wide-eyed.

"Well, look what the cat dragged in," Lejeune drawled.

"Leaving so soon, Jack?" Beth cooed. "I was just about to put the kettle on for tea." She lifted the damp hair off her neck.

"You're a real piece of work, Kirby. You were supposed to be training this guy, not setting him up to take a fall. Chief McNeil spelled it out crystal clear that anything you discovered on your fact-finding mission was to go to me. Yet you didn't call and you didn't write." He glared down his nose at her. "You're off jogging on company time while your protégé tips off Buckley."

"Miss Kirby was there but had no idea what I had planned. Once she realized, she tried to stop me." Michael wedged himself between the two adversaries.

"Yeah, then she should've tried harder." Lejeune pushed past him down the stairs. "If Buckley's in the wind, this is on you, Kirby."

Michael opened his mouth, but Beth held up a hand. "Stop. Don't say another word. Let him blame me. It's better if he doesn't hate both of us." She backed him into the office as Maxine arrived from the alley entrance.

"What did I miss? You two look like a battle was fought and lost."

"Your analogy isn't far from the truth." Beth dropped into one of the visitor chairs.

Michael pulled the second chair closer. "This is my fault, and I apologize."

"What did you do, Michael?" Maxine loomed over him like a brooding hen.

Ignoring her, Beth responded to him. "Lejeune is right. I should have explained word-for-word what Chris said and left nothing to chance. You're still in training."

"What does Chief McNeil have to do with this?" Maxine whispered next to Michael's ear.

"Nothing, Miss Maxine. I acted on impulse without thinking. Now Beth caught Detective Lejeune's wrath instead of me."

Beth scraped her hands down her face. "Nate put me in charge, so the responsibility was mine. Jack has every right to be mad."

"Are you okay, sweetie?" Maxine pressed the back of her hand to Beth's forehead. "You might be coming down with a bug."

Beth smiled at the older woman. "I'm fine, thanks, but I think I'll head to my cubicle and update my résumé."

"No way," said Michael. "If anybody loses their job over this, it should be me."

"Both of you get a grip," said Maxine. "When our fearless leader returns from his honeymoon, he'll be in such a good mood he'll overlook anything but capital murder. Which reminds me, did you talk to Nate during your walk from Buckley's?" she asked Beth. "And why did you make her walk?" Maxine asked him. "Did she drip ice cream on your new upholstery?"

Michael answered first. "No, ma'am. Beth walked to get her quota of Fitbit steps."

Beth smiled at his answer. "Nah, I didn't want to talk to Nate until Michael smoothed things over with Jack." Suddenly, the ping of her cell phone was accompanied by the whir of the fax machine.

"Anyone want to bet those two communications are related?" Maxine hurried to retrieve the fax.

"It's probably a text from Nate, along with a faxed resignation for me to sign and return before I leave the office." Beth pulled her phone from her pocket and tapped on the screen.

"What is it?" demanded Michael and Maxine after several moments of silence.

"It's an email from the state medical examiner. The second autopsy has been completed." Beth read certain key phrases aloud. "Neck bruising has been ruled inconsistent with self-inflicted death. What's more, traces of ketamine have been found in the toxicology screen of the victim's blood. Paul Dean was drugged at the time of his death, yet no drugs were found on his person or in the vicinity of the body." Beth sucked in a breath before continuing. "Dr. Pallota's original conclusion of death-by-suicide has been overturned. Paul Dean's death has been reclassified as a homicide. Appropriate law enforcement personnel have been sent copies of new autopsy results including toxicology report. They have been instructed to submit all physical evidence taken from the scene to the state crime lab for further examination. Duplicate copies have been faxed to the office of Price Investigations, in care of Elizabeth Kirby, representing Alice Dean, widow of the deceased. Respectfully submitted, Dr. Anna Diab, Hinds County, Mississippi." When she reached the end of the email, Beth shoved her phone in her pocket and looked at her fellow employees. "Anybody have something to say?"

Maxine wrung her hands, her earlier exuberance gone. "I would say hooray, but how can we cheer the idea of Reverend Dean being murdered?"

"I would say Mrs. Dean was right all along," murmured Michael. "Now you and I will bring a murderer to justice."

Beth met his eye with an unreadable expression.

Maxine pulled the faxed transmission from the tray. "These will point you in the right direction."

Beth shook her head. "Why don't you study them first, Mike? I need a few moments alone." She staggered to her cubicle.

Michael took the reports from Maxine. He longed to follow her down the hall but had to respect her wishes. Once again, he'd forgotten that his partner and the reverend had been close. It was bad enough to think someone you respected took their own life, but it was even worse to think your friend had been murdered in cold blood.

FORTY

*B*eth closed the flimsy partition separating the back cubicles and laid her head down on her desk. For several minutes she let every memory of Paul and Alice Dean, along with their daughter, run through her mind like an old home movie. She'd never seen the pastor in anything but a good mood. How often he stayed after services to chat with old ladies, rebellious teenagers, or postpartum new mothers. Patient, thoughtful, kind—that was Reverend Dean. Yet somebody strung him up in a cobwebby shed with no more compassion than they would have for a side of beef. Beth let her tears fall until they pooled on the metal desktop. Then she slipped down the hallway and out the back door before Michael or Maxine could ask another question.

How could this case get so messed up?

Despite the fact that she wore slacks and loafers, Beth broke into a run. She didn't stop until she doubled over with a side stitch and her feet hurt. Then she turned around and walked slowly back, inhaling deep, yoga-style breaths with every step. Unlocking the alley door with her key, Beth returned to her cubicle far more centered than when she left. She knew what she had to do. Nate needed to be updated on the case. He was the one paying their salaries and expected to be kept in the loop. On her desk lay a copy of Paul's second autopsy. Helpless to stop herself, Beth picked it up and began to read. For fifteen minutes she was oblivious to ringing phones, traffic noise on the street, and the emptiness in her gut. She soaked up the terminology with morbid fascination, silently pronouncing medical terms as though she'd be quizzed tomorrow.

"Beth!" Maxine's voice finally pierced her shell.

"Yes?" She dropped the final sheet atop the others.

"Didn't you hear me yelling? Nate has been trying to reach you. He said your phone goes straight to voice mail. You'd better call him back right now. He didn't sound happy."

Michael squeezed next to Maxine in the doorway. "Want me to talk to him first? If Nate's mad, it's because of what I did."

Beth tapped the ME's reports into a neat pile. "No, just sit there while I call." She pointed at a box of old files that needed to be stored. "Thanks, Maxine."

When the assistant had ambled back to her desk, Beth punched Nate's number into her phone. He answered on the first ring—a bad sign if there ever was one. "Hi, Nate. How's life on the Gulf of Mexico?"

"Peachy. How are things going upstate?" The tone of Nate's voice confirmed Maxine's assessment of his mood.

"I take it you heard from Jack?"

"Oh, no. It's much worse than that. I heard from Chris McNeil. The chief took time from his busy day to call because the people I left in charge don't seem to understand chain of command."

Beth contemplated putting the conversation on speaker, but inside the tiny cubicle there was no need. Michael could hear every word. "I can explain everything. I think Chris overreacted because Jack got him fired up—"

"McNeil didn't overreact, Beth. He was calm, cool, and confused as to what went wrong. He said you told him about the trip to Denver when you came to his office and that he made it clear you were only to gather facts, evidence which could be presented to the DA if there are criminal charges down the road. You indicated you understood the limitations of a private investigator in a potential police matter." Nate spoke slowly without raising his voice, yet the tension between them spanned hundreds of miles.

Michael leaped to his feet and tried to wrestle the phone from her hand. "Could you hold on one moment?" Beth elbowed her partner in the ribs with little reaction.

"No, actually I can't. Isabelle and I are in the middle of something right now. I trust you'll talk to Chief McNeil and Detective Lejeune and get this straightened out."

"Since it's getting late, I'll call them first thing Monday morning. Tell Isabelle I said—"

"No, Beth. You and Mike will go to the Natchez PD right now. I don't care if you sit there all night, but you'll face the music in person. I'll be back in touch soon." Nate hung up without mentioning the weather or asking for an update on the case.

Beth locked eyes with her partner. "He hung up before I could tell him about the autopsy results."

Michael stuck his hands in his pockets. "Sounds like he and his wife are busy. Why don't we wait a few hours and then send him a text? I can scan the new report and send it as an attachment."

"Good idea about sending a text, but we'll hold off on the report unless Nate asks for it. He might not want it floating through the ethers."

"So you and I are off to see the Wizard?" Michael backed out of her cramped cubicle. "Too bad you're not wearing ruby slippers."

Beth managed a weak smile. Facing Chris in front of Michael was worse than flying monkeys clawing her back. She really liked her new partner and would prefer not groveling at the feet of her old boss. "We might as well get this over with. Let's make extra copies of Reverend Dean's autopsy just in case."

At least when they reached the police station, Sergeant Mendez didn't complain about them not having an appointment or put them through a preliminary interrogation. "The chief has been expecting you, Miss Kirby. Best not to keep him waiting," Mendez said with a smug grin.

"Let me do the talking," Michael whispered in her ear. "I won't let you take the fall for this."

"No way. Nate put me in charge of the Dean case, so the responsibility rests squarely with me."

"I acted without consulting you first. That's what I need to—"

If the hallway to his office had been longer, they might have been able to finish the argument. But because Natchez had a small police station, and Chief McNeil was standing in his doorway, Michael's final words hung in the air. "Should I catch up with email while you two decide upon an explanation?" he asked, his gaze drifting over them like a cold breeze.

"No. We're ready." Beth walked in as though approaching the gallows. "Chris, I would like to apologize on behalf of Price Investigations. It was my job to see that our new agent understood procedures, and I left too much at his discretion."

"Miss Kirby had no way of knowing what I had planned. I take full responsibility." Michael gripped the back of a leather chair.

"Stop and sit down, both of you." Chris pointed at two chairs. "I understand it was a lack of communication without intention to interfere with a police investigation and that it won't happen again. However, rest assured that if it does happen again, Detective Lejeune will bring charges against one or both of you. Charges that I will be unable and unwilling to circumvent."

They both nodded agreement.

"Make sure Detective Lejeune has everything you collected on this scam charity, even if you're unsure of its importance. It will be the FBI's call whether evidence is pertinent or not."

"I understand, sir," said Michael.

"And, Beth, I strongly suggest you stay out of Jack's way. Do the job Alice is paying for in regards to clearing her husband's name of financial misfeasance. If the building fund of Calvary Baptist has been absconded by a fake charity, the Financial Crimes Division will do everything in their power to recover the money."

Beth and Michael exchanged a glance. "I'm afraid we have bigger problems than just missing money. An hour ago I received word from the Mississippi medical examiner. Dr. Diab finished the second autopsy along with a full tox screen. Paul's official cause of death has been changed to homicide. I thought you would have heard by now." Beth's clothes suddenly felt one size too small.

Chris's face registered a flicker of displeasure. "That report would have gone straight to Detective Lejeune, despite the fact a private party requested the second autopsy. I trust you indicated that he was the lead investigator on the criminal case on all paperwork you submitted to Jackson?" His focus landed right between Beth's eyebrows.

"Of course I did. Besides, the ME's office knows who works in Homicide in Adams County."

"Then I'm sure Jack has already received the report. I'll take a look at it when he comes back to the office."

"In that case, we shouldn't take up more of your time." Beth stood, eager to be away from the man she'd wanted to spend her life with. "Rest assured we won't step over the line in the Dean case again."

"There's one more thing, Beth...and you may not want Mr. Preston to hear it." Chris bobbed his head at Michael.

"I can't keep secrets from my partner, not if I want him to learn the good, the bad, and the ugly of PI work."

"Suit yourself. Just make sure you dot every *i* with my new head of Homicide. Jack doesn't like you, Beth. That's obvious. You probably think it's because you were promoted first." Chris shifted his weight in the chair as though uncomfortable. "But the truth is that Jack had a crush on you a long time ago. Everyone knew it but you. When you focused your attention...elsewhere, he took it personally. I can only offer some friendly advice—stay out of his way."

"Thanks. That's what I intend to do." Expecting the riot act, part two, Beth felt blindsided by Chris's warning. She hurried out of his office as though someone pulled the fire alarm at Morgantown Elementary. "Sorry. I guess you didn't need to hear that," she said to Michael once they were outside the municipal building.

He had wasted no time with polite fare-thee-well's either. "Any clue how many times you apologized today?"

"I don't know...nine or ten?"

"I believe forty-two, more than the sum total of your adult life."

Beth burst out laughing. "For a second there I thought you had actually counted. Oh, man, take me away from this town—someplace warm, maybe on the water. Definitely where I haven't made a fool of myself yet."

"How about the DQ south of town? They have great chili dogs and a partial view of a retention pond."

"Perfect. Nobody knows me at that one. Full speed ahead, Scotty."

As soon as they buckled up, Michael peeled out of the parking lot. "I doubt they can catch us in this car. Watch how much better you'll feel after chili dogs with a soft-serve chaser."

"I feel better already." Beth leaned back and closed her eyes, marveling at how the world improved with each passing mile.

FORTY-ONE

*T*hat evening, Beth entered a kitchen smelling like chicory coffee and fresh-baked dessert. It was a welcome change from the usual odor of fried catfish or boiled cabbage and onions. "Is that apple pie I smell?" she asked, letting the screen door slam behind her.

Her mother turned from a sink full of soapy dishes with a cheery smile. "Yep. I baked three this afternoon. How 'bout I cut you a slice?"

"We have French vanilla ice cream too," added Pops, his callused fingers wrapped around a coffee mug. With his bib overalls and plaid shirt, her father brought to mind the famous *American Gothic* painting, minus the pitchfork.

"I'll wait and have my pie for breakfast." Beth slipped into the chair next to her dad. "I just devoured two chili dogs along with a strawberry milkshake."

"Should I get you the Mylanta or a stomach pump?" asked her mother.

"Neither, actually. I feel fine. When Michael falls off the health food wagon, he doesn't mess around. He opted for a three-pack of chili and onion dogs."

Rita carried two mugs to the table. "Your new partner seems to be working out."

"He still has more to learn, but we're getting along." Beth reached for the coffee. "I'm not sure where I'll put this, but it smells wonderful."

"You think Nate might keep you in Natchez once this case is finished?" Rita studied her daughter over her mug.

The case. For a brief moment, Beth thought about confiding in her parents that Alice had been right, but she came to her senses. Her mother would have that tidbit spread across the county by tomorrow, which would hardly be professional discretion. Besides, she had fixated on the case enough for one day. She longed for mindless chatter followed by an hour of television reruns and then dreamless sleep.

When Beth glanced up, her parents were still waiting for an answer. "He might. It all depends on who hires our agency next. Lately, Natchez hasn't been a hotbed of wayward spouses, runaway teenagers, or shady business dealings."

"Thank goodness." Rita popped Stan's neglected crust into her mouth.

"That's good for our Christian souls, but bad for the PI business." Beth eyed the pie. A thin slice seemed to be calling her name. Despite being full, she knew how seldom her mother baked and how spectacular her pies were. Suddenly, the crunch of gravel and a flash of headlights provided timely distraction.

"Who could that be at this hour?" Clucking her tongue with disapproval, Rita directed the question at no one in particular.

"I'll go see. The longer I smell that pie, the tighter my waistband gets." Beth scrambled to her feet. The visitor was probably Michael making sure things were copacetic. His mistake with Buckley was her fault. She should have told him about her conversation with the chief and spelled out PI limitations.

Unfortunately, the car that stopped inches from her mother's prized rosebushes wasn't a shiny new Charger. Jack climbed from his county-issued sedan with the friendliness of a bear awoken midway through winter hibernation.

"You're really a piece of work, Kirby!" he snarled as she stepped onto the porch. He shrugged into his sport coat to cover his shoulder holster.

"Good evening, Jack. Did you hear through the grapevine that my mother baked her famous Dutch apple pies? I believe there's a piece inside with your name on it." Beth closed the distance so their conversation wouldn't be under the kitchen window. There was a time when she'd thought him nice looking, although his attitude was never her style. Tonight he looked like a lion bearing down on an antelope.

Lejeune slicked a hand through his hair, the whites of his eyes sharp against his suntan. "*Have a slice of pie?*" He mimicked her inflection. "You can't possibly be this stupid."

Beth refused to let him rile her. "To either confirm or deny, I need to know what you're talking about."

"Can you explain why I had to hear from a Vicksburg detective that Reverend Dean's death was ruled a homicide?"

Beth stared at him without blinking. "Someone from Vicksburg called you with the ME's decision?"

"No, Kirby. Detective Russell asked why *she* was sent the new autopsy and the request for physical evidence instead of me. Paul Dean died in Adams County, not in Warren. I looked like a fool. When I called my chief, he said he'd been hand-delivered a copy. Of course, you would use any reason to visit your boyfriend." His face was contorted with rage.

Beth ignored his juvenile terminology and concentrated on something more important. "You didn't get an email from the ME, along with a faxed copy of her report?"

A muscle in his jaw twitched. "Don't play games with me, Kirby. Nobody sent the report because you failed to list me as the lead detective on the case. You are so—"

"No!" Beth interrupted, her voice rising. "I put down your name and the fax number for the Natchez PD. It should have been sent to your attention. I have no idea why it went to Detective Russell in Vicksburg!"

"I'll tell you what happened." Jack jabbed his index finger precariously close to her chest. "You…are…incompetent. Always have been, always will be."

Rankled by his unfair description, she slapped away his finger. "I'm telling you it was some kind of snafu at the ME's office. Your name was listed along with mine on Alice's request for a second autopsy. Chris only received a copy because Nate ordered Michael and me to apologize for our misstep." She refused to let Michael take the blame just to mitigate the present situation.

"Sounds like your new boss isn't any more thrilled with your performance than your old boss." His grin contained more malevolence than humor. "Know something, Kirby? I don't believe a word you say. I'm giving you one last warning to stay away from my case."

"I have a right to do the job I'm being paid for," she snapped, losing patience.

"Sure," he drawled, "just so you remember you're no longer a detective. You're not even on the force. And if I find proof that this was no *clerical error* at the ME's office, I'll have you arrested for interfering with a police investigation. We'll see how a Class B misdemeanor looks on your résumé when Price fires you." He stomped back to his car and peeled down the driveway, sending gravel in all directions.

Beth walked back through the kitchen door feeling as though she'd been kicked in the gut. One look at her parents told her they had heard every word of the conversation.

"Your piece of pie is in the blue Tupperware, ready to heat for your breakfast." Her mother wrung her hands, while her dad squeezed her elbow as she walked past.

"Get some sleep, daughter," he said. "The world will look a little rosier tomorrow."

"Don't worry about me. That was just Jack overreacting, same as usual. Good night."

Seeing the pain on their faces hurt worse than Lejeune's unfair conclusion. Just once before she died, Beth wanted to make her parents proud. Inside her bedroom, the last thing on her mind was sleep. Beth had never seen Jack so angry. If she'd been a man, she would probably be nursing a bloody nose or picking herself up from the sidewalk. She considered calling Chris or Nate, but she dismissed the notion. The truth about the mix-up at the ME's office would eventually come out. Until it did, any action on her part would seem like rationalizing or groveling or asking someone else to fight her battles. Not one of which would help her career.

After several minutes of self-pity, she punched in the number of her only friend in town.

FORTY-TWO

*M*ichael had just completed his evening workout and stepped into the shower when his phone rang. It was probably his mother since he hadn't called her in two weeks. Or maybe it was Nate, making sure he understood the error of his ways with Buckley. Preferring to hit the sack without a sour taste in his mouth, Michael decided to let voice mail pick up. But at the last moment, he reached for his phone. He was glad he did when he saw that his partner was calling.

"Hi, Mike. It's Beth. I hope I'm not interrupting anything."

"Nothing that can't wait, as long as you don't start whining about heartburn. You made your choice regarding the chili dogs." Michael shut off the water and shrugged into a bathrobe.

"My indigestion has nothing to do with food." Her tone was oddly subdued.

"Did Nate call back and blame you for my actions? Because I won't let—"

"No, I haven't heard from him or Chris since we left his office."

"Tell me what's on your mind."

She hesitated. "Promise me you won't do anything hasty. I...I don't want you to try to fix this. I just want to talk and you to listen."

"My weapon is locked in my trunk, and I'm too tired to throttle anyone with my bare hands. So you have my word." Michael muted the television.

After another brief hesitation, Beth described the unfortunate misunderstanding that her former partner was blowing out of proportion. By the time she finished, Michael wasn't sure if Lejeune was a power-hungry cop desperate for recognition, or an insecure male, unable to deal with the woman who had spurned his affections. Or maybe a combination of the two. Considering his track record with relationships, he was treading on unfamiliar ground.

Michael listened patiently without interrupting, but when he heard crying on the other end, his protective instincts kicked in. "Tell me what I can do to help. Would you like me to talk to Lejeune?"

"No, I appreciate the offer, but it won't help until Jack calms down. Tomorrow morning I'll call the ME's office and find out what happened. That report should have gone to Natchez Homicide. I sure hope my contacts in Vicksburg didn't confuse the issue when I asked them to speed things up in Jackson."

"Don't take the blame, Beth. It could have been an honest mistake."

"Or someone resented a PI's involvement in the case. Perhaps someone wanted to tweak Jack's nose," Beth said, sniffling.

"You're probably not the only one to run afoul of Lejeune in Mississippi."

"Maybe the truth will come out, or maybe we'll never know. But tonight I needed to vent and didn't know who else to call."

In the silent room Michael heard his heart thump against his ribs, reminding him how important their friendship was. But never in a million years could he admit that. "How about if I shoot the guy in the leg? I could say I was cleaning my gun in his front yard when the crazy thing went off. Plenty of people will testify to the likelihood."

Beth released peals of laughter. "Jack is a crack shot. If he got the drop on you, I could never live with myself. And I don't have that many friends."

"Let's get your mind off Lejeune and back to the case. Tomorrow you and I are taking a road trip. Go to early church and then be ready by eleven o'clock. I've got a lead." Michael started to pace his living room. *Why on earth did I move into so small an apartment?*

"I'll be waiting at the curb. Where are we going?"

"All in good time, Miss Kirby. Get a good night's sleep," he said before ending the call.

ᴗ

When he arrived at the Kirby residence, Beth was standing in the driveway with the biggest purse Michael had ever seen. "Good morning," he greeted, pushing open the car door.

Beth jumped in and buckled her seat belt. "You were awfully mysterious last night. Are you going to share where we're going or blindfold me? Mom only sent provisions for one day." She held up a soft-sided cooler.

"We're going to Hattiesburg. That will put some serious miles on the Charger, but you should be home by suppertime in case Rita is frying muskrat livers."

"Good, because I didn't pack an overnight bag, and muskrat is sautéed, not fried." Beth pulled two wrapped sandwiches from her purse. "Speaking of food, Rita fixed us bagels for breakfast. Are we allowed to eat in your new car?"

In the past his answer would have been different. "Yes, of course." He accepted one of the bacon, cheese, and egg calorie bombs. "It smells wonderful. Tell your mother thanks."

For several minutes they ate and watched the scenery. Then Beth turned to face him. "Okay, why are we going to Hattiesburg?"

"To talk to another Baptist minister who was recently fired and faces theft charges. We know that Reverend Dean was one of many contributors to Spare the Children. So I ran a search of Mississippi churches in the news. There were plenty of dead ends until I came across the name Daniel Huff."

"I stand in awe of your cyber skills," Beth said as she adjusted her seat to a more comfortable angle.

"Reverend Dean and Reverend Huff of Hattiesburg could be the tip of an iceberg. Most churches are reluctant to slander a man of God in the media. If there's an unexplained misfeasance, most congregations would probably prefer not to broadcast it. However, an uptick of resignations in church leadership across the state can't be a coincidence. Whoever set up Reverend Dean probably duped this pastor as well. We need to find out for sure, and find any other victims."

"Somebody was bound to catch on if this is a scam." Beth carefully brushed crumbs into a napkin.

"That's why time is of the essence. Elliott Rayburn might be getting ready to cut and run."

"Which would make him a dangerous man." Beth looked stricken, as though she were somehow responsible.

"Let's not get ahead of ourselves. We'll start in Hattiesburg with Reverend Huff and take it from there." He checked his watch. "Since we still have a couple hours in the car, mind if I change the subject?"

"Talk about anything you want. How's the training coming for the Iron Man competition?"

Reluctant to get too excited, Michael happily described his new workout regimen. Unfortunately, when they arrived at their destination, they found the middle-aged preacher reluctant to talk despite yesterday's conversation.

"I'm not sure what you want from me, Mr. Preston." Reverend Huff spoke through a six-inch opening in the doorway. "Like I told you on the phone, I've been advised by my attorney not to speak to the media."

"We're private investigators, not the media. Anything you say to us will be kept confidential. We believe that you might have been victimized by the same charity as our pastor, Reverend Paul Dean of Calvary Baptist of Natchez."

Huff seemed to wilt before their eyes. "Whether that's true or not, it's no longer relevant. Part of my plea deal to a lesser offense is based on not drawing more attention to my mismanagement of church finances."

"You're pleading guilty to a crime?" asked Beth, her tone somewhere between innocent curiosity and appalled disbelief. "Did you steal the congregation's money or not?"

"Of course not," he snapped. "I held a position of trust and responsibility, and yet I can't explain what happened to the money."

"This is actually very simple," said Beth. "Our pastor smelled something fishy and demanded his investment back. When the charity refused, Reverend Dean started kicking up a fuss. Apparently, you would rather go to jail than make any noise."

"You have no right to judge me, young lady!" Huff exclaimed before slamming the door in their faces.

"Oh, I have plenty of right!" She continued the conversation one decibel louder. "Our minister was murdered in cold blood because someone at the charity didn't want to give back the money. Maybe your case has nothing to do with what happened in Natchez, but if the people you trusted happen to be Spare the Children out of Denver, then we have plenty in common. And I strongly suggest you not plead guilty for something you didn't do!" Beth was shouting at this point, while Michael stood back and watched. For half a minute they held their breath until the door opened wide.

"They told me we would save young lives while earning interest on our investment." Huff looked and sounded like a broken man.

"That's what Rayburn told Reverend Dean too," said Beth. "Was Elliott Rayburn who you dealt with?"

"No. I usually communicated with a company out of Jackson."

"D.K. Financials, right?" asked Michael, exchanging a look with Beth.

"Yes, that was it. One of their agents, a Rachel Stewart, said she would furnish quarterly statements and act as my local contact. Then she stopped returning my calls and has since changed her number."

Michael felt the bottom drop from his gut.

Because the name meant nothing to his partner, Beth forged ahead. "Are you ready to help us now, sir?"

Huff nodded. "Come inside. I'll tell you everything I know. I don't care about the plea deal anymore. This church was my *life*."

Beth stepped across the threshold. "Since you're still alive, there's still hope. And now you've got Price Investigations on your side."

FORTY-THREE

Bay St. Louis

Following their instructions precisely, Nate and Isabelle turned down a street narrowed by double-parked cars, neglected trash cans in the ditch, and plastic cones marking the location of potholes. "Are you sure we're in the right place?" asked Isabelle.

Nate glanced at the dashboard GPS. "This is the address Johnny Herman gave me on the phone. I don't think he'd steer us wrong after agreeing to help and telling us to come on Saturday."

"In that case, Mr. Herman lives on the saddest block in Biloxi."

"That's not very nice, Izzy." Nate pulled into a short driveway. The retired PI recommended by Art Lewis had been more than willing to talk to them. In fact, Mr. Herman sounded excited about Nate's ideas. Maybe retirement wasn't everything it was cracked up to be.

Isabelle coaxed a few wisps into her ponytail. "If more young gamblers saw how old ones ended up, they would quit a lot sooner."

Nate stared at her, dumbfounded. "Why are you being so judgmental? We have no idea if his present circumstances have anything to do with gambling."

"Why else would he be living here? According to the head of

security, Mr. Herman was a successful investigator." She frowned at the litter-strewn vacant lot next door.

"Plenty of people weren't adequately insured when Katrina hit and ended up losing everything. Maybe you should wait here in the car. I'll keep the windows rolled down so nobody calls the SPCA."

"Very funny. Honestly, Nate. We know that Mr. Herman was a big gambler. Probably even the luckiest card sharks end up flat broke if they stay in the game long enough. I'm just saying that seeing this neighborhood could be a cautionary tale for Craig." Climbing out of the car, Isabelle smoothed down her sundress.

Nate rolled his eyes and mimed a zipper across his lips. This wasn't a good time to argue with her. Besides, the row of tiny, three-room cottages with patchy weeds instead of grass *was* depressing. Apparently, not everywhere along the Gulf Coast had recovered as nicely as Bay St. Louis. Nate knocked on the front door and waited. A few moments later, a seventyish man with a bent spine and white hair opened the door.

"Mr. Herman? Nate and Isabelle Price from Natchez. I spoke with you on the phone."

"Yep, that's me. Been expecting y'all. Come on in." A hacking cough punctuated his invitation.

Isabelle smiled as she stepped inside, her normal temperament restored. "It's so kind of you to see us, sir."

"Pleasure's mine, ma'am. Don't get much company now that my boy lives in Texas. He's got himself quite a brood out there, two boys and three girls. The airfare east would set them back an arm and a leg." Herman tapped both appendages of his analogy. "Make yourselves comfortable."

"Those five grandchildren must be a blessing to you, even if they are miles away." Isabelle sat primly on the sofa.

"Oh, that they are." Herman lifted a framed photograph off the mantel. "Here's my son's family."

While Isabelle perused the seven smiling faces, Nate assessed the room. Although the furnishings weren't up to *House Beautiful* standards, the home felt warm, welcoming, and filled with love. "Is Mrs. Herman around?" he asked. "I wanted to offer her my compliments. I'll bet those are her handiwork." Nate pointed at the purple and pink flowers in the window boxes.

Herman lowered himself into the recliner, his smile fading. "No, she passed two years ago this Christmas. But you guessed right— my wife planted those boxes. I do my best to keep them alive, but Betty had the green thumb. Heart of gold and thumb of green. I had that inscribed on her tombstone right above, 'Waiting for the Lord's return.'" His voice cracked with emotion.

"We're so sorry for your loss," said Nate. "Forgive my impertinence."

Herman's brow furrowed. "Don't know much about impertinence, but I love talkin' about my Betty. She was the light of my life." He pushed to his feet and headed toward the door. "Come out back with me. Those flower boxes out front ain't nothing compared to her garden."

What Nate and Isabelle discovered was a secret retreat, enclosed with a redwood fence, transected by flagstone paths, and illuminated with strings of tiny white lights. There was a fishpond in the center with a wrought iron table and chairs, but it was the flowers that took your breath away. From the ornamental trees to the fragrant shrubs and down to the groundcover, everything in the yard was blooming.

"Wow!" Nate and Isabelle's responses were identical.

"That's what everybody says," Herman said, chuckling. "This is what Betty wanted, so this is what she got. Took several years, but it was all worth it."

"From the street no one would guess your little paradise is back here," said Isabelle without thinking. She blushed with embarrassment. "I hope you don't take that wrong."

"That's also what everybody says, and that's how we wanted it. Didn't want teenagers tearing up my hard work just to be ornery."

He pointed toward the chairs in the shade. "Have a seat if you don't mind the heat."

Isabelle plunked down. "Don't mind if I do. I love it out here. And if you want to talk about Betty, we've got plenty of time. What did she think about your being a card shark?"

"Izzy!" Nate sounded shocked. "That's none of our business. We came to ask Mr. Herman—"

"Hold up there, young man. She's asking because she's a wife who was once married to a compulsive gambler. I know the story—Mr. Lewis filled me in. She's curious, and I don't mind talkin'. Don't get much of a chance to these days." With a grin aimed solely at Isabelle, Herman sat down at the patio table.

Nate had no choice but to do the same.

"You're probably thinkin' our reduced circumstances are because of my playing poker. Not so. I never wagered much at the tables, just the allowance Betty gave me for being good." He winked at Nate. "Whenever I won big, I'd buy something we needed, like a new mattress or a set of tires. And if I lost? It would be a long time before I saved up enough to hit the casino again. I never gambled the mortgage payment or grocery money the way some fools do."

Herman turned his gaze skyward, where seagulls wheeled on warm air currents. "No, we sold our big house on the water and spent all our savings on her cancer treatments. Insurance refused to cover them because they were still *experimental*." His inflection conveyed fury over the ruling. "But I wouldn't have it any other way. Those treatments gave her several more good years. When we moved here, Betty transformed the backyard into a healing place. She gave the orders, like every wife knows how to do, and I did the heavy lifting." He laughed from deep inside his belly.

Nate glanced at Isabelle, who sat so still she might have been hit by a mysterious bout of paralysis. "A dozen landscapers couldn't have done a better job," he said, encircling her shoulders with his arm.

Johnny Herman met his gaze. "Yes, sir. My Betty got her healing place. She went to the Lord filled with grace and not a bit of pain. This is where I'll stay until I join her."

"That's the most beautiful story I ever heard," Isabelle said, wiping tears from her face.

"Yes, ma'am, it might be, but don't you worry. If I can help your ex-husband straighten himself out, I will. We want him to have a good life, like you have with Nate and I had with Betty."

She eked out a weak, "Thank you, Mr. Herman. We'll be eternally grateful for your help."

"Ah, that ain't necessary. After all, I like poker and haven't played in quite some time. With the Golden Magnolia staking my game, I'll be sitting in high cotton." His hoot spooked several sparrows from their perch. "You tell Art Lewis I'll stop by Monday afternoon. If there's a high-stakes game in one of the poker rooms, one of us should be able to wrestle an invite. Knowing Art, he'll even throw in a free buffet."

Nate took Isabelle's arm and helped her to her feet. "Don't forget, Mr. Herman, if you ever have need of a PI or are ever in Natchez, give me a call."

"I'll keep that in mind. Now why don't you take your wife out to dinner? We both know women love meals they don't have to cook."

"That's exactly what I'll do." Nate shook hands, and then Isabelle hugged him tightly. After they left, it was an unusually quiet drive back to the B and B, both lost in their own thoughts.

Isabelle didn't speak until Nate parked in their designated spot. "If I ever act so high-and-mighty again, I want you to whack me with a phone book."

"I can't imagine that happening, not in light of my numerous personal shortcomings."

She stared straight ahead, her lower lip trembling. "I've never been so ashamed of myself in my life."

Nate kissed her cheek. "You are human, dear wife. Perfection is the domain of angels, not us mere mortals."

"After we get Craig straightened out, could we do something nice for Mr. Herman?"

"You do realize we'll be on our way home soon."

"I know, but if we have time?" Isabelle look at him with moist, shiny eyes.

"Why not? We can always hang out at the beach after we retire."

FORTY-FOUR

Natchez
Monday

I t wasn't easy for a person to remain hidden for long. Not in a low-population state like Mississippi. Especially not from someone who knew your friends, your former employer, your social history, and your professional affiliations. And certainly not from your former fiancé.

The hard part yesterday had been interviewing the Hattiesburg minister without revealing that he *knew* Rachel Stewart from D.K. Financials. Michael could have confessed that to his partner on the drive back to town. Surely he could have found time between discussing who had the best shot at the SEC championship and where to stop for a caffeine break and said: *By the way, Elizabeth, this crooked Rachel Stewart is the same Rachel who nearly stood me up at the altar and single-handedly broke my heart.*

Michael might have had the time but not the guts.

His second difficult challenge was convincing Beth that he should go alone to Jackson to question Miss Stewart, while Beth collected and organized their file on Spare the Children to turn over to the Natchez PD. Scams that crossed state lines and international borders were the FBI's jurisdiction, but private investigators shouldn't be the ones handing over evidence.

"You're the forensic accountant on the team," she'd complained. "Shouldn't you be the one putting together the file for Chris?" Her question had been legitimate.

"Why can't I come along when you interrogate Miss Con Artist? Why should you have all the fun?" Another excellent question Michael had no answer for.

"Please, Beth, could you just once show some faith in my decision-making abilities?" His response, although rather underhanded, had been effective. His partner reluctantly agreed as long as he provided a full update on his way home.

In comparison, tracking down Rachel Stewart, with her accounting degree from Auburn and mutual friends both were in contact with, had been easy. Even finding her present employer, D.K. Financials, in an industrial section of town wasn't much of a challenge. For ninety minutes Michael watched the entrance of the storefront operation to no avail. After his equally uneventful drive to Jackson, he began to doubt the wisdom of his plan. Then God was merciful.

Rachel parked next to the curb and exited her vehicle carrying a giant cup and a takeout bag. Even unscrupulous charlatans get hungry by two o'clock in the afternoon. As she clicked the lock on her Cadillac and headed toward the door, Michael intercepted her path.

"Hi, Rachel. What a surprise seeing you here." He stuck his hands in his pockets. "Nice car. The last time I saw you, you were driving a Jeep with a hundred thousand miles on the odometer."

She blinked her unnaturally blue eyes. "Mike. What are you doing in Jackson? Have you been following me?" Her expression of shock morphed into irritation as though she frowned at gum stuck to her shoe.

"I assure you I'm not looking for work." He straightened his spine. "My new job led me to D.K. Financials. Imagine my surprise to find you here." He paused and watched the first crack appear in her haughty facade.

"This company offered a great salary and better benefits. If you could leave Anderson Accountants, why shouldn't I?" Rachel tightened her grip on her soft drink. "I love living in Jackson. Did you think I would stay in Brookhaven forever?"

"Actually, I haven't thought much about you since we broke up." It was a bald-faced lie, but it felt good to say the words. "As I said, I'm following a lead for the case I'm on."

A second crack appeared in her demeanor. "What kind of *case* are you talking about? You're an accountant." She gave the word a distasteful inflection despite sharing the same credentials as him.

"After you broke off our engagement, I made a few changes in my life. I'm a private investigator now in Natchez. I love what I do. Working in the field got me away from that backstabbing, gossip-spreading, competitive pack of jackals. But hey, that's just my opinion. Some people working in offices are probably quite nice."

Frowning, Rachel took a step back. "Look, Mike, it's great seeing you again, but I need to get to my desk. I wish you well in your new career." She turned and reached for the door handle.

"Thanks, but it's *you* I came to see. Let's step inside. I also have a few questions for your boss. You know, the boiler room operator for D.K. Financials?"

Rachel's perfect features contorted with rage. "How dare you demean what we do? We are legitimate fund-raisers, licensed and registered in this state. We provide funds for a humanitarian charity that serves children across the globe." She braced the door open with her backside.

"The fact that you're registered proves nothing, so save the pep talk for the next naive priest or minister on your list. I represent the widow of one of your targets, Reverend Paul Dean of Natchez."

Suddenly the chameleon's sneer turned into a smile. She moved toward him, letting the door swing shut. "Why don't we go somewhere private to talk? You have the wrong idea about D.K. Financials, but I haven't helped the situation with my attitude." Shifting her lunch, Rachel placed a hand on his sleeve.

Michael glanced down at her manicured fingers and smiled. "You're right. We've gotten off on the wrong foot. Let's sit down with your director and talk this over."

"Please, Mike, is there any way to avoid speaking to Mr. Roush? He feels terrible that Reverend Dean took his own life and holds me partially responsible." Rachel's voice dropped to a whisper.

"Care to elaborate how it could be your fault?"

"The company policy is specific. I'm to encourage donors to be generous and to give the charity the longest possible term on their investment. Most pastors aren't savvy about normal market fluctuations, so I'm also here to calm jittery nerves during downturns."

"Is that how you were trained to handle Reverend Dean?" Michael crossed his arms.

"Yes, and I tried my best. But he insisted that we refund the original amount." Rachel set down her lunch long enough to wipe away a tear. "I tried to explain his investment would suffer a serious loss if he cashed out early, but Reverend Dean became irate. He shouted at me and called me names. He was totally out of control. I never heard such language coming from a preacher before."

Michael clenched down on his back teeth. He was certain Paul Dean had never uttered a curse word in his life, let alone to a woman over the phone. "What did you do?"

"I hung up on him. That's how I was raised. I planned to call him in a few days after he had a chance to calm down. When we heard about his suicide, I felt just…just awful." Rachel covered her face with her hands, accidentally kicking over her drink. Coke and ice splashed down the steps.

"I'm surprised news of a suicide reached all the way to Jackson." Michael laid a steadying hand on her shoulder.

"What?" she asked with confusion.

"How did you find out Reverend Dean was dead?"

She shrugged. "I think Mr. Roush told me. That's why I'm hoping you won't say anything to him. Mr. Roush said I should have immediately complied with Reverend Dean's wishes. I should've notified the comptroller to cut a check for the balance at the end of the day. The company doesn't want unhappy investors badmouthing the wonderful work Spare the Children has done. Mr. Roush said he'll fire me if I cause any more trouble for the firm." Her lower lip trembled as she spoke. "Please, Mike, take pity on me. I can't afford to lose this job. You have no idea how expensive it is to live here. That's just one of the things I miss about Brookhaven." She attempted a halfhearted laugh.

Michael shrugged. "I have no desire to jam you up, Rachel, despite our past…differences, but I need copies of correspondence with Reverend Dean for his widow. By the way, whatever happened to the church's money?"

"Honestly, I don't know. The balance is probably still invested for the rest of the term." Her hypnotic eyes locked with his. "I'm afraid to ask too many questions. You understand, don't you?"

"I'm beginning to." Michael glanced at his watch. "As long as I provide some kind of answer to my client, your boss doesn't have to get involved. Mrs. Dean and the church elders need to know their money is still hard at work saving kids. Why don't you fax copies of your correspondence with the pastor to this email address?" Michael handed her a business card. "I'll do my best to assure discretion on our end."

"Of course. Give me a few days, a week at the most, to get everything together without arousing suspicion." Rachel tucked the card in her purse. "Before you go, may I ask you something?"

"Sure, what's on your mind?" He feigned a carefree attitude while his stomach tightened into a knot.

"Would you have dinner with me tonight? You can't believe the great selection of restaurants in Jackson. We're not in the Mississippi Delta anymore, Toto." Her laughter sounded almost childlike.

"Thanks, but I need to get back to Kansas." Michael headed down the stairs with the beginnings of a headache from her perfume.

"I hope you don't hate me for what I did. If there's one regret I'll take to my grave, it's leaving you so abruptly."

Michael felt an old familiar pain in his gut. "Forget about it, Rach. I survived the trauma and walked away unscathed. Look, not even scarred or disfigured." He slicked a hand through his hair, now longer and better styled than his former buzz cut.

Her gaze traveled from the top of his head down to his Italian leather loafers. "You look great. Have you been working out? This new career must be the best thing that ever happened to you. Or is it a new woman?" She sounded coy as she squeezed his arm.

Memories—some good, some horrible—flooded back with her touch. It took every ounce of fortitude not to bat her hand away as if it were a horsefly. "I have no plans to walk down the aisle anytime soon, if that's what you're asking, but I love Natchez. I've got new friends, new routines, and a better outlook on life."

"I'm truly happy for you." She bent down to retrieve her empty cup. "But I'd still like to buy you supper. I could answer the rest of your questions while you could assuage some of my guilt over Reverend Dean. Is there anything I can do for his family? I want to at least send flowers to his wife. Please, Mike, let me make things up to you."

For a few moments, he considered her invitation. After all, he couldn't think of a better way to discover the extent of her deviousness than to gain her trust—yet something in her coy drawl sent his self-preservation meter into the red zone.

Shame on you for dancing me around like a puppet on a string, but if I let you do it again…shame on me.

He glanced at his watch again, as though he had a pressing appointment. "Can I have a raincheck on dinner? There might be a few more questions after I get your email, but I don't mind driving back to Jackson to have dinner with a beautiful woman." He forced a smile.

"Give me a call anytime. Here's my new cell number." She scribbled a number on a corner of her lunch bag.

"I'll do that. Good luck with your new job. Oh, and maybe you should send D.K.'s last two statements for Calvary Baptist along with your correspondence with Reverend Dean. Even though probate is months away, those should relieve Mrs. Dean's worries that she will be held responsible for any church losses." Michael tipped an imaginary hat, a throwback from his nerdy days that refused to die, and walked toward his car.

"I'll send those out as soon as I can," called Rachel, waving like a prom queen.

Michael slipped behind the wheel, feeling he needed a shower despite unusually cool temperatures. He felt disloyal to Beth, even though their relationship was strictly platonic. Most of all, it felt like he just danced with a three-headed serpent, who was wearing a silk dress and stiletto heels.

FORTY-FIVE

*B*eth jumped when her phone rang. She answered on the second ring. "It's about time you called, Preston. I've been chomping at the bit to hear your news. What was she like— this Rachel from D.K. Financials? I'm hoping you didn't tip your hand before you found evidence on that little crook."

"Simmer down before you hyperventilate," he said, his voice muffled as though on speaker.

"Are you back to Natchez yet?"

"Not by a long shot. I'm tied up behind a road repair crew. Did you finish organizing our file on the charity scam?"

"Of course I did. I'm not an idiot. It's ready whenever you go see Jack. Me, I'm staying at least five hundred feet away from that madman." Beth listened to chuckling on the other end. "But let's not talk boring facts and figures now, not when you met the enemy face-to-face. Any chance this woman might have had a hand in Paul's death?"

Beth waited expectantly but heard only silence. "I can't hear you, Mike. Unless you're in heavy traffic, take me off Bluetooth and put the phone to your ear. I want to hear every detail about your trip to Jackson."

Michael cleared his throat. "I staked out D.K. Financials until Miss Stewart showed up. She must work strange hours because she was carrying her lunch."

"Okay…that's certainly fascinating."

"Truth is I didn't *meet* Rachel. I…actually knew her previously."

"You knew her from where? Stop being so cryptic and spell it out for me." As soon as Beth asked the question, cogs started to turn. When her memory scanned every past association for that name only one answer came to mind.

"No," she murmured. "You can't possibly mean your coworker at the accounting firm. Your former girlfriend?" She cupped her hands around the phone to evade Maxine's keen hearing.

"One and the same. My former fiancée, to be exact. Rachel was a good accountant. Too bad she's taken her talents to the dark side."

Beth searched unsuccessfully for the right thing to say. "I can't put this together. Did you know before you left this morning? Is that why you didn't want me along?"

Michael hesitated a moment too long. "I suppose so. Her name is fairly common, but when I factored in her vocation and the fact Rachel left Anderson six months ago, I suspected it might be her. Truthfully, I didn't want our initial showdown to be in front of witnesses."

"You didn't bloody her nose, did you? Did the other swindlers have to pull you apart?"

His laughter sounded more genuine this time. "No, nothing dramatic like that. The meeting went well. I told her I was investigating Paul Dean's investments on behalf of his widow, and that I had tracked the church's account to her at this address."

"Did you get the name of her supervisor at D.K. Financials? Which one of them was more worried about your questions?"

"Her boss's name is Mr. Roush, but we talked outside her office. Rachel said if there's any more trouble connected to Paul Dean, she might lose her job."

Beth stared at a picture of playful otters on the wall. "Why would you care if Rachel got fired? Her conniving led to Paul's death…or worse. For all we know, she might have been the one kicking the stool out from under his feet." Beth felt the muscles in her neck tighten as she spoke the words.

"I realize that, but we gain nothing by tipping our hand too soon. Wasn't that one of your first lessons?"

"So what did Miss Heartbreaker say other than plead for mercy with her crooked employer?"

"Could you not reference our past in every other sentence?" Michael asked. "Let's stay focused on the present."

"All right. Did Miss Stewart talk about her relationship with Calvary Baptist Church?"

"Yes. She acknowledged that Reverend Dean requested the church investment be returned and that she initially refused. Rachel counseled patience during a market slump, but the pastor became irate and started cursing at her—"

"Paul would never do that!"

"Calm down. I know that, but I wanted to see where this was headed. Rachel said she was giving Pastor Dean a cooling-off period but had planned to refund his money in a few days. Then her boss heard about the suicide, and Rachel ended up in hot water for pushing the man too hard."

"And you believed this bag of bologna?"

"Of course not, but I acted like I did. Rachel agreed to send me copies of her correspondence with Calvary Baptist."

"She's not dumb enough to give you anything incriminating." Desperate for fortification, Beth marched to the coffeemaker by Maxine's desk.

"Probably not, but we won't know until we see the emails. Rachel also invited me to dinner, but I declined. She insisted that I take a rain check."

"Oh, really?" Beth swigged the coffee black without her standard cream and two sugars. "What else did little Rachel have to say?"

Michael didn't seem to pick up the sarcasm. "Let's see…she said I looked great and that she could tell I'd been working out."

"Very observant of her. Anything else?"

"She said she would regret breaking up with me until the day she died." His inflection was downright melodramatic.

Beth locked gazes with Maxine. "Are you falling for Rachel's manipulations? She's trying to con you into divulging how much you know."

"I realize that, Beth, but why not play along? If she doesn't send us something the feds can use in the email, I might just accept her invitation. Maybe I'll wear a wire the way they do in the movies."

Beth set down her coffee before she crushed the Styrofoam cup. "That wouldn't be a good idea."

"Why not? Since I'm a private citizen and not law enforcement, I don't need a court order to tape our conversation. Any confession on her part most likely would be admissible."

"I'm not talking legalities. You need to avoid her like the plague."

"Do you mean conflict of interest?" Michael sounded genuinely confused.

"I'm talking about your having dinner with a woman you once loved. Rachel had you wrapped firmly around her finger. What makes you sure you won't fall under her influence again?" Beth hadn't meant to phrase it exactly like that, but unlike in an email, she couldn't highlight and delete to express herself correctly.

Michael released a whoosh of air. "Wow, nice to know your faith in my abilities remains ironclad."

"You're a fine PI, Mikey, but you're also a man, subject to male pheromones or whatever they're called." Beth spotted Maxine slashing a finger across her throat, but the damage was already done.

"I'm going to forget you said that. Instead, why don't you make arrangements to present our evidence to Chief McNeil and Detective Lejeune?"

"You want me to face the Natchez police department alone?"

"There's no reason to wait for me since I'm still ninety minutes from home. And unlike you, I have full faith in your ability to act professionally with someone you were once romantically involved with."

"Okay, maybe I deserved that, but later on, why don't we grab a sandwich and compare notes?"

"No, I'll pass. I'm going to delve into Rachel's bank account. I would love to know if the woman I *dream about every night* could possibly be a murderer." He ended the call before she could say another word.

Beth slumped into a chair and laid her head on Maxine's desk. "Am I the stupidest person you know?"

"At the moment, yes." Maxine refilled her coffee mug. "While I get Chief McNeil on the phone, you go pull yourself together." She pointed at the bathroom.

Beth walked in, turned on the taps, and washed her hands and face. When she reached for the towel, Maxine stood in the doorway, the cordless phone in her outstretched hand.

"Chief McNeil is on the line if you're back to reality."

Beth mouthed her thanks and closed the door. "Chris? My partner and I have compiled a file on Spare the Children International. Their fund-raising tactics in Mississippi came to light during our investigation of Paul's mur—" She stopped just shy of the line because she was no longer a cop or homicide detective. "In the course of our investigation on behalf of Alice Dean."

"Detective Lejeune is here in my office. I'm putting you on speaker."

"Thank you. This concerns him too." Her unnecessary comment grated on her ears. "We've compiled investment statements sent to Paul along with copies of email correspondence between the Denver charity and Calvary Baptist. As you suspected, this case has federal implications because the organizers ripped off churches in at least five states."

"You got proof that other churches were scammed, Kirby?" Cordial as always, Jack barked the question in the background. "Or you just talking out of your hat?"

"In addition to the file my partner put together, we have a minister in Hattiesburg willing to testify that he was a victim of the same scam. He's facing charges right now for theft of church funds, a crime he didn't commit."

"Why bother with judges and lawyers when we got Beth Kirby, who knows more than a dozen Supreme Court justices?" Lejeune's cackle rubbed Beth's nerves raw.

"All right, enough," said Chris. "Are you prepared to turn over what you have to us?"

"I can be there within fifteen minutes."

"We'll be waiting. Thanks for the update." He clicked off, leaving Beth staring into the bathroom mirror.

Should I comb my hair? Put on fresh makeup? At least brush my teeth? In the end she brushed her teeth and drove to the station on autopilot. Once the clerk had buzzed her into the station, she walked down the hallway as though a prisoner on death row.

Chris, in his immaculate suit coat without a hair out of place, stood when she entered the room. His greeting was cordial but his smile held no warmth. Across the desk, Jack remained rooted to the chair, his expression bored and annoyed.

"This is everything that could be helpful in a financial crimes prosecution, including a taped interview with Reverend Daniel Huff of Hattiesburg. Mr. Preston and I will be available to answer the FBI's questions down the road."

"How extraordinarily helpful of you, Kirby," said Jack. "Now will you butt your nose out?"

Beth addressed the chief. "Our client is Alice Dean. Because she had nothing to do with the church's investment, our involvement with Spare the Children International is finished."

Jack tapped an index finger on the bulging file. "And you've given us *everything* to turn over to the feds? The state crime lab reexamined the physical evidence, and their high-tech equipment found a drop of sweat on the stool and a partial print on the rope. So, you're not hiding any secrets up your sleeve?"

"I've given you everything." There was only one acceptable

answer to his question. Yet as soon as she gave it, apprehension crawled up her spine like a spider.

Beth couldn't wait to get out of the station. Even though she took the long way home to clear her head, she couldn't stop thinking about her conversation with Michael. Why on earth had she implied he couldn't be trusted around Rachel? Even though Chris was polite and professional, his presence made her just as uncomfortable as Jack did. Her romantic allusions were long gone. Whatever attraction he once held merely embarrassed her now.

But, apparently, she wasn't done being a fool.

FORTY-SIX

*I*t wasn't the traffic through a construction zone spiking Michael's blood pressure. Even after he turned up the radio, his conversation with Beth kept running through his mind on a continuous loop. Just when he thought they had reached a place of mutual respect, she could still find it within herself to ask, "What makes you sure you won't fall under her influence again?"

Wasn't he capable of using his past history with Rachel Stewart to help solve their case? He could no more fall in love again with that cold, calculating viper than with the girl who sat behind him in eighth grade homeroom. But after weeks of physical workouts and months of classes, both off and on the firing range, his partner still saw him as weak. And that hurt just as much as Rachel's declaration: "I don't want to spend the rest of my life with you."

When Michael finally passed the last yellow barrel, he rolled down the window and stepped on the gas. He needed time to think and some distance from his partner. As much as he would like to speak his mind, a cooler head would be better for their future. If they did ever close the case, Beth might return to Vicksburg or move to the south of France—somewhere she wouldn't bump heads with Detective Lejeune. In the meantime, Michael planned to learn what he could and keep his personal life personal. Dwelling on Beth's lack of confidence in him wouldn't help any more than believing Rachel regretted breaking off their engagement.

A mistake I'll take to the grave, indeed.

By the time Michael reached Natchez city limits, he'd lost the bad taste in his mouth from fickle women. He drove straight to the Grand Hotel and headed for the fitness room. After a grueling workout, followed by a cold shower, he was back to normal. What he needed now was an order of crawfish étouffée from Cotton Alley and he'd be ready for what he did best—work.

Michael left his takeout food on the counter, popped open a Coke, and turned on his laptop. After scanning and deleting the usual assortment of emails, he completed his daily report for Price Investigations. He was ready for dinner in front of the TV when the chime of a new email caught his attention—an email from Rachel that would change the course of his evening and the case forever:

> *Great seeing you today, Mike. Attached are copies of the statements sent to Paul Dean on behalf of Calvary Baptist Church. If there's anything else I can do to help Mrs. Dean, just say the word. Don't forget o plan a return trip to Jackson in a week or two. I'm not comfortable with how we left it, and I'd like a chance to make things right. Rachel.*

Michael downloaded the statements and compared them to the copies provided by Elliott Rayburn's assistant, same as those in the file turned over to Natchez PD. Then he sat back and smiled. *Give people enough rope, and they don't usually make hammocks.* When his phone rang some time later, his attention was still riveted to his computer.

"Hello?"

"Thanks for taking my call, Mike. I was afraid you might ignore me. Not that I don't have that coming." Beth sounded unusually contrite.

"I didn't check Caller ID before answering." Michael set the crawfish étouffée in the microwave and pressed the button.

"Oh…okay, but I'm still grateful. I would like to make up for the stupid things I said with an extra cheese, black olive, and double pepperoni—just how you like it. Then we can compare notes on what we found out today."

"Do you think forgiveness can be bought with a deluxe pizza, Miss Kirby?"

"I'm hoping it will work."

"Thanks, but I already picked up crawfish from Cotton Alley. It's in the microwave now."

"Great. I can bring over my pizza and we can share both of them—a cross-culture smorgasbord."

Michael wasn't the type to refuse an olive branch, but he hesitated nevertheless. "I do have news, but it can wait until tomorrow. Why don't we meet for breakfast?"

"So you still hate me?"

"We're not in junior high anymore," he said, releasing a weary sigh. "I'm not pouting over our conversation, but it's been a long day and I'm tired."

"Okay. I'll take my pizza and go home. Eating alone will give me a chance to contemplate the errors of my ways. At least, that's what Mom used to say."

"Wait. Where are you?" Michael pulled back the curtains at the front window. Sure enough, Beth's car was parked across the street. She flashed her headlights as her answer. "Have you already bought the pizza?"

The driver's window lowered and the corner of a box appeared.

"For heaven's sake, come upstairs." Michael hung up and scrambled around his apartment, picking up discarded clothes and empty soda cans. By the time he changed the towel and wiped toothpaste off the bathroom mirror, Beth was at the door. She walked in with the pizza and two grocery bags.

"I take it you finished contemplating your errors. What's in the bags?"

"Before you stands a reformed woman bearing gifts of power drinks, vitamin water, protein bars, and dark chocolate. But first, a super-charged pizza." Beth spread her bribes across his counter. "I'm really sorry I doubted you about Rachel."

Michael divided his crawfish between two plates. "I forgive you, so let's forget it. Tell me about your meeting with Lejeune and the chief. I hope no one had to separate you two with Tasers."

Beth picked up her plate and took a bite. "Thanks for sharing your étouffée." Then she summarized the transfer of evidence over to law enforcement. "As usual, Jack acted like a junkyard dog tied just beyond reach of a steak," she said in conclusion.

"At least we followed protocol." Michael finished his half and took two slices of pizza.

"Now it's your turn. What did you learn from Rachel about her role at D.K. Financials?"

"Better than anything we could have hoped for. I played down our work for Alice Dean. I implied we merely wanted to separate the reverend's financial affairs from those connected to the church in preparation for probate of his estate." Michael paused to gauge her reaction.

"Sure, so Alice would know where she stands financially." Beth took a bite of pizza but kept her focus on him.

"Exactly, but I didn't mention that we had statements from Elliott Rayburn. Apparently, no one at Spare the Children told Rachel they already provided copies of Calvary Baptist's account. Now we have our lucky break." Michael set down his plate.

Beth's brows knit together. "Sorry, but you'll have to spell this out for me."

"The copies that Rachel emailed me didn't match the ones

provided by Elliott Rayburn. In fact, those that D.K. Financials sent to Reverend Dean clearly showed a steady erosion of principal. I think I know why Rachel didn't want me talking to her boss. And I better understand why Reverend Dean had started to panic. Half of the church's money was gone, at least on paper. Rachel probably had some kind of arrangement with the guy, payola for each church she lined up in the South. D.K. Financials provided a different set of statements to Spare the Children."

"So Elliott Rayburn isn't the crook here?"

"Doubtlessly the executive director lives very well on the money he raises for charity. These organizations operate in a gray area of the law. It might not be ethical to keep a cut of the funds, but it is legal. From what I could find out, the bulk of the money goes overseas to orphanages and outreach centers."

"And Rachel and the Jackson storefront boiler room?"

Michael couldn't help but smile. "Somebody at D.K. Financials is setting up for one big score before hightailing it out of the country. Her boss could be packing his bags right now."

Beth set down her piece of pizza. "You've got my full attention."

"Not only do I have proof two different statements were being created for Mississippi clients, but I have proof Rachel accepted thousands of dollars directly from George Roush, her employer at D.K., far beyond even the most generous salary and benefits package."

Beth's eyes practically bugged from her head. "How on earth did you get copies of her bank statement? You just saw her *today*."

"Remember what I said about some things not being ethical but still perfectly legal?" Feeling his cheeks grow warm, Michael bit into another slice to hide his discomfort.

"Put down that pizza and talk to me, Preston. What did you do?"

He chewed and swallowed. "If you recall, I'm the former fiancé of our person of interest. Like many engaged couples, she and I opened a joint account for wedding expenses and to save for the future."

"Don't tell me your name was still on that account."

"Nope. When Rachel broke the engagement off, she sent a check for the amount she felt I was entitled to and then removed my name. We had opened the account at her favorite bank, not mine, and she kept the account open." Michael cracked his knuckles one by one. "Lazy Rachel never changed the password."

"You hacked her bank account?" asked Beth, awestruck.

"Well, yes. I could claim that I was making sure everyone we owed money had been paid back. You know, to protect my credit rating."

"Aren't you quick with a rationalization? You just earned yourself more pizza." Beth handed him the box. "This story is getting good."

"Rachel's account contained over thirty thousand dollars. That might not be enough to start over in a new town, but if Roush is expecting a final payday, Rachel's probably expecting one too."

"D.K. Financials was already skimming profits from the fundraising. Then they cooked the books for select Mississippi churches with substantial sums to invest. George Roush was wiping out their accounts one by one and paying Rachel a cut of the loot."

Michael wiped his hands on a towel. "Granted, some of this is conjecture on my part, but I've also got proof Rachel paid off Buckley, probably to keep him quiet. The feds need to act fast before the thieves disappear. Rachel bought an airline ticket with her debit card. Her flight to the Maldives is in ten days."

"Those are islands in the Indian Ocean, right?"

"Exactly, and they have no extradition treaty with the U.S. I can't imagine Rachel spending the rest of her life there, no matter how beautiful the beaches. Probably once interest in her dies down, she'll move back to the States under a new identity." Michael crossed his arms behind his head.

However, the expression on his partner's face was anything but joyous.

"What's wrong? I thought you'd be glad my siren-temptress was planning to run away even faster this time. Rachel's offer of a candlelit dinner was just a smoke screen."

Beth scraped a hand through her hair, frowning as though her tooth ached. "I told Natchez PD we were handing over everything on the pyramid scam. Now you've come up with additional evidence for Jack."

"Are you *never* happy, or is this your idea of training the newbie?" Michael flung the kitchen towel across the room. "No matter what I do, it's never quite what you had in mind."

"Settle down. It's just that Jack will use anything to discredit my ability to work with law enforcement." She picked the towel off the floor.

"You're worried how you'll look to Chief McNeil, your old heartthrob?"

Beth's nostrils flared. "I suppose I had that coming, but no. I'm more worried about my future with Price Investigations. A PI must be able to get along with the police or they're worthless."

Michael carried their plates into the kitchen to diffuse the tension. "Sorry. I guess I'm still sore about your not trusting me with Rachel."

"No more apologies for the rest of the day." Beth rose to her feet. "I'll let you get back to your evening while I take that second set of statements and Rachel's bank deposits to Jack."

Michael grabbed hold of her sleeve as she walked past him. "Elizabeth, there's something I need to get off my chest. I hope you don't see me as weak and easily fooled by women. I used to be that man, but I'm not anymore. I'll probably never fall in love again, but if I do, I plan on keeping my eyes wide open." He released her shirt, but she didn't move.

"Falling in love isn't a sign of weakness, Mike. It's a sign of being human. I've always been a little envious of how open you are. That's the last thing you should change about yourself."

"I can't even imagine what the first would be." Michael tapped the papers into a pile and slipped them into an envelope. "Even after we turn over the new evidence to the police, you and I aren't done with Miss Stewart."

Beth lifted an eyebrow. "Care to elaborate?"

"Rachel was on the payroll at D.K. Financials and also getting separate kickbacks from George Roush. How far would she go to protect the biggest fish on her hook?"

"You think Rachel murdered Paul?"

"She could have incapacitated him with drugs. According to the toxicology report, ketamine was found in his bloodstream. That's a strong tranquilizer."

Beth shook her head. "Then she lifted him onto a stool, twice, because it didn't work the first time? You never mentioned that Rachel was an Olympic bodybuilder."

"There might be holes in my theory, but Reverend Dean was demanding the church's half-million dollars back. He was about to bring down their house of cards. Maybe someone helped Rachel, or she could have hired a hit man."

"How would a sweet girl from Brookhaven know where to hire a hit man?"

"Everything and everyone is available on the Internet. That's why I plan to get my hands on Rachel's DNA. If the Mississippi Crime Lab runs it against evidence from the rope and stool, who knows what we'll find?"

Beth stifled a laugh behind a coughing jag.

"Speak your mind, Kirby. What's so funny?"

"That's a great idea. But if you're right, how will you explain to your mother you were engaged to a murderer?"

"Could have been worse. Who knows what plans Rachel had for me down the line? Anderson Accountants carried a two-million-dollar life insurance policy on each employee, payable to the spouse."

Shrugging into her sweater, Beth picked up the envelope. "Okay, I'm on my way to the station."

Michael blocked her path at the door. "It's late now and we're both tired. Lejeune and Chief McNeil have probably left for the day. Why don't you take tomorrow off while I deliver the file alone?" He plucked the envelope from her hand. "Use the time to bring Nate up to date on the case, or go out to your uncle's and kill some Coke cans, or maybe have your hair cut."

"What's wrong with my hair?" Beth tugged on one curly lock.

"Nothing, but I can talk to Lejeune first thing in the morning and then head straight to Jackson. Let me take the lead on this." Michael opened the door for her. "Go home, partner, and get some sleep. I'll call Rachel to see if she's available for a late lunch or early dinner tomorrow. The next time you see me, I'll have several samples of her DNA."

FORTY-SEVEN

Bay St. Louis

Isabelle took at least a dozen deep breaths on her way from the employee restroom into the lounge area in an attempt to calm her nerves. Per Mr. Lewis's suggestion, she put on twice her usual amount of makeup and had practiced balancing a tray in one hand for an hour. Per Mrs. Doucet's insistence, she wore the highest heels she'd brought on vacation.

Mrs. Doucet delivered instructions to the next shift with a take-no-prisoners attitude: "Remember, no gum chewing, no counting tips in front of customers, no eating, and no drinking anything other than bottled water. Never argue with players or intervene during their disagreements. Pay absolutely zero attention to a player's hand while serving drinks. If a player requests a special food not on the buffet, call down to the kitchen. It will be sent up immediately. Security will always be close by, but basically you are to remain as invisible as possible. Any questions?" Mrs. Doucet glanced around from one woman to the next.

Isabelle had so many she didn't know where to start, so she simply shook her head. "No, ma'am."

"Good, Isabelle and Mindy, you're needed on the second floor. Hostesses in the main poker room have been working for four hours without a break." She scurried off to give instructions to a group of buffet servers about to go on duty.

"We're on," said her new partner, Mindy. The young, fresh-faced woman led Isabelle toward the main playing floor. "Let's hope tips will be better today than yesterday. I didn't even clear two bills."

Isabelle pushed the button for the elevator as she mulled over the amount "two bills." "I'm confused as to how we can serve drinks if we're not allowed to set them on the table and we can't look at a player's hand. Won't there be a lot of spillage?"

Mindy gaped at her, bewildered. "You're joking, right? A player's hand refers to his or her cards. Some poker players worry that you'll signal what cards they're holding. That's why you shouldn't look too curious."

Isabelle silently scolded herself. "I knew that. I was just teasing."

"Yeah, yeah." Mindy rolled her eyes. "Just don't spill a drink on the felt or on a customer. I've seen newbies fired for less. This could be the best-paying job you'll ever get."

And the shortest in duration, Isabelle thought as the door opened.

Inside the poker room, the noise from the blackjack and roulette tables faded. The seven or eight players concentrating on the game barely glanced up as the new hostesses passed through the door.

"Gentlemen and lady," the dealer nodded to the sole female. "There will be a shift change among hostesses if any of you wish to reward superb service."

The two ladies Isabelle and Mindy were replacing glided around the table accepting gratuities. From their expressions, Isabelle assumed the split would surpass that of Mindy's mediocre previous day.

"Have a good one," said the taller of the two.

"Break a leg." The smaller girl stuffed bills into her clear plastic tote and headed for the door.

As the senior employee on duty, Mindy took charge at the buffet table. In a quiet voice she said to Isabelle, "We have ham, turkey, pastrami, and corned beef. Swiss, Monterey Jack, Colby, and smoked cheddar. Italian, whole-wheat, and Jewish rye. We'll call down if someone wants gluten-free. For salads, we have potato, pasta, coleslaw, and Waldorf." She pointed a red-nailed finger at a pair of rolling tables on wheels. "Players who want a snack can have one without leaving the game." Mindy walked to the beverage cart to continue her tutelage. "We serve coffee, tea, and soft drinks, plus beer, wine, and top-shelf liquors. Again, if someone wants a fancy cordial, it's a phone call away. You do know how to make standard cocktails, don't you?"

"Of course, I reviewed Mrs. Doucet's bar guide all last night." Isabelle tapped the napkins into a neat pile. *While Nate insisted this was the worst idea I ever had.*

"Any chips we're given during the game go in here." Mindy pointed to a basket tucked between the sweetened lime juice and lemon wedges. "At the end of our shift, we divvy up. Okay?" The girl's dark eyes sparkled.

"Sounds good." Isabelle placed a tablet and pen on her tray.

"I'll take the first spin around so you can watch me." Mindy flew into action, starting at the end where apparently the bid was not. She patiently waited behind the chairs of players as they considered their options. She didn't write down anything and yet seemed to have no trouble remembering every request.

Isabelle's stomach churned with apprehension. She had trouble remembering a grocery list of four items.

While Mindy mixed and delivered the drinks, Isabelle studied the seven players: a thirtyish, well-dressed lady and six men, including Johnny Herman, who winked at her when no one was looking. One man looked barely old enough to gamble, two appeared to be in their seventies, and one gentleman had to weigh four hundred pounds if he weighed an ounce.

"Don't stare at Mr. Malloy," warned Mindy. "It annoys him. If Big Sam likes you, his tip will match your salary for a week."

"Good to know," whispered Isabelle. But it wasn't Big Sam who had captured her interest. The sixth man, totally focused on the game, looked very familiar. Even with long hair, a thick mustache, and dark glasses, Isabelle would recognize her ex-husband anywhere. Amazingly, huge piles of chips sat in front of him.

With no one wanting a snack, Isabelle tried to follow the action but soon gave up. Texas Hold'em wasn't a game she could learn in one shift.

"That's too rich for my blood."

"I bet you're holding threes."

"I'll call and raise you five."

"Okay, you're up," said Mindy, breaking her concentration. "Make your round, but remember not to interrupt the play." Her warning struck more fear than a teacher's command, *Time's up. Turn in your exam.*

With pen and tablet in hand, Isabelle worked her way to Craig's chair. "Would you like something to drink, sir?"

"Sweet tea with—" Craig sputtered to an abrupt stop. "What in blazes are *you* doing here?"

"I work here, sir. This is my first day on the job." Isabelle held her pen poised over her tablet. "Was that sweet tea with lemon?"

"This is so not possible," he muttered.

"Say, friend, you here to play poker or catch up with old girlfriends?" Johnny Herman punctuated his question with a chuckle.

"I call." Craig's cheeks flamed bright red. "Sorry. For a moment I thought I was looking at my ex-wife."

Everyone laughed as the bid passed to the next player.

"Your drink, sir?" Isabelle asked.

"Know what, sweetheart? Skip the tea. Fix me a sandwich—ham, cheese, and turkey, and stack it up tall. Gimmie some salad too. Just nothing with nuts. I'll eat after this hand."

"You get the sandwich started. I'll take the drink order." The ever-efficient Mindy appeared at her side.

On wobbly legs that had nothing to do with her high heels, Isabelle tottered toward the buffet table. One quick glance at the poker table confirmed her suspicion. Despite his dark glasses, her ex-husband was glaring daggers at her. Refusing to become intimidated, she made a sandwich Dagwood would have been proud of. On the plate she added mayo and scoops of coleslaw and Waldorf salad. *Funny how you remember someone's favorites even after several years.*

By the time she placed the plate on one of the rolling tables, Craig had risen to his feet. "Gentlemen, ma'am, with your permission I'll sit out a hand or two." He pushed his chips into a pile.

"Hurry back, Craig from Tennessee. You have temporary custody of lots of my money." Big Sam laughed, but his smile didn't quite reach his eyes.

"I'll be back before you know it, Mr. Malloy." Craig nodded at the other players and approached Isabelle looking as if he might burst into flames. He whispered in a voice only she could hear. "I don't know what you're up to, but you need to get out of here."

"Yes, of course," she said. "I'd be happy to get you some sweet tea." Isabelle marched off to the beverage cart and took her time filling the order. When she returned with the unrequested drink, Craig had already eaten half his sandwich.

"I can't believe you have nothing better to do on your honeymoon," he hissed between mouthfuls of salad.

"Nate and I are on a humanitarian mission." She brushed crumbs into the palm of her hand. "I'm an actor on the stage of life."

"No, you're a crazy person who's rapidly turning me into one." Craig shoveled in another forkful of food.

"Are you in a big hurry, sir?" Isabelle modulated her tone because Mindy was eavesdropping.

"Yes. I'm eager to get back to the action and away from someone who resembles a former thorn in my foot." Craig threw down his napkin and shoved away his plate.

Isabelle returned to the drink cart, where Mindy was ready with an admonishment. "Stay away from that player. He doesn't like your looks, and Big Sam doesn't like bad vibes at his game."

"Why should I be worried about this Big Sam guy, other than the big-tip angle?" Isabelle wiped condensation from the cooler with a fresh cloth.

Mindy was ready to explode. "Because he's the biggest whale in professional poker—no pun intended. Mr. Malloy brings tons of money into this casino whenever he's in town, and the Golden Magnolia wants to keep him happy. Were you born yesterday, Isabelle?"

She rubbed her forehead. "I think so."

"Big Sam organizes private games, and the house gets a cut. One of those pots could buy you a new house, silly girl." Mindy produced a glorious smile as the security guard approached the cooler of Cokes. "Just handle the sandwich bar while I serve drinks," she ordered.

Isabelle would have happily followed Mindy's instructions if only the poker room hadn't erupted into chaos.

Craig suddenly threw down his cards and grabbed his throat with both hands. "What have you done?" he gasped. "I told you nothing with nuts." Craig's eyes bugged from his head, while his cheeks turned pale. When he struggled to stand, he fell back into his chair.

What is he talking about? Craig used to eat Payday bars and Rocky Road ice cream like they were going out of style. While Isabelle watched helplessly from behind the cold cuts, other casino employees sprang into action.

Security guards rushed into the room as the dealer helped Craig to his feet. "Paramedics are on their way, sir. They'll be here shortly." The dealer supported one of his arms, while a guard took hold of the other.

"No paramedics," Craig wheezed, his words labored and slurred. "Just get me to the restroom. I have an Epi pen."

Without a moment's hesitation, the staff half lifted, half dragged Craig into the private bathroom for the high-stakes area.

Epi pen? Her ex-husband wasn't allergic to anything. Craig had been known to eat week-old Moo Shoo Gai Pan with no adverse effects. Isabelle glanced around the room. The young gambler looked bored, the rest of the players concerned, and Big Sam looked furious—at her.

"Mindy, let's have a round of drinks," called Big Sam. "But I'd like you and you alone to make them."

"Coming right up, sir," Mindy said. Then to Isabelle she whispered, "What did you give that guy?"

"Yes, what did you give him, Miss Price?" This question came from Mr. Lewis. He'd slipped into the room during the melee.

Isabelle's knees felt weak. "Turkey, ham, and Swiss cheese on Italian bread. Coleslaw and that apple salad on the side."

"Waldorf salad contains raisins, celery, eggs, and *walnuts* in addition to apples," said Mindy.

"I didn't realize that. I've never made it at home."

"It's your professional responsibility to learn the ingredients of what you serve. Information is available at the start of each shift." Mr. Lewis looked down his Roman nose at her as if he thought she had tried to murder the man.

Not that she didn't have good reason to in the past. "I'm so sorry, sir."

For the next minute—the longest in her life—everyone watched the door to the restroom until Craig emerged. Looking pale, he walked shakily back to the table.

"Sorry for the drama, folks," he said when he reached his chair. "I'm fine, but I need to lay down a while. Mr. Malloy, can I take a rain check on the game?"

"Sure, no problem. I'm glad you're all right. Come back when you're feeling up to it."

"Thank you, sir." Craig hung on to the table while the dealer cashed out his impressive pile of chips. Then he slowly shuffled from the room as every pair of eyes followed his progress.

"If we're all in agreement, why don't we take a one-hour break? " Big Sam struggled to his feet and approached the bar. "Forget the drink, Mindy, but this is for you." He laid down a chip.

From where she stood Isabelle could see a five followed by two zeros.

Mr. Lewis addressed the whale rather solicitously. "Why don't we get some lunch, Sam?"

"Sure, but let's clear something up before we go. I don't want *that woman* anywhere near me." Mr. Malloy pointed a stubby finger in Isabelle's direction. "If she's on the floor, I'll play down the road."

"I understand, sir." Mr. Lewis turned to scowl at Isabelle. "You're fired, Miss Price. Collect your wages and turn in your uniform downstairs."

Although she hadn't been planning on a long career in casino service, she'd never been fired in her life. "I'm so sorry. I hope that player will be okay." Sobbing, she reached for her clear plastic tote containing her lipstick and tissues.

"Wait," said Mindy. "I'll go cash in the chips and give you your share."

"No, they are all yours. I consider this a lesson learned." Isabelle cast a teary smile at her short-lived partner and hurried toward the elevator.

Downstairs in the employee lounge, she pulled on her capris and T-shirt and threw the uniform into a hamper. Not bothering with her hourly wage, Isabelle sprinted through the casino to the parking lot. With any luck, she could catch up with Craig before he left. After scanning the parking lot for five minutes, she gave up and headed to her car.

Inside her vehicle sat both her current husband and ex-husband. Neither man looked happy as Isabelle climbed into the backseat.

"I can't believe you let her walk into a dangerous situation," said Craig. "Poker players take the game very seriously. We're talking about a lot of money."

"If by *her* you mean *me*, nobody *let* me do anything." She poked her finger at Craig's shoulder. "And since when did you develop a nut allergy?"

Craig swiveled around. "You are crazy, just as I suspected."

"Everybody calm down," Nate demanded. "You are not going back in there," he said to Isabelle. "That room had security cameras and I had a plant in that game," he said to Craig, sounding smug.

"A plant? Tell me what's going on or I'm outta here."

"Relax," said Nate. "We know you're up to something, and we want to help. I asked a retired poker player to join the game to keep an eye on Izzy. That Big Sam character is filthy rich and a little scary."

"Keep away from Malloy and stay out of this casino. I mean it, Nate. Mind your own business or I'll have security bar you from the premises." Craig tried to exit, but Nate was too quick. He jerked him back inside like a rag doll.

"If I'm barred, Cassie will start making a ruckus outside the poker room, begging you not to squander the rent money."

"Cassie is here? You involved my wife?" Craig grabbed ahold of Nate's shirt.

"No, she involved us. Make no mistake about it. And she's not leaving Bay St. Louis without you."

Craig released the fabric. "Please, Nate, take Izzy and Cassie home. I've fallen down a hole I can't crawl out of. All your good intentions will only get me killed." He dropped his face into his hands.

"Not if you let us help you before it's too late." Isabelle placed a hand on his shoulder.

Nate did too. "Trust us."

His simple declaration seemed to turn the tide. Without looking at them, Craig started to talk. "I just received an invitation to the big game Sam Malloy organizes in every town he visits. I have no choice. I must win big to pay Mickey Pierce what I owe him."

Isabelle's pity evaporated. "Your old loan shark from Nashville? You borrowed from that creep to start gambling again?" She pounded on the back of his seat.

"No, Izzy, I didn't." Craig turned to face her. "But Pierce came to my office to collect on an old debt I never paid in full. He said if I didn't help with his 'sure way to win,' he would make my life miserable."

"Why didn't you go to the police?" asked Nate.

"And say what? A man I owe money to wants to be repaid? I've heard the stories. Pierce starts by poisoning your dog or torching your garage. One of his goons once pushed a man's mother down a flight of stairs, but there's never a way to tie it to Pierce." Craig looked from one to the other. "He said a seat at Big Sam's table can pay the debt in full, and then I'll never see him again."

"What happens if you lose?" asked Nate. "Then the money he staked you will be added to your tab. I don't care how good you are, Craig. The cards might not fall your way."

"I can't lose, not with these." He pulled a pair of dark glasses from his pocket and handed them to Nate. "Don't touch the lenses."

Nate held them up to inspect. "Good grief! What are these—night vision?"

"It's a type of infrared. Pierce bought a prototype from some teenage genius and used it in Shreveport and then in Tunica. Now we'll put them into play at the Golden Magnolia." He tucked them back into his pocket.

Isabelle clucked her tongue. "How will that work? You think the poker room will be pitch-dark and only you will be able to see the cards? You're not this stupid, Craig."

He ignored her insult. "They're not night vision goggles. Every deck of cards used by this chain of casinos comes from the same manufacturer. Mickey paid an employee to mark certain decks with a special ink. Wearing these, I'll know what everybody is holding once those decks are put into play." Craig pulled out his regular pair of sunglasses. "The shades don't look much different from the ones I always wear."

"And you fell for this *Star Wars* baloney?" Isabelle shook his headrest with both hands.

"Like I said, it worked twice before. Pierce sets up a different player in each town and has already taken a couple million off Big Sam. That's why Sam is itching to play again tomorrow. He thinks his luck is about to change. This will be my only chance to get out from under that loan shark's thumb. I'll give him my winnings, and I swear I'll never gamble again."

Isabelle looked at Nate, who seemed to share her sense of foreboding. "Did you use those glasses to win? I saw that you had a huge pile of chips."

"No, today I won fair and square. Imagine that. Pierce arranged for a marked deck to appear to make sure I knew what I was doing, but I faked the allergic reaction before it came into play. I needed to get you out of there before you ruined everything."

"You big faker." Isabelle pulled a lock of his hair. "I was worried you were dying."

"You shouldn't have been in there," snapped Craig. "I told you to mind your own business. At least my stunt won me a return invitation to Big Sam's game. Pierce won't have any trouble getting his special decks into play. And that's where the big money can be won."

Nate finally spoke up. "You were very close to going to jail instead of back to some high roller's big game."

"What do you mean?" Craig's grip on the armrest tightened.

"If you had cheated today, you would be under arrest, the same as Pierce and anybody else connected to this screwball scheme. I told you security was watching Izzy, but they were also watching you. Casinos prosecute cheaters to the full extent of the law."

"In that case, I'm a dead man or worse. They might hurt Cassie." Craig sounded on the verge of tears.

Isabelle wrapped an arm around him. "When security checks the cards, they'll know you didn't cheat."

"Don't you get it? Mickey Pierce is a well-connected man. When he finds out I ruined his perfect plan, I'll never be able to stop looking over my shoulder."

Nate shook his head. "Since you haven't cheated yet, we can find a way to get everything we want."

"What do you have in mind?" he asked, his voice hopeful.

"Let's just say Izzy and I have friends in high places too." Nate started the engine. "Stay in touch with us. In the meantime I'll drop you off at your car."

"Thanks, Nate. You too, Izzy."

"Don't mention it," she said.

We're an odd threesome, she thought. *But sometimes you just have to play the hand you're dealt.*

FORTY-EIGHT

Natchez
Tuesday

Beth stumbled down the steps, still groggy even after her morning shower. In the kitchen her mother worked a crossword puzzle. "Good morning, Mummy." Beth used her favorite childhood nickname. "Where's Pops?"

Rita peered over her reading glasses. "Probably in the bathroom now that you're finally done in the shower. We have to be in New Orleans by one o'clock. He's getting a second opinion that his benign prostatic hyperplasia truly is benign."

Beth stopped pouring and held the coffeepot aloft. "Why didn't he pound on the door or shut off the hot water tank?"

"Because you're no longer a teenager. If we don't treat adult children with the dignity they deserve, they'll move out. Then we'll be denied that fat room and board check each month." Rita's belly shook as she laughed.

"Sounds like you read that somewhere." Beth sat at the table with her coffee.

"Heard it on *The View*. Usually one of those gals knows what they're talking about. That's why they have four."

"Why is this the first time I'm hearing about Pops needing a second opinion about something that sounds serious?"

"Because your dad doesn't want you to worry, and because there's nothing to worry about. The second opinion just gives us a chance to check out a new buffet restaurant by the zoo."

"Adult children need to be kept in the loop. Check with the gals on *The View* if you don't believe me."

Rita passed her a plate of blueberry muffins. "I will. Why aren't you at work?"

"My partner told me to stay home while he drops off evidence and goes to Jackson to take his former fiancée out to lunch." Beth broke off a piece of muffin.

"That charming little Michael Preston? Why are you letting him see his old flame? You should have sharpened your claws and tagged along."

"Michael and I are partners, nothing more. So please don't stop at a mother-of-the-bride store while in New Orleans." Beth leveled her sternest expression. "What can I do to occupy my mind while you're gone?"

"Are you worried because Michael's seeing his old girlfriend?" Rita whispered with tender concern.

Beth snorted. "I've got more on my mind than romance. Give me something physically demanding."

Rita threw her crossword puzzle in the trash and set her mug in the sink. "Well, since you volunteered, I would love someone to rototill the garden. Everything is done growing out there. If the clumps are broken up and weeds turned under, the garden will be ready for spring planting."

"I'm just the woman for the job." Beth finished her muffin in two bites.

"Wear safety glasses and throw any stones you find into a bucket." Her mother kissed the top of her head. "Dig around in the fridge. There are plenty of leftovers for your lunch and dinner. We'll be back before dark."

"Don't worry about me. This adult child can stay home alone without something bad happening." Beth refilled her mug and took a quick scan of the newspaper. Within the hour, her parents left on their day trip.

Dressed in holey jeans and a ragged Saints T-shirt, Beth was soon ankle-deep in a thick tangle of weeds and decaying vegetables. *Who knew a person could get trapped in pumpkin vines just like water hyacinths in the swamp?* She would need a machete to chop the mess before running the tiller.

"Doesn't anybody answer the door at the Kirby household?"

A gruff voice cut through Beth's contemplation of her task. Wiping sweat from her eyes with the back of a glove, she stared into the face of Detective Lejeune. "My parents went to a doctor's appointment. What can I help you with, Jack? Surely I can't be breaking the law in my mother's backyard."

"Was that supposed to be funny? If so, your one-woman comedy routine has reached the end of the line." Jack pushed up his sunglasses and shifted his weight on the uneven ground. "Put down the shovel and get over here." Even for a man who sneered instead of smiled, he looked particularly loathsome.

"It's a hoe, not a shovel. Care to tell me what this is all about?"

The detective rested his beefy hand on his weapon. "I'll tell you after you put down the hoe."

Wordlessly, Beth held the implement at arm's length and dropped it between rows of cabbage plants.

"Elizabeth Kirby, you're under arrest for obstruction of justice. Step out of the garden and put your hands behind your back. You have the right to remain silent. Anything you say can and will be used against—"

"Stop!" she shouted. "I know the Miranda warning." Beth glanced around, praying the neighbors weren't outside. She feared local gossip more than his bullying. "What is the matter with you, Jack? I didn't *obstruct* anything."

"I'm not telling you again. Walk toward me nice and slow." He unsnapped his holster.

Blowing her breath out in a huff, Beth lifted her palms and

approached the madman. "Do you have a warrant?" she asked, although she knew the answer.

"Of course I do. Unlike you, I know my job. Hold out your hands." When she stood in front of him, he snapped a cuff on one wrist.

"You've got to be kidding me." Beth struggled to get away. "Let's go down to the station and sort out whatever has tipped you over the edge."

He yanked her by the arm and snapped on the other cuff. "You think Chief McNeil will pull your fat out of the fire? He witnessed you interfering in my investigation. I asked you point-blank if we had everything to give to the feds and you said yes. I asked you if you were hiding anything up your sleeve. 'Oh, no, not little ol' me,' you said. Then the other half of the Price tag team drops off new copies of the Baptist Church account. Even someone as incompetent as you should know that's obstruction. You're going to jail, Kirby. With any luck, you'll stay in the county to serve your sentence. Maybe I'll bring stale cookies on visiting day...or maybe not." He dragged her through the yard to the street, where a patrol car sat idling.

As expected, several neighbors happened to be walking their dogs or retrieving mail as Beth was propelled into the backseat like a bag of laundry. They stared at the spectacle as the car drove slowly down the street. Beth rode downtown as though she'd been knocked windless. No one spoke—not her, not Jack, not the new patrolman, who stole glances at her in the rearview mirror. At least when they reached the station, Beth was hustled through the back entrance, down familiar hallways, and placed in a holding cell. Fortunately, her new roommate, who was asleep on her bunk, wasn't someone Beth had previously arrested. *In a former life.*

Beth sat on the metal chair facing the green wall and pondered her options. One by one she ruled out calling her mom, her boss, and her partner. Her parents were on their way to New Orleans, doubtlessly worried about prostate cancer. Nate was enjoying his honeymoon with his bride and in no mood to hear that his veteran employee was in jail. And Michael was currently collecting DNA evidence to bring a potential murderer to justice. No time to post bail for his training instructor. Briefly she considered calling Kim, Cheryl, or Nina. Yet once again she'd neglected to stay in touch with her friends. Her promise of lunch or a movie had never materialized. So instead, she climbed onto the top bunk and contemplated all the ways she'd gone off track, with the case and with life in general.

With so much to contemplate, Beth dozed off, only to dream about spoons sharpened into blades, group showers with nasty women, and poisoned cookies delivered by her archenemy.

FORTY-NINE

When Michael had shown up at the police station early Tuesday morning, both Chief McNeil and Detective Lejeune were already out on the road. With little time to spare, Michael sealed the yellow envelope of account statements and left it with instructions that it should go to Detective Lejeune ASAP. Briefly he contemplated explaining to the chief's second-in-command how he came by the new evidence, but then he dismissed the notion. The man looked as though he had enough on his plate already.

"Have Detective Lejeune call me if he has any questions." Michael placed his business card atop the envelope.

Within minutes he was driving northeast on Route 9 but in no particular hurry. He needed time to think, a chance to mentally prepare to meet someone capable of great evil. A woman likely responsible for a minister's death, either directly or indirectly.

Rachel wasn't happy when he'd phoned last night, especially because he'd woken her up. "Do you know what time it is, Preston?" she huffed.

"Yes, ma'am. It's almost eleven. But I wanted to thank you for sending the statements so promptly."

"You're welcome. Give me a few days to track down those emails, and then I'll be in touch."

She was about to hang up when Michael blurted out, "That will be fine, but I want to redeem my rain check for dinner."

"*What?* Dinner was hours ago." Impatience edged her words.

"I'm hoping we can have dinner tomorrow. Since my boss left town, I've been working way too hard. This would be a good chance for us to catch up." Michael thought a half-truth would sound more believable than complete fiction.

Rachel yawned into the mouthpiece. "As much as I'd like to, I gotta work from one to nine. No time for dinner."

"How about a quick lunch if I promise not to make you late?" Michael gave her no chance to decline. "The problem is, I don't think copies of the statements and your correspondence with Paul Dean will satisfy my client. Mrs. Dean would like assurance that Spare the Children doesn't expect *her* to fulfill any monetary commitments."

"The statements clearly indicate the account belongs to Calvary Baptist of Natchez, not Reverend Dean personally."

"I agree. It's black-and-white from where I stand, but maybe you could sign an affidavit that her family has no obligation, especially because quite a bit of money seems to be missing."

Michael's last four words hung in the air before Rachel changed her tune, literally and figuratively.

"Why don't you pick me up outside my office at eleven?" she drawled. "Two hours should be enough time to catch up on each other's life. Bring whatever document you want me to sign." Rachel ended the call without wishing him a good night.

With their evidence in police custody and several hours before his date, he did a quick search of Rachel Stewart on his laptop and then slept like a baby. By the time he headed north the next morning, he knew that she rented her furnished apartment on a month-to-month basis and her car had been leased by D.K. Financials, who held the title and registration. Other than a closetful of clothes, Rachel had nothing anchoring her to Jackson. She would have no trouble making a quick getaway once the pyramid tumbled to the ground.

As he pulled up in front of D.K. Financials, Rachel climbed from her Cadillac. "Right on the dot," she called with a cheery smile. "That's one of the things I love about you, Michael."

He walked around to the passenger side to open her door. "That's me, Mr. Punctual."

"And you're a gentleman. I don't remember the last time a man opened my door." Rachel ducked into his low-slung car. "When did you get this fancy thing? I don't remember your driving anything like this."

"I bought it as part of my self-improvement program. Where are we going? Your choice, my treat."

"Take a left at the light." Rachel turned to face him. "Everyone needs to make changes, but you were just fine the way you were."

Although the traffic was light, Michael kept his eyes on the road. "If you were so happy, Rachel, why break our engagement right before the wedding?"

"It wasn't because of your shortcomings. It was due to my own personal unhappiness." She placed a hand on his arm. "Turn left at the stop sign."

"Care to elaborate? Today is about catching up and being honest with each other." He glanced at her, but she was staring out the window.

"When you asked me to marry you, I was so happy to say yes, but then, as we got closer to the wedding, I took a good look at my two married sisters and started to panic. Their lives are nothing but an endless loop of cooking, cleaning, and chauffeuring kids to soccer practice. My one sister who kept her job simply added sleep-deprived and stressed-out to her lifestyle. Ugh, I couldn't imagine that for myself." Rachel shook her head as though dispelling the mental image. "Turn into the next plaza on your right. A Terrace in Tuscany serves the best Italian cuisine in town."

Following her instructions, Michael spotted the restaurant at the end of the row. "Couldn't you have figured that out *before* we put down deposits everywhere in town?"

"That is my one regret," she whispered. "I made the right choice by not getting married, but I'm sorry I hurt you, Michael. You could be the only man I'll ever love."

He ignored the manipulative lie as though no more consequential than a radio commercial. "Shall we go inside? I can smell the garlic and sweet basil even in the parking lot."

Inside the dimly lit bistro, Michael waited to resume serious conversation until after they had ordered. "Does this accounting firm that specializes in nonprofits have what you were looking for?"

Her response was an unexpected burst of laughter. "Hardly. Jackson might be bigger than Brookhaven and have more restaurants, but it has basically the same family-oriented mind-set. Plus my work here is just as boring as it was at Anderson. I want excitement and adventure before I'm too old to enjoy it." She blotted her lipstick on the linen napkin.

Michael realized that was probably the most honest thing she had ever said. "So what's next on your agenda? Any plans for the future?"

Her eyes turned luminous in the candlelight. "Yes. That's why I need you to reassure Mrs. Dean. Not that I have no compassion for a grieving widow, but I can't have her causing a ruckus for me."

"Care to elaborate?" Beneath the table, Michael's hands bunched into fists.

Rachel took a piece of crusty bread from the basket. "A few weeks ago I applied for a position at a global consortium of accountants. Their clients are either wealthy individuals or international corporations. Every one of them places discretion high on their list of requirements. I recently found out they've narrowed the field to three candidates. I can't tell you how much I want this job. The consortium has branches in Rome, Paris, London, and Tokyo. If hired, who knows where I could be sent? I would travel the world on private jets, be able to set my hours, and have conversations without catty secretaries listening in. D.K. has been no different than Anderson in that regard."

"Sounds like the opportunity of a lifetime, but I fail to see what Mrs. Dean has to do with your career aspirations."

Rachel leaned toward him as though about to divulge state secrets. "With competition so fierce, I don't want my potential employer to find out about my misunderstanding with Paul Dean. That's why I need to keep my current boss out of the loop. Who knows what George Roush could put in my employment file?"

A misunderstanding with Paul Dean? Michael dabbed his bread in the olive oil for distraction. He had forgotten how self-serving Rachel was. Living in a big city had done little to nurture compassion or empathy.

She took a bite of bread. "Please smooth things out with Alice Dean, at least for a few weeks. This new job can get me out of Mississippi forever. If you help me, I'll be more than grateful. Who knows? Maybe one day you'll be ready to put these cotton fields in your rearview mirror, and I'll be in a position to help you. There's a whole world out there if you could stand working with me again. The woman who stupidly let the best man she'd ever met slip away." Rachel settled back as the waitress delivered a huge salad and a heaping platter of smoked meats, cheeses, and olives.

"I don't believe Mrs. Dean will present any problems." He forced his lips into a smile. "Why don't we get started? All this talk about the future made me hungry."

It was a bald-faced lie. Talking with the conniving scammer had nauseated him, but as Rachel pointed out, appearances were everything. Michael ate a portion of salad and tasted several different meats and cheeses. He feigned interest when she gave updates on a few mutual friends.

Then, at the appropriate moment, his hand knocked over her water glass into her lap. Michael apologized profusely for his clumsiness, and when Rachel left to pat herself dry a bit more privately, he slipped her lipstick-smeared napkin and water glass into plastic bags. He quickly scanned the room, stowed the evidence in his briefcase, and replaced the napkin and goblet from an empty nearby table. When she returned from the restroom, he was refilling her water from the carafe.

"I apologize again, Rachel."

"Don't mention it. Soon I'll be good as new."

Thank goodness for shadowy bistros where patrons minded their own business. If any of the waitstaff or fellow patrons had witnessed his sleight of hand, no one made mention. Soon Michael dropped off the three-headed serpent at her office amid a flurry of air kisses and false promises to stay in touch.

Then he was on his way back to Natchez, eager to see Beth, the antithesis of Rachel in every possible way.

FIFTY

Bay St. Louis

Tuesday evening, Craig walked into the casino's coffee shop and scanned the assortment of patrons. Some were winding down after a day in the spa or at the slot machines. Others, like him, had just awoken from a midday nap and were anxious for the games to begin. He had no trouble spotting Nate Price. The guy sat hunched over a cup of coffee looking far less confident than he had in today's meeting with casino security, the head of the poker room, and the retired card shark.

"You look worried." Craig slipped into the opposite side of the booth. "Did my ex try to poison you with her cooking?"

Nate grimaced. "You forget that we're staying at a B and B. Besides, you're the one who needs to pull off the Big Sting, and you look terrible. Not at all like Robert Redford in that old movie."

Craig motioned to the waitress for coffee. "I couldn't sleep because I was rehearsing every possible contingency in my mind. I am ready to take on Big Sam and every other high roller looking to separate this particular fool from his money." He rubbed his knuckles as though preparing for a fistfight.

Nate sipped his coffee. "It's not too late to back out."

"Why would I do that?"

"Because it could get dangerous. Lewis said the buy-in is a

quarter-million dollars. Maybe Big Sam can absorb that kind of loss, but some players could be staking their life savings on a card game."

"Like I said, fools and their money. Gamblers usually lose in the long run. Unfortunately, it took me a long time to figure that out."

"If one of those players finds out you hastened the inevitable, you could have more enemies than Mickey Pierce."

"Weren't you paying attention? I don't plan to cheat."

Nate shook his head like a stubborn child. "What if the special decks don't show up?"

"If I lose Pierce's money waiting for the marked cards to appear, that's on him. Pierce is in charge of those decks." Craig smiled at the waitress, who was ready to take their order. "French toast, bacon, eggs over hard. And keep the coffee coming."

"How about you?" she asked Nate.

"Nothing, ma'am. Just coffee." Nate appeared to be chewing on a sour lemon.

"Either spit out what's bothering you or relax. Nothing will go wrong."

"What if you get caught up in the action and use those crazy glasses to win hand after hand? Lewis was very clear. If you use any illegal means to cheat on casino premises, you'll be prosecuted to the full extent of the law."

A jolt of anger spiked up Craig's spine. "I was at the meeting, remember? Like I told security, I don't plan to cheat."

Nate met his gaze. "I know you love poker. And I read gambling can be as strong an addiction as alcohol or drugs. Maybe I was wrong to set this up. Isabelle and I don't want to enable you."

Craig took several deep breaths. "You're not the one who set this up. I did so that I can get out from under my debt to a mobster. I'm truly amazed the Golden Magnolia is going along with the idea. They could have as easily turned me over to the police and washed their hands of me and my personal problems."

"Having possession of those glasses isn't a crime. If they work, they can catch everyone connected to the ring. But there are so many things that could go wrong."

"You've always been a man of faith, Nate. Try having some now." Craig glanced at his watch. "You're right about gambling. My addiction destroyed my first marriage. I won't let the past destroy my second. Despite what I told Cassie in Nashville, I love my wife more than life itself. I can't live with the possibility of Pierce's thugs coming after her."

"But if you're playing against the house, I heard the house always wins."

Craig sighed. "Look, I'm grateful to you and Isabelle, but you know nothing about poker. You only play against the house at the table games on the casino floor. In real poker games, you're playing against other players. And I'm better than the average Joe."

"If you gamble only until the marked cards appear, how can you be sure you'll have enough to pay Pierce?"

"I won plenty yesterday before Izzy showed up and spoiled my concentration. As for the rest? Let's just say I've become a man of faith too." Craig pushed up from the table just as the waitress delivered a plate of hot food.

Nate clamped a hand on his arm. "Where are you going? There's plenty of time before the game starts."

"Your negativity is bringing me down, old buddy. I'm going out to the marina to clear my head."

"But you need to eat. That game could go all night." Nate sounded anxious.

"You worry more than your wife." Nevertheless, Craig forked the eggs in between slices of toast, topped it with strips of bacon, and wrapped it up in his napkin. "I'll eat this sitting on the dock of the bay. Someone ought to write a song about that." Craig winked and strolled out the door.

Once he was away from Nate, Craig lost some of his bravado about the game. He hadn't liked Johnny Herman during the meeting with casino officials. The guy had made several judgmental comments he didn't need. Plenty of people had good reason to berate him, but not that old-timer. Why did Nate think a former poker pro would be helpful to his cause? But as long as Herman stayed out of his way and didn't do anything stupid, there shouldn't be a problem.

Ninety minutes later, wearing his spiffiest clothes along with a wire to transmit every word said during the game, Craig headed to one of the poker rooms on the third floor. He took a final glance at Cassie's picture, tucked it next to his heart, and knocked on the door. One of the executive hosts opened the door with a broad smile.

"Mr. Mitchell, come in. Glad you're feeling better." Big Sam's booming voice matched his girth.

"Thank you for letting me come back, Mr. Malloy. I'm honored to play with a man of your reputation."

"Don't know about my reputation, but this is a fair game. We might not all be friends here, but we're all gentlemen…and one fine lady." Sam bowed to the well-dressed woman Craig had met last night.

Ms. Hardesty was sipping a flute of what looked like champagne. Most likely it would be her only glass. Few serious players imbibed in alcohol during games because it dulled their faculties. And considering the quarter-million-dollar buy-in, this game was for serious players only. Nevertheless, a tuxedoed professional stood at the bar. When Sam walked over to greet another new arrival, Craig perused the snack table: caviar on toast points, grilled shrimp and asparagus skewers, a veal pâté served with crackers, and warm prime rib sliders. Although rich people probably didn't call tiny sandwiches "sliders."

Craig asked for a Coke at the bar and stood back to assess the other players. He immediately locked gazes with Johnny Herman. *That old man is watching me.* Craig frowned and occupied himself with the appetizers, trying not to attract attention.

"If everyone will take their seats, please," announced Big Sam.

"We're ready to resume play. Feel free to sit out a few hands whenever the spirit moves you. Any questions?"

There were none.

Craig took a position three seats away from Johnny Herman and next to Ms. Hardesty. The woman was wearing a wedding band on her right hand. *What did that mean—widow? Married, but temporarily estranged?* He forced his concentration back to his task at hand. Because that's what this was—a job for the evening that would restore the life he'd come to love. Nate and Isabelle might not believe this—and he couldn't blame them—but he would never gamble again after tonight. No matter what the outcome. He felt neither the anticipation of nonstop, heart-pounding action nor the exhilaration over the prospect of vast riches.

Craig felt nothing but cold, unmitigated fear that failure would seal his fate with Cassie forever. He could not fail. As he settled into the high-backed upholstered chair, Craig uttered a simple prayer for deliverance from his past and grace for the future.

For several hours he played poker to the best of his abilities. Often he won, sometimes he lost, but the pile of chips in front of him continued to grow. The special decks—those marked with a certain ink visible only to him—failed to appear. His luck wouldn't last forever. He'd played poker long enough to know that, but what could he do? He hadn't won enough to pay Pierce everything he owed him.

Surprisingly, the tiresome retired gambler, who had been so critical of him this morning, seemed to throw down his cards at inappropriate times. Maybe he was wrong, but Craig possessed a sixth sense for these things—Johnny Herman had folded several winning hands.

Finally, the first egg from the golden goose appeared in the dealer's shoe. As each card was dealt facedown around the table, Craig could easily see who had been given a queen or an eight or the ace of hearts. Like magic he knew exactly what each player had, along with the face-up cards on the table. And he knew exactly how to bet.

With this incredible advantage, all Craig needed was four or five more hands. Then he would have all the money he owed Pierce. He knew what he'd promised Nate and Art Lewis, but a few extra winning hands could rid him of a nasty loan shark forever.

This wasn't addiction. This was a chance of a lifetime. Yet somehow that tiresome old man sensed Craig's golden opportunity had arrived.

"Know what, Tennessee?" Mr. Herman slurred as though drunk, yet Craig had seen him drink only black coffee.

"My name is Mr. Mitchell, sir," said Craig, mildly unnerved.

"Yeah, whoever you are," continued Herman. "I'm tired of those dark glasses. Like you're some kind of Hollywood celebrity. If it's just the same to you, I like to see the eyes of everybody I'm losing money to."

Craig cleared his throat. "It's *not* just the same to me. These are prescription glasses that I'm required to wear."

Herman scooted his chair back from the table. "That's baloney, boy. I've seen you play on the casino floor all week with no dark glasses. You saw the cards just fine." His smile was almost a sneer. "I want those shades gone so I know who I'm playing with." The tiresome old man turned his focus on Big Sam, as did Craig and every other player at the table. As their organizer, it was his decision.

Craig held his breath. He needed to win a few more hands. Yes, he wasn't supposed to cheat, but only he knew exactly when the marked cards appeared.

Big Sam sipped his drink while considering the conundrum. One by one he assessed his invited guests and then folded his arms over his chest. "I played with Mr. Herman years ago when I was starting out." Sam nodded at the old man. "I know you're an honest player." Then he refocused on Craig. "But I never laid eyes on you, Mr. Mitchell, before yesterday. So if Mr. Herman wants no sunglasses at the table, then I say no sunglasses at the table." Sam thumped his fist on the felt, an unnecessary punctuation to his command.

Craig knew the host's decision was final. If he argued, he would be asked to leave. So he removed the glasses and tucked them inside his sport coat. "Of course, sir. My apologies for the disruption."

Tension at the table immediately abated. Two players called drink orders to the bartender, giving Craig a few moments to consider his options before the next hand. He could continue to play. After all, he'd been winning before the marked cards surfaced. Glancing at his chips, he estimated he was within a few thousand of his target.

Or he could cash out and leave somewhere he no longer belonged. He and Cassie would figure out how to make up the difference and rid Mickey Pierce from their lives forever. That would be the right thing to do.

"How about a drink, Mr. Mitchell?" Sam Malloy slapped him on the back. "No hard feelings?"

With a queasy stomach and rubbery legs, Craig rose to his feet. "None whatsoever, sir, but I feel the vibes have turned against me. Cash me out, please." He pushed his chips toward the dealer. A minute later he stuffed the bills into his pocket and strode toward the door.

"*Vibes*...what a bunch of hooey," muttered Mr. Herman. "Come back when you wear big-boy pants."

Craig didn't care about the retired gambler's opinion of him. He cared what Cassie thought and what he thought of himself. Tomorrow he would find a Gamblers Anonymous meeting. But tonight he needed to find a church—any church—and lower his head in prayer. God had delivered him from himself.

Riding the elevator down from the high roller room, Craig's eyes filled with tears. By the time the doors opened onto the lively casino floor, he was sobbing like a baby. *Johnny Herman pegged me correctly.* He started walking, away from the bright lights of the casino, and kept on walking for miles. Several hours later, he was shaken awake by a burly maintenance man.

"I need to lock up in here, sir. Is there someone I can call for you?"

Craig gaped at his surroundings. "Where am I?"

"Main Street United Methodist Church. Are you all right?"

"Yes, I'm perfectly fine. I came in to pray and must have dozed off." Craig staggered stiffly down the aisle.

"Having a tough week?" the man asked when they reached the door.

"You could say that, but things are looking up." Craig stepped into a night that had grown much cooler.

"God bless you, friend." He waved and locked the door behind him.

Craig peered left and right, confused. For several disoriented moments, he couldn't remember where he had left his car. Then a familiar voice called out from the street.

"Hey, Tennessee, need a ride back to the Golden Magnolia?" Johnny Herman stuck his head out the window of his vehicle.

"What on earth are you doing here?" Craig snarled.

"I've been waiting to give you something, sonny."

Craig walked to the annoying man's car, stopping a foot from the driver's side.

"This is for you and Cassie." Herman shoved a banded stack of hundreds out the window.

"How do you know my wife's name is Cassie?" He chose probably the least consequential of his pack of questions.

"Nate told me. He and Isabelle have been worried about you. Get in. I don't want you walking down the street with this much money."

"How did you know where I was?" Inconsequential question number two.

"Nate followed you when you left the casino. He thought you might want some privacy when you went inside the church. I took over waiting for you to come out when I cashed out of the game. What happened? Did you fall asleep in there?"

Craig climbed into the car and sighed wearily. "Yes. All that stress wore me out."

Herman tossed another stack of money into his lap before driving away from the curb. "Add this to what you still need to pay off that guy. I only kept playing for your sake."

Staring at the money, Craig chose the big question: "Why would you do this for me, a total stranger?" A hitch in his voice betrayed his emotions.

"You ain't no stranger, Mr. Tennessee. I used to be you, once upon a time."

Craig placed the money on the console. "Thanks, but I can't take money from a senior citizen. You can probably put it to good use."

Herman braked to a sudden stop. "Nope. I don't need it. I gave the Golden Magnolia back the amount they staked me. I just added an extra twist to Nate's original plan. Now stop arguing and do what I tell you. Boy, I see why you and Isabelle didn't last—you're both cut from the same piece of stubborn cloth."

"That is the truth." Grinning, Craig picked up the money and tucked it in his coat. "Thank you, Mr. Herman. I'll never forget this, and I won't let you down."

"I know you won't, sonny, because I'm going to be keeping tabs on you."

FIFTY-ONE

Wednesday

Nate let his bride sleep in the next morning. When he heard her stir, he opened the shutters and flooded their bedroom with sunshine.

"Goodness, Nate. What time is it?" Isabelle bolted upright.

"Eight fifteen. You have forty-five minutes to shower and dress. Craig and Cassie are joining us for breakfast."

"Craig *and Cassie*?" she squealed, swinging her legs out of bed. "What have you been up to behind my back?"

Nate tossed her a bathrobe. "All questions shall be answered on the east verandah. I'll wait for you there. Don't be late." He closed the pocket doors behind him.

For the first time in their marriage, Isabelle appeared ten minutes early. "Okay, spill what you know." She dropped breathlessly into her chair.

Nate shrugged. "I would have, dear wife, but the Mitchells are here." He pointed at Craig and Cassie on their way up the walk.

Isabelle stared at the couple while Nate folded his newspaper.

"Mrs. Russo, I believe we're ready for breakfast," he told their innkeeper.

"You two look...absolutely joyous," Isabelle said to their guests.

"Don't sound so surprised," said Craig, taking Cassie's elbow. "Miracles do happen, Mrs. Price."

"You be nice, Craig." Cassie wrapped her arms around Isabelle. "If not for these two, we might not have our happy ending."

"I don't know how to say thank you." Craig offered Nate his hand, but when he started to shake, Craig pulled him into a man hug. "If there's any way I can repay you…"

Nate felt his cheeks flush. "Someday I'll ask for tickets to the Grand Old Opry."

Everyone laughed and sat down as Mrs. Russo delivered four plates of breakfast. "Dig in, folks. Today I whipped up my specialty."

Nate picked up his fork. "Can you two spend the day with us? We're heading to Mobile for some sightseeing."

Cassie and Craig exchanged a look. "We've taken up enough of your honeymoon. The Prices will spend today alone."

"No spying from behind potted plants," added Craig. "No surveillance, and no worrying about us. The Mitchells are fine." He kissed the back of Cassie's fingers.

"What will we do?" Nate winked at Isabelle.

She rolled her eyes and nibbled a piece of toast. "Mind if I ask what happened at the big game?"

Craig took a long gulp of coffee. "Johnny continued to play and win after I left. He returned what the casino had staked him and gave me the rest. I paid the loan shark and got him off my back forever. I tried to return what was left over to Johnny, but he said to donate it to Mississippi's GA helpline." Craig began to eat his omelet.

"What about Mickey Pierce and his crazy glasses?" asked Isabelle. "Will he get away with this?"

"Let him eat, Izzy." Nate patted his wife's hand. "We didn't invite the Mitchells over to interrogate Craig."

"No, she has a right to know." Craig dabbed his mouth. "When I paid Pierce my winnings and returned the glasses, I was afraid he would say that he wanted me to get into another game with Big Sam. Malloy will be in Biloxi in three weeks for a tournament, but Pierce told me he will have another player in place ready to take a few million off the guy. That crook never uses the same player twice, so I'm off the hook."

"He won't get away with this, will he?" Isabelle demanded.

Craig smiled. "Biloxi police, along with casino security, will be waiting for whoever uses those glasses in the high-stakes poker room. Those glasses will be retired before they're put into mass production."

Isabelle picked up her fork and began to eat. "Thank goodness you didn't cheat."

Craig locked gazes with Nate. "That is the truth."

"What's next for you two?" Nate asked.

Cassie, who had been eating and listening while her husband talked, set down her fork. "I cashed in my plane ticket, and we're driving back to Nashville today. I can't wait to get home. Not that Bay St. Louis isn't the sweetest town on the Gulf." She glanced around guiltily.

"I plan to beg for my old job back as a law clerk and eventually get reinstated as an attorney. In the meantime, I want to live a quiet life with my beloved wife." The look he gave Cassie left little doubt as to his sincerity.

"If it will help, I'll testify before the bar association that you helped law enforcement capture a band of card cheats. I'll even bring Johnny Herman to Nashville with me. That guy needs to get out more." Nate shared a smile with his wife as he said that.

"You would do that for me after I caused so much fuss on your honeymoon?"

"I would. What are family and friends for if not to create a little drama in life?"

Craig gave Nate his second meaningful gaze. "Not that I'm not grateful for the offer, but I hope that won't be necessary. I don't want to talk or even think poker ever again. But my home will always be open to you and Mr. Herman. I can't thank the three of you enough."

When the silence grew uncomfortable, Nate did the only thing he could—attack his breakfast with a vengeance.

After a tearful goodbye to Craig and Cassie, they walked down to the beach and dug their toes into the powdery white sand. "What's going on with you, Izzy?" asked Nate, sensing something was wrong. "Are you sad about leaving in a few days?"

"No. I love Natchez, and I'm eager to go back." Isabelle slipped her hand into his. "I just hope I didn't ruin our first vacation as man and wife."

"Are you joking? What second husband would want to miss this kind of excitement with husband number one?"

She pursed her lips. "You're not disappointed we didn't have more…private time together?"

He laughed. "We still have three more nights at this lovely B and B to help nature take its course."

"If you're referring to makin' babies, Mr. Price, we might as well watch a movie tonight."

He stopped short. "What exactly are you saying?"

"Have you heard about those little kits from the drugstore? If the stick turns a certain color it means one thing, but if—"

"Spit it out, Izzy," Nate interrupted.

"It turned a lovely shade of blue with a plus sign. We're pregnant."

"Does blue mean a boy?"

"Not necessarily. It's too soon to tell, but the Price family will soon be three."

Nate picked her up and swung her around. "Let's go home early. We need to go house-hunting and buy a minivan."

"*Simmer down*, Mr. Price. We've got at least seven months to prepare. Today we're going to Mobile, and tonight you're buying me something fattening for dinner. After that, we'll sit on the porch and discuss baby names."

"And then?" Nate lowered his wife to the ground.

"Who knows? We still have the most romantic suite in Mississippi. Let the games begin. And I'm not talkin' cards."

FIFTY-TWO

Natchez

*L*ooks like you won't be our overnight guest after all, Kirby."
The officer delivered his heartfelt regrets with a loud clang
of metal against the bars of her cell.

Momentarily confused, Beth bolted upright and peered around
her dismal surroundings. Then she remembered Jack tramping
through her mother's garden and dragging her away in handcuffs.
"More's the pity, Sergeant. Perhaps we can rendezvous later in the
week." She shifted onto her belly and slid off the top bunk, trying
not to wake her roommate. During one of their chats, Beth learned
that the young woman had been arrested for shoplifting for the
third time from the same establishment.

"Look who's here, your partner in crime." Sergeant Mendez
unlocked the cell door and stepped aside, revealing Michael leaning against the dingy wall. He was wearing workout clothes and a
worried expression on his face.

"I was at the gym, Elizabeth. I came as soon as I heard. I planned
to call you later."

"Right about now you look like a Ralph Lauren model, Mikey,"
Beth said as she squeezed past the cop in the doorway.

"Could you two take the reunion somewhere else? I'm trying
to catch some sleep here," her roommate complained from under-
neath the blanket.

"Sure thing," said Beth. "Nice meeting you, Wanda. Good luck in court."

Michael's smile lines deepened. "You certainly make friends quickly."

Beth walked down the hall to the personal property room. "A gal needs pals on the inside. Did you bail me out? How much did they ding you for?"

"Nary a dime. You've been released on your own recognizance, but I was fully prepared to put up my car title if necessary."

Beth got in line at the clerk's window. "For your new Charger? I'm not worth it, considering I'll soon be out of a job. Nate will fire me the moment he hears about my arrest."

Michael scanned the hallway in both directions. "Let's not discuss it until we're someplace private."

"Good idea." Most people were minding their own business, but a few cast withering looks at her. Beth avoided eye contact with others as she waited for her belongings to be returned.

As soon as they reached the parking lot, she inhaled a deep breath of warm, humid air. "Ah, freedom. Seems like I was locked up for months instead of hours." Beth hurried to his car and jumped in the moment he unlocked the doors.

"Are you hungry? How about coffee and a sandwich? Got a place in mind?"

"Yes, yes, and anywhere not frequented by off-duty cops." She slouched down in the seat.

"Let's cross the bridge into Vidalia. I bet nobody knows you there, so we can avoid the paparazzi." Michael wiggled his eyebrows comically.

"This isn't a joke. They charged me with felony obstruction, which could be bumped up to federal court if the FBI feels I impeded their case in any way."

"Calm down. It's not as bad as that." Michael turned onto the ramp to the bridge. "At best, what you did was interfere with a police investigation, which is a class B misdemeanor. You can probably plea that down to disorderly conduct and get off with community service. Along with time served, of course. Maybe they'll have you scrubbing graffiti or picking up litter." He leaned over to bump shoulders.

"Remind me to laugh uproariously the next time you sprain an ankle. I can't believe you find the demolition of my career amusing."

"Chief McNeil was the one who called me at the gym after he ordered your release. He was furious that Lejeune got the warrant behind his back, especially after I explained how and when I came by the new information."

"Once again, Chris had to come to my rescue." Beth scrubbed her face with her hands.

"Hey, I'm the one who rode my white horse to the station. If you prefer, I can take you back to your comfortable suite with Miss Sticky Fingers. Just say the word." Michael sounded duly offended.

"Sorry. Being tired, hungry, and crabby does nothing for my people skills. Please don't take me back to the slammer."

"Didn't they give you anything to eat? Even a PI has constitutional rights." He braked at the end of the bridge."

Beth chuckled, giddy from fatigue. "They delivered supper while I was asleep. When I woke up, I discovered that my roomie had eaten both trays. All she left me was the Jell-O. Thank goodness it was lime, my favorite."

"This restaurant serves the best twenty-four-hour breakfast in Vidalia. They make great burgers and fries too."

"I'll take all of the above." Beth staggered from his car toward the neon-lit door.

Inside, none of the patrons paid them any attention. Once they had slipped into a back booth, a waitress appeared immediately with coffee and menus. Beth ordered a club sandwich with fries without even looking. "Okay, I'm ready for your update."

"Same for me," said Mike to the waitress. Turning back to Beth, he said, "Unfortunately, neither your favorite detective nor McNeil were at the station when I dropped off the new statements. Lejeune didn't wait for an explanation. He just overreacted. When McNeil heard, he called my cell and told me where you were. Why didn't you notify your parents or one of your friends? Then you wouldn't have had to wait until I got back."

"My parents went to New Orleans for the day, and none of my friends have cash sitting around to post bail. How did you do in Jackson? Is your engagement back on?" She took a long sip of coffee.

"That's not remotely funny, but I'll let you slide for now. I just delivered samples of Rachel's DNA and fingerprints to the chief. He'll see that they're sent to the crime lab for comparison against those found at the murder scene. Because I emphasized that Rachel is a flight risk, the Natchez investigation should get immediate priority."

Beth refilled their mugs from the carafe on the table. "I'm impressed, Preston. You've handled yourself very professionally on this case."

"I had a good teacher."

She shook her head. "I can't take any credit. What happened today is proof I'm incompetent, just like Jack said."

"Don't let him undermine your confidence, Kirby. He's hated you for a long time. Chief McNeil said that once he speaks to the DA, all charges against you should be dropped, providing we're both willing to cooperate with the federal investigation—and there are no further missteps with the murder investigation." Michael pointed his finger at her.

Beth stared out the window as a cat slinked between cars under the yellow glow of a streetlight. "You have my word I'll stay out of Jack's way. If one of us needs to communicate with Homicide, it will be you."

"Sandwiches will be out in a jiffy, folks, but you can start on these now." The waitress delivered a heaping basket of fries and bottle of catsup and then hurried away.

Beth pulled out a fry hot enough to burn her fingers. She dropped it back in the basket and said, "I need to call my parents.

They should be home by now and are probably wondering as to where I am. Not that they don't have enough to worry about already."

Mike grabbed her wrist as she pulled out her phone. "They don't have to know about today, Elizabeth. Like I said, within a couple of days all of this will all go away."

She met his gaze. "The neighbors saw me dragged off in hand-cuffs, Mike. Mrs. Patrick probably was waiting on my parents' glider when they got home with cell phone pictures to show them. Nothing escapes her attention on Meadowsweet Avenue."

Michael doused his side of the basket liberally with catsup. "At least Nate never has to know. Maxine doesn't live in your neighborhood and wouldn't snitch even if she did. She likes you, same as me." He winked and began eating.

"I need no better friends, but Jack will make it his mission to tell. My former partner would love to see me tar and feathered or sent downriver bound and gagged."

"Stop reading Mark Twain and look on the bright side. We might have cracked the case. McNeil has already contacted the FBI Financial Crimes Division. A special agent should be here tomorrow to look at the evidence. You and I need to stay by the phone in the office. As soon as Natchez PD hears from the crime lab, they will know how to proceed. This is only conjecture at this point, but the feds might use Rachel in a sting to bring down her boss at D.K. Financials and anyone else connected to the scam."

Beth choked on a French fry. "Sounds like the cops are only worried about the investment fraud. What about Paul's murder? Surely they won't let Rachel walk away after killing an innocent preacher who only tried to serve his congregation."

"Take it easy. Drink some water before you hyperventilate. Murder is a capital offense in Mississippi. No one's walking away from that. We don't know if her DNA will match what was found on the rope and stool. I got the feeling at lunch that Rachel might be arrogant and greedy, but I doubt she's a murderer."

"So in addition to getting DNA samples, your lunch went well?"

"Couldn't have gone better. She thinks I still cry myself to sleep over her. But don't worry, I don't. Your partner is no longer an idiot."

The waitress thumped plates onto their table. "See, folks, I told you it wouldn't take long."

Beth gaped at sandwiches so huge, they could feed a village. "Apparently you and I have reversed roles. But our symbiotic relationship might not last much longer—one case and done. Assuming Nate doesn't fire me, he needs PIs in Natchez. Even once the gossip dies down, Jack will hobble me here indefinitely. I can't expect the chief or you to run interference forever." She compressed her triple-decker sandwich and took a bite.

"We'll cross that bridge when we come to it. The future is in God's hands, not Detective Lejeune's. In the meantime, let's concentrate on these sandwiches. This meal will cost the company at least fifteen bucks."

FIFTY-THREE

Friday

For three days Michael remained more or less in the loop with Natchez PD and Special Agent Jessica Fonteneau of the FBI's Financial Crimes Division. Nate assigned Beth to a missing person case, which got her away from the office for a few days. When Michael's partner returned from Nashville, where she'd gone to track down the twenty-year-old woman, he finally had something good to report.

Beth walked into the office just as Maxine was leaving for the day. "I'm b-a-ack," she crowed. "Did anybody miss me?"

"I've been counting the hours, dear heart." Maxine squeezed Beth's arm on her way out the door. "I just made a fresh pitcher of tea."

"I'm glad you're here," Michael said, hiding how much he really had missed her. "Tell me your news first. Did you find the missing college kid before she could do much damage?"

Beth rolled her eyes. "The girl wasn't covering her tracks very well. She went to Nashville for a bachelorette party. At least she hadn't eloped with her boyfriend as her parents had feared. Trouble is, she took her grandfather's credit card along with her. She decided to pay for a suite at the Grand Ole Opry Hotel and wine and dine the bride-to-be and other girls." Beth pulled up a chair next to Michael's desk.

"And she thought this was a good idea?" He suppressed a grin.

"Her grandfather just had hip replacement surgery and will be out of commission for a while. Miss Bridesmaid thought she could spend to her heart's desire and then report the credit card stolen. The bank would issue a new card and remove the charges from Grandpa's account. Aren't cards being replaced after each and every security breach?"

"It doesn't quite work that way."

"I know it and you know it, but not this bridesmaid. She didn't know her mother was monitoring Grandpa's account online. A few months ago, he'd been duped by a fraudulent GoFundMe scheme. When I tracked the girl down in Nashville, her parents had already cancelled the Visa card. They made arrangements to pay the hotel what she owed, but Miss Bridesmaid will be paying them back long after this wedding is a sweet memory."

"Once again, justice is served by Price Investigations." Michael offered Beth a high five. "I also have news, but I'm hungry. Want me to tell you while we get something to eat?"

Beth leaned back and stared at the ceiling. "As appealing as that sounds, I'm having dinner with my parents. They deserve a better explanation than the one they got the night you sprang me from jail. I told them they would hear the whole story when I got back to town."

"You did nothing wrong, Elizabeth. How's your dad?"

"They're still waiting for bloodwork results, but so far the second doctor agrees with the benign diagnosis. What did you hear from the police?"

"McNeil received the crime lab's results: Miss Stewart's DNA and fingerprints didn't match those found at the scene." He paused to let this sink in. "Whoever was with Reverend Dean when he died isn't in the law enforcement data banks. But the FBI arrested Rachel at her home in Jackson on charges of illegal wire transfers, conspiracy to commit fraud, and more. She's being transported to Natchez as we speak. Apparently, she's willing to cooperate with homicide detectives in exchange for a reduced sentence on federal charges."

"They won't let her off, will they?"

"Absolutely not, but if she helps catch the murderer, maybe she won't die in jail. The FBI has located another Mississippi church that suffered a significant loss. D.K. Financials had been planning to wipe out every account they had access to, but in the meantime they were helping themselves to three accounts for current overhead."

"Three victims, not just Paul and Reverend Huff of Hattiesburg?" Beth asked.

"Special Agent Jessica Fonteneau spoke with a finance director in Greenville, Clay Whitfield. According to their last statement, his church suffered a fifty percent loss of principal. Mr. Whitfield is willing to help the FBI catch all the crooked fish."

"And Elliott Rayburn? Will he go to jail?"

"Most likely not. The investigation is far from over, but apparently Spare the Children had been turning over seventy-five percent of monies raised to orphanages in Nigeria, Bangladesh, Rwanda, and other sub-Saharan countries. Rayburn merely took a healthy percentage for his services."

Beth looked sick to her stomach. "Does *everyone* have their hand out these days?"

"The Internet makes it so much easier to steal. The person collecting money door-to-door for charity used to be one of your neighbors. Now all you see is an email or a slick website."

"Where does this leave us? Should we tell Alice that Natchez PD has booted us off the case?"

"When the investment sting takes place, we'll both be there as consultants to the police. Rachel gave Special Agent Fonteneau the impression that she trusted me. I'm not sure why."

"Maybe she regrets breaking off the engagement."

"Nah, she's just scared and thinks I'll be her champion. If it helps to close the case, I'm willing to play along."

"It will give you closure at long last." Beth rose to her feet. "Why don't we pay Alice a visit tomorrow? If we let her know what's going on, maybe she can start sleeping better."

"Good idea. Right now, why don't you call your mom and wrangle me a dinner invitation for tonight? I'd like to be *your* champion with your parents over this arrest debacle."

Beth ducked her head, but not before Michael spotted her blush. "Fine, but if rabbit stew and stuffed turnips are on the menu, don't say I didn't warn you."

FIFTY-FOUR

When Michael picked up Beth on Sunday morning, they drove to the station in relative silence. Alice hadn't been available Saturday, so this was the first time they had seen each other since dinner with the Kirbys Friday night. Neither of them knew quite what to say. Michael had explained the reason for Lejeune's overreaction and Beth's innocence in the trumped-up charges. Rita and Stan had insisted they never doubted their daughter's innocence for a moment, which was reassuring to hear, but some of Rita's thinly veiled comments were harder to take in stride: "Seems to me like you two are a perfect match, and I'm so glad Betsy found a nice man for a change."

"We're *work* partners, Ma," Beth had said. "Can't you let Michael enjoy his dinner in peace?"

"Of course, dear. I was referring to your job. I never did like Jack Lejeune."

When they pulled into the parking lot for Natchez PD, Beth asked, "Any idea what we're walking into? What did Chris say on the phone?"

Michael turned off the ignition. "It was Lejeune who called. He said to come to the conference room and to not be late. We'll be briefed by the FBI agent in charge."

"Does he know I'm coming?" asked Beth, half inside the car, half out. "The last time we met, his hand was on his weapon."

"He does, so stop worrying."

Michael locked their firearms in the trunk. Once they were buzzed in, he led the way down the hall with Beth on his heels. Chris McNeil and a uniformed officer rose to their feet when they entered the conference room, followed by Lejeune and a second detective. A thirtyish, well-dressed woman remained seated but smiled politely. *FBI Special Crimes*, he thought.

"Come in, Mr. Preston, Miss Kirby. This is Special Agent Jessica Fonteneau from Baton Rouge. She's taken over the investment scam case and will be assisting our Homicide Department today. You already know Jack, and this is Lieutenant Baxter and Officer Pratt. Mike Preston and Beth Kirby work for Price Investigations here in town," McNeil said to the agent.

"How do you do, ma'am," said Mike.

"Thank you for letting us join the investigation, Agent Fonteneau." Beth smiled at her and then at the other gentlemen. She managed to avoid eye contact with Jack.

After almost everyone shook hands and sat down, Agent Fonteneau was first to speak. "I want to thank you for giving our team a great starting point, Mr. Preston, Miss Kirby. We've already obtained warrants to seize funds later today before any money can be wired out of the country."

"Later today?" Michael asked, hoping a consultant was allowed to ask questions.

Chief McNeil took the floor. "We don't want to tip anyone off too soon. Miss Stewart agreed to let us record the phone conversation between her and her boss at D.K. Financials last night. When they meet this afternoon, she will be wearing a wire."

"Rachel will be your bait?" asked Michael.

"Yes. She agreed, provided less-serious federal charges are brought against her." Agent Fonteneau retook control of the briefing. "Would you care to hear her conversation with George Roush?"

"You bet we would," said Beth, with plenty of enthusiasm.

Lejeune cleared his throat but kept his attention on Agent Fonteneau as she switched on the machine.

"George? It's Rachel." The voice of Michael's ex-fiancée filled the room. "Hope I'm not calling too late."

"Late isn't the problem. Care to explain where you were today? I didn't appreciate your telling my assistant you had a head cold. Next time, talk to me personally if you'll be away from the office. We're getting down to the wire."

Michael caught Beth's expression from the corner of his eye. She was practically levitating from her chair.

"I took several remedies to lessen the symptoms," said Rachel in a nasally voice. "They seem to be working. I'll be back in the office on Monday, bright eyed and bushy tailed." She coughed, perhaps for effect.

"What is the matter with you? I need you here tomorrow. I don't care if it is a Sunday!" Roush thundered. *No way will this guy win any boss-of-the-year awards,* Michael thought.

"There's a slight problem, but it's nothing I can't handle. I got a call from the finance director of a Presbyterian church in Greenville. Unfortunately, I gave Clay Whitfield my cell number when I set up the account. What a mistake. He's screaming about his church's money. He says he'll contact Mississippi's attorney general if we don't return their initial investment in full."

Roush uttered a foul word that revealed much about his professional demeanor with employees. "And you said *what,* exactly?"

"Relax. What can the attorney general do? Have one of his minions send a form letter asking for clarification of the complaint?"

Rachel's choice of words indicated D.K. might have received just such a request in the past. "I told Whitfield I would bring him an updated statement showing their losses were a temporary glitch and that the church has nothing to worry about. I have an appointment with him at two. That's why I won't be in the office until Monday."

"I can't believe you sound so lackadaisical about this! The attorney general can cause serious problems for us, which we certainly don't need."

"That's why I'm buying us more time. That financial director likes me. The guy stared at my legs during our entire appointment."

"Considering his church is kicking up a fuss, let's not depend on your *legs* to prevent disaster. I'll pick you up, and we'll go talk to him together."

There was only the briefest hesitation before his sly ex-fiancée answered. "Oh, dear, I'm afraid I'm already in Greenville. I drove up to spend the night with a friend. I haven't seen any of my sorority sisters in ages—"

"Rachel! What were you thinking?" Roush peppered his question with additional profanities. "We have the biggest score ever on the line, and you want to touch base with an old college pal? I thought you were sick!"

"The medication is working, and I might never see my friend again." Rachel's drawl was sticky sweet. "Besides, we have absolutely nothing to worry about."

"Hold on a second," snapped Roush. "According to Google, there's a coffee shop within a mile of Mr. Whitfield's house. I'll meet you at one fifteen and we'll talk to him together. No arguments, Rachel. Forget about your girlfriend and get a good night's sleep. You'll need your A-game tomorrow to keep this finance director from ruining everything we've worked for."

The line went dead, and Special Agent Fonteneau switched off the machine. "Today the FBI and the Natchez PD will bring their A-games as well. Rachel will be wearing a wire when she meets her boss and also during their appointment with the finance director. We'll get the evidence we need to convict Roush on fraud charges. Miss Stewart requested your presence, Mr. Preston, in case things turn dicey. For some reason she trusts you. You and Miss Kirby will ride in the surveillance van with Natchez PD. I'll ride with Chief

McNeil and Detective Lejeune. If there are no additional questions, shall we hit the road? We don't want to be late."

It was a rhetorical question. Agent Fonteneau immediately shoved her folders into her briefcase and strode out the door with the officers at her heels. Michael and Beth exchanged a glance and followed the entourage into the back lot, where the unmarked van sat idling, the techs already in place.

During the drive to Greenville, the van driver played a radio talk show so loudly conversation was impossible. For that, Michael was grateful. He had no idea why Rachel trusted him or thought he would somehow be on her side. When the surveillance team was in place near the coffee shop, the driver turned down the radio and closed his eyes to wait.

Beth scooted closer to him on the backseat. "Sorry if my mom made you uncomfortable at dinner the other night."

Michael smiled. "I'm fine with your mother. In fact, I really like your parents."

"Embarrassing my friends, especially if they happen to be male, is Rita's personal A-game."

"Would it help if I shared some of my painful moments at the hands of Margo Preston? But you must promise never to divulge a word you're about to hear."

Beth nodded, placed her left hand over her heart, and lifted her right hand as though in court. "I swear," she mouthed.

Michael outlined the highlights from his days of science fair competitions and blue ribbons for hamster 4-H projects. His mother never understood that those accomplishments weren't quite as newsworthy as gridiron achievements. Before Michael launched into one particularly dreadful article in their church's newsletter, the cop motioned for them to be silent. The two technicians who had been dozing with headsets on sprang into action as Rachel and an older man entered the coffee shop. In the background, Michael heard the din of conversation, but the microphone picked up the targeted dialogue perfectly. In short order Rachel's voice filled the surveillance van.

"He's expecting us at two o'clock, Mr. Roush. There was no reason to meet me here. I know how to handle a client."

"Like you reassured Paul Dean?" said George Roush.

"Pastor Dean must have been suffering from depression or else—"

"We can't afford any more mistakes, so stop talking and listen." Roush barked the words in a harsh whisper. "You will follow my instructions to the letter. Everything we've worked for is at stake."

"What do you want me to do?"

"Wait until Whitfield invites us in and we're sitting down in his living room. Then ask for coffee. If he says he has none, ask for tea or something cold. Once he brings out some refreshment, send him back to the kitchen for sugar or cream. You must think of *something* that's not on the tray. Can you handle that, Rachel?"

"Of course I can, but what exactly are you planning?" She sounded scared, something Michael had never known her to be.

"While he's out of the room, I'll put enough tranquilizers in his cup to send him to dreamland." Roush emitted a scornful laugh.

"There's no need to drug him, Mr. Roush. I know I can buy us the time we need by talking to him."

"We can't take that chance. Within twenty-four hours, money from our targeted accounts will transfer beyond the reach of anyone in the U.S. and we'll be on a flight out of here. If Whitfield calls the attorney general, you and I will go to prison for a long time."

"What if Mr. Whitfield wakes up before the funds transfer?"

"You really are a little ninny, aren't you?" Roush snorted. "The drug will only last a couple hours, but it'll be long enough to get him to the garage, where the disgraced finance director decides he can't live with his shame."

Two or three seconds of silence passed, while Michael and everyone in the van held their breath. "Are you going to kill him…hang him like you did Paul Dean?" Rachel asked.

"Keep your voice down. Of course I'm not going to hang him. How would that look? When Whitfield falls asleep, we'll put him behind the wheel of his car and turn on the ignition. Carbon monoxide should take care of the rest as long as the garage door is closed. Let's get going. Leave your car here and ride with me. I want to be early to catch him off guard."

The sound of boisterous children nearby obscured part of Rachel's reply. "…kill not one, but two preachers and still live with yourself? You've never even met the man."

"Whitfield ain't no preacher. He's a pompous church elder who holds the purse strings too tightly. You'd think it was *his* money or something."

"Count me out. I might be a thief, but I've never killed anyone."

Rachel had decided to stand up to him, rather belatedly in Michael's opinion.

"You will do what you're told. If we get caught, you're going away as an accessory to murder. That carries the same sentence as if you pulled the proverbial trigger, so don't get self-righteous with me."

When Michael heard Rachel crying, he felt a pang of pity for a girl who was kind to animals, who took off a semester from college to tend her dying grandmother, and who once told him he was the smartest man on earth. Somewhere Rachel had gone astray and would now pay the price.

Michael and Beth watched the scammers leave the coffee shop and climb in Roush's car. As the police van followed at a safe distance, Beth stared out the window, her eyes glassy with moisture. They both had known Paul Dean's death wasn't a suicide, but hearing a heartless killer admit the truth drained every bit of color from Beth's face.

"We'll get him, partner." Michael reached for her hand.

Without meeting his gaze, Beth squeezed his fingers.

Parked across the street under a century-old tree, the van's occupants watched the scene play out: A paunchy, balding man opened his door to admit a murderer and his ambitious accomplice.

Thanks to modern technology, they listened to harsh accusations and angry threats from Clay Whitfield, followed by Rachel's tearful excuses and profuse apologies. A stern browbeating by Roush to his employee was thrown in for good measure. Then Rachel promised to return the Presbyterian church's investment in total, but could she have a cup of coffee to settle her nerves in the meantime?

During the next few difficult minutes, Michael longed to shout: *Don't drink the coffee* as though this was some horror movie on TV.

Clear as a bell, the van occupants heard Rachel ask for Sweet-n-Low instead of sugar. Then the entire drama was over too soon in Michael's estimation. Law enforcement emerged from the bushes and entered the house before ketamine could be consumed by Whitfield...or any other hapless victim. Detective Lejeune arrested the owner of D.K. Financials and dragged him toward the waiting patrol car with more force than necessary. *Is that how he manhandled Beth?* Michael forced the image from his mind.

Surprisingly, Officer Pratt allowed Rachel to approach the two private investigators standing on the sidelines. With her hands cuffed behind her, she stopped in front of Michael. She turned her luminous blue gaze on him—eyes he had once thought he would wake up to for the rest of his life.

"Did I do good?" she asked.

Michael clenched down on his molars. "You might have reduced your eventual sentence, Rachel, but I wouldn't describe ruining three men's lives and eroding people's faith in charitable causes as 'good.'"

Her head reared back as though slapped. Then she focused a venomous glare at Beth. "Who are you looking at?" she demanded.

"Who, me?" Beth stepped forward, hooking her thumb toward her chest. "Nobody. Absolutely nobody."

FIFTY-FIVE

Monday

*B*eth bounded down the steps with more energy than she'd had since her release from jail nearly a week ago. Nate would be back in the office today, well rested after his honeymoon. He would be apprised of everything that took place in his absence—the good, the bad, and the ugly. If she was to be fired, she might as well get it over with. Maybe Walmart could use another greeter, or Nate might have seen "Help Wanted" signs somewhere along the coast. It would be nice living close to the beach with powdery white sand, bumper-to-bumper traffic, and the occasional hurricane. At least her conundrum of whether she and Michael would remain partners would soon be over.

"Are you whistling?" asked her mother, dropping her newspaper onto the table.

"Yep. I'm in such a good mood I'll resist the impulse to drive across the neighbor's pansies." Beth filled her to-go mug to the rim.

"You would do that to Mrs. Patrick after what she tried to do for you?" Rita arched an eyebrow as she put a plate of waffles on the table for her daughter.

"What did that busybody ever do other than spread malicious gossip in the neighborhood?" Beth forked a waffle from the plate to eat dry.

"Well, let's see. That nosy busybody was so upset you got hauled away in handcuffs that she tried to bail you out. She had to take two buses to her bank to empty out her Christmas Club and another bus to city hall. Unfortunately, she thought that's where you paid someone's bail. After her daughter picked her up and they found the right place, you had already been sprung from the slammer." Rita poured maple syrup on her second waffle.

"People still open Christmas Clubs?"

"That's all you have to say, missy?"

"Everything else is unbelievable."

"Well, believe it. Nancy Patrick wants to be a character witness in court if you need her." Rita waved her syrupy fork through the air. "I don't know why you think everybody hates you, Betsy. Maybe you should talk to a therapist about your low self-esteem."

Beth choked on her dry waffle. "That will be at the top of my to-do list. But right now, I need to get to work. Wish me luck. You could be seeing more of me starting tomorrow."

Rita caught hold of her arm. "Stand up for yourself, daughter. Make sure Nate knows what a good PI you are and how hard you worked for Mrs. Dean."

"If all else fails, I'll ask Mrs. Patrick for an affidavit." Beth brushed a kiss across her mother's gray head as tears clouded her vison. *What is it about female emotions?* Crying when you're sad was one thing, but this was altogether different.

Beth walked into an office that looked like New Year's Eve and Fourth of July rolled into one. Red, white, and blue streamers crisscrossed the ceiling, bouquets of helium balloons adorned each desktop, and a huge banner proclaimed "Welcome back, Nate and Isabelle."

Closing the door behind her, Beth spotted a tray of colorful cupcakes which spelled out the same greeting. "Did you bake those, Maxine? They look yummy." She reached for a particularly gooey one.

"Of course I did." Maxine slapped her hand away. "What do

Isabelle's pals at Realty World have that I don't? But we're waiting for Isabelle to start eating."

"After the week Beth had, I think she can have one now." Nate walked out of his office and enveloped her in a loose hug. "How ya doing, Kirby? My bride stopped at the doctor's office, but she'll be here soon with enough pictures to bore you to tears."

"I'm fine. And you look great, Nate—all tan and healthy. Ready to tackle the next Natchez missing person or corporate espionage case? Where's Preston? I hope he's not late on your first day back."

Michael carried a pot of coffee from the kitchen. "Present and accounted for."

Nate held out a mug. "I'll wait for Izzy to share the honeymoon saga. Right now, give me an update on the Reverend Dean investigation."

Beth held her breath, hoping Michael would take the lead.

He didn't let her down. "Special Agent Fonteneau said the assets of D.K. Financials have been frozen pending the conclusion of their fraud case. Then the U.S. district judge will appoint a trustee to divide up the funds between the churches burned by the scam. Elliott Rayburn assured the FBI he would personally replace any shortfalls from his own assets. He feels terrible about not vetting George Roush more thoroughly."

Nate pulled the letter *I* cupcake off the tray. "Sounds like raising money for offshore charities can be lucrative these days."

Because Maxine didn't slap his hand, Beth helped herself to an *e* cupcake.

"So far, homicide detectives have found no proof Rachel had anything to do with Reverend Dean's murder," continued Michael. "But Roush's DNA will undoubtedly match the drop of sweat on the stool and a partial print on the rope. He must have had trouble retying the knot with gloves on. Right now Roush is only talking to his lawyer, but he'll be prosecuted both locally and in federal court."

"And Miss Stewart?" asked Nate. "Sounds like you dodged a bullet on that one."

Michael's face flushed with color. "She's in federal custody in Jackson. I've had no further contact with her, nor do I plan to have any." He focused his honey-brown eyes on Beth. She concentrated on not dropping cupcake crumbs on the floor.

Suddenly, the door swung open and Isabelle appeared. "Who just dodged a bullet? You had better not be bad-mouthing *me*, Mr. Price." She set several bottles of fruit punch on the table and eyed the cupcakes. "Who are Nat and sabelle? Do I know them?"

"The two luckiest people on earth," said Nate.

"We're all here. Let the games begin." Maxine clapped her hands wildly. "Any good news you care to report from your doctor's visit?"

Isabelle's mouth dropped open. "Are there no secrets in this company?"

"Not in a PI firm this good." Nate wrapped an arm around his wife's waist. "I heard from Mrs. Dean. She is very happy with how you two handled her husband's case. She invited Isabelle and me to dinner later this week and said we could use her as a reference anytime."

"That's good to hear." Beth pretended to wipe sweat from her brow.

"Beth was a very good teacher," said Michael.

"Does that mean you two are willing to remain partners?" Nate looked at Michael first.

"I'm willing. I still have more to learn," he said.

All eyes turned to Beth. "I'm the one with plenty to learn. So yes, I enjoy working as Mike's partner. I'm just not sure Natchez is a good fit for me." Beth felt her gut drop the moment she spoke the words. "Maybe if you get an out-of-town case?"

"I might be able to get you both out of Dodge for a while." Nate exchanged glances with Isabelle. "Ever been to Savannah? I hear it's a lovely city. Price Investigations has just been handed a case with a fee so generous we can't refuse. I would go myself, but my bride is eager to sleep in her own bed. Any cases that come up in Natchez I can handle alone."

"How did you land a case in Savannah?" asked Michael.

"On the day we spent sightseeing in Mobile, a street thug ripped off a lady's purse right in front of us—"

"Actually, it happened across the street," interrupted Isabelle. "But my hero took off after the thief, caught him three blocks away, and returned the purse to the rightful owner."

"The woman was very grateful and offered a reward—"

"Which Nate turned down, but he said if you ever need a PI please keep my agency in mind." Isabelle smiled at her husband. "Did I mention she was very rich?"

Nate rolled his eyes. "This woman was on business in Mobile, but she kept my card. Then she called me a few days later about a job for us in her hometown of Savannah."

"You want us both to go to the East Coast?" asked Beth, incredulously.

"I do. With the daily per diem for expenses, I can put you up in decent accommodations. It wouldn't be fair for one partner to get a vacation and not the other."

Michael scratched his scalp. "I'm confused. Are you giving us a free trip or a new case to work?"

"Consider it both. Plan to be gone for at least a week, but the case shouldn't take longer than a couple days. I'll pay for the rest of your expenses while you take some R and R."

Beth felt her old fear of getting too close to someone at work rear its head. "I don't know, Nate. I don't exactly deserve an all-expense-paid trip after getting thrown in jail." She held her breath.

Nate scoffed. "That happens to every PI sooner or later. Ask me sometime what jail was like in New Orleans, and Nicki came awfully close to seeing the inside of a Memphis holding cell."

Michael approached Beth until he was inches from her. "It's time for me to play my get-out-of-jail-free card. I'm entitled to stick my nose into your business one time. I say we *both* need a trip to Savannah."

With all eyes on her, Beth had little alternative. "Should I go start packing now, or do I have time for another cupcake?"

"Have all the cupcakes you want," said Nate. "Nobody's leaving the office until you hear all about our very long, very convoluted honeymoon."

"And watch our PowerPoint presentation. I've loaded in all of our photos, and we can't wait to share them with you." Isabelle started lining up chairs.

As for Beth, she couldn't think of anywhere else she would rather be.

DISCUSSION QUESTIONS

1. Why does Beth Kirby feel so alien in her hometown? Why has she distanced herself from her friends, her church, and even her family?

2. Following his broken engagement, Michael Preston endeavors to overhaul nearly every facet of his life. Have you ever undertaken such a major reinvention? What triggered the decision?

3. What looks suspicious about Reverend Dean's death to the PIs despite the coroner's conclusion?

4. Craig Mitchell's gambling ruined Isabelle's first marriage. Why is she so intent on helping someone who doesn't want help?

5. A private investigator must walk a narrow line with local law enforcement. What makes Detective Lejeune especially resentful of Beth's interference in his case?

6. Why would church personnel be easy marks for scam artists?

7. What was in the quarterly statements that made Michael suspicious of D.K. Financials?

8. Why is it nearly impossible to cheat a casino?

9. A series of bad choices created a mess in Craig's life. What one good choice does he make in the poker game that turns his life around?

10. Much to her dismay, Rachel Stewart no longer has power over Michael. What has changed inside him to bring this about?

ABOUT THE AUTHOR

Mary Ellis is the bestselling author of a dozen novels set in the Amish community and several historical romances set during the Civil War. *Midnight on the Mississippi*, *What Happened on Beale Street*, and *Magnolia Moonlight* are books in a romantic suspense series, Secrets of the South.

Before "retiring" to write full-time, Mary taught school and worked as a sales rep for Hershey Chocolate. Her debut book, *A Widow's Hope*, was a finalist for a 2010 Carol Award. *Living in Harmony* won the 2012 Lime Award for Excellence in Amish Fiction, while *Love Comes to Paradise* won the 2013 Lime Award. Mary and her husband live in Ohio.

⁓

Mary can be found on the web at
www.maryellis.net
or look for
Mary Ellis/Author on Facebook

Midnight on the Mississippi

What Lies Beneath the Black Water of the Bayou?

Hunter Galen, a New Orleans securities broker, suspects his business partner, James Nowak, of embezzling their clients' money, but he's reluctant to jeopardize their friendship. After James turns up dead, Hunter realizes his unwillingness to confront a problem may have cost James his life.

Nicki Price, a newly minted PI, intends to solve the stockbroker's murder as she establishes herself in the career she adores. As she ferrets out fraud and deception at Galen-Nowak Investments, Hunter's fiancée, Ashley Menard, rubs her the wrong way. Nicki doesn't trust the ostentatious woman who seems to be hiding something, but is the PI's growing attraction to Hunter—the police's only suspect—her true reason for disliking Ashley?

As Hunter and Nicki encounter sophisticated shell games, blackmail, and death threats both subtle and overt, danger swirls around them like the mysterious dark water of the bayou. Only their reliance on faith and fearless determination give them hope they will live to see another day.

What Happened on Beale Street

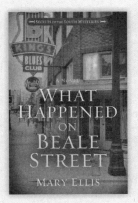

How Can Music So Beautiful
Hide Something So Deadly?

A cryptic plea for help from a childhood friend sends cousins Nate and Nicki Price from New Orleans to Memphis. When these two private investigators arrive at Danny Andre's last known address, they discover signs of a struggle and a lifestyle not in keeping with the choirboy they fondly remember.

Danny's sister, Isabelle, reluctantly accepts their help. She and Nate aren't on the best of terms due to a shared past. Can they get beyond painful memories to find her brother?

And what on earth was Danny involved in besides becoming a rising star as a sax player? Nate and Nicki follow clues into dim and smoky clubs, trail potential stalkers, and challenge dangerous men with connections to underworld drug trafficking. To complicate things, the hotel they are staying in has its own secrets. Confronted with murder and mystery in the land of the Delta blues, the cousins and Isabelle will have to rely on their faith and investigative experience to solve the case and not lose their lives.

Want another entertaining and romantic
murder mystery involving the dedicated
and engaging sleuths from
Price Investigations?

Don't Miss

Sunset in Old Savannah

Coming soon to your favorite retailer

To learn more about Harvest House books and
to read sample chapters, visit our website:

www.harvesthousepublishers.com

HARVEST HOUSE PUBLISHERS
EUGENE, OREGON
